REDACTED AFFAIRS

BOOK ONE OF
RISE OF THE PEACEMAKERS

Kevin Ikenberry &
Kevin Steverson

Seventh Seal Press
Virginia Beach, VA

Chris Kennedy/Seventh Seal Press
2052 Bierce Dr.
Virginia Beach, VA 23454
http://chriskennedypublishing.com/

Publisher's Note: This is a work of fiction. Names, characters, places, and incidents are a product of the author's imagination. Locales and public names are sometimes used for atmospheric purposes. Any resemblance to actual people, living or dead, or to businesses, companies, events, institutions, or locales is completely coincidental.

Ordering Information:
Quantity sales. Special discounts are available on quantity purchases by corporations, associations, and others. For details, contact the "Special Sales Department" at the address above.

Redacted Affairs/Kevin Ikenberry & Kevin Steverson -- 1st ed.
ISBN 978-1950420438

For My Girls.

— Kevin Ikenberry

This one is for my wife, Stacey. She'll tell you, there is some of me in the personalities of several of the characters. She's probably right. She usually is.

— Kevin Steverson

Chapter One

"I'm telling you, Jyrall," Larth said, "you gotta try it."

"I will not," the big Besquith answered while looking over and down at his weasel-like partner.

Larth, a Zuparti, had been born without fear. The lack of natural paranoia inherent in his species labeled him as insane among his race. In fact, he had actually been diagnosed as such on more than one occasion. Rumor was the Peacemaker Selector, Hak-Chet, threatened Larth's prior schoolmaster with investigation by the Enforcers while requesting Larth by name four years ago. Jyrall knew Larth didn't believe that, but like most stories around the Peacemaker Academy, there was likely more truth to the story than not. Whatever the cause, Jyrall's unlikely best friend walked at his side through the corridors of the Academy. Around them, giddy classmates of all known races jostled and called out to each other as they headed to the Accessions Briefing. Today they would learn their initial assignments beyond graduation. The final two weeks of their tenure at the Academy had officially started.

"I will not dip perfectly good fish into a tomato puree. Ever," Jyrall said for the third time, shaking his head. "The entire galaxy knows the wonderful concoction known as tartar sauce is the only acceptable sauce for fried fish. It must not be desecrated with…what did you call it? Gatch-up?"

"Ketchup…it's ketchup!" Larth exclaimed. "Besides, who made you the galaxy's leading expert on fish?"

"I am a connoisseur of the Earth product, fish, I'll have you know!" Jyrall laughed. "I have been consuming them since the day of my birth."

"You're as crazy as I am." Larth laughed and licked the last of the ketchup from his paw. Occasionally, Jyrall believed his partner and friend's diagnosis was spot on. Like now, for instance. Larth was truly crazy. There could be no denying it. The little Zuparti laughed. "Even if your Gamma gave you a thing for tilapia."

He referred to the fact that the Gamma in Jyrall's clan had fed him fish as an alternate to meat due to allergies when he was a pup. When his clan Alpha had ordered the pup, who could not eat properly, discarded, his Gamma had refused, feeding him fish and formula from Earth, and raising him with the rest of the pups in his clan. It had been the only time he knew of that his clan's Gamma had openly disobeyed their Alpha. Since it was so out of character for the Gamma, the Alpha had allowed it, resulting in the largest Besquith in the clan. When a pup had no competition for food, he grew quite large for their already large race.

While the allergy had long since been cured and was irrelevant now, the thought of eating meat still turned Jyrall's stomach. He couldn't eat the way the rest of his race ate because of it, and as a result, was considered as insane as his partner. There were plenty of other ways to take in the necessary proteins to maintain one's health. Jyrall's preference was fish. As far as he was concerned, the contribution of fish from Earth was as important as any other system's contribution, regardless of what it was. Art, medicine, and technology were all good stuff, but a good fish sandwich was hard to beat. Especially with tartar sauce on it.

"Well, explain your love of fish tacos, then?" Larth asked, knowing he had his partner dead to rights. "Or is that just because it's Peacemaker Francis' favorite food?"

Jyrall rolled his eyes. "Gods, you are insane."

"You won't eat ketchup, but you'll eat salsa? It's the same thing, Jyrall. Admit it."

"Salsa is not gatch-up!" Jyrall exclaimed. He looked up away from his partner in time to see Captain Dreel step into the next intersection. Dreel was large for a Besquith himself, but he still had to look up at Jyrall. The captain stared at them with his paws resting on his hips, waiting for them to approach.

Captain Dreel had been one of their best, if not intermittent, instructors for their first three years at the academy. Among other subjects, he had been instrumental in hand-to-hand combat training, and the Besquith had tossed them both around many times. Later, as they progressed, Larth had been able to hold his own for a surprising amount of time before being defeated by the instructor. Size did matter in some things. In that same line of thought, Jyrall had been able to beat the smaller Besquith instructor by the end of year two at least half the time. He remained their favorite instructor, though they had seen less of him of late. The situation with the Mercenary Guild and the siege of Earth had pressed the senior Peacemakers into more complex, secretive duties.

"Sir," Jyrall said. "I didn't expect to see you until the graduation ceremonies in two weeks."

"We were just on our way to the Accessions Briefing, sir," Larth said. "We'll know our first assignment this afternoon. We planned on getting front row seats since we'll be there early. You know, 'Early is on time. On time is not,' and all that." Larth was quoting the instructor in front of him about arriving to his lessons.

"It is," agreed Captain Dreel with a pleased sigh, "for some things. For others, exact timing is crucial. One of those times is right now. Follow me." He turned around and headed down the corridor he had come from, away from the lecture hall assigned for the afternoon's briefing.

With a shrug to his partner, Larth said, "Roger that, sir," and turned and followed him.

Jyrall followed closely behind the Zuparti. "What exactly does 'Roger that' mean?"

"You really should watch more GalNet shows," Larth answered, "especially the old ones from Earth. It means 'yes,' 'affirmative,' and sometimes 'hell yes,' I gathered."

"Then why didn't you just say that?" the big Besquith asked, shaking his head and grinning.

They followed Captain Dreel deeper into the corridors of the Peacemaker Academy until they stopped at a door. It wasn't the door to the office of the head of the Academy. It was the door to the guild master's campus office. Neither of the soon-to-be Peacemakers knew why they were there. Guild Master Rsach hadn't been seen on campus for a long time. Rumor had it the entire High Council had been out of sight for a while. The persistent rumors said they were in hiding, and that Rsach probably wouldn't be attending the graduation ceremonies, either, for security reasons. Even with Enforcers patrolling the exterior of the Academy, and the whole of the planet's security forces created from the ranks of Peacemakers, present and past, Guild Master Rsach was too much of a target in the rapidly disintegrating Union. No guild master had ever missed graduation.

Captain Dreel paused before opening the door, leaning against it to listen with his sensitive ears. Jyrall held his breath and looked around the deserted corridor with his widest, most sensitive vision. *Find the enemy when they do not want to be found.* Jyrall heard nothing and wondered if Dreel had determined the same. Satisfied, the captain opened the door and motioned for the two candidates to enter ahead of him. They walked in, still wondering why they were there instead of attending the Accessions Briefing.

To their surprise, Guild Master Rsach stood by the central desk in the dimly lit office. He put his slate down and motioned for them to come in. "Jyrall. Larth. Please, come in. You're just the two I came to see. Let me congratulate you both on graduating from the Academy."

"Thank you, Guild Master," Jyrall said.

"Thank you, sir, but graduation isn't for a couple more weeks," Larth blurted.

The guild master rippled several arms and looked toward Captain Dreel. Dreel held a small cube with three green dots glowing steadily. The anti-listening device was elSha made and part of the standard Peacemaker deployment kit. The lights indicated it was working, effectively jamming every possible listening frequency. Any interested parties would have to be inside the office already if they wanted to hear the conversation. Dreel nodded at the guild master, and the Jeha continued speaking.

"Not for you two." The guild master turned his millipede body and reached out with several arms to pick up some items from his desk. "Much like your confirmation mission, the situation has changed. Your iridium badges, please," he asked.

Jyrall and Larth each reached into an inner pocket. Larth reached into the angled pocket of his candidate coveralls. Jyrall's was on the vest he wore in lieu of the standard coveralls, as there were none large enough for him. Each of them took out the temporary badges they had carried since the incident on the Marloch Trading Station the year before. They'd stopped a potential terrorist attack from happening on Earth, and the guild master had declared it to be their commissioning mission, well ahead of schedule. It wasn't the first time a mission of its type had sufficed for a commissioning mission, but none of their classmates or instructors, other than Dreel, knew about it—nor would they ever. Like their classmates about to embark on their own missions, Jyrall and Larth retained the badges to be traded for Peacemaker Coins during the graduation ceremony and the actual Peacemaker Badge they had each designed and could not wait to hold.

Can this really be happening?

With trembling paws, they handed their iridium candidate badges to the guild master. He twisted again and placed them on the desk. He turned toward them again, and there was a ripple of pride through his body.

"I am greatly honored to commission you, Peacemaker Jyrall." Rsach placed a coin on the Besquith's hand. Jyrall nodded, afraid to speak. In that moment, feeling the coin on his palm, all he wanted to do was roar in celebration.

"I am greatly honored to commission you, Peacemaker Larth," Rsach said, repeating the ritual. Jyrall saw his friend's eyes glisten as his paw clasped the coin tightly. For the first time, Jyrall looked at the coin as if he'd never seen one before. Centered on the coin was the suspended diamond sigil of the Peacemaker. Most outsiders believed a Peacemaker's badge was the source of the greatest honor. They were mistaken. The coin was part membership card, part diploma, and all honor. Since the first Peacemakers, the coin was the true mark of the Peacemaker's commitment to "Secure and Protect" the Union. The badge was the necessary symbol of authority on the lawless frontier.

They both looked up after studying the coin for a moment, each lost in their own thoughts. The guild master held out matching platinum badges for them. Jyrall tilted his head slightly in question, but reached out to take the badge, as Larth was doing. The badges weren't the ones they'd designed. Each Peacemaker got to design the image of the tree on their badges. Usually, it was a tree native to the planet a Peacemaker hailed from.

The two badges, like the coins, had the sigil of the Peacemaker Guild tree on them. With an intake of breath, Larth realized what the badges meant. "We will be assigned directly to you, Guild Master?"

"You are, Peacemaker," Guild Master Rsach said. "I have a mission for you two. You are designated partners from this moment forward. Is this agreeable to you both?"

Jyrall spoke first. "I am honored to share the duty with my friend, Guild Master."

"I wouldn't have wanted it any other way," Larth said softly. He looked up at Jyrall and winked. The Besquith returned it.

"Then officially partnered you are. This decision suits you both," Rsach continued. "You will go immediately to the Parmick System. There's a mining outpost on the planet Parmick, once owned by a legitimate business. The mine has recommenced operations, but we don't know under whose direction. You will investigate the situation there. We've lost contact with the local Peacemaker, so we're no longer receiving the intelligence we need. The occasional loss of communications with an individual Peacemaker is to be expected; however, the barracks commander reported electromagnetic interference as the cause of disruption via StormWatch this entire time. I cannot immediately risk sending a Blue Flight to the barracks to talk with the commander there, and the situation on Parmick is serious enough that it requires direct investigation now. That's where the two of you come in. No one knows who you are. No one will be expecting you. If you follow the procedures you applied on Marloch last year, you'll likely gain more intelligence faster than we could if I sent Enforcers to the colony."

"Yes, sir," Jyrall said. "Will we be briefed on the full situation as it now stands before we depart?"

"We could study the brief while our supplies and gear are drawn and a ship is assigned to us," added Larth, thinking ahead to the next several weeks.

"It will be loaded onto your ship," assured Captain Dreel. The Besquith hesitated for a moment and glanced at the guild master. "Honored Rsach, I would ask that the Peacemakers know our greatest concern. Whether or not it has any bearing on Parmick, I believe they need to know the whole situation."

Rsach studied them both for a moment. Jyrall couldn't help but wonder if the guild master was still measuring them, even with their new assignment. He turned to Dreel. "Captain Dreel, you are correct. I value your judgment."

"Thank you, Guild Master." Dreel nodded solemnly.

The Jeha stepped closer to Jyrall and Larth. His voice was little more than a whisper. "What you need to know right now is, Kr'et'Socae escaped from the detention center on Kleve several months ago. We have suppressed that information for obvious reasons. He was confirmed to be on Araf and was behind the recent attack on Victoria Bravo."

Attempting to keep their surprise in check, both silently nodded their heads. Kr'et'Socae was the only Enforcer to be decommissioned and imprisoned for murder. The escaped Equirri was a formidable opponent in his own right, yet the physiological enhancements an Enforcer often received made him even more dangerous.

"His location is unknown at this time, and the silence from the mining outpost and the regional barracks doesn't ease my mind about the situation on Parmick," said Guild Master Rsach. "You two, watch each other's backs and get us the information we need. Go pack your bags and meet Captain Dreel at the starport. You leave immediately via Blue Flight. Do you have any questions?"

Jyrall shook his head, but Larth said, "Why us?"

The guild master made a sound somewhere between surprise and admiration. "You truly have no fear, Peacemaker."

"It's the most obvious question. Is it what we did on Marloch? The fact no one knows us? Or something else?"

Rsach glanced at Dreel, and there was a deep, rumbling chuckle from the captain. "This is a situation where one Peacemaker might not be enough, Larth. Until we know more, it's better that we send a pair of highly intelligent, seasoned Peacemakers. Given the situation, we cannot be sure our Peacemakers aren't being watched by the Mercenary Guild in their sectors," Dreel replied.

"Then why take us via Blue Flight?" Jyrall added and then hesitated. "Wait, you're not taking us direct to Parmick, are you?"

Rsach shook his head. "No, Peacemaker. We'll take you forward to Zeha on official business. From there, the MinSha will arrange transport for you to Parmick."

Dreel's smile was unusually wide. "Before you ask, Larth, this MinSha planet and its queen are allies with us. Lieutenant Francis has seen to that arrangement personally. She has the highest confidence in Queen Taal and her forces. That's enough assurance for the High Council."

"As well as my own," Rsach said. "I wish you well, Peacemakers. Set the terms and honor all threats."

"Thank you, Guild Master," they each managed to mumble. Dreel steered them from the office and into the corridor. He squeezed their upper arms once and nodded at them.

"Best of luck," the captain said.

"Do Besquith believe in luck?" Larth asked.

"Only the luck we make," Jyrall said.

"Well stated, Peacemaker." Dreel leaned closer to Jyrall. "I am proud of you, pup."

For a moment, Jyrall wondered if his chest would burst from pride. As quickly as the thought faded, he realized he and Larth were alone again.

Still holding their badges and coins, they glanced at each other several times as they walked the quiet corridors to their room. They couldn't help but grin, though they both knew the seriousness of the assignment they'd been given.

"Don't even say it," Jyrall warned.

"Oh, I'm going to say it," said his partner. "Performance Punishment. When you're good, you get the bad…and we're good."

"Good assignment, bad assignment," Jyrall answered, "it doesn't matter. What matters is Honoring the Threat and Setting the Terms."

"And kicking ass," Larth added.

"There is that," agreed his friend with a toothy grin. "Should we grab a bite to eat before we depart? I imagine the cafeteria will be pretty much deserted with Accessions going on now."

"Great idea," Larth chittered. "I'll grab some ketchup for the road and—"

"You will do no such thing," Jyrall said, menacingly. "If you do, I'll be forced to escalate this in the form of tartar sauce in everything you eat during the trip."

Larth blanched. "That's not fair! It's disgusting and not fair, Jyrall. Just because you have a taste for weird Human condiments doesn't give you the right to force feed it to me."

"Keep your damned gatch-up away from me, and you won't have to worry when I'll strike, Larth. You might not be afraid of anything, but you have sensitive taste buds that can be easily tainted. Tartar sauce could be my greatest ally." Jyrall grinned.

"Fine, fish boy. I still say this is because of Peacemaker Francis and fish tacos."

"You wish." Jyrall slapped his partner on one shoulder. "By the time this mission is over, you'll be a fan of fish."

"In your dreams, Snarlyface. In your dreams."

* * * * *

Chapter Two

Peacemaker Academy
Ocono

Rsach waited until Dreel closed the office door and turned around before allowing himself a moment to relax. Clandestine missions were not his favorite, and the need for so many of them at this critical time for the guild taxed both energy and health more than he cared to admit. Unlike his friends on the High Council, though, young Captain Dreel had never seen the guild master in repose. Yet the need for clandestine operations far outweighed any measure of personal dignity Rsach maintained. As a Jeha, personal dignity was not a critical trait. Rsach's experience as a guild master and, more importantly, a leader gave him a certain perspective. Sometimes a subordinate needed to see behind the veil of command.

"Guild Master? Are you ill?" Dreel's monstrous visage was concerned and still.

So much for how to start the awkward conversation.

"I am well, Captain Dreel. I apologize for alarming you, but I feel I have your trust, and in this place," he motioned with his many arms, "I can be both truthful and easily seek the counsel of others."

"You would have my counsel? Guild Master?" The surprise in Dreel's voice made Rsach bark a quick laugh.

17

"I would. You have earned my trust on more than one occasion." Rsach nodded solemnly at the Besquith. "You were correct to want to warn the young ones about Kr'et'Socae. Whether his hoofprints are on this silence or not, we cannot be too careful. Hence my desire to speak with you."

The Besquith nodded stiffly. "I am ready to carry out your orders."

"That's not what I'm asking," Rsach snapped. "The last thing I need, Captain Dreel, are more officers telling me 'yes,' when I need to hear their thoughts, their opinions. While a guild master has the ability to rule their guild and its people, I would prefer to *lead* them. That requires insight and motivations be known. I would have you know my thoughts, and I would like to know yours."

"Guild Master, please," Dreel swallowed. "I am many things, but a counselor is not my—"

"Nonsense." Rsach shook his head, and there was a touch of a smile on his curled maw. "You and Kurrang have given me an advantage I hadn't thought possible. Your plan to organize the Enforcers is ambitious, and necessary. We will need them, and I authorize you to begin the second phase of your plan once we depart Ocono. Your belief in those two young Peacemakers rivals the first time you came to me about Jessica Francis—do you remember that conversation?"

"I do," Dreel replied. "When Hop'Ta the Horrible wanted Jessica expelled for making a perfect score in marksmanship on her first attempt. I remember his incoherent, squeaking rage all too well."

"And I remember what you said, almost verbatim. You said that Jessica exemplified what a Peacemaker should be and, Human or not, she was the kind of being you wanted at your shoulder. For a

Besquith, those words remain powerful. You see yourself in those young ones, and that's a good thing for our operations going forward. We need the right Peacemakers in the right positions, Dreel. Your candor will be in as great a demand as your leadership skills, especially when your units are ready for deployment."

"Thank you, Guild Master." Dreel nodded and his posture relaxed. The Besquith grinned. "I believe we can have combat ready squads—no more than eight Enforcers each—ready within a few weeks."

Rsach nodded. "We may not have that kind of time. I recognize that may prohibit the fully intermixed squads you designed. Yet having a squad of a particular species could prove advantageous in the right situation."

"It would not be ideal." Dreel stared into the space between them for a long moment. Rsach knew the young captain's earlier hesitation had been replaced with the calculation of a trained tactician. "Under the current time constraints, we would merely have to use the right ones for the right tasks."

"Which brings me to my next point." Rsach drew a breath. "Kr'et'Socae will not be taken easily. He has the remnants of a force at his disposal, and there are reports of thousands more in his control. Face-to-face combat will not be something he wishes to engage in for the short term. What forces he has are reconsolidating as we speak. Finding them is your first task, Captain Dreel."

"I understand, Guild Master," Dreel replied. "The presence of a large force, wherever they are, constitutes a larger problem. We have to assume he will intimidate the Information Guild, and maybe the Cartography Guild, but he would appear to be severely lacking in other areas."

"Indeed. Finite resources." Rsach's body rippled unconsciously. "How is he paying his forces? Feeding them? Getting fuel for his ships? Those are no small tasks, even for the smallest of mercenary companies. An army of more than ten thousand? That requires credits and a support network spanning the galaxy. He cannot have both."

Dreel nodded and his grin turned into a broadening smile. "What do they mine on Parmick?"

"Red diamonds," Rsach said. "Officially, the mines were abandoned by the Tellus Mining Consortium more than a hundred years ago. Parmick has been a prospecting hub for decades, as well as a place for mercenaries and pirates without a place to go. It's the kind of place where Kr'et'Socae could make his presence known."

"And you've sent someone he will never expect." Dreel chuckled, but it sounded like a snarl. The Besquith shook his head. "Jyrall and Larth will investigate and see what turns up."

Rsach nodded. "At the very least, they will determine why our reports from the region have dried up at the barracks level. I suspect I know that answer already, though. There are many in our ranks who have turned on their oaths."

"They have tarnished our sacred honor, Guild Master."

"They will be punished, Dreel. You have my word on that." Rsach turned toward the small window overlooking the quadrangle between the halls of the Academy. Ocono was a temperate planet, much like Victoria Bravo and Earth, and the warm spring days were gorgeous and calm after weeks of winter storms. "Once your mission is underway, you may be tempted to chase down our traitors. I must caution you to let them go."

"Why?" Dreel asked. "They have stolen our honor."

"They have, yes. But I want you to understand that they have chosen the short-term reward versus the value of long-time service. They have failed to play the 'long game,' as our Human counterparts would say. Leaving your path to serve the honor you carry like none other would do the same."

Dreel stiffened, took a deep breath, and then sagged slightly forward. "I want to ensure they will be punished, Guild Master. Should your location or the High Council's be revealed, I fear the guilds may come for you."

Rsach nodded solemnly. "They will, Captain Dreel, but not yet. They believe we're on the run. They believe we will do what we have always done and let tensions ebb while seeking to preserve the fragile unity of the Galactic Union at the negotiating table. They do not consider us a threat; much less will they honor us. We have the advantage in their ignorance."

"Are you suggesting we press forward?" Dreel squinted. "That goes against our very charter."

Rsach rippled a dozen arms and shook his head violently. "No, Dreel. Think. Through your efforts, we are gathering the Enforcers. Our barracks commanders have already started to comply with my order to consolidate our own forces. Our fleet has done the same. We are preparing for a greater threat than one guild sequestering a planet and holding a species hostage. Peepo will ultimately fail. We both know this. You yourself have commented on the Human ability to adapt and overcome in any given situation. The Humans will undoubtedly rise against Peepo. When that happens, the Mercenary Guild will fail from within. If that happens, the Union could destabilize."

Dreel rubbed a paw over his long face. "If that happens, the guilds could go to war."

"I fear they will. That means we must prepare ourselves for the coming conflict and ensure we honor the current threat. Whatever Kr'et'Socae's motivations and plans, we must be a step ahead of him, Captain Dreel. We cannot afford to fail."

* * *

Hangar One
Ocono

Jyrall ambled into the nearly deserted hangar carrying two monstrous cylindrical bags in each of his arms, a rectangular hard case for weapons slung across his back, and a smaller bag with its strap looped around his neck. The load would have crushed anyone else, even his fellow Besquith. There was some discomfort, but Jyrall moved with an unnatural grace, without a sign of strain. There were six shuttles in the main hangar, lined up abreast behind the open bay doors that let in the fresh breeze and the smell of flowers blooming in the springtime warmth. Jyrall slowed his pace and breathed deeply through his nose, savoring the scent of the outside. Soon enough he'd be locked into a spacecraft for hyperspace transit. The weightlessness and the boredom didn't bother him—the scents of space flight did. Most species developed a tolerance for the smells of others in a tight space over time. For Jyrall, there was no greater torture in the universe.

Ahead, Larth ambled out of the open rear deck of a shuttle. In his paws was a small case Jyrall recognized from their dormitory room. Larth's entire collection of personal effects fit in the small bag.

"Overpack much?" Larth grinned at his partner.

Jyrall growled. "I drew the weapons and both our field kits. And, I might add, I'm three times your size, and therefore require three times the equipment."

Larth chittered a laugh. "Oh, I'm sure that's it. Didn't you take anything to storage?"

"Of course I did." Jyrall set the two large bags on the shuttle ramp and worked the one from around his neck. "I put all your contraband food items in the common room, too. They shouldn't be able to trace all of it back to you."

"Not me, they won't," Larth agreed. "There's no ketchup there. I brought all the packets."

"You didn't!" Jyrall said. "I warned you about it. It's tartar sauce for you."

"Nope," Larth said, full of confidence. "I brought a little insurance policy with me. You like fish so much, you heard of sardines? I may or may not have acquired a can of it. In mustard sauce…maybe. You sneak tartar sauce into any of my food, and I'll crack the can and crawl into a space you can't reach with your big ass, and we'll see how your nose likes it after a day or two."

"Okay! Truce!" Jyrall laughed, holding his hands up in surrender. "Still, they shouldn't be able to trace it to you."

Larth cocked a furry eyebrow. "You put a sign on it, didn't you? My contraband?"

Jyrall tried not to smile, and failed. "Of course, but I didn't sign it or even write your name on it."

"What did you do?" Larth motioned with one digit for more of the story. "Who did you blame it on?"

"I merely said it was a gift," Jyrall opened up his arms and shifted his weight from foot to foot clumsily, "and I signed it 'Director Aarrtraa.'"

"You didn't!" Larth screeched. The Oogar dorm director was somewhat of a legend at the Academy. The Oogar had retired from active service with the guild nearly twenty years before and was said to have been a close friend of the legendary Enforcer Hr'ent. His methods for enforcing the rules of the dormitory had known no boundaries. He was part clean freak and part drill instructor, and the candidates paid the price for demerits and contraband through extra duty hours and cleaning details.

"Down to the handprint." Jyrall laughed. "When everyone figures out who did it, because we're gone and all, I hope they aren't too mad at us."

"Who cares? We won't be here to deal with it, and Aarrtraa could use a little laugh." Larth wiped his mouth with back of one paw. "Of course, he *won't* laugh. He's too prim and proper for that. But everyone else is headed out on their commissioning missions and…"

Jyrall watched his friend as his words trailed off. The Zuparti was correct, though. Soon, the upperclassmen would be gone on their final missions before graduation. The two of them, however, had completed their commissioning mission more than a year before and were coin-wielding members of the guild.

Gods. I'm a Peacemaker.

"You okay, Jyrall?"

The big Besquith turned to his friend. "Reality setting in, you know?"

"I do. We're Peacemakers now, partner." Larth grinned, his eyes glistening with pride. Jyrall returned the smile and they nodded at each other. They'd completed the unlikely gauntlet together, and their friendship would continue beyond graduation. There might be updates on StormWatch or other venues, or potentially additional training courses, but most of their friends would never be seen again. That distance didn't mean their classmates weren't brothers and sisters, nor were they forgotten. They were together in spirit, and that would be all that mattered.

But not for us, my friend. Our lives are in each other's hands now.

Jyrall shook off the thought. "You ready for this, Larth?"

"As ready as I can be, Snarlyface."

"I wish you wouldn't call me that," Jyrall grunted. "You can certainly do better than—"

Movement in the shuttle caught his eye. Captain Dreel appeared in the passenger compartment and watched them for a moment. "Sometimes I wonder what I'm walking in on with you two. You banter like a mated pair."

"He started it." Larth pointed at Jyrall.

"I said you could do better than calling me," Jyrall glanced at Dreel, "Snarlyface."

Dreel put his clawed hands on his hips, tilted his head toward the roof of the shuttle, and laughed long and hard. After a moment Larth and Jyrall laughed as well, and the tension Jyrall had felt creeping into his bones fell away. As he recovered, Dreel looked at Jyrall.

"This may come as a surprise to you, Jyrall, but my roommate in the Academy also had a select nickname for me. He knew it got under my fur to the fullest extent, and while he used it sparingly, it was effective to get my attention. I used one for him, too. He was also a

Zuparti, and I never got a chance to see him again after graduation. He taught me the value of friendship, and I envy the two of you going on this mission together. You can call each other anything you want, just don't say Peacemaker outside these walls. Maintain your cover as long as you can, but be prepared to take control of the situation at all times."

Jyrall pointed at the gear. "I drew our weapons and two full field kits for this mission. We're prepared—"

"No," Dreel said. "All that equipment stays here, including your weapons."

"No weapons? That's crazy!" Larth came to life. "I know crazy, and that's crazy. That's sending us out on a suicide mission."

"What did I tell you about weaponry in my very first class as your instructor?" Dreel asked with a grin.

"A Peacemaker can find and use anything for a weapon. When the time comes and the situation changes, the weapons available change, too," Larth replied. As he finished, he nodded his head with every word. "I understand, sir. I'm going to miss those pistols, but I understand."

Jyrall met his mentor's eyes. "I understand."

"Now, I do want you two to do something." Dreel motioned for them to come closer. "Face each other and greet each other officially, as if you'd never met before, right at this moment. Let the customs and courtesies flow now, where it is safe. From here on, you cannot indulge each other in this manner, even in private."

Jyrall squinted but didn't ask the question threatening to erupt from his lips. Instead, he lowered his gaze to Larth's and nodded. As the words formed, Jyrall knew what Dreel wanted them to do. The words were both simple and difficult at the same time. Emotions threatened to break into the mantra and disrupt the exchange. Peacemakers weren't much on ceremony, but the official greeting was different. For the first time, they were Peacemakers, and everything had changed.

"Peacemaker Larth, well met," said Jyrall.

"Well met, Peacemaker Jyrall."

Dreel put a hand on each of their shoulders. "Now, you understand."

"I do, sir," Jyrall replied.

Larth shook his head. "Dammit. What is that phrase?"

"What are you talking about?" Jyrall asked.

"It's from one of the Human movies we watched in Species Appreciation. Followed their early astronauts. Oh, dammit! One of them was always saying something in agreement that was caustic, vulgar, and funny as hell. I can't remember what it was, and it would have been perfect for this moment. You know, flying off on our first mission under the gaze of our mentor, who would have shaken his head and smiled at my perfectly timed wit. And I can't remember the punch line."

Dreel squeezed them both and leaned over to Larth. As he spoke, he deliberately winked his right eyelid. "Fucking A you can't, Peacemaker. Set the terms, and safe travels."

* * * * *

Chapter Three

Reception Hangar
Zeha
Ares Minor System

The commercial shuttlecraft's doors opened, and fresh, humid air filled the compartment. In a matter of seconds, the stale recycled air and its horrible scents vanished and gave Jyrall's senses a very brief respite before the scents of a new planet overwhelmed him. Two weeks of almost constant hyperspace travel grated on his every last nerve. The short stopover in the Kateris system to allow the Blue Flight to rendezvous with a Besquith Thrust Core and debark them to their first conveyance hadn't lasted more than an hour. Head thick and feeling woozy, Jyrall blinked several times and made himself acknowledge that gravity was present. As the world tilted to the left and started to spin, Jyrall closed his eyes and felt blindly for the edges of the external hatch. As his fingers found purchase, he took a long, deep breath and tried again to open his eyes.

Larth stood there looking up at him. "You okay?"

"You know how much I hate hyperspace."

"You hate space in general," Larth chittered. "It will pass. I'm sure we can find a stimtab around here that would clear up your head."

Jyrall shook his head and didn't immediately feel dizzy. "I'll be okay. Just give me a minute."

"By the looks of it, you won't have that long." Larth wasn't looking up at him anymore. Jyrall carefully turned his head toward the tarmac beyond the shuttle's door and saw a single male MinSha prancing in their direction. "Even money that's Lieutenant Colonel Tirr."

Jyrall squinted, but the effort didn't bring any improvement. "No bet."

"You always say that."

Jyrall turned back to his partner. "You're almost always right."

"Almost?" Larth placed a paw over his chest in mock surprise. "That's as close as you've come to saying that I'm always right."

"There was that Zuparti in the—"

"Hey!" Larth frowned. "I had no idea she wasn't entirely a she, okay?" One of the peculiar ironies of the Zuparti genetic structure was a very small percentage of recessive genes sometimes combined. About 0.002 percent of the entire Zuparti population were hermaphroditic. That fact wasn't widely known outside of the Zuparti homeworld, and for an off-worlder like Larth, discovery came as quite a shock.

Jyrall smiled but didn't say anything. "Time to get serious."

"Are you saying I'm not serious?"

"No," Jyrall said. "I'm telling myself it's time to get serious. Like from this moment forward. Once we leave Zeha, we're on our own."

Larth didn't say anything. After a moment, he squeezed past Jyrall's hulking frame and bounded down the passenger ramp toward Tirr. Jyrall stood fully upright and took two deep breaths, using a centering technique from the Peacemaker Guild to help control his reaction to renewed gravity. Feeling only slightly better and with the world turning only slightly, he followed his partner down the ramp and into the cool evening sunlight.

At the bottom of the ramp Larth waited, and as Jyrall arrived, he fell into step with the Besquith. They rapidly closed the distance to the MinSha officer, who paused, clasped a foreclaw to his thorax, and nodded. "Well met, Peacemakers."

"Well met, Lieutenant Colonel Tirr," Larth replied. "I'm Larth."

Tirr nodded and looked up at Jyrall. "You're Jyrall."

"I am. Well met, sir."

Tirr made a rasping sound like a chuckle. "Please, I insist you call me Tirr. Dreel said you couldn't be missed. I believe I underestimated your size by an order of magnitude."

Jyrall grinned. "Very difficult to hide in a crowd."

"On the contrary," Tirr replied. His compound eyes twinkled as he said, "The last thing you'll do is blend in, and that can play to your advantage in your assignment. Hiding in plain sight, Peacemaker. Given your cover stories and the implanted identities you received, it will bode quite well for you to get all the attention and allow your partner to gather the relevant intelligence."

"I'm not an intelligence operative, sir." Larth frowned.

"Nor did I say you were, Peacemaker." Tirr turned to the Zuparti. "Everyone on that colony with half a brain will expect Jyrall to be an Enforcer, based on his size alone. He'll be challenged constantly. You, Larth, have the advantage."

Larth nodded, but said nothing for a change. Jyrall knew the look on his face. Larth's lack of fear didn't mean his partner lacked intelligence. He'd seen the wisdom in Tirr's words and was reevaluating the mission even now.

Time to get serious, indeed.

Jyrall turned to Tirr. "When do we leave, sir?"

"Your ship is about two days out. You have time to stretch your legs, eat well, and rest," Tirr replied. He kept speaking, but Jyrall wasn't listening. Up the long slope behind Tirr, the winding trail that disappeared into the thick forest had been vacant. Now, it held two female MinSha, trailed by four others with very large bladed weapons in their claws.

"Peacemaker?"

Jyrall looked at Tirr again. "Yes, sir?"

"I asked if something was wrong?"

Jyrall motioned with a small twitch of his head. "Who are they?"

Tirr didn't bother to look. "Queen Taal, her chief of staff, Keshell, and the Queen's Guard. Technically they're my guard, as I command them, but I'm still considered on assignment to the Peacemaker Guild."

"And what assignment is that?" Larth asked.

"With respect, Peacemaker, you don't have a need to know what my assignment is," Tirr replied without a hint of tone in his voice. "I serve your guild master through an agreement with Queen Taal that was brokered by Peacemaker Francis. That's all you need to know. Should the time come, I will tell you. Until such time, it's best that you perform your mission with no further details of the operation at large."

"Fair enough," Larth grunted. The disappointment was palpable enough that Tirr's antennae bounced in amusement. Jyrall had to cough to cover the smile threatening to break across his features.

"There are parts of your mission that I am unaware of, Peacemaker Larth," Tirr said quietly. "What matters now is that you're here, and, until your ship arrives, you are both guests of Honored Queen Taal. I trust you're aware of the protocols involved in talking with a MinSha queen?"

"We are," Jyrall said. "We're also aware that Peacemaker Francis had a run-in with one of her guards. Are we going to find ourselves in a similar situation, Tirr?"

"No, you will not. MinSha females are stubborn creatures, my friends, but they're not stupid. I doubt any of them will ever distrust a Peacemaker in the performance of their duties again." Tirr walked toward the approaching entourage. "Please, follow me. I will make the formal introductions."

As they walked up the slope in shimmering twilight, Jyrall kept his eyes forward and heard Larth speak out of the side of his mouth.

"Why am I suddenly thinking this just went from bad to worse?"

Jyrall ground his lower jaw. As much as he didn't want to admit it, he was starting to feel the same way. While Tirr was pleasant enough, and serious, there was something else. After a moment, Jyrall recognized it as tension, and he tried to relax, but could not.

"Just do me a favor, will you?" Larth whispered.

"What?"

"Keep Tirr between you and the Queen. They eat the males who piss them off. If this goes to entropy, I have a plan," Larth said. "If he's in front of us, and you're in front of me, she'll have to get through the two of you first."

Jyrall bit back a bark of laughter with a sudden cough. Tirr glanced over his shoulder, his face impassive, although his antennae wobbled in displeasure, and kept walking. "What makes you think she'll want to eat you?"

"You never know." Larth grinned. "She'd definitely want to eat you first. I'd be like a snack, but you're like three full courses."

Jyrall smiled ominously. "She'd have to catch me first."

Larth chuckled. "Can a Besquith outrun a MinSha Queen?"

"I don't have to outrun a MinSha Queen. All I have to do is outrun *you*."

* * *

Small Freighter

Entering Zeha Atmosphere

"**H**ey, man, who are we again?" Keaton asked his co-pilot.

"Dude, I told you twice." His brother, Ricky, laughed. "We're the ship named *Night Moves*. You write these things and can't remember which one I picked out of them. *Night Moves*."

"Right on," Keaton said, rolling his neck. "Call ahead and find out exactly where we're going. I have the coordinates, but they may have a hanger preference."

"Yeah, the last thing we want to do is land where we're not expected," Ricky agreed. He sat forward and straightened the rumpled, soft Jacksonville Generals t-shirt he wore. A few errant crumbs of their dinner floated up and away in the microgravity. "I mean, it's been, like, forever since the war, and Captain Dreel says there are no issues with us, but I would prefer not to have to fight it out with a whole planet."

"We're good, man," his brother assured him. "Pops told us a long time ago we can trust the Peacemakers."

"I know that. I'm just not sure I trust the MinSha," Keaton replied.

"Gate Control, this is *Night Moves*, clearing emergence point and requesting contact information with Zeha approach control. Over."

A few seconds passed. Keaton wondered if they'd reawakened the sleepy-sounding gate controller from his drowsy watch. "*Night Moves*, acknowledged. Standard Ku band channels for approach are 10.21 gigahertz and 11.24 gigahertz. Initiate contact before 800 kilometers altitude."

"He means below that altitude, they'll come up firing." Ricky laughed before clearing his throat and calmly replying, "Zeha Gate Control, *Night Moves* acknowledges. We are clear and switching."

"Is that supposed to make me feel better?" Keaton flexed his grip on the controls but didn't look at his brother. "They'll assume we're hostile inside 800 kilometers?"

Ricky shook his head. "Nah. They'll consider us hostile until we make contact and send the Peacemaker's codes. That whole 800-kilometer thing is when they'll fly up and smack us out of the sky."

Keaton turned to his brother and frowned. "Call them. Now."

"All right, all right, man." Ricky grinned and tapped the communications display. "Zeha Approach, this is *Night Moves* in your sky at 1200 kilometers altitude. Requesting vector to main reception hangars. We have business with the royal family on behalf of the Peacemaker Guild. I say again, we have business with the royal family on behalf of the Peacemaker Guild. Over."

The response was immediate. A terse, high-pitched voice replied, "*Night Moves*, transmit your code clearance package immediately."

"Zeha Approach, transmission commencing." Ricky tapped the communications panel quickly, and the data package transmitted. "This is the part where I lean over and say something about hoping the code works."

"Shut up, Ricky," Keaton replied. After a moment, he grinned. "It was kinda overused though, wasn't it?"

"You think?"

"I do. The old man's movie preferences, like his advice and training, taught us how the galaxy works," Keaton replied. After a moment, his smile grew wistful.

"*Night Moves*, Zeha Approach Control. Clearance codes accepted. The royal family welcomes you. You are directed to the main reception hangar at this time. After atmospheric interface, assume a heading of 274 and follow UHF navigation beacon at 1128.75 megahertz. Acknowledge."

"Zeha Approach, *Night Moves*. Copy 274 at atmo and 1128.75 megahertz for nav beacons. Many thanks for the vectors."

"Copy, *Night Moves*. Expect a little turbulence on the approach. At thirty kilometers, Reception Control will contact you on this frequency. Zeha Approach, out."

"*Night Moves*, out," Ricky replied while his brother continued to fly the ship. They were silent until the first licks of ionized plasma licked at the forward surfaces of the ship. There was a little buffeting, and they felt gravity taking effect, pulling them down into their seats.

"I still miss the old man," Ricky said after a few quiet minutes.

"Yeah," his brother said, looking over at his near twin. "Times like these, I do, too."

* * *

Queen's Chambers
Zeha

"They are awfully young," Queen Taal mused. Her antennae bobbled in concern as she looked at Tirr and her chief of staff, Keshell. "We are merely to provide secure transportation? No weapons? Additional warriors?"

Tirr tilted his head and his antennae shook in a negative response. "No, Honored Queen. They require nothing from us for the completion of this mission."

Keshell flinched. "This mission? There will be others?"

Tirr looked up at the Queen, whose ruby eyes glittered. "I expect this is as good a time as any, Keshell. I have kept something from you, the act of which can cause distrust and discord. We cannot have that going forward."

"Have I disappointed you, Honored Queen?" Keshell's voice was soft and unsure. "Have I lost your trust?"

Queen Taal chittered a laugh. "No, you have not. In fact, your handling of this request from the Peacemaker Guild has given me any assurance I needed, about not only my staff but the military forces under our immediate command. Both are about to be placed in harm's way."

"Harm's Way?" Keshell's antennae thrashed in uncertainty. "I am unfamiliar with that system."

"It is a saying, Keshell," Tirr interjected. "From Earth. It means that conflict approaches, and many of our warriors will find themselves at risk and their lives in jeopardy."

"Indeed," Queen Taal replied. "The actions I am about to undertake could strain our relationship with the homeworld and the other royal families. I know it will strain our relationship with the Mercenary Guild, the Cartography Guild, and the Information Guild, but I believe we have no choice. The Peacemaker Guild must be protected."

Keshell turned to Tirr. "This is why you have *Victory Twelve* at the secure facility? For a mission I was not aware of?"

Tirr glanced at the Queen out of habit, but she merely watched him. He turned to his friend. "Yes. At the request of Lieutenant Francis and Guild Master Rsach, I have a mission of my own. I originally thought it would be easy enough to accomplish myself. However, I realized there was much more I hadn't considered. Our Honored Queen and I discussed this at length, and decided there was too great a risk."

"At which point," Queen Taal interjected, "I gave Colonel Tirr the ability to form a combat operation with two inherent missions. The first is to protect the Peacemaker Guild's High Council. With the clearance of the guild master, the finest of our Peacemakers, twelve warriors of the highest caliber, are the personal bodyguards of the High Council members, with the exception of Lieutenant Francis."

"Who is protecting her?" Keshell blurted.

Tirr turned to his friend and his antennae went rigid. "That I'm not allowed to tell you or the Honored Queen. All I know is, she's sufficiently protected. I have the assurance of the guild master, and I take him at his word."

Keshell opened her mouth to speak but closed it quickly. "One can surmise based off what we know of the first battle at Victoria Bravo."

Taal nodded. "Then nothing needs to be said. The second mission, though, is much more dangerous and troubling. It has direct ties to both Victoria Bravo and to Jessica's first mission. Are you familiar with the Dream World Consortium, Keshell?"

"No, my Queen."

"They market themselves as building stable worlds for multiple species to colonize and work together in harmony. Terraforming and climate control are within their grasp, and they've used the technology well. While their success rate has been impressive, there have been failures, and many lives have been lost. Jessica's first mission on Araf was in response to a failed contract, and the efforts of two mercenary companies to try to eradicate a colony of Altar. During the latest conflict at Victoria Bravo, before its establishment as a free trade zone, the Dream World Consortium was implicated in both the attack and attempting to help the enemy forces take down the colony there." Taal gestured at Tirr to continue.

"What we know comes from the Peacemaker Guild and their intelligence sections," Tirr replied. "We don't know what the Dream World Consortium is doing, but they've started doing far more exploratory testing and research than actual colonization and terraforming operations. A tenfold increase in research missions, versus one known planet opened for colonization in the last six months. They've launched 150 missions, including a mission to Earth itself."

"Why would they go to Earth? It's a perfectible habitable planet, isn't it?" Keshell asked. "Are they establishing a baseline of data?"

"Perhaps," Tirr replied. "Or it's something more. I've been tasked to find out what. I'm taking the first echelon of Guards and a small support force disguised as a research team aboard *Victory Twelve.*"

"That makes no sense, Tirr." Keshell shook her antennae. "*Victory Twelve* is Lieutenant Francis' ship, and it's registered to the Peacemaker Guild."

"Technically, it's registered to Intergalactic Haulers," Tirr replied with a hint of humor in his voice. "The company was never fully disbanded."

"It's still something anyone with GalNet access can determine," Keshell replied. "And unless you're planning to—Oh! This is a ruse?"

"A feint, but a feint with purpose," Queen Taal said. "With an echelon of warriors, Tirr can handle a combat situation until assistance arrives. By following the Dream World Consortium teams under the guise of looking for the lost assets of Intergalactic Haulers, we can maybe ascertain what the Dream World Consortium is attempting to do, and we could potentially draw attention away from Force 25. They've started their sweep of the outer worlds as they look for Jessica's father. Whatever we can do to assist them— indirectly of course—is best."

Keshell considered for a moment. "And the young ones out there? Their mission is both dangerous and deceitful, is it not?"

"The gathering of intelligence is seldom a bloodless, easy affair," Tirr said. "Their mission, from what I understand, is of the utmost importance to the Peacemaker Guild. There's a possibility those behind the last attacks at Victoria Bravo are in play where the Peacemakers are headed. The latest Peacemaker class graduates in less than two weeks. The hope is no one will expect them."

"But we know hope is not a strategy, Tirr," Queen Taal said. "That's why we act now, and we're prepared to mobilize the full complement of our forces for operations, Keshell. As Tirr departs, you'll set those plans in motion."

Keshell nodded. "I understand, Honored Queen. When must our forces be ready?"

"Far sooner than I'd hoped, I fear. Far sooner."

* * * * *

Chapter Four

"**A**m I seeing things, or does that look like *Gray-lich*?" Larth asked.

Larth stood on the tarmac with Jyrall, waiting for their ship to land. Aside from the MinSha younglings handling the landing pad operations, they were alone. Tirr and the other representatives of the MinSha royal family hadn't come to welcome the ship as they had the young Peacemakers. Part of it was the need for secrecy. The other part was the secure reception hangar lay some four hundred kilometers away from Queen Taal's chambers, and it was a closely kept secret, even among the MinSha. Nobody had told them what the MinSha did there, and they knew better than to ask. After a quick, disconcerting meal with the MinSha, they'd boarded a shuttle and flown to the outpost, with a quick blessing from Tirr and an assurance they would see him soon.

The ship's impending arrival cured any sense of boredom or idle curiosity about their new location. They'd been given the heads up when it entered the system, and when it hit the atmosphere. Local sunset had occurred a few minutes before, and the Zeha sky was a deep violet, with thin wisps of high clouds a bright orange and pink toward the western horizon. The calm, moist air surrounded them. The ship grew larger as it decelerated and descended to the tarmac, pirouetting effortlessly onto the landing pad with its engines oriented the way the ground controllers wanted. The ship hadn't hesitated, merely responded to the controls from the MinSha receiving team with ease. Impressive as it was, both young Peacemakers focused on the actual hull for a shred of positive identification. They'd had no idea what type of ship they were being issued. Captain Dreel had skirted the subject and only let them know it and its crew would be just what they needed for their mission.

"I don't doubt you see things," Jyrall answered. "I don't think you are right now, though. That ship looks quite similar to *Graylich*."

Graylich was the small freighter involved in the terrorist plot they'd stopped a year earlier. Jyrall had disabled the engines, keeping it on the station before the firefight that took out the two Peacemakers in that district. They had both been accepting bribes and furthering the Mercenary Guild's objectives against humanity.

"Well, I guess a small freighter is as good a ship as any," Larth said as they watched it flare and land. "It should be good cover. The pilot's pretty good; it came in quick and landed smoothly."

"It was impressive," agreed his partner. The Besquith tilted his head slightly and focused. Comparing it to his memory, he looked closer at the ship. "I see a couple of bulges and what looks like a few hatches added to the ship, if it is *Graylich*. Whoever added the hatches did a good job matching them with the old exterior."

"I didn't even notice them," admitted Larth with a shrug. "But then again, I didn't get a real good look at the ship like you did."

"Come on, let's go meet our crew," Jyrall said as they walked toward the ship. He could have stepped it out, but he maintained an easy pace for the Zuparti. It was habit, after three years of training together. Other times, when speed was necessary, Larth had perfected a shuffling jog and kept up with Jyrall's long strides. It wasn't needed now.

They stood far enough away to allow the ramp on the back of the freighter to come down, and they watched it lower. Larth noticed Jyrall stiffen as his partner looked into the dark recesses of the hold. The lights came on in the cargo area, and Larth saw why. Two figures walked down the ramp to the tarmac. They were nearly the same size, and looked strikingly similar to each other, though if you looked closely, the differences were there. A tiger's stripes are always unique. The two coming toward them looked like six-foot-tall bipedal tigers from Earth.

Larth whispered out of the side of his mouth. "Aren't they Pushtal? What in the wild hell fire is going on around here?"

"Shhh," Jyrall whispered back. He stepped forward. "Well met, I'm Jyrall."

They stopped a short distance away. In the tense moment, one spoke. "Well met, Peacemaker, I'm Keaton."

"And I'm Ricky," the other Pushtal said, raising a hand in greeting. "Dang, if Captain Dreel wasn't right. You're a big'un, huh?"

The ice was broken. Larth grinned; he already liked Ricky. "Well met, Larth is the name. So you're working with us? As in the Peacemakers?" He folded his arms. "Oh, I gotta hear this story."

"I'm interested as well," Jyrall admitted.

"Board your ship, Peacemakers," Keaton said, indicating the ramp. "We'll give you the half-credit tour and point out a few things."

The lights remained on as the ramp closed. The first thing Jyrall noticed was the size of the cargo area seemed smaller. There were bulkheads in place that hadn't been there before. He wondered if it was the same ship or one made similar. The hold was empty. Something was missing, and it wasn't cargo. Jyrall tried to place it, but nothing came to mind.

"So, this is your ship," Keaton began. "As I'm sure you surmised, we're your crew. I'm the pilot, and I program a little. My brother Ricky is the co-pilot and all-around maintenance guy. Unless we get into a really tight spot, don't let him fly her. He's pretty good with the weapons systems, but don't give him the stick, man."

"Whatever!" Ricky said, grinning and exposing his sharp teeth. "I can fly her just fine. And don't let Keaton fool you, he can do more than program a little. He's been hacking systems since we were cubs. It used to drive our old man crazy. Except when he'd hack some of the sites on the GalNet and we'd watch the old Earth shows and concerts. That he didn't mind."

"Wait, what?" Larth said, becoming excited. "You two like Earth-made GalNet shows?"

"Well, hell yeah," Ricky said. "We were raised by a Human. Pops was an old man by Earth standards when he fought off the ship we came from. Our biological parents weren't much better than pirates. We were the only survivors. From what he told us, we weren't much bigger than a handful each when he saved us."

"Really? Pirates," Larth said. "I mean, everyone knows Pushtal are prone to that kind of thing, but you two work with the Peacemaker Guild."

"We do," answered Keaton. "Look, we have no memory of other Pushtal. As a matter of fact, as far as I'm concerned, I'm glad we don't. Being a pirate isn't an honest living. The old man taught us to earn our own way through life. Taking from others ain't right; it's for cowards."

"No McCoy has ever been called a coward and the one saying it stayed upright for long," Ricky quoted the man who raised them. "We speak English. Hell, I wouldn't understand another Pushtal if he spoke right to my face. Pops always told us, 'It's not who you are, it's who you think you are and how you act that defines you, boys. Don't ever let some sumbitch tell you different. You two are McCoys, through and through.'"

"I miss the old man," Keaton said, staring off for a moment. He shook off the memory and said, "Enough of memory lane. After time finally got him—God knows nothing else could kill him—a Human Peacemaker came around a few weeks later, gave us her condolences, and directed us toward a job at a ship repair facility. Kind of a hush-hush operation in the Torgero system. We'd been doing some freelance work as well as helping the old man with his small mining operation in the Aspara system. Anything to make an honest credit."

"Was it Jessica Francis?" Jyrall asked. Out of the corner of his eye, he saw Larth cover a grin with a paw. "The redheaded one?"

"Naw, she had dark hair—about shoulder length. Sinclair was her name."

"Nice," Larth said as he turned to wink at Jyrall. "I knew she was still operating out there somewhere."

Jyrall nodded. He'd surmised it, too. In the upheaval of the current Galactic Union, no Peacemaker could sit idle. "You guys did all these modifications yourselves?"

"We had some help," Ricky said, his arms wide. "But we were a part of refitting this entire ship. We've known we would be part of your team for a year. This baby has missile launchers, defensive lasers—a decent offensive one for its size—a projectile gun for close stuff, a hidden arms room, and some other hidden compartments in case we have to vanish. It has an escape pod for four, capable of entering an atmosphere and landing on a planet. The projectile gun comes with that, since it doubles as the gunner's seat for it. There's some ramped-up engines, and best of all, it has its own shunts."

"A year?" Jyrall asked. He glanced at Larth, who met his gaze but said nothing.

"Give or take a little, yes. We didn't know it would be you two specifically, but the guild master had a mission in mind, and he wanted us to fly it. All we needed was the right ship and a few specific new features."

"Impressive," Jyrall commented, going over all he'd just heard. He twitched his long chin at the ship. "What's her name?"

"Right now she's squawking *Night Moves*," Keaton replied, "but I have four other identification programs ready should we need it. She was *Graylich* when we got our paws on her. Captain Dreel said you had a bit of history with her."

Larth and Jyrall grinned at each other. It was a good sign. Around them, the MinSha ground crew sprang into action, moving several pallets of provisions toward the ship with speed and efficiency. There wasn't much time until launch. "Show me the weapon's console and the other modifications," Jyrall said.

"Where's that arms room?" Larth asked. He looked up at Jyrall. "Priorities, man. Priorities."

* * *

Volvok

Tecran System

The freighter *Rygg's* outer hatch opened with a rush of air that generated a brief flash of vapor at the edge of the circular door before evaporating. No sooner had the outer ramp deployed than a small Zuparti—wrapped in what appeared to be several ratty blankets—bounded, shivering, down the ramp. Rubbing its paws together and stamping its tiny paws on the ground to generate warmth, the golden-furred being glanced around the reception area for a familiar face before repeating the effort to sense security or Peacemakers. There were none, and Ch'tek breathed a sigh of relief. Sixteen days aboard *Rygg* had been more than enough spaceflight for a while. After securing clandestine transportation off Victoria Bravo, Ch'tek had been along for the ride, first to Karma, where he didn't leave the spacecraft, and then direct to Volvok. *Rygg* carried spare parts and medicinal supplies on its manifest. What he paid for secure transit, Ch'tek was sure, far surpassed what anyone would pay for its wares. The move had been risky, but there was no other game in town to get away from Victoria Bravo before they'd found him. A Peacemaker warrant for arrest garnered far more attention than he'd wanted and moved his timetable immeasurably forward.

Squinting against the early morning sunrise, he stared across the containers strewn around the tarmac and saw another Zuparti about a hundred meters away, leaning against a rust-colored container bearing the markings of Zendt Logistics. Still huddled in his blankets, Ch'tek made his way across the tarmac to the familiar face. He didn't wave or acknowledge the other's presence, and as he stepped closer, his counterpart didn't greet him, but merely fell into step beside him.

"This has gone awry, Ch'tek."

He ground his lower jaw. "I am well aware of that, Emop."

"The Consortium's board is concerned you've lost sight of the original intent. First your reckless experiment with the Canavar egg, and then nearly being compromised at Victoria Bravo?" Emop chittered disgustedly. "If the Peacemaker Guild ties you to Kenos and the failure at Araf, this entire operation will fail."

"Kenos was an idiot. His plan to eradicate the colony brought the Peacemakers' scrutiny in the first place." Ch'tek shook his head. "And yes, it was bad luck that Jessica Francis was there to intercept the egg. Her former husband was an idiot. What she saw in him, I don't know. That woman is formidable, Emop. I think another Peacemaker could have been bought, and the Altar moved without incident. Humans should never have been allowed into the Peacemaker Guild. They were bad enough in the Mercenary Guild, as the dirty-fighting, credit-grubbing bastards they are."

Emop nodded once as they walked. "You shouldn't have attempted the Canavar egg operation."

"How else was I supposed to divert attention from our initial operations at Ghinzz, Snowmass, and Ferega-Two?" Ch'tek sighed. "We managed to get teams onto those planets for surveys without anyone batting an eye. Then we pushed on to twelve more worlds. And more after that. In the last year, we've surveyed more than ninety planets. In the first sixty years of the Consortium, they managed half that number."

"Perhaps we've tried to accomplish too much?"

"No." Ch'tek glanced up. They were approaching the terminal building, and the rising sun slowly pushed through the bone-chilling cold of spaceflight on his frame. "We have no idea of a...timetable."

Much less if this entire thing is a bust, Ch'tek mused. The entire gambit and sixty years of work were based on a possibility that was little more than faith. The very idea that they could profit from something so unlikely—

"We must cover our tracks." Emop took a deep breath. "There are those familiar with our inner circles who could be swayed. The war with the Humans has caused lines to be drawn in strange places. Allegiances and secrets have become liquid assets. We have to ensure that the Consortium's intent is kept hidden."

"Only a few of the board know the truth, Emop."

"There are others who promised secrecy long ago, Ch'tek. What if they're found and swayed? What if the Peacemakers investigate the Consortium in earnest this time? What might they find? We must do something." Emop was silent for a long moment. Ch'tek said nothing as he waited for Emop to ask the question he'd danced around during their walk. It came after another deep breath. "The mission at Victoria Bravo was a failure, wasn't it? They didn't get the server to orbit?"

"No," Ch'tek replied. "I'm not sure they were meant to."

"Meaning what?"

"I think our benefactor may not have actually needed the server to get what he wants. There was no better Enforcer at finding targets who didn't want to be found." Ch'tek chittered a laugh. "I believe Kr'et'Socae has nearly everything he needs, save for one thing."

"Funding," Emop replied. "With forces and resources under his command, he'll have to do something fast to secure credits. Do you know what that might be, Ch'tek?"

"No, I don't. Ultimately, it doesn't matter. We have our own business to attend to. As part of our agreement, however, I will have to inform Kr'et'Socae of the entire situation."

"He does not have a need to know everything."

"I believe he does." Ch'tek curled one side of his mouth under. "This is about more than the location of Peacemaker Francis' father. He doesn't matter, mark my words. This is about Kr'et'Socae going after the Peacemaker Guild. He has the skeleton of an army, a few ships, and some powerful allies, but he needs credits. When he gets them, he's going to kill Guild Master Rsach and the entire council."

"How do you know this? Or is it just a premonition?"

Ch'tek shook his head. "I don't know this. I can only speculate that a disgraced Enforcer, put away for life by the guild he thought would back his actions, would want a measure of revenge. His actions on Drecht Four were no different than what Jessica Francis did on Araf and on Victoria Bravo. She chose a side and initiated combat actions. How is that making peace?"

"The situation forced her to choose a side."

"Since when do Peacemakers choose sides?" Ch'tek seethed. "They were supposed to be arbitrators. Kr'et'Socae must see this, and he will take it on himself to punish them. The Equiri sense of honor, when wronged, is dangerous. There is no more dangerous being in the galaxy right now than Kr'et'Socae. What's worse, Emop? The Peacemakers are looking for him, and they aren't going to find him. They know he's behind this, and they can't catch him."

"What are they going to do, then?"

"They'll try to trap him somehow. But they'll be looking in the wrong place." Ch'tek looked up again at the rising sun and felt the warmth on his face. Everything about being out of a spacecraft was good. With some proper food and rest, he'd be able to initiate the next phase of his plan. "All we have to do, Emop, is maintain contact with his elements and provide what we can. He will do the rest."

"Meaning what?"

"Those former members of the council? We're going to exterminate them." Ch'tek grinned. "Because he needs the credits, Kr'et'Socae will jump on the chance. When he does, we'll see what he's really up to and make our move."

* * * * *

Chapter Five

Mining Operations Building
Parmick
Parmick System

Barlung snatched the heavy metal door open, ducked his massive frame through it, and slammed it shut behind him, with a clang that vibrated the foundation. Several heads whipped around in shock as the noise echoed off the concrete walls. Almost all of them quickly looked back at whatever they were doing beforehand. A couple of Goka in the room went back to cleaning their weapons, working hard to get the dust out of the small places.

Several Lumar sat quietly around the large stone slab acting as the conference table. There had been a double armwrestling match before their leader emerged from the operations area, but it was discontinued. Credits bet on it slipped quietly into the various owner's pockets and pouches as they prepared to hear the displeasure surely coming their way. Hopefully, it wouldn't be complicated orders; too much detail tended to confuse them. They preferred it when the boss just demanded the miners work harder or longer shifts. They were good at carrying out those type of demands and making it happen.

Hired muscle bereft of brains. Barlung held his breath for a moment and let it out in a long, frustrated sigh. Across the room, his two lieutenants rose from their own card game and rumbled toward him.

Instead of supervising the mines at shift change, they were relaxing. Again. Barlung stomped toward them and met them in the middle of the room.

Cartrule and Frooth looked slightly up at their larger leader. "Bad news, Boss?" rumbled Frooth.

"We need more production!" Barlung growled. "The output this last week has been pathetic. What kinda mining operation are you two running? Did you let them take breaks this last week?" The Oogar's voice rose until he nearly screamed at every occupant in the room. Several flinched but no one spoke for a long moment.

"No, Boss, no breaks," Cartrule answered for his fellow overseer. "Just the mid-shift stoppage so they can eat and recharge their tools."

"Yeah, well, Nay-Thok ran the numbers, and they're way off where we should be," said the big Oogar menacingly. "From now on, only half stop to eat. They can rotate so the equipment doesn't shut down at all." He looked over at the Lumar in the room. "You knuckle draggers hear that? Only half eat at a time. Make sure those on shift now get the word."

"Yes, Boss," one of them answered. "They can only eat half of their food."

"Hr'ent save me," Barlung growled under his breath. He shook his head and stared at Cartrule and Frooth. He pointed at them with a large paw. "You two figure out how to get the damned Lumar to understand your orders and find ways to get more production out of the labor. What am I paying you for if you're not doing your jobs?"

"We got it, Boss," Frooth, the lightest colored of the three purple Oogars, assured him. Frooth stood an easy seven and a half feet, but he was a head shorter than Barlung. The former mercenary had been wounded several years before and drifted from one job to another. They'd served a tour in the same company and had been friends forever, and while Frooth had always been exceptional in a fight, his style of management bordered on non-existent. Cartrule, on the other hand, wasn't much of a fighter, but he knew how to handle situations. Yet he deferred to Frooth more often than taking his own stand. Barlung had hoped the two of them could handle the demands of the mining operation. Under normal circumstances, that might have been the case, but with usable output falling below expectations, it was difficult. Then again, how was he supposed to get more than red diamond dust out of a defunct, barren mine?

"Good," Barlung said, slightly calmer.

"We'll take care of the change." Cartrule nodded. His eyes bright and jaw firm, Barlung had no qualms believing the junior Oogar. He quickly surveyed the room and felt the fur on his back ripple in rage.

"Hey!" Barlung shouted at the two Goka. "You two put those back together and get back out there. We only have two in the towers right now. If any more of the workers escape, you two alone will answer for it. Get out there."

"Moving, Boss. We're moving," answered the closest Goka as they quickly reassembled their weapons.

"You two go make sure the shaft is producing something," Barlung said. "If we don't get anything else out of it by tomorrow, we'll try another. I need to get over to the lab and see what kind of quality last week provided. Nay-Thok tells me the quality is okay, but he would feel better if I verified. He doesn't want to venture out."

"He never does," commented Frooth with one side of his maw turned under.

"It's not his job," warned Barlung. "You let me worry about him. On second thought, Frooth, call your friend, that Zuul over in Town, and see if there're any takers on the posted mining jobs. If there are, tell them whatever you need to, just get them to come for an 'interview.' Once we get them here, we'll make *them* accept the job and the work conditions, or they can help fill in that last shaft like the others who gave us a problem."

"I'm on it," Frooth replied.

"If no one else has come into the system for work, we may have to consider getting some of the locals," Cartrule suggested.

"Yeah?" Barlung asked. "Who's going to convince them? We got the miners on lockdown, and we can do the same to any others who come into the system, but most of the residents of Town aren't going to come quietly. There're at least three different factions using Town as their base of operations. They maintain a truce and just stay out of each other's way. We're not walking in there with demands for labor, that's for sure. They might get the idea they need to work together and challenge me. Then we'll have to kill everyone, and that's not in the plans right now. Not to mention all the others based out of Town."

"You idiot." Frooth laughed at his counterpart, Cartrule. "There's a reason the rest of the Goka company is contracted to guard our hanger, the ship, and the courier's ships. Town is full of ex-mercenaries, AWOL mercenaries, mercenary wannabees, smugglers, pirates, and half a dozen other undesirable types from all over the galaxy. None of them are going to fall for the 'mining job' bit. If you take anyone in the colony, from the shops or other business the locals use, without all three of the factions' approval, it'll get ugly.

What's your plan? Snatch the waitresses out of Pete's Dive Bar and put them to work in the mines?"

Frooth continued, "The last time you said something smart to one of the waitresses, she broke a mug over your head. Idiot."

"It was a lucky shot," complained Cartrule. "She grabbed the mug and threw it before I could react. I was going to pound her, but all four of the other waitresses had their hands on their weapons. She'll get hers…one day."

"That's why you don't go to Town anymore," Barlung said as they walked out into the bright light of day. The Parmick system star was shining with a slight red tint through the clouds, and the breeze was only blowing slightly today. On Parmick, there was always wind blowing. Often it stirred up clouds of dust around the mining site, covering everything in a layer of slate gray grime.

The workers they could see across the valley, coming and going from one of the six shafts dug into the mountainside, were coated with it. Some of it came from deep in the shaft being worked, but most of it came from the swirls of dirt flying around the valley. The legs of the four overwatch towers close to the shaft openings were permanently covered in the dust.

"You did say if we met the quarterly goals, we could have a night on the town. I'm ready to go back to Pete's." Frooth elbowed Cartrule. "If nothing else, to watch you get your hairy ass kicked."

"Why you two would go into that place again is beyond me," Barlung continued. "We're supposed to keep the success here under wraps, not get drunk on whatever swill they serve in Pete's and run our mouths. You're lucky I didn't put you to work in the shaft after that little incident."

Barlung turned away from his lieutenants and headed toward the only modern looking building at the mining site. He needed to check the quality of the last group of red diamonds and find out how much more was needed for the next batch. Undermining the currency of the Galactic Union could work up a thirst, but there was nothing he wanted in Pete's Dive Bar or any of the other establishments on Parmick. Soon enough, he'd be off this godsforsaken rock and back to civilization, with a hefty retirement account.

Soon enough.

* * *

Pete's Dive Bar
Town, Parmick

Cora cleaned another table and ran through the numbers in her head again. At the rate she and the rest of them were saving credits, it would still be another year or more before they could book passage and get out of this system and back to Earth with the gear they had remaining. They could probably do it in six months if they were willing to leave their gear behind, but she couldn't leave the Mk 7 she'd inherited and had fought in for the last couple of years behind.

It was old and outdated, with a few scars, but it was hers. She wouldn't leave it behind, and she couldn't ask the others to do it if she didn't, especially now that Nileah and Lisalle had repaired it and the other two damaged machines.

For the thousandth time, she thought about the circumstances that had stranded her and her squad on this cesspool of a colony on the far side of the galaxy, with no means to get back to Earth, and debt mounting from their boss/landlord, a man little better than an outright thief.

* * *

One Year Earlier

Planet Naar
Tecran System

"**S**taff Sergeant McCoy," Colonel Joshua Talmore ordered, "shore up that flank, or they'll roll us up like home grown tobacco and smoke us out."

"Yes, sir," Cora answered through the link in her mech. She switched over to the designated squad frequency and directed her troops to shift over and behind the large boulders on the side of the hill. She verified none of them were silhouetted on the ridge, creating an obvious target for the oncoming horde of KzSha at least two companies in size.

She'd never fought against the KzSha race, but everything she'd read indicated they would take no prisoners. The four-foot insectoids were ruthless in battle, and they were coming fast to take the hill and the compound at its summit. It was supposed to have been a fairly easy contract for the small company from Western North Carolina, a break from the contract before that, which had reduced the unit from battalion-size to little more than a company-sized element.

Despite the impending fight, Cora smiled to herself. *Stay below the ridgeline.* Her last instructions to her six troops. Funny, since the unit she was contracted with was called Talmore's Ridge Runners. Her squad knew the deal, though. They were hillbillies through and through.

With a quick scan, she checked the placement of her all-female squad. The colonel had no qualms about women in mechs, or even in combat, for that matter. He had, however, worried about their safety in a unit full of men, many of whom could not be described as gentlemen. Within a week, he knew better, as the women fiercely stood up for themselves to the point that none of the other squads wanted them. He decided on strength in numbers and placed the women together. It had worked out well through several contracts. Despite the squad being comprised of older Mk 7 CASPers, they fought well together.

The unit didn't have the most modern equipment, but they got everything they could out of what they had. Unless they started getting more lucrative contracts, they would never pilot Mk 8s. Cora didn't mind too much. Her mech was actually hers, unlike most of the unit members. It was a gift left to her by an uncle on her eighteenth birthday, years ago. Sent from wherever he was at the time, it must have cost a fortune to ensure she received it. It was the best gift she'd ever gotten, and she'd promised herself that only death would separate them.

Watching the enemy jump and sort of fly up the hillside toward them, Cora gave the command to open fire, and the other six members of her squad immediately began to whittle down the enemy ranks. The KzSha returned fire with their laser rifles as they came. She didn't have time to see how the rest of the company faired. They had the high ground, but the enemy continued to climb, getting closer and closer through the sheer numbers of troops they threw at them. Her own ammunition indicators were already yellow. She frowned.

It's gonna be close.

"Look out, Withers!" she heard her team leader, Sergeant Nileah, cry out as one of the other members received a rocket in her mech's torso. It penetrated in a spot the older mech had been repaired before, and Withers was gone. There were just six of them left holding the flank.

Over the company net, Cora heard some of the battle happening as orders were given. Most of the commands were to the opposite flank and the center of the main line, where the weaker commanders fought. The colonel typically left her alone and gave her full authority for her given sector of fire. As it was, Cora simply fought the battle. Moving, firing, and communicating with her remaining CASPers came easily, and they fought like demons.

After several minutes, she no longer heard the colonel on the net. She continued to engage the enemy, and noticed their enthusiasm and numbers were dwindling, when another of those portable rockets came spiraling in and struck Jackson right where her head would be in the cockpit of the mech. With a flash, multiple lasers hit the mech, and it toppled face first and slid partway down the hill.

Shit! They were down to five. She didn't have time to grieve as she snapped her sword out on the arm of her mech and prepared for close combat.

The KzSha withdrew quickly, firing sporadically as they sought cover behind their fallen comrades, stacked in piles. Cora saw them regrouping and reached for her transmit button without a second thought.

"Runner Six, Blue One. Enemy withdrawing by fire and preparing to counterattack. Over."

There was no response, so she tried again.

"Runner Six, Blue One. Did you hear me, sir? Enemy falling back in my sector. Over."

After fifteen seconds, a new voice cut in. She recognized the executive officer's voice immediately. "Copy, Blue One. Hold the line. Out."

Cora wanted to ask where the colonel was, but there were a million possible answers and, really, it wasn't that important. She had to take care of her soldiers and execute her orders. The colonel had said, and the executive officer had reminded her, to hold the line.

That's just what we're gonna do.

She selected the squad's internal radio frequency and pressed the transmit button. "Blue Team, sound off with status and equipment check."

"One, this is Two. Fuel is green, ammo is yellow. Armor is stable," Sergeant Nileah replied.

The next voice was slightly higher pitched and excited. Specialist Lisalle Jones easily won the title of most amped up for a fight. "One, this is Four. Fuel is green, ammo is amber. Armor is stable."

For a split second, Cora wanted to reprimand Three for lack of radio procedures, but the stark realization that Three had been Withers slammed her jaw shut with a click.

"One, this is Five. Fuel is green, ammo is amber. Armor is Condition Two."

Cora frowned and touched a direct laser connection to Five. "May, what's going on?"

"Took a high velocity round to the left shoulder. My MAC is FUBAR, and I lost a big chunk of exterior armor and one camera. I've got rocks for cover at my position, so I'm okay." Specialist May Bolton was as good as they came. She was the youngest of Cora's soldiers and the only person on the team not from North Carolina, but from Flag Pond, Tennessee.

Close enough.

"Copy," Cora replied. "Keep your young ass down as much as you can, Honey."

"Roger, One."

"One, this is Six." Private First Class Kellie English sounded bored. Where her wingman, Lisalle Jones, was exuberant in combat, English took it deathly serious, and she was damned good at her job. "My states match the others. Armor is green."

"One, Four. I've got forward movement in the sector. Here they come!"

Her squad fell into the routine of battle with ease. The KzSha attempted to take the hill twice more before they were completely devastated. The high ground was a force multiplier nigh impossible to overcome without artillery or air-to-ground support. The KzSha had neither. Cora and her team collected their dead and waited for transport in virtual silence.

Later, inside the compound where the local governor lived, the staff sergeant learned of Colonel Talmore's death, a lucky hit by one of those rockets. The unit executive officer was now the owner of the company, as the colonel had no heirs. It wasn't good. Cora had never trusted the man. He was from a big city farther north and seemed…slimy.

The contract was fulfilled, and they were relieved by a battalion-sized unit of Jivool to protect the governor of the colony. She had no doubt the Aku wanted protection because they were hoarding something valuable, but that wasn't her concern. The four women under her leadership mattered far more than anything an alien could want. Together they boarded the old ship to head back to Earth. Before they launched, Cora decided to find another unit. She planned to announce the dissolution of her contract the moment the ship touched down.

As the ship slipped into hyperspace, she learned Major Smith had decided to go to Parmick instead of Earth. That didn't sit well with her entire unit, and she let him know. Gathered in a staff meeting that had proven to be very one-sided, Cora ground her teeth and said what everyone else was thinking. "Parmick is a joke," Cora said in the meeting. "If it's another contract you want, there are far better places to find one than a backwater colony that far out on the rim, sir."

"My decision is final and above your pay grade, Staff Sergeant," the major said with contempt. Command was already going to his head. "I'll decide where we're going and what missions we'll take. Your opinions are understood, but they are simply that. Opinions."

After a week in Town on Parmick, Cora was ready to be anywhere but there. The night before, the company—now called Smith's Troopers—prepared to deploy for some mission the new owner had secured, gods knew what it was, and the whole company crowded into Pete's Dive Bar for a last liberty call. Reluctantly, Cora and her squad joined them and secured a table as far from the center of the action as possible. She'd been engrossed in watching a replayed rugby match from Earth and hadn't seen the situation change.

"We could be friends, you know," the drunken major slurred into her ear, startling her.

"Sir, you're drunk," Cora said, disgusted. "Go back to your table."

"We could be *really* good friends," he insisted and put an arm around her. He grinned wide and his eyes glinted in half-lidded humor. "You're pretty good looking, you know? Or do you hillbillies call that 'purty?'"

"Sir, you're drunk. Go back to your table. Please." The volume of her words sent her squad mates into action. They sat forward, all of them surveying the room and preparing to protect her. It gave her a sense of pride that almost overcame her sudden fear.

Embarrassed, Smith looked over at the table where his friends in the unit sat and watched. The men jostled and pointed, even catcalling him. Smith laughed, tossed back the remains of his drink, and leered at Cora. He grabbed a handful of her ass and said, "You should rethink my offer, Staff Sergeant, or it's back to private for you. Maybe worse."

Without thinking, she whirled, threw his arm off her shoulder, and punched him between the eyes, knocking him to the floor. As he struggled to get up, Cora whispered to Nileah, "Take the squad and get our mechs off the ship. If any of you want to ship out with them, you can, but I'm not."

The four women stood and headed toward the door with the eyes of their entire company on them. A burly man stepped in front of them at the door, and Cora's heart raced. Sergeant Jerund was hardly the man she'd expected to give them trouble. Of the rest of the unit, the maintenance NCO, Jimmy-Ray Jerund, was probably the only decent member besides the five of them. They had a lot in common, and he always acted like a respectable southern gentleman around them, never hinting at more than friendship or trying to slip inuendo into conversations.

He hailed from Rabun County in the mountains of northeast Georgia, and was sometimes the brunt of hillbilly jokes himself, despite having the ability to fix dang near anything with almost nothing. Cora watched him talking with her soldiers quietly. His eyes flitted to her once, and he looked back at the others. Through the din of the crowded bar, she couldn't hear what he said, but the four women passed through the door and into the night. Sergeant Jerund stood by the door for a long moment, his face stern and his arms crossed, as if silently signaling the others that the women weren't to be touched. Fast, almost too fast to see, he winked at her and hope surged. Was it too much to hope he'd given the others the codes? The ship was unmanned and only locked down at the debarkation point. Major Smith hadn't bothered to pay off the security guards, and the unit's passive security measures were easily defeated. That was proof the new commander was an even bigger idiot than Cora had thought.

Cora turned her eyes back toward the bar in time to get hit in the head with an empty mug. She saw stars and felt the blood flow down her face. Without thinking, she kicked out, catching the commander between the legs. He howled as he dropped to the floor. Clutching his genitals, he pitched over on his side and vomited explosively. His new executive officer and the company sergeant major picked him up, scowling at her, and dragged him back to their table. Cora waited for them to retaliate, but all they did was stare and continue their hushed conversations. She vowed to never forget Smith's face and the promise therein to either get what he wanted or kill her. There was no way he was going to do either, to her, or to any of the women in her squad. They had to leave. Cora grabbed a napkin and dabbed at the wound on her head, but kept watch on the others. No one moved. When Smith and his core staff stood to leave a half hour later, the rest of the unit slowly filtered out of the bar after them.

Sergeant Jerund remained behind. He went to the bar and grabbed a handful of napkins and a pitcher of cloudy ice water. Turning toward her, he kept his face straighter than he'd ever done and closed the distance quickly. He set the pitcher down on the table and dabbed one of the napkins in the water before handing it to her.

"Thanks," Cora said. "What did you tell them?"

"How to get your gear out and where to hide it." Jerund's voice was serious and low. "Sit here until last call. I'll make sure no one's out there to blindside you."

"I owe you one, Jimmy-Ray."

Jerund winked at her again. "Time'll come, Cora. Time'll come. You be safe out here."

"You, too."

She watched him go, then turned her attention to the wound on her head. Direct pressure stopped the bleeding after a couple of minutes, and with careful touches, she felt the edges of the wound and grimaced. It would need stitches at a minimum, and it would likely scar.

That sonuvabitch managed to leave his mark in one way or another, huh?

Anger rose, and she let it come. She'd always tried to do her best and take care of her people without letting anyone take advantage of them. Smith had done just that, and while she'd made sure her people were clear of the line of fire, and she'd ultimately made the bastard pay for hitting her with a cheap shot, she'd failed to take care of herself.

Never again, Cora. You were raised better than that.

The rest of the night passed quietly. Cora sat alone, tracing her fingers around the top of her water glass until last call before walking to the door.

"Come back soon," the owner called to her from behind the bar.

Not likely. First thing tomorrow morning, we're finding a ride and getting the hell off this rock.

She joined her squad at the loading docks where the remaining CASPers, low on fuel and without ammunition, sat ready for storage. Each of the women had a simple footlocker for their belongings, and there were a couple of spares with other equipment from the squad bay. There hadn't been time to do more. It took the last of their collected credits to secure a private storage locker for the equipment, but it had been worth it.

When Smith and the company left early the next morning, they hadn't bothered to try and find the missing squad. Staff Sergeant Cora McCoy and her squad, formerly of Talmore's Ridge Runners, were stranded on a planet in the middle of nowhere, with no chance of getting off of it unless they signed on with some of the worst units ever put together. Units that were little more than pirates and who knew what else, using the colony as their base of operations. They needed a job to earn credits, but not one that compromised their sense of honor and decency. She started asking around.

* * *

Present

Pete's Dive Bar
Town, Parmick

With a sigh, the tall brunette brushed the hair out of her eyes. Cora could feel the almost completely healed scar just below her hairline on her forehead. She moved on to the next table and collected the mugs sitting on it. May and Kellie were doing the same across the room, in between fetching drinks for the few patrons in the bar, a Human and two aliens of a race she didn't recognize.

Pete sat at the long bar, the stump of his right leg resting on the barstool beside him, doing something on his slate. He was probably figuring out how to cut the alcohol even more to increase his profits. Anything for an extra credit, including paying next to nothing for his help in the bar. *Once a pirate, always a pirate, thought Cora.*

"Cora?" Pete slurred. He stared at her with one eyebrow cocked comically and a half-smile on his thin white lips. "Time to take the deposit."

She nodded, but didn't say anything. Every day, Pete packaged up the previous day's earnings, minus his meager salary and the staff's paltry share, and sent them to Barlung's accountant and second-in-command. In the days following the bust of the mining operations, civilization on Parmick had devolved until the strongest faction prevailed. The Oogar and his lieutenants had assumed control of Town about the same time they acquired the defunct mines and pressed every possible soul into service in the slate gray tunnels, searching for red diamonds. They ran Town like the mobsters on the old holo-videos from Earth.

Pete closed the black case. He held up an attached explosive bracelet and snapped it around her wrist. Only Nay-Thok had the other key to open the case, and the explosive inside was far greater than it would take to sever her wrist. She didn't know how powerful it was, but it was a risk she couldn't take.

"You best hurry back," Pete said. "Happy Hour starts in thirty minutes."

"I will," Cora replied. The case was heavy, and the metal cuff tight on her wrist.

"You'd better, girl," Pete snarled. "Don't cross me."

* * * * *

Chapter Six

Mining Operations Center
Parmick

Nay-Thok rested on a specially constructed chair, watching a bank of six monitors showing various shafts of the central mining operation. The Jeha's eyes flittered from one to another, searching for anything amiss. Seeing nothing, he turned his attention to the monitor showing the front entrance and saw the Human woman approaching. For a barely literate pirate, Pete managed to keep to the dictated schedule with relative ease. By three o'clock in the afternoon, every day, his earnings and slate records for the bar were due. Any failure to submit the credits received, minus the allowable payments for salaries, would be met with a visit from Barlung's friends. The last time they'd gone there, for pleasure and not business, one of the Human females working in the bar had surprised Cartrule with a mug to his thick head. Ever since, the two Oogar longed for payback. Pete, out of what little good sense he seemed to have, realized that crossing Barlung would have far greater consequences than he'd originally thought. So he clasped the explosive case to one of the females and marched her on foot to the mining entrance every day.

Nay-Thok rippled forward in recognition. *He's sent Cora today. A most unexpected pleasure.*

Whoever she was or had been before she arrived on Parmick, Cora fascinated the Jeha. The other Human women at Pete's Dive Bar were smart and polite, but Cora never failed to surprise him. She was more articulate and self-assured than the others, and there was considerable intelligence behind the vacant stare she tried to put on. On numerous occasions, he'd caught her looking around the office, sweeping it with the eyes of a professional for anything of value. The first time, he'd thought her to be nothing more than a common thief. But when she took no action and showed restraint, it piqued his interest further. Clearly he had no physical want or need for a Human female, and as much as he wanted her to talk more and expand upon the glimmer of interest she'd shown him, Cora remained mostly silent.

I wonder who she really is.

And if she can be bought.

All things have their price.

On the monitor, she approached and raised her hand to touch the intercom button. Nay-Thok snapped the switch to open the door and leaned forward to speak into the small microphone at his chair. "Please come in, Cora."

He waited to see if there was a hint of surprise, contempt, or any other emotion on the brunette's face, but her expression never changed.

Such a fascinating Human! Really quite the enigma.

He rippled in anticipation and gathered the explosive case key from the wide desk to his right. As the office door opened, and Cora stepped inside, he wiggled a dozen arms and sat up, raising his eyes to her level.

"It's nice to see you again, Cora."

Cora nodded. "Nay-Thok. Pete sends his regards."

"I'm certain he does." Nay-Thok wanted to laugh, but didn't. "What has he brought for me today? Is it better than the previous day's take?"

"About the same," Cora replied. "There are two new ships on approach to the planet. Should be a good night tonight."

Nay-Thok considered this. Many species, after leaving the confines of a spacecraft for the first time in days, wanted a private place of their own. They would arrive, disembark from their shuttles, and immediately look at the local lodging opportunities. He knew his managers were already changing their vacancy signs at the lower priced options. The luxury boxes and suites were almost all open, and the price a mere ten percent higher than it had been with no ships on approach. Those who wanted their privacy would gladly pay for a few nights, no more than three, before they'd seek more affordable lodging. Even then, his managers would adjust the rates enough to ensnare those who remained behind when the ships departed. The restaurants and bars would do well at their normal prices, with the obvious cuts to costs like watered down spirits and employing food concentrates. Every new ship brought profit. Profit was all that mattered.

"For his sake, I should hope so. I don't like falling below expectations," Nay-Thok said. "Barlung could get upset if it continues."

Cora didn't respond to the threat. "I'll make sure Pete knows your wishes."

"Does this please you? Coming here instead of being in the bar all day?" As soon as he said it, Nay-Thok held his breath. He'd overstepped his bounds.

"I get to walk outside every day. When the winds aren't howling, it's almost pleasant," Cora replied. "Not like Earth, but enough so I don't mind it."

He said nothing in response. His agitation faded as he realized he had created an opening for her to talk about home. Maybe not today, but soon. He would learn more about the young woman yet. Nay-Thok held up the key. "Come here."

She stepped forward, holding the heavy case in her right hand. Nay-Thok watched her hoist it easily and set it down on the open counter between them with hardly a sound. Control and restraint never failed to grab his attention, and the young woman exuded it with quiet confidence. She left her hand hovering over the case with the heavy metal cuff dangling from her wrist to the wide handle. Nay-Thok leaned forward with a ripple of his many arms and worked the specially made key into the lock. The cuff beeped, and a series of lights flashed green before the cuff opened.

Cora quickly withdrew her wrist and rubbed at the bright red welts it left behind on her skin. Nay-Thok watched the lines on her wrist with great attention. "Do you need something for your wrist?"

"No, thank you. It'll be fine."

Nay-Thok returned his gaze to her bright green eyes. "Can I get you some refreshment?"

"I have to get back."

"Ah, yes," Nay-Thok chittered. "Happy Hour. Why is it called that? Do you know?"

Cora shrugged. "No idea."

Nay-Thok spun in his chair, contorting his body, and gestured to the monitors. "I suppose it's to provide a smile to the miners? Something to make them happier about their station?"

"I suppose," Cora said. Her eyes danced from monitor to monitor, taking in the sights. "With only so much time off, they don't come into the bar as often as before."

"Indeed," Nay-Thok replied. "Our schedules are tight, and work must come first. You understand that, I'm sure."

"I must be going," Cora said. Her eyes fell on his and for a moment there was nothing more he wanted to do than keep her there and force her to talk, not out of malice, but genuine curiosity. The young woman knew far more than she let on, but if she were delayed more than a few minutes, the old pirate at the bar might harm her. For what it was worth, Nay-Thok didn't want that for the interesting Human. She truly had potential.

"You must. Tell Pete I would like you to deliver the deposit every day, Cora. I find you trustworthy," he said. The last part wasn't exactly true, but he knew if he told her she fascinated him, there would be no chance for further conversation. Humans and their feelings were a galactic conundrum.

Cora almost grimaced. Her lips pressed into a momentary thin white line. "I'll let him know, Honored Nay-Thok."

His antennae bounced, and his body rippled with the unnecessary display of respect. "I hope you have a decent evening, Cora."

"Thank you," Cora replied. "We'll do as best we can."

Nay-Thok lowered his voice. "I expect nothing less, Cora."

As she left, he watched every moment until the cameras could no longer follow her. It was a long time before his full attention returned to the mines and the counting of his money.

* * * * *

Chapter Seven

Night Moves
Ship Operations Center
Hyperspace

"I think I've finally figured out what was missing when I first boarded the ship," Jyrall said.

"Missing?" Keaton asked, looking over from the pilot's seat in the operations center. "I don't know that there's room for much else on this girl. We put everything in her we thought a Peacemaker Team might need." He glanced back over the instruments before looking back. "I mean, we had to leave some room in the hold to make it appear as if she still hauls cargo."

Jyrall grinned. He liked that the Pushtal wasn't trying to make excuses if there was something amiss. Having been trained in individual observation and body language, Jyrall knew many races gave away what they truly thought, as opposed to what they were saying. Given the fact Keaton and his brother were raised by a Human and held the mannerisms of that race, Jyrall knew his tone showed he truly wanted to know if they'd missed something that might be essential to any upcoming missions, yet still maintain their cover.

"It's not that, my new friend," Jyrall said. "What's missing, in this case, is a good thing."

"Well, now you've got me confused as a squirrel on a telephone pole," Keaton said. "Ain't no nuts up there."

"What?" Jyrall asked, wrinkling his snout in confusion. "I know what a nut is, but what is a telephone pole? Or a squirrel, for that matter?"

"It's—aw, shoot," Keaton admitted. "Larth mentioned you'd never watched many Earth GalNet shows. It's something mountain folk said years ago. Pops used to say it all the time." He shrugged apologetically. "Seriously, what's missing?"

"The smells," Jyrall said, settling back into the copilot seat and adjusting the harness so it fit his huge frame a little better. "I mean, don't get me wrong, I still smell things. But it's nothing like other ships I've had to spend time in, and it's a far cry better than the last owners had her smelling."

"Oh." Keaton grinned. "Yeah, that's my doing. I made sure Ricky doubled up the environmental filtering system. I can't stand a stinky ship. Microgravity, for me, is no big deal, but if you add a bunch of smells mixing in with each other—no thanks."

"Well I, for one, appreciate the extra filtration," Jyrall said. "I'm no fan of space travel, and hyperspace can really get to me sometimes. An atmosphere that doesn't overwhelm my sense of smell along with it makes it bearable."

"Ricky said it was a waste of time," Keaton informed him. "That dude can just ignore smells like nobody I know. I guess it comes with being a technician and mechanic. You should smell some of the oils and grease that gets in his fur when he's working on something. Something sprays all over him from a hose or whatever, and he just wipes his face with a dirty rag and keeps working. I'd have to go clean myself off if it was me."

"Does he get fixated on something and refuse to let it beat him," Jyrall asked, "even if it's an inanimate object?"

"Yes!" Keaton exclaimed. "It's almost as if he's in competition with what he's working on. He gets it in his head that he's making or fixing something, and that's it. How did you know?"

Jyrall grinned. "I know someone just like him. Larth refused to believe he could only become an expert shot with his dominant hand. He spent more time on the range than anyone in our class, proving he could do it with both hands. Once he accomplished that, he set out to prove someone could use two weapons at once. I swear he learned to hit the center circle without aiming down his sights. He draws his pistols as quick as any cowboy on the old Earth shows called westerns."

"Really?" Keaton asked with a grin of his own. "A gunslinger. We love the westerns. Pops had a collection, and the ones he didn't have I got for him off the GalNet. Your friend a John Wayne man? Or old Charlie Bronson? Maybe even Yul Brenner and his boys? No, no, I got it. He's an Eastwood fan, right?"

"I have no idea what you're talking about, Keaton." Jyrall felt himself smiling in response to his new friend.

"Oh, you will, Peacemaker. You sure will."

* * *

Night Moves
Arms Room
Hyperspace

"Hey!" Larth exclaimed. "What do we have here?" He placed a box on the repair table set up in the corner, opposite the rifle racks on the bulkhead.

"Those are special," Ricky said. "Pops said they belonged to a friend a long time ago." Ricky opened the top drawer on the repair desk and shuffled around until he found what he was looking for. He held out a small key ring with two keys on it. Actual keys.

Larth hopped up on the stool, tilted the flat box up, and saw the keyhole on the front. He realized the box and whatever was in it had to be pretty old. The first key he tried worked, and he heard the muffled click of the mechanism unlocking. He opened the box, and his eyes widened. He quickly looked up at Ricky's grinning face.

"They look just like 1911s…but they're *my* size!" Larth exclaimed.

Nestled in the foam in the box were four black pistols. They looked like miniature versions of the famous Colt 1911. Larth had seen them on countless videos and shows on the GalNet. The weapons were legendary, and some Human mercenaries carried them still. There were several in the arms room he'd looked at and placed back on the shelf. The 1911 style was not a pistol Larth could ever hope to use effectively due to his small stature, but the ones in front of him looked like they would fit his small paws perfectly.

"Those are Llama MicroMax .380 1911s," Ricky said. "They were made in the early 2000s. Somewhere around 2017, I think. Pops taught me and Keaton how to shoot with them when we were young. Of course, we outgrew 'em. They ain't no bigger than a toy for us. But I figure they're the right size for you."

Larth reached in and selected a pistol. He checked to see no magazine was in place, then pulled the slide back to ensure there was no round chambered. ".380, huh?" he asked. "That's kind of a small round isn't it?"

"Well, yeah," Ricky admitted, "but they're effective. I modified the chamber and barrels on these years ago. They've been reinforced and dipped. I reworked everything to ensure they worked better than they did when they came off the assembly line. We McCoys load our own ammo—always have." He nodded toward another corner of the arms room to some equipment Larth was unfamiliar with. "We got some rounds for them that'll move at about 1100 feet per second, and when they hit, the core fragments. Leaves a nasty hole."

"Interesting, what about against armor?" Larth asked, looking down the sight.

"Got it covered," Ricky said. "It ain't like the rounds available when they were made. There's liquid propellants now that push a round at close to 2200 feet per second. I mean, sure, there's some armor out there, both natural and worn, that'll be hard to get through, but that's the same with most any projectile weapon. I reckon you just have to hit the right spot."

"That I can do," Larth assured him. "Where're the magazines?'

"Under the first layer of foam," Ricky said, pointing at the box.

Larth lifted the foam with three of the pistols still in it and counted magazines. They were laid out, filling the bottom of the entire box. He counted twenty-four of them. He picked one up, thumbed it to check the spring, and inserted it into the pistol. With the magazine in, the grip was perfect for him.

"So, can I use them?" Larth asked. "I'll take good care of them."

"Why, sure," Ricky said. "That's why I showed them to you. Hell, we can't hardly get a digit into the trigger guard on 'em anymore. There's a couple belts with holsters on 'em somewhere around here." He looked in a locker and found what he was looking for.

Larth put the belt on and adjusted the holsters to sit right on his hip. He slid the weapon in and stood there for a second. Suddenly, in a move that boggled the mind, his hand was up at waist level gripping the pistol. It was almost faster than Ricky could follow.

"Get the hell outta here!" Ricky said with a huge grin, showing all his sharp teeth. "Do that shit again."

Larth grinned back at his new friend and put pistols in both holsters. This time he drew both pistols in a blur of movement. Ricky just shook his head and asked him, "I seen it on video before, but I ain't never seen it in person. So are those the two you want?"

"Two?" Larth said. "No, I want all four. Can you help me rig holsters under each arm?"

"Oh yeah, we can make 'em, all right," he assured Larth. "You're about to be one bad ass gunslinger. We gotta figure out where to put the magazines, too. Hand me that slate, will you? I'll sketch it out."

* * *

Night Moves
Operations Center

"I wonder what those two are doing back there?" Jyrall asked. "They've been kind of quiet."

"Ain't no telling," Keaton said with a shrug. "Either they're still in the arms room, or Ricky is showing him something he's working on or wants to make. For all we know, he's figured out how to make the ship fly even faster. I swear he thinks he can turn a wrench on anything and make it better."

"My guess is they're still in the arms room," Jyrall said. "Larth is going to have to hold every weapon in the inventory at least once. It didn't take me long to find a pistol."

"I noticed," Keaton said, looking at the weapon in the holster strapped to Jyrall's thigh. The CT-75 Paladin was an artillery piece of a pistol. At .75 caliber, there was almost nothing the weapon couldn't stop. With liquid propellants and targeting gyroscopes, in the hands of a strong and qualified operator, the pistol had a maximum effective range of up to two hundred meters. Jyrall hefted the massive pistol with ease and had reached for the holster without looking for additional weapons. He knew the weapon was more statement than actually useful, but Lieutenant Colonel Tirr's advice was on his mind. A large weapon went with the idea that he'd be seen as a greater threat and attract attention. That would give Larth a greater opportunity to investigate. "You got yourself a hand cannon if I ever saw one."

"It fits my hand," Jyrall explained. "Not many do. And I fired it pretty well at the Academy." He looked over the instruments in front of his side of the cockpit. "I wanted to tell you, that was a good decision, using the shunts when we left the system instead of using the gate so no one knows our destination. Going through the gate could have left a way for someone to ascertain our plan."

"It seemed like a good time to use them," Keaton answered. "Where we're going, we don't want anyone to suspect you're the law. I hacked a system or two building a history for the ship. You two are going to have a reputation to uphold—undercover and all that. Me and Ricky have to act like normal Pushtal. Nobody's gonna suspect anything about us. I figured we didn't need to take no chances before we got there."

"I like the way you think, my friend," Jyrall said. "We're going to be a good team."

"Right on, man," Keaton agreed. "I'm starved. I wonder what we should eat. You like fish? I got some frozen catfish in the galley. You ever had catfish? It's good eatin'."

"Oh, yeah." Jyrall grinned. "We're going to make a *great* team. I'll cook." He unstrapped and pulled himself up out of his seat. "Cooking in microgravity should prove interesting. Do we have any blackening seasoning on board?" He pulled himself out of the cockpit area using the straps fixed to the bulkhead.

Keaton laughed. "I'm offended, Peacemaker! You think we'd have catfish and not be able to blacken it on this ship?"

Jyrall hung from a strap and turned back to the young Pushtal. "Jyrall. Please, just call me Jyrall. It's not like our lives are going to depend on it or anything."

"Gotcha, Jyrall." Keaton nodded. "Never thought I'd be calling a Peacemaker by their first name."

"Why? We aren't scary." Jyrall blinked. "Well, not all of us."

"It ain't that." Keaton shook his head. He smoothed back the fur on top of his head in an all-too-Human gesture. For a Pushtal, it looked almost ridiculous. "The Old Man taught us Peacemakers were the one good, true thing in the galaxy. That they could always be trusted. That you was always interested in what was fair and just. With some of the things we've seen, it's hard to believe anybody in the galaxy can be trusted all the time. I guess it's all about respect, you know? Calling you Peacemaker seems the right thing to do, because it's respectful. I know I need to call you Jyrall, though. Hell, I'm rambling, man."

Jyrall knew exactly what Keaton meant, and the words bubbled out of him faster than he thought they would. "At the Academy, we spent many hours on respect and diplomacy. Many of our peers didn't make it through that phase the first time because they couldn't separate the needs of different situations until they'd experienced them. For some of them, that problem was solved during our first field exercises in squad-level tactics. Once they saw their peers, and in some cases our superiors, in a situation where the field was level, everything changed. They learned they could be respectful and…at ease with each other when necessary. Do you understand?"

Keaton nodded. "Makes sense to me. The Old Man used to say you never knew somebody until they were in the shit with you."

"In the shit?" Jyrall chuckled.

"Yeah." Keaton grinned. "That whole being there together thing? It's an expression."

"I have much to learn." Jyrall shook his head. "I think I'll start with cooking in hyperspace. I'm starving."

"You do that, Jyrall. I think you're gonna be fine," Keaton called after him. "The spices are in the second drawer under the water dispenser. Make yourself at home!"

* * * * *

Chapter Eight

Town

Parmick

Cora walked down the shoddy road toward Pete's Dive Bar, her eyes on the dusty black and gray gravel. The cloud-filled sky and occasional drops of black rain soured her mood as much as Nay-Thok's request that she deliver the bar's daily take personally. Jeha in general gave her the heebie-jeebies, but one who stared and followed her every move like a stalker set off every internal alarm she possessed. As much as she hated it, there was a part of her that relished the opportunity to see the inner workings of Barlung's operation on a daily basis. There could be something gained from reliable intelligence. If there was someone willing to pay, that would be one thing, but she knew the real reason the situation intrigued her was leverage. Since landing on Parmick, the reminders of leverage were all around her. That she walked the streets of an alien world and not southern Appalachia didn't matter. Mining operations, legitimate or not, never changed. She'd lived the first seventeen years of her life in one and had vowed never to return.

Her first memory was a company meeting day. The Warwick Mining Corporation's discovery of a coal vein deep under the Appalachian Mountains brought a period of unrivaled opulence to parts of western North Carolina. The investors in Asheville and Charlotte made millions of dollars, which they quickly transferred to credits, and soon left the planet behind. In the small rural towns, already reeling from a century of recession and the loss of their workforce to the cities and the mercenary companies, Warwick and its competitors quickly became the entire town. The corporate-friendly politicians came first, and then came new roads, buildings, even recreational facilities, all paid for from company profits to the community. Yet the stores and mercantile shop were forced out of business as the company pushed their employees and their families to only use certain businesses and local professionals. Lawyers, doctors, and even the morticians either bought into the company's practices or fled.

Within a decade of the Murphy Mine development, the town of Murphy was a beautiful, modern city surrounded by company housing that barely met the codes and regulations the company guaranteed. Those houses, built on a grid of dusty gravel roads, were increasingly filled with dirty, disgruntled men and women. As the mine paid less and less for their time and their loads, the townspeople's grumbles were silenced by the company. The message had been clear—either accept the terms given and survive, or leave. With no ability to save their earnings under the oppressive prices of the company stores, survival was key. Warwick and its competitors had rural America over a barrel, and there were no unions or organizations strong enough to combat them.

Parmick was the same. When it had been a legitimate mining operation, Town had been built almost as an analog to the mining towns of Earth. When Cora was a child, her mother had told her stories passed down from the coal miners of her own family, of places far away that no longer existed. Somewhere in her lineage, a distant relative had been born in Dawson, New Mexico. Cora tried to find it on a map, only to learn it was no longer there. The only thing standing where the entire town once stood was a cemetery filled with identical white iron crosses marking the graves of miners killed in multiple disasters that struck the mine during its operation. The town formed, grew, and died alongside whatever they could pull from the ground. When what came out of the ground couldn't keep the mine safe or the people employed, it disappeared. Parmick would likely be no different.

When the legitimate mine had closed because its revenue couldn't cover its expenses, Barlung and his team took over. As she walked, Cora snorted.

What's the old saying? Here comes the new boss, same as the old boss?

A legitimate mine could be somewhat counted on to maintain safety standards and protect the lives of its miners. Barlung's illegitimate operation did neither. As she rounded a corner, two large and familiar figures stood over another laid out in the street. Cora froze and partially hid behind the corner of a dilapidated building that had once housed a credit exchange.

"You owe us credits," the small Oogar named Frooth said over a cowering Jivool. The much smaller bear-like creature lay in the black mud with its paws around its head in a vain effort to protect itself. The larger of the two assailants, Cartrule, rained blows down on the stricken alien.

The Jivool murmured something that didn't satisfy Cartrule, and the Oogar swung again. The sickening crunch of bone-on-bone resonated all the way to Cora's position, and she flinched back against the masonry, wondering what she could do, if anything.

A second or two later, a young child's scream echoed down the street. Cora stuck her head around to see a tiny Jivool cub ambling down the middle of the street. The cub didn't appear to be wearing a translator, and Cora couldn't make out what it was screaming, but her mind quickly filled in the blanks.

"Let's grab the cub." Frooth laughed. "That'll make Ledram pay up faster."

"Good idea," Cartrule replied as he leaned over to hit the Jivool again. "You hear that, Ledram? We're gonna take your cub and keep it until you pay up. If you don't pay up, we'll have us a feast!"

Red filled Cora's vision, and she looked down at her feet for a weapon. There was a meter-long length of partially bent rebar, and even though she knew it was a bad idea, she grabbed it and stood up slowly. Still hidden behind the crumbling corner of the building, she took a deep breath.

Come on, Cora. Toughen up. You can—

"That's enough."

Cora ducked around the corner and bit her lower lip to keep from gasping in surprise. She recognized the voice, but it had been a while—maybe months—since she'd heard it. The ant-like Altar Peacemaker Rekk stood at the opposite end of the street with an Altar rifle held across his bulbous abdomen.

Frooth laughed. "What do you think you're doing? Go back to your office, Rekk. We'll handle this."

"No, you won't harm another citizen," Rekk replied and stepped forward. "This has gone on long enough."

Frooth glanced at Cartrule. "Look who finally found some courage."

Cartrule moved toward the Peacemaker, leaving the Jivool behind in the mud. The cub raced to its father and gently patted his face. The adult Jivool didn't move, and Cora felt her breath hitch in her chest as Cartule spoke. "That or he's decided to go back on his deal with Barlung. Either way, that's a death sentence."

"I'm not afraid of you," Rekk replied. "I have a job to uphold and citizens to protect. When they're on your property, in the mine, I can't intervene. But out here I can, and it's time I do."

"We own this whole rock, Peacemaker." Frooth shook his head from side to side. A stream of drool whipped and flashed. "You have no jurisdiction, remember? You surrendered your post. That's what you called it, right? Your post."

"I'm taking it back."

"Over my dead body," Cartrule said and stomped forward, with Frooth at his side.

Before she realized what she was doing, Cora ran into the street for the Jivool. As she closed the distance, the cub looked up at her with wide black eyes. Cora put her finger to her lips, hoping the cub understood the idea of being quiet. It said nothing. She watched the two Oogar running toward the stationary Peacemaker. The Altar hefted the rifle and pointed it at Cartrule.

"Stay where you are."

Cora looked down at the Jivool Ledram. She'd seen him around town several times, but never in the bar. The little cub murmured the same thing over and over again. She knew it was the equivalent of "Daddy," and it steeled her resolve.

"Ledram?" she whispered. "Can you hear me?"

The Jivool's eyes opened in a flash. "Cora McCoy?"

He knows my name?

"Can you get up? We have to go."

"Yes, I can." Ledram rolled over and gathered his cub in one arm. "Thank you, Cora."

"Get out of here. On the next ship if you can," Cora pleaded.

"I cannot. They'll come for me again," Ledram said. "I'll pay them, but we won't eat for a week."

Cora ground her teeth. "You will, too. I'll make sure of it. Now, go."

The Jivool scrambled down a side street. Cora stood and made her way back to the wall. The two Oogar had stopped in the street about thirty meters from Peacemaker Rekk.

What are they doing?

"Now what are you going to do, Rekk? Shoot us down in the street? Peacemakers can't do that, if I remember right," Frooth said.

"You're trapped by your own procedures. You want to find a peaceful solution. We're being peaceful," Cartrule said.

Rekk shifted the rifle's barrel. As he did, his antennae bobbed, as though he was confused and trying to ascertain what to do next. For a brief moment, he looked away from the two of them.

Whap!

A flash of blue light came from behind the Altar and to the right. A wide hole appeared in his chest cavity. His arms fell limp, and the rifle clattered into the gravel a half second before Peacemaker Rekk toppled forward in a heap.

Gods!

Cora ducked forward and found a hiding place behind a trash container. Through the metal slats she could see the Oogar standing still, as if in shock. She raised a hand to her face and clasped her nostrils shut at the ungodly stench from the container, but kept her gaze focused.

"You idiots!" Barlung appeared from the alley the bolt had originated from. "I told you before—no shakedowns in public. Hit them at the store on our ground. That's where you make them part with their credits. Out here, they gain sympathy. Sympathy breeds trouble."

"We own this town, Boss," Frooth replied.

Barlung raced forward and reared to his full height above Frooth. "We own the town, but not the citizens, Frooth. Until we own all of them, we can't get them working against us. You understand that?"

Frooth looked away. "Yes, I do."

"Now get your asses back to the mine. The next shift starts in thirty minutes, and I want to make sure every miner loads the scale at two for one today. Nobody makes a profit, get me?"

"What about the Peacemaker?" Cartrule asked.

"Get rid of the body. Use the smelter at the mine. I want no trace of him to remain. When you're done with that, clear out his office and domicile. Leave his personal effects, but anything that looks official, smelt it, too. I want that done by midnight tonight. You're as guilty of his death as I am. There will be questions, and in time, the Peacemakers will send someone to find out what happened to him. If he honored our deal and didn't send any reports, our window may be long enough to get what we need and be gone when they come looking for him. He's the least of our troubles."

Cartrule and Frooth turned back to the empty street. "You let Ledram get away, Cartrule."

"I did nothing of the sort, Frooth."

"Don't worry about him." Barlung stared down the street and seemingly right through Cora's hiding place. "I'll handle that situation personally. The situation has changed."

* * * * *

Chapter Nine

Night Moves
Hyperspace

"We'll emerge into the Parmick System in about twenty minutes," Keaton said. "Anybody got any questions on the backgrounds I provided for the ship—or us?"

Keaton was in the pilot's seat, and Jyrall in the copilot's, while Ricky and Larth floated effortlessly behind them, each with a hand on a strap. They'd grilled each other on the information for the last day to make sure it was second nature. For the two Peacemakers, it was easy to slip into another persona after all the training they'd received.

For the brothers, it was going to take a conscious effort. Due to their upbringing, they were, for all intents and purposes, a couple of good ol' boys from the Appalachian Mountains on Earth, despite the outward appearances of their actual race. They were McCoys, through and through, and for them to behave any differently than southerners would take actual acting on their part. They said they were up for it, but Ricky admitted there may be a slight problem.

"It's called southern chivalry," Keaton explained to Jyrall. "At least that's what Pops called it. I can't count the stories he told us about him and his brothers going to go see someone after they heard a fella did a woman or young'uns wrong. Even when they were just teenagers."

"When he was fourteen, he beat a fella down with a chunk of farwood when he saw the black eye of a classmate," Ricky chimed in. "Said he couldn't stand to see a girl carrying the mark of a drunk man. He told us he stood over the girl's father and waited on the law, figured he'd go to jail. Instead, the lawman gave him a ride back home clear across the valley up into the holler before he took the unconscious man to the hospital."

"Impressive," admitted Jyrall, "given that he was only a fourteen-year-old Human and what kind of size difference there must have been between him and a full-grown man. But…what's a 'far wood?'"

"Firewood—a piece of a cut tree," Keaton said with a shrug of his shoulders. "It's the accent."

"Looky here, y'all," Ricky said again. "You know I don't start fights, but I don't walk away from 'em either. Hell, I'm a mechanic, not a soldier, but I am a McCoy. I'm just sayin, iffin I see any female get treated wrong, I may just have to set someone straight. Keaton, you know how Pops felt about that. He said, 'if a woman is a soldier or the law, it's different 'cause they know things can get rough. But a civilian woman being disrespected, or God forbid, shore 'nuff abused, you got to step in and straighten a bent fella out.' You know he did."

"I know," Keaton admitted, "but we're going in all incognito. We have a part to play. How about you just keep a mental note and then you straighten 'em out once we accomplish the mission?"

"How 'bout, I just whup 'em for some other reason, cause that's what a Pushtal would do," Ricky reasoned. "If I'm playing the part, I need to have a hair trigger and just be ornery anyway."

"He has a point," Larth admitted. "Pushtal aren't pleasant types." He looked over at Ricky. "I love a good fight myself, and I can't stand to see anyone wronged. But there's a time to fight, and a time to take notes. Believe me, if I see it, I'll want to be right beside you, but we have to play our parts and accomplish the mission."

"I'd appreciate if both of you refrain from unnecessary fights," Jyrall said. "Violence is not always the answer. Insertion, investigation, and diplomacy is what needs to happen here. With that being said, the reputation of this colony precedes itself. There'll be many instances where someone needs a good left hook, but that's not what we're going there for. We play our parts, we find out what happened to the Peacemaker on site, and we'll go from there. With that also being said, I will admit, a little brawl may help solidify our reputations." He winked at the two floating behind him.

"Yes!" Ricky exclaimed with a grin. "Somebody does a woman wrong and that somebody is gonna tote an ass whupping."

Jyrall grinned and shook his head. He thought for a moment and said, "Okay. One last time. This is the ship *Night Moves*. We mostly work the other side of the galaxy. We've hauled some items lately—successfully, of course. Anyone who looks us up will be able to find that."

"Not easily," Keaton added, "if it was right out in the open, it would be suspicious."

"Right," Larth said. "You own the ship," he indicated Jyrall, "and we work for you. These two are the muscle—not that you need any. I handle the actual financials for you, supervising the loading and unloading. I go by the name Switch. If anybody asks about it, you guys just be vague. Tell 'em something like, you don't want him to flip the switch. Let 'em wonder."

"I'm using the name Varkell," Jyrall said. "Known as One-eyed Varkell behind my back. I'll be wearing the patch on my right eye. I still think it's an amazing piece of technology. It was genius, putting a micro camera in the stitching of the leather with a screen on the back side. I can hardly tell it's not what I'd see without it on." He held up a reddish-brown leather patch, similar to one Larth had worn while in disguise the year before.

"Aw, hell, I don't know about genius," Ricky said. "I just made it so it can't be noticed, it's Keaton's programming that makes it work right."

"You know, I bet I could write an aiming program wirelessly connecting that cannon you wear to the patch," Keaton thought out loud. "It would show you exactly where the pistol is aimed on the screen."

"Nice," Ricky agreed. "I can put a sight on it with a zeroed-in micro camera."

"What?" Larth laughed. "Come on, he's a good shot with the naked eye. Besides, one should know at all times where a pistol is aimed, even if you're not looking through the sight. You just sorta feel it. They're like a part of you, you know?"

"Hey, I'm a pretty fair shot, and so's Keaton," Ricky said, "but we gotta look down the sights and aim the dang thing. Are you saying you can hit where you want when you whip a pistol out? Every time?"

"Not everyone can hit the target all the time, especially when it's chaos all around you," Jyrall said. "Larth does a vast majority of the time, though. If he misses, it's close enough to keep their head down, that's for sure."

"Well, that's good to know," Keaton said, checking his instruments again and making a slight adjustment. "We're known as Rylon and Zarr. We won't say anything—ever. We just growl and snarl and show some teeth when people speak to us. We won't speak when outsiders are around or if there are cameras around—which there'll most likely be. Most have never heard a Pushtal speak, but someone in that colony may have. Hell, there may be some Pushtal who use it as a base of operations, as bad as that place is. If anyone asks, you just tell 'em we don't talk, and haven't as long as you've known us."

"We should probably learn Pushtal at some point," Ricky observed, "at least a few words and a sentence or two."

"We're about to come into the system," Keaton announced. "In three, two, one."

Everyone felt it when they emerged into normal space in the Parmick system. For the brothers and Larth, it was a few moments of slight disorientation. Jyrall, on the other hand, shook his head and held a large paw to his head. "I hate that," he said.

"You all right there, Snarlyface?" Larth asked. "You gonna be sick?"

"Sick!" Keaton said alarmed. "Please, not in the operations center. I mean, it's your ship, but…"

With a deep breath, Jyrall looked up. "It'll pass. I hate hyperspace transitions."

Larth looked over at Keaton. "When you land, make sure it's on the far side of the tarmac, away from any buildings, so Jyrall has time to get his feet back under him."

"Roger that," answered Keaton with a wide grin. Larth couldn't hide his grin at the answer.

They traveled for another day toward the fourth planet in the system. As it grew larger in the viewports, it looked like many other habitable planets across the galaxy. There were greens, blues, and obvious brown wasteland in a couple of areas. The colony was located where some of the obvious green met the edge of a mountain range, the other side of which indicated wasteland. It was near a bay opening into an ocean, but not right on the shoreline, and a river ran partially through the area to meet the shore.

When they entered the atmosphere, Keaton handled it with great skill. Larth asked no one in particular, "Town—they actually named the town Town. I wonder what genius thought of that?"

"It ain't too original, that's for sure," agreed Ricky, "but it's as good a name as any, I reckon."

After touching down with a delicate touch, proving all of his piloting skills, Keaton went through the shutdown procedures. It was midafternoon local time. They stood in the cargo area, and Ricky activated the ramp. Outside, dust swirled on the breeze like tiny dust devils.

"Hang on," Ricky said. "I got an idea."

Jyrall and Larth glanced at Keaton, who shrugged. Ricky dug into a container mounted to the hull of the ship inside the door.

"Got 'em." Ricky held up two respirator masks in his hands. He handed one to Keaton. "We can wear these. Even if there are cameras, we can talk if there ain't people around, and no one will be able to see it."

Jyrall nodded and waited for the brothers to don their masks. When they were ready, he said, "Let's go."

They exited the ship, Jyrall with his eyepatch on and the hand cannon at his side. Larth wore his belt with the two holsters and, hidden under a vest, two more holsters under his arms, unnoticeable to the casual observer. Both Keaton and Ricky had slings across their chests, with rifles pointed downward across their back, and laser pistols in holsters on their sides. The four of them looked like a group not to be trifled with, exactly the image they wished to portray.

Keaton pulled a small device out of a pocket and sent a code to raise the ramp and lock the ship down. Not only would it not open if someone tried to force their way on board, the engines wouldn't start without the proper command code. It could also be performed on a hidden panel in an unused berth, should the remote get lost, stolen, or damaged.

"Let's head into town," Jyrall said, feeling better by the minute now that he was off the ship. "We'll take the route we talked about and walk by the location of the local Peacemaker's office. Nobody stare; I'll look from the patch without turning my head and see what clues I can pick up. It may be something as simple as he's sick and bedridden; who knows."

"Doesn't look like a booming place to me," Larth said, looking across the tarmac.

"Yeah, no signs of a growing colony," Keaton observed as they walked. The respirator muffled his voice slightly, but there was no exterior sign he was talking.

"What in the hell is up with the dang wind?" Ricky asked. "It ain't let up yet."

"You should have felt it in the controls on the descent," Keaton said. "I really had to compensate."

"You see that?" Jyrall asked Larth, nodding his head and pointing with his snout.

"I see it," Larth answered. "There are half a dozen guards around that hanger if there's one."

"Reckon whose hanger it is?" Ricky asked, adjusting the strap across his chest.

Larth replied, "Whoever they are, I'm guessing they'll tell us before long."

"I see cameras up ahead. Good thing I remembered the masks," Ricky told his brother. "We're supposed to be mute."

"It was a good idea. I figured we'd be glassed," agreed Keaton.

"What does 'be glassed' mean?" Jyrall asked.

"It means being observed through a lens of some kind," Larth answered. "You know, a scope? A camera? You really should watch more GalNet shows. You're killing me."

* * * * *

Chapter Ten

"Emergence confirmed. All systems nominal and hyperspace shunts disengaged," Dreel said as he leaned forward to tap a series of commands into the ship's main instrument panel. "Toscatta Gate Control is asking for clearance and intentions." His deep, gravelly voice rose slightly in pitch from surprise.

"It appears the Cartography Guild finally has their guard up." Kurrang harrumphed and leaned forward against the straps holding him in the command couch. "We're broadcasting standard codes, aren't we?"

"Affirmative," Dreel replied. "Standard codes on standard frequencies."

"Any interference in the spectrum?"

"Negative. I think they're being overly cautious." Dreel frowned. "Either that or they suspect we're lying about who we are."

"You think they suspect something?" Kurrang asked. "Do you think the word has spread that fast about Kr'et'Socae's escape from Kleve?"

Dreel shrugged his massive shoulders. "It's possible. Nothing spreads faster than gossip. It's a miracle we kept it quiet for eight months, but it had to get out."

"It's unfortunate, if that's the case," Kurrang said. "There's also the possibility they're simply using a higher measure of security with the threat against them at Victoria Bravo."

"It's difficult to say," Dreel replied. With a sneer, he adjusted the headset over his angular head so the microphone sat next to his snout. "Toscatta Gate Control, this is Peacemaker Blue Flight in your space at three five zero decimal two six and eight thousand kilometers. Authentication transmitting now."

Kurrang tapped his console. "Codes out."

Dreel nodded, but didn't say anything. Toscatta was home to two habitable planets, both with substantial agricultural conglomerates at work to provide food for hundreds of species from their specially engineered biomes. Known simply as Toscatta One and Toscatta Two, the second planet also held one of the three largest Peacemaker Regional Barracks. There should be no question as to who they were or what their intentions were.

"Blue Flight, Toscatta Gate, you are cleared direct approach to Toscatta Two. Maintain standard approach procedures. Have a good morning."

Kurrang coughed. "Gods, I will never get acclimated to differing times at the next point of arrival."

"Look on the side of opportunity," Dreel said, looking at the Tri-V screen to his right. "It's 0130 local time at the barracks. We'll be able to approach under the cover of night."

"And wake the whole barracks."

Dreel laughed. "My friend, if they've paid any attention to StormWatch and the latest intelligence packages, they're not sleeping right now."

Two hours later, the Blue Flight settled to the tarmac outside the Barracks Reception Center. Not only was the barracks commander present, wearing the red sash of his office across his chest, but there was also what looked like an entire squad of Peacemakers in full weapons and combat armor.

Kurrang tilted his chin up and jutted it at the formation. "All this ceremony for us?"

"Not ceremony, at least I don't think that's what they're doing. Not with weapons and armor," Dreel replied with a grin. "When times are the most difficult, security is paramount."

"You're quoting the standard operating procedure again." Kurrang half-smiled and turned to his friend.

"It's only been a hundred years since you read it."

"One hundred and thirteen, if you must know." Kurrang shook his head and looked again at the formation through the forward windows. "What am I not seeing out there?"

"Something you won't see," Dreel replied.

"Enforcers."

Dreel smiled wide, his teeth glinting in the cockpit light. "I know where they are. Well, I have a reasonably educated guess as to where they're stationed."

"Says the Deputy Prime Enforcer." Kurrang grunted. "I should hope you know where they are."

"You never worked with us before?"

Kurrang shook his head. "No. In my time as a Peacemaker, I only met a few. I can't remember any of their names, except one. Everyone knows his name."

"Where did you meet Hr'ent?" Dreel asked.

The legendary Oogar was one of the most influential officers in the early days of the Enforcers. As the first being to undergo extensive nanite therapy to quicken his reactions and amplify his strength, Hr'ent had become the Prime Enforcer very early in life and had filled the position until a decade ago when he'd retired from active service. Yet his service to the guild, and to his friend Guild Master

Rsach, was far from over. As a consultant and confidant, Hr'ent remained involved with the guild through his post on Luna. When the Mercenary Guild attacked there, he had let them come. The official report said he and the other Peacemakers left in the consulate died while the perpetrators got away. In reality, the legendary Enforcer's minimal security team quickly found and dispatched the infiltrators while he himself disarmed and defeated their leader before allowing the planted explosives to detonate. Gravely ill, Hr'ent and the other elderly and compromised Peacemakers called to action a final time did their duty. For Dreel, there was no better example of courage and commitment to the guild. He hoped to even fill one of Hr'ent's mighty footprints when his own career culminated.

Kurrang spoke slowly as if conjuring the memory, "On Ocono, right out of the Academy. They tested me for Enforcer, only to find out the nanites wouldn't take. My system performed at its very peak. There was nothing to be gained by the therapy, and with the guidance of the time, only those who'd had a successful nanite and surgical regime could be Enforcers."

"A short-sighted policy that had no bearing on anything." Dreel grunted. "Many exceptional Peacemakers were barred from being Enforcers."

"And yet that policy still remains."

"For now," Dreel conceded. "I see a time when the policy will change. Times change, and our bodies adapt to the procession. Until then, augmented Enforcers are our best chance to go up against Kr'et'Socae."

"He was augmented, wasn't he?" Kurrang asked, but he was already shaking his head. "Of course he was. There's more, isn't there?"

"Kr'et'Socae took exceptionally well to the therapy, Kurrang. He is the most powerful Enforcer in the field," Dreel replied. "Even I wouldn't be a match for him in one-on-one combat. It's best we take him down with allies at our side."

"Which is the reason we're here. Recruiting."

Dreel coughed and smiled. "Oh, I don't have to recruit the Enforcers, Kurrang. They're a weapon system. To effectively use a weapon system, one simply must do three things. First, understand the weapon system's capabilities and limitations. Second, understand how to best employ the weapons system in any number of given scenarios and, third—"

"Point them in the right direction and fire." Kurrang nodded. "Do you want me to download the intelligence packets from the Gate?"

"No." Dreel waved a large paw from side to side. "I don't wish to open any of our data packets to Gate Control from this time forward. We're gathering and preparing to employ Enforcers, and I won't risk any unnecessary connection. That's why we have the only shunt-capable Blue Flight in the guild at our disposal. Yes, the Cartography Guild can report where we are, but they don't know where we're going. That means they're typically several days behind in reporting our whereabouts to anyone who might be listening. As soon as this mission is complete, we'll return to the standard gate-required ships, and this one will continue a deception mission until the end of hostilities."

"You really have thought this out," Kurrang said. "That makes you the complete opposite of Jessica Francis."

Dreel howled with laughter. "My friend, you honestly believe she doesn't have a plan?"

"Jessica may have a plan, but she tends to make things up as she goes."

"A formidable skill." Dreel nodded. He raised a long finger and pointed at the TriRusk. "Which, I might add, is precisely why we pursued Humans for the Peacemaker Guild in the first place. For more years than you might believe."

"But she was the first Human." Kurrang's wide brow furrowed.

"We tried for a long time. Almost succeeded a few times. But Jessica was something special." Dreel sighed and smiled as softly as a Besquith could, which wasn't much. "When the time comes, she will be again. And we're going to be right there with her and the others. Enforcers and all."

"I must admit, I like the sound of that." Kurrang chuckled. It sounded like a distant thunderstorm.

"So do I, my friend. Let's introduce ourselves and get started." Dreel stood and stretched slowly with the return of gravity. "We'll get our intelligence update and then brief the barracks commander."

Kurrang looked again outside. "I've never seen a Flatar as a barracks commander."

"You've never met Gnaxx," Dreel replied. "You're in for a new experience."

"And why would that be?" Kurrang slowly undid his own straps.

Dreel placed his massive paws on his hip joints and stretched backward slightly. "Let me put it this way. I've never thought much about the Flatar without their Tortantula. I mean, in a combat situation, I believed the Flatar would be worthless without their ten-legged companions."

"I would tend to agree," Kurrang said. His lower jaw worked like he wanted to say more, but he didn't.

"Gnaxx changed all that, Kurrang. I've worked with him before, and the best definition of him is actually a Human one."

Kurrang frowned. "Which one?"

"He's a sonuvabitch, my friend. The exact one we need right now," Dreel replied. "If we're going to do this—I mean organize the Enforcers for combat operations in any type of unit structure that has a chance of success—there was only one place to start. That would be Gnaxx."

* * *

Pete's Dive Bar
Parmick

Cora pushed through the door of the bar as Pete shuffled forward to turn on the sputtering, humming neon sign outside. Ten seconds later, the awful, blaring horn signifying the change of shifts at the mine sounded. Since mine operations were continuous, no matter what, and with little regard for any type of calendar, there were no up or down days at the bar. The miners would cash in their hauls for the day, and walk down the hill from the mine to slake their thirst at the only watering hole in Town, paying exorbitant prices for watered-down drinks and shitty beer.

The miners who didn't manage to score enough red diamond dust, or anything else of value, would belly up to the bar within ten minutes to spend the remainder of their previous hauls for a beer or two and leave by nightfall. The ones who came later, pockets filled with chits and, in some cases, actual credits, would drink well into the night. A few would come to their senses and leave before the credits ran out. The rest would drink until they could drink no more, or get into a brawl over week-old sports games from Earth and Aspara or any other perceived slight. Once the bar closed at 0300 local, Cora and the girls would sweep up the trash, mop up the blood and vomit, restock the bar, and collapse into their racks around dawn. Like the miners, they hadn't had a night off in forever, but when the miners had a good day down-below, Cora and her squad picked up enough tips to move them one step closer to leaving Parmick behind for good.

The bar door opened much sooner than any of them expected. Cora looked up from behind the bar to see Ledram amble in, his dark eyes intently staring at her. He clambered between the scattered tables and chairs and onto a stool at the bar.

The Jivool licked the outer edges of his maw and settled both forearms onto the bar. "Water, please."

Cora fished out one of the bottles of water—the filtered ones reserved for the higher paying customers—and set it on the bar.

"On me," she said, keeping her voice low.

"Thank you," Ledram replied. He took the bottle and drank from it greedily. He wiped his maw with the back of one furry paw. Cora tried not to stare. The Jivool's curly fur looked impossibly soft, except for the places where the black mud from the street remained. Barely fifteen minutes had passed since the two Oogar thugs had threatened his life and killed Peacemaker Rekk. Cora kept her face straight. There hadn't even been time to tell the others, and there was no one in authority to whom she could report the Peacemaker's death. Barlung and his brutes seemed to hold Parmick in a vise.

Cora chewed on the inside of her lower lip for a moment. The Jivool obviously wanted to talk. Otherwise, he wouldn't have sought her out after what happened in the deserted street. Before then, she'd seen him maybe two or three times during her team's time on the planet, surely not more.

And he knew my name.

She tried to brush the thought away and reasoned there were only so many Humans on Parmick. Immediately she knew that was bullshit, too. There were at least fifty Humans in the mines, and another fifty or so in the remaining mercenary companies and support roles around Town. Of the total population, the Human element was only about one percent, but there were enough she'd believed she blended in until he'd called her by name.

"Is your cub okay?"

Ledram stared at her for a moment. His translator seemed to take a long time deciphering the words. "Yes, my cub is well. A bit frightened, but he's fine. Thank you for your concern."

"No problem."

"Is that something Humans tend to do? Care for children so much?" Ledram asked. "I've seen several instances where Humans appear more concerned for children than themselves, and race and species mattered not."

Cora shrugged. "The good ones."

Ledram considered the words and then chuckled. "Then I was right to come. You can be trusted."

The way he spoke brought up a memory from her childhood. Her family's farm was a place where nothing mattered but family. In the kitchen at the great, round, weathered table, any topic could be discussed without reprisal, fear, or emotion. She learned to have a discussion there, and the first rule of talking was to listen. Sometimes all a person needed to do was pause, look thoughtfully at the other person, and wait. If someone really wanted to talk, they would.

"You're familiar with the conditions in the mine?" Ledram's voice was little more than a whisper.

Cora nodded and gave a little shrug. "I know enough."

The truth was something more like every manifestation of hell imaginable.

"It's as bad as you've heard, and even worse than you might imagine." The Jivool took a long drink from the water bottle and wiped his maw again. "We scrape the walls and ground for red diamond dust and the occasional gems. We go for hours without food or water. They shake us down every day, strip us and inspect us to make sure no diamonds or dust leaves the mine. Anyone who steals disappears and is never seen again."

"Didn't they know what they signed up for?"

"That's another thing; anyone who runs afoul of Barlung's thugs ends up in the mine. That's how I got there, and if they keep paying twenty percent on every credit, I may never get out." Ledram frowned. "There are many others like me working down there. Former soldiers. Mercs."

The Jivool leaned closer, and Cora huddled in as well. She could smell him—a warm scent not unlike cedar wood.

"We've had enough," Ledram whispered. "And we're going to do something about it."

Cora kept her face still despite the bolt of electricity that ran down her spine. "When?"

Ledram shook his head. "When the time is right."

Cora squinted at him. "But how will I—"

"Remember this password, Cora. Keep it in your mind, and tell no one. Strength together. When you hear that from me or one of my messengers, we will act." Ledram looked over his shoulder. She knew he could see the other women staring at them. "Aside from your close friends. We may need all of your assistance and your...tools. Do you understand?"

"I got it." Cora nodded. "What do I do with it?"

"You'll see very soon." Ledram finished off the bottle of water and straightened up on his stool. "Thank you for the water. I'll contact you soon."

Without another word, the Jivool slid off the stool and ambled toward the door. He was halfway across the floor when the first rush of miners slammed open the doors and raced for the bar. In the sudden rush, Cora lost sight of the small, bear-like alien. As the night wore on, she even managed to put aside the confusion he'd managed to plant in her mind. For the time being, only the credits mattered. Every tip put them a little closer to their goal.

Cora McCoy didn't think about Ledram's secret for several days, but the password for whatever he had planned stuck in her mind.

Strength together.

* * * * *

Chapter Eleven

Town Starport

Parmick

As they came through the dilapidated fence surrounding the tarmac and landing area of the starport, Jyrall noticed there was no local government security at all. Glancing to his right, he saw darkness in every window in the control tower. *No wonder we didn't have to make landing arrangements with the planet before entering atmosphere.* "This place has definitely seen better days," he said to the group.

"It's a rat hole," said Ricky in a barely understandable murmur through his mask.

"What?" replied Keaton from behind his own respirator.

"A rat hole," murmured Ricky once again.

"Oh, a rat hole," Keaton whispered. "I thought you said asshole. I was thinking the place is bad, but that's a little harsh."

"Me, too!" Larth said, holding back a laugh. "I thought he said asshole!"

"You assholes keep quiet," Jyrall said, attempting to maintain a straight face. "We're supposed to be the baddest thing that ever walked through this starport."

When they turned off the side street onto Town's main street, they started to see more activity. Some of the storefronts appeared to have businesses, if not exactly the businesses that were originally in the spots they occupied, but businesses all the same. The first one they passed was a pawn shop of sorts in what appeared to have once been a restaurant. The tables displayed a variety of objects, from tools to weapons, instead of the normal slate menus or eating utensils.

They passed two more buildings before they came to an actual restaurant, judging by the smells emanating from it. It was set up in an old mining hardware store, with stools pulled up to what would have been the front counter or the parts look up area. Jyrall shook his head, puzzled.

Larth looked across the street and saw several SleSha standing around the front of what appeared to be a bar. In fact, the board nailed sloppily above the door said Pete's Dive Bar. The large wasp-like aliens were known to be exceptional pilots. At least the intelligent ones were; the drones and troops of the race weren't particularly intelligent but were good in combat. They would mindlessly obey orders and fight as if possessed.

"There's a spot we can find information from some locals," Larth said, nodding his head across the street. "It looks like the local watering hole."

"Yeah, we'll come back down that side," Jyrall agreed. "The local Peacemaker's office is up ahead a couple of blocks; from the information we have, it's beside the only credit exchange in town. We'll go in, and I'll break some of the larger credits into smaller stuff and distribute it between us. It'll look like I'm paying wages, in case anyone in the exchange is observing."

"You know they will be," Larth cautioned. "A place like this? The security guard in the exchange may try and rob us later."

"Good point," Jyrall said. He glanced back at Keaton and Ricky trailing them. They were looking around as good security should. "You two keep an eye on the security in there, but don't look too intimidating. They may think we're in there to rob the place."

"Gotcha," Keaton said through a hand.

"If the guard looks too closely, I'll give him the ol' stink eye," Ricky assured them, using the same face-wiping trick to speak clearly this time.

Larth snorted at this, and Jyrall asked himself, *What in all the gods of the universe is a stink eye? An old stink eye? An old one has to be worse than a new one, for sure.* "We're going to have to talk about maintaining identity on these missions," Jyrall finally said. "You two are supposed to be quiet, not making Larth giggle like an adolescent."

"It ain't me," Keaton said, pleading his case. "It's that greasy-fingered wrench turner that's doing it."

Suddenly the wind kicked up and sent swirling dust devils chasing each other down the main street like living cones of grey. There weren't many beings moving about. It was still early in the afternoon so they were probably working in the mines. Observing with a determined look on his face as they walked past several Humans, mercenaries by their appearances, Jyrall noticed many beings wore goggles of some type. *Not a bad idea,* he thought as he realized all the windows they'd passed had been dusty with layers of grime on the outside of the sill.

They passed by the Peacemaker's office—the emblem was stenciled on the door—and Jyrall looked over without turning his head. He saw the office lights were on, but there was no sign of Peacemaker Rekk. There was nowhere for him to hide, either. It was a small, one-room office with a few doors leading off into a very small building. It didn't even look like there was a holding area for detainees, unless the space was bigger than it seemed from the outside. It didn't make sense. Maybe prisoners were kept in the town's local law office building, wherever that was. From what he could see, the office was clean and neat, as it should be, and looked as if it was regularly occupied.

We'll have to find him sooner rather than later.

The exchange Jyrall was looking for was the next building after the Peacemaker's office, and without slowing, Jyrall turned and walked up the three steps to the entrance. Jyrall didn't worry about the other three waiting outside because of their weapons. In a place like Parmick, not even the credit exchange would demand a weapons-free zone.

Larth and the brothers followed Jyrall inside. The lobby seemed unusually quiet. Jyrall attributed it to the lack of constant wind blowing outside. Glancing left and right to get his bearings, he noticed a guard on either side of the door sitting at small kiosks. Two more guards were positioned on each end of the counter, where there were two openings in a barrier for conducting business. All four were Blevins, a race Jyrall and Larth had encountered the year before. Blevin weren't one of the thirty-seven known mercenary races in the galaxy. They were, however, often hired as trigger-happy security. The humanoid race was roughly the size of Humans but would never be mistaken for one with their leathery skin, vaguely reptilian heads, and six-fingered hands.

All four were armed with pistols and appeared alert, but didn't take exception to the fact Jyrall and his crew entered the credit exchange armed. He did see an increase in vigilance on their lizard-like faces. It was to be expected; a Besquith accompanied by two Pushtal called for that, but they were concerned with the wrong one. Jyrall almost flushed as he realized the truth in Colonel Tirr's prediction. All the attention was on him; Larth was forgotten. Little did they know, Larth, the smallest of them, could probably take all four guards down before they finished drawing their weapons.

Jyrall and Larth walked up to the counter, and Keaton and Ricky stayed back, watching the guards watch them. A Jeha stood up from a desk with several monitors, rippled over, and waited expectantly.

"What are your rates?" growled Jyrall.

"It depends on the transaction," said the bored banker. "Are you looking to open an account?"

"Not hardly," scoffed Larth. "I'll bet this place doesn't even insure accounts, Boss."

"No bet," said Jyrall. He turned back to the window and said, "What's the charge for making change?"

"Five percent," answered the Jeha. Jyrall noted the millipede-like alien rippled in anticipation. All the body language courses they'd suffered through in the academy were already paying dividends.

"Robbery!" Jyrall boomed and stared hard at the banker for a few moments with his good eye. "Have him break a thousand-credit chit into twenties and pay the boys for the week," Jyrall ordered, disgusted.

Larth stepped up and produced a thousand-credit chit embedded with a small red diamond. He tossed it up on the counter, which was almost shoulder level on him. "You heard him, give me twenties," he demanded. "We got places to be."

The banker picked up the piece and looked closely at the stone. He produced a specialized jeweler's eyepiece from somewhere on his person, passed it up through several of his pincers to one of his eyes, and looked long and hard at the red diamond. Satisfied, the chit disappeared below the counter, and he started counting out the change. Before he handed it over, he asked, "Name please?"

Larth was still trying to figure out why the chit he'd provided was inspected so closely and was caught off guard for a moment. "What?" he asked.

The Jeha paused before handing over the change. "I said, name please."

"None," Larth replied.

"None? Just None?" he asked, sliding the stack over.

"No," Larth answered with a sneer. "None of your business." He took the stack and turned away.

As he counted out two hundred credits to each of the brothers, Ricky decided one of the guards was showing too much interest in the act. Staring at the Blevin, he showed some teeth and let out a low, menacing growl. It rumbled from deep inside his chest and had the desired effect. The leathery skin of the guard paled visibly, and he found something else to look at across the lobby.

Jyrall looked back as they were leaving and saw the Jeha speaking into a handheld device, watching them go. The teller acted strange during the whole exchange, so he filed it away in the back of his mind as something to think about later and maybe discuss with Larth. Something was amiss, and Larth had likely seen more than him.

The wind had eased, so they were able to get a good look around without having to squint from the dust.

The town was dilapidated and, overall, pretty run down. Traffic was light, so after a battered old cargo carrier on actual wheels rumbled by, they crossed the street and turned to go back toward Pete's Dive Bar.

They saw several Humans and SleSha walk into the bar together. They acted as if they knew each other. The Humans, and what he could see of the SleSha's work belts, were filthy. Blackened faces and hands stuck out from under sweat-stained coveralls the color of wet ashes.

"Awfully friendly," Jyrall said quietly. "Either they serve in the same company or they labor together in some way."

"It's still early," Larth commented. "They must be day drinkers."

They stepped through the door of the bar and looked around. It was a decent-sized place, with the obligatory bar along one side lined with stools. There were tables scattered about the floor with some mismatched chairs, and several Human women fetched drinks back and forth to four occupied tables. The group of Humans and SleSha were just settling in.

Jyrall stomped up to a table that had a large, stout chair on one side, fairly certain it could contain his bulk. He eased into the chair and winced when it squeaked slightly. Larth watched closely, and Jyrall knew why. Larth had seen several chairs fail underneath him in the past, and it was always good for a laugh. Larth seemed a little disappointed when it held.

The bartender, a middle-aged man who looked like he'd been around the galaxy a few times, shouted at a waitress to get a move on. She gave him a dirty look, adjusted the belt and holster at her waist, and ambled over.

"What can I get y'all?" she asked.

"Four beers," Larth said. "You got Earth beer in this joint?"

"We got some on tap," she answered. "It ain't real cold, but it's wet."

"Good enough," Larth answered.

When she walked away, Keaton leaned forward and whispered, "She said y'all."

"That's slang, right?" Jyrall asked.

"That's Southern slang," confirmed Ricky.

A loud crash came from near the bar. They all turned their heads sharply toward the noise. Three tables over, the group of men and SleSha laughed uproariously. One of the men still had his leg stretched out where he'd tripped their waitress. The blonde-haired woman stood up cursing. She wiped herself off and glared at the patrons.

"Get that cleaned up!" shouted the bartender. "It's coming out of your check, May!"

Ricky started to stand, but Keaton grabbed his arm and pulled him back down. Larth saw him do it and realized Ricky was close to blowing their cover early on the first day. Something needed to be done about what had just happened to settle Ricky's anger, so he stood himself.

"Those were our beers," Larth said, hands on his hips as he glared at the table.

"Yeah? What of it, pipsqueak?" the man who had tripped May asked.

Larth was moving before he could think. At a dead sprint, he caught the man with a right square in the face. Larth wasn't very big, but the momentum and the height of his jump made for a powerful strike.

Larth passed over the man as the chair toppled back, and he ran around another table to come back to the stunned group. The downed man struggled to untangle himself from the chair and slipped in the spilled beer. The man's four friends hesitated for a moment, then knocked over their own chairs and stood as one, ready to fight.

Now Jyrall was close enough to grab one of the SleSha and throw him against the bar, knocking over several stools. There was a loud crack when the SleSha hit, and it wasn't wood breaking. Jyrall turned to see the brothers fighting two of the Human assholes, when he felt a blow to his back as the remaining SleSha broke a chair against him, the impact moving him slightly. Baring his teeth, he struck without claws and knocked his opponent several feet into a table. He stalked after him.

Larth timed it perfectly; as the man he'd hit sat up, finally free of the chair, Larth caught him with a running knee, knocking him unconscious. Jyrall saw the last Human drop from a combination of strikes from Keaton. The brothers could hold their own in a fight.

The bar was deathly quiet. None of the other groups had interfered in the fight. The bartender stood open-mouthed, looking at the devastation. Barfights happened; that was why there were mismatched chairs and tables everywhere.

"Barlung's not gonna like this," the bartender said finally. "Those were some of his couriers." He pointed at the five individuals laying in states of semi-consciousness. Both the SleShas obviously had broken limbs and were buzzing in pain.

"Yeah?" Jyrall growled. "When you talk to him, you tell him he owes Varkell and his crew a beer."

Ricky walked over to the bar and stood in front of the bartender. He showed some teeth and growled softly.

The bartender backed up against the mirrored wall, nervous. "What's he want?"

"Pete?" Larth asked. "Is that your name? Pete? You own this dump?"

"Yeah," answered the man, licking his lips and looking around.

"I think he expects *you* to pay for our drinks, not the waitress," Larth advised, looking down at the claws on one hand. He looked back up. "I'd advise you to make it so. These two," Larth indicated the two Pushtal staring across the bar, "are not the ones to have upset at you."

They finally settled at their table and watched the group of beaten Humans and aliens help each other out of the bar. Their waitress finally brought them their beers and whispered, "Thanks, Honey."

* * *

Mining Operations Center
Parmick

"What do you mean, you don't know who they are?" screamed Barlung.

The five standing before him in the large room in the mining headquarters shrank back visibly. They made their way straight to Barlung to explain themselves and why they wouldn't be able to make the first leg of the run the next day. Not only were they afraid of losing the easy credits for the run, they were doubly afraid of losing their lives with a simple command from the boss.

"You were beat down by just four other beings?" demanded Barlung, even though they'd told their story twice already. "And one of them was a Zuparti? You've got to be shitting me!"

"Yes, Boss," answered the man who'd started the whole thing, both eyes sporting impressively swelling and angry gouges. His voice was nasal from the swelling in his nose and cheeks. "They had a Besquith and a couple of tiger-looking guys."

"Pushtal? They had Pushtal?" Barlung said as if he was talking to himself. "You go clean up. You'd better be ready for the run in three weeks, if you know what's good for you."

After the group left, Barlung walked to the door of the operations center to talk to Nay-Thok. He wanted to know more about the four and knew Nay-Thok could get the answers. He had a powerful computer system and knew how to use it.

Barlung was surprised when he walked into the room. It was as if Nay-Thok had read his mind. "Varkell. The Besquith is named Varkell. I've found over a hundred references to One-Eyed Varkell and his thugs in the GalNet archives over the last five years. They're quite the crew."

On the main screen, a camera feed showed several views of Pete's Dive Bar. The only view with sound was the one over the bar itself, focused on the register. Nay-Thok kept an eye on everything everywhere in town, especially the businesses they got a cut of.

"Give me a few minutes, and I'll find out more," the Jeha said, manipulating his computer system.

Barlung observed the four sitting at the table. The Besquith was huge, easily the biggest Barlung had ever seen. One eye was missing, covered by the patch. Looking closer, Barlung decided he was still much bigger than the Besquith on screen. Besides, it was a known fact that cameras made one appear larger than they actually were.

The idiots were right. There were two Pushtal sitting at the table. *Interesting.* The last of the four, the Zuparti, was talking. Barlung couldn't hear what was being said, but it was obvious by the movement of his hands, he was discussing the fight. Barlung shook his head and turned back to Nay-Thok, waiting patiently.

After a few minutes, Nay-Thok looked up. "Varkell's ship is called *Night Moves.*" He pulled up an image of the airfield and zoomed in on a ship parked on the far side, well away from their hanger. "It's a small freighter, and they specialize in moving goods…with no questions asked. I had to do a deep search for the Besquith's name. I followed a couple hidden links, hacked into a syndicate's files from the other side of the galaxy, and found they have a name for themselves in that area among those who move things without public knowledge."

"Why are they here?" Barlung demanded.

"I can't see that," admitted the Jeha, "which tells me they're good at what they do. I wouldn't doubt they probably know of this colony and think they may be able to get some work in the area. I suggest you go to Pete's and get them working for us before they find a run they want elsewhere."

"I'll go talk to him," Barlung said, turning toward the door.

"Very wise of you to go now," Nay-Thok said to his back as Barlung paused. "You can catch them while they're still in a good mood. From what I've discovered, we're lucky those five idiots lived to tell of the fight."

* * * * *

Chapter Twelve

Pete's Dive Bar
Town, Parmick

Jyrall looked up when the door opened and saw a huge Oogar duck through the doorway. Glancing at Larth, he knew his partner had also noticed the big Oogar. The brothers didn't see him, as their backs were to the door, a position Jyrall never let himself sit in. Come to think of it, neither did Larth. At times, the two of them may have looked strange using the same corner of a table instead of across from each other, but neither cared. Old habits and academy lessons died hard.

Conversation dropped to a minimum, and Pete looked nervously over at their table, as though expecting the worst. He glanced back at the door several times, looking for Barlung's lieutenants, or at least several of his guards. When none followed, he looked puzzled. Even the waitresses kept glancing at the door.

Barlung made his way to their table and stood there for a moment. The brothers were alert now that he was standing at their table, but neither moved. Larth calmly took a sip of his beer. Jyrall just stared back at the Oogar. If the purple alien thought his size and presence would intimidate them, he was wrong. They didn't bother to stand, though they already had a plan to fight the imposing figure.

"You mind if I join you, Varkell?" the Oogar finally asked.

Though surprised the Oogar already knew his alias, Jyrall didn't let it show. "If you can find a chair that'll hold you. Be my guest."

The big Oogar looked around and walked over to an occupied table. The Jivool sitting in the biggest chair there quickly vacated it, and Barlung dragged it over to their table. He scooted up between Larth and Keaton.

Barlung looked over at Pete and said, "Bring me a water. A bottled water."

Jyrall was surprised when Pete came around the bar using a crutch; one of his legs was missing from the knee down. It was something he hadn't noticed with the bartender half hidden behind the bar, and Jyrall chastised himself. Not even a Peacemaker could see everything. Pete set a huge bottle of water down in front of the Oogar and limped away.

"You have me at a disadvantage," Jyrall said. "You know who I am, but I don't know who you are. If you're going to sit at our table, you'd better give up your name."

"The name is Barlung. I run things around here," the Oogar said, opening his bottle.

"Do you?" asked Jyrall with a subtle challenge in his voice. "There's a lot of places in town, the mines, the airfield, and all the rest," Jyrall continued, taking a sip of his own drink. "Hard to believe one individual runs it all. I suppose you have the local Peacemaker under your control as well?"

At this Larth laughed. "Yeah, right, Boss, a high and mighty Peacemaker playing nice in a place like this? Whoever has this area probably has a full detention center. Where are they? This system? The next? You know they're around here somewhere, poking their noses into everyone's business. That's all they're good for."

"Yeah. If they get close, we move on. Halfway across the galaxy if we have to," Jyrall agreed with a shake of his head.

"The local Peacemaker hasn't been a problem," Barlung said. "As a matter of fact, I think he's gone back to the Academy for some kind of new training. Who knows how long he'll be gone."

"The academy, huh?" Larth said. "Better than around here."

"For argument's sake, let's agree you run some things around here," Jyrall said. "I know the mines used to produce red diamonds and other precious metals. You're digging out scraps, right? Does all of it get shipped to the Merchant Guild and accounted for to help keep the galaxy economy straight...or does some of it need to make its way elsewhere?"

"That's a pretty bold question," Barlung remarked coldly. "What makes you think the mining operation here isn't by the book?"

"Pffftt," Jyrall remarked. "If I ran the mines, the Merchant Guild would know only what I want them to know. Tell him, Switch."

"Only a fool would send it all out all legal-like," agreed Larth. "Our business is our business. The only ones who see our books are me and the boss. It's nobody's business what we do with what we make or how much we make."

"I see," Barlung said, thinking for a moment. "Speaking of how much you make...the crew you four...damaged, was supposed to make a run for me. A couple of containers of mining equipment, you understand."

"Yeah?" Jyrall said. "Well, they're out of business for a while. I have half a mind to go find their ship and relieve them of it. They're lucky they're still breathing. If I wasn't looking to pick up a little business around here, they wouldn't be."

"I still need the equipment shipped," Barlung commented.

"Where's it going?" Jyrall asked.

"To the starport in the Miderall system," Barlung answered. "It gets off-loaded onto another ship to continue its journey."

"Miderall, huh?" Jyrall looked over at Larth.

"Easy run, Boss," Larth said looking at a handheld slate. "Nearest Peacemaker isn't even based in that system, from what I can tell."

"Five thousand credits, and you provide the F11, since you run things around here," Jyrall said. "I don't want to know what the equipment is. I don't care. But if it damages my ship with leakage or radiation, you will."

"That's pretty steep," commented Barlung. "That's more than I normally pay."

"Yeah, well, you pay idiots," Larth said. It was a test, and the Oogar merely stared in return.

"Half up front, the rest on delivery," Jyrall stated and drained his mug.

"How do I know you won't take the half and skip out with my equipment?" Barlung asked.

Jyrall stood up to his full height, and Keaton and Ricky did the same. Larth just sat and shook his head. "That was the wrong thing to say," he said, to no one in particular.

Barlung was taller than Jyrall, but not by much. He was beginning to think perhaps he should have brought a few guards with him. "I'm just asking," he remarked. "You got any references?"

"It's none of your business who we hauled for in the past," Jyrall said threateningly. "Just like it'll be nobody's business if we haul for you."

"That's what I like to hear," Barlung said, standing himself. "I'll have the payment delivered to your ship at noon tomorrow with instructions for delivery. It'll be hard credit. The exchange in town is crooked. I should know, I run it." He turned and walked away without looking back.

Jyrall glanced around the bar. Everyone seemed to be minding their own business, except one of the waitresses. It wasn't May. This one was dark-haired and had a seasoned look in her eyes. She looked away and continued wiping down the table.

* * *

Night Moves
Parmick Starport

The next day, at noon, a hauler pulled up next to the open ramp of *Night Moves*. Jyrall stood there with Ricky as they watched some dusty miners load four containers onto the ship under the watchful eyes of four Lumar guards. One of the guards handed Jyrall a box. Inside was half the fee and the name of the captain and ship they were to contact upon arrival at the trading port in Miderall.

A wheeled tanker showed up minutes later to fill the ship with F11. The specially trained crew deployed and got to work. *Night Moves* would be on its way shortly. Jyrall didn't want to admit it, but it was an efficient process. He and Ricky walked up the ramp and closed it behind them.

"If that's mining equipment in those boxes, it's really small," Larth said, looking at the boxes. "I bet it's red diamonds."

"No bet," Jyrall said, flipping his patch up on his forehead.

"That's what you always say!" Larth complained. "That Barlung is running some kind of scam. I don't doubt whoever receives this load will take it to his hidey hole, wherever that is."

"You're probably right," Ricky said. "The guy is as crooked as they come."

"I have most of the message we drafted last night ready to send to Captain Dreel," Larth said. "Now that we know which ship we're delivering it to, we can send it before we make the transition."

"There's no guarantee he'll get it in time," Jyrall replied, "even with a Blue Flight at his disposal."

"There's actually a regional barracks in Miderall. Next planet out from the star, but still in the habitable zone. They can relay the message. Maybe they'll just send support?"

Jyrall shook his head. "Not with the general recall orders, remember? If they come, they'll have to come with a large force, and that's not something Rsach wants."

Larth stroked his chin with one paw. "Yeah, I see what you mean. It's Dreel or nothing. Do you want me to hack the Peacemaker's Aethernet connections? I can transmit StormWatch through there."

"No, I guarantee it's compromised." Jyrall let the words trail off as a plan came to mind. "Two jumps. We'll transition to another location first, and tell Barlung we wanted to make sure we weren't being followed."

"Tell him? Before we go?" Keaton asked, his brow furrowing in confusion.

"No, after. He never gave us a timeline. So, we use the first jump to give us time to message Dreel. The second jump gives him time to respond with Blue Flight, provided the Cartography Guild plays along." Jyrall nodded to himself. *It could work.*

"Done deal." Larth grinned. "I'll get the message ready. Keaton? Reprogram the navigation, and we'll be in business."

"We can't afford to drop our guard at all," Jyrall rumbled. "We should inspect the ship one more time and maintain security until we're off planet. I don't trust Barlung or his cronies."

"Neither do I, Snarlyface. The sooner we're off this rock, the better."

"Once we get off the planet, I'll work on the sight for that cannon," Ricky said. "I still think I can link it to the view inside your patch."

"After we figure out how to get into the containers without leaving a trace," Jyrall said.

"Now you're talking," Larth said, rubbing his small paws together. "Somebody hand me a pry bar."

"You might want to wait until we break gravity," Keaton cautioned before he headed to the operations center. "Besides, I should look at the access pad and see if I need to reprogram it after we open it."

"Hellfahr, for all we know, they might blow up in our face if we open one without the right code," Ricky said. "I ain't trying to get blowed up."

"I guess," Larth said, disappointed he had to wait. "If it did blow up in our faces, we wouldn't have time to feel it. I mean, I'm just saying."

"You're not wrong." Jyrall laughed. "Stay the hell away from the containers until Keaton takes a look."

"Yeah, stay away from them," agreed Ricky. "Peacemaker or not, you'll get us all killed."

* * * * *

Chapter Thirteen

Night Moves

Hyperspace to Miderall via Krifay

"It's kind of strange, being able to leave a colonized planet without having to clear it through anyone," remarked Keaton, looking over at Jyrall. "It reminds me of home."

"It is unusual," agreed Jyrall from the copilot's seat as he adjusted his safety harness in preparation for the upcoming microgravity. For him, the less movement the better during the transition from a planet's gravity to actual space.

"I kinda like it," said Larth from behind them. "It helps with our cover. We don't ask anyone when we can come and go. It fits us."

"Hey, Ricky," Keaton asked over the ship's internal comms, "we good back there?"

"Yep," Ricky answered a moment later. "I finished checking the hull, and it's good to go. Nobody could get inside without us knowing even if they wanted to. I ran three different sensor sweeps on the cargo, too. It's clean."

"All right, prepare for liftoff," Keaton advised.

"Haul ass, man," replied his brother.

"Like a bootlegger." Keaton grinned and hit a switch.

Several minutes later the G-forces eased off and they were in space. The ship was moving at a good speed and had plenty of power to spare, should they need it. Once they were a safe distance into the star system, Keaton would engage the shunts, and they'd be on their way.

"Once we get to Krifay, we should set down away from everything so I can get in some range time with my new pistols," suggested Larth. "I want to really get the feel of them."

"That's a good idea," Jyrall agreed. "It's been a while since my familiarization fire. I'd like to see what this can do." He patted the huge pistol on his side.

"A lot," Larth said, grinning, "including straining even *your* wrist."

"Oh, it'll probably kick, but I think I can handle it," Jyrall assured him with a slight smile.

"That's why I carry a smaller laser pistol," Keaton said. "Not much kick to it."

"Those rifles you two had weren't lasers," Jyrall said, "and they weren't small."

"Yeah, those are a couple of the Barrett M107s Pops acquired," admitted Keaton. "They're old, but they're good weapons. We reload those rounds, too."

"What are they?" Larth asked. "50 cals, right?"

"Yeah," said Keaton, looking back. "We have plenty of rounds for them, since Frank uses them."

"Who?" Jyrall asked, confused.

"Frank and Stein. Didn't Ricky tell you about them?" Keaton asked with a funny look on his face. "I thought he did. Once we get into hyperspace, we'll go back so he can show you."

"He did mention some kind of security rovers, but I thought he meant just for perimeter detection or something," Larth admitted.

"What are they exactly?" Jyrall asked, now more than a little curious.

"Oh, no," Keaton said shaking his head. "Sorry, Peacemakers, but I'm not going to tell you. I'll let Ricky do that. After all, it's some Ricky Shit." He smiled. "Thirty seconds until we transition," he added as he observed a screen and made an adjustment.

Once the transition was complete, they made their way to the cargo hold. Ricky was bent over a waist-high, eight-foot-long tracked machine of some sort. It was ugly, really ugly. It had mismatched, chipped paint, and the sides and the front were different types of metal, clearly from different sources. There was a hatch open on the top, and he was adjusting something inside. He pushed back, stopping at the end of the tether he'd connected to a ring on the side of the vehicle, shaking his paw.

"Dang thing bit me!" he exclaimed.

"What?" Jyrall asked alarmed. "Just what do you have in that thing? If it bites, don't let it out!"

"I think he means it shocked him," Keaton explained.

"Oh, well that's different, then," Jyrall said, relieved.

Larth looked down and shook his head. He looked up and said, "You're a Besquith and one of the biggest Peacemakers in the galaxy. You're incredibly strong and near unstoppable in a fight. You far exceeded standards in many of the classes and training we received in the Academy. Yet you're still afraid of small creatures that bite. You're killing me over here. You know that? Killing me."

"I'm not afraid of things that bite…I just don't like them," Jyrall said defensively. "That's all. Nobody wants to be bitten by anything. That's perfectly reasonable."

"Makes sense to me," agreed Keaton.

"It shocked me a little, that's all," Ricky explained. "No disrespect, Jyrall, but come on. Even if I had a pet in there, a little nip wouldn't hurt you none. Unless it was pizzen. Then you would die, I reckon."

"Pizzen?" Jyrall asked.

"He means poison," Keaton translated.

"All right, I'm laying down the law right now," Jyrall said, standing as tall as he could in microgravity while hanging on to a strap. "Nobody—and I mean nobody—is bringing any creature on this ship that may be venomous. Or may bite me, with poison or not."

Jyrall stood with one hand on his hip as his partner and the brothers laughed at him. "I mean it," Jyrall exclaimed, attempting to keep a serious look on his face. They laughed even harder. He finally shook his head and grinned himself.

If you can't beat them, join them.

"So, Keaton said to ask you about—what was it?" Jyrall thought for a moment. "Frank and Stein."

Ricky's face lit up. "Well, this is Frank." He indicated the tracked object in front of him. "I put magnetized tracks on him so I could work on him in micro gravity. He has two .50 caliber machine guns. They're chain-fed, and the composite barrels are chemically cooled, though in a pinch they can be air cooled. They just can't maintain full auto for long bursts if it has to go to air. Check it out."

Ricky pulled a small device off his belt and hit a button. The hatch on the other half of the top opened, and both hatches continued until they were level with the top. A stand came up, and a weapon with two barrels pivoted up and toward the front. Covered belt guides went down into the body of the rover. Ricky hit another button, and a front hatch dropped, revealing four missile tubes. A final push of the button, and a small mast rose behind the guns and started rotating.

"Cool," said Larth, rubbing his paws together. "Can I operate it when we get to Krifay? We're going to get in a little range time."

"Sure," Ricky said. "We'll have to load it. It ain't loaded now, since I had to do a little tweaking."

"What type of missiles go in those tubes?" Jyrall asked, indicating the front of the vehicle.

"Those are standard CASPer missiles," Ricky answered. "Mk 6s and Mk7s use them. Don't know about the new Mk 8s. Never saw one. Pops had a whole supply of missiles for his Mk 7. He hoarded weapons and ammunition, you know. He shipped his CASPer off to Earth about eight or nine years ago, if I remember right. He said he was too old to operate it, and there was some kin back home that could use it. He didn't send the missiles, though. So, since we had a supply of them, I figured why not?

"Stein is over there," he continued, pointing to an open space that served as a garage for the two tracked vehicles; only one slot was occupied. "He has a missile rack that comes up. Five wide, six high. Thirty of those babies. Easy to reload, too. Just open the back, slide them in, and close it. The backs have open slots for the exhaust but close around each one enough to hold it in place. Kinda like loading missiles on a mech. I pieced a couple old tommy gun parts on him, so he has two machine guns that are drum fed. They're .45s, but what can you do? I could put a .50 on him, but I didn't want to tear down any of the good weapons in the arms room."

"Tommy guns?" Larth blurted excitedly. "Really?"

"Are they both remote operated?" Jyrall cut off his friend's excitement and stepped over to look at the one Ricky called Stein. It was just as hideous as the other, except this one had a large square box welded to the top of the body. The box was too wide and a little overbalanced on one side.

"They are," Keaton confirmed. "They can be operated by camera remote from the ship's operations center, linked to a slate, or to a handheld computer. I also programmed them to operate in their own defense. You just have to put in restrictions and any pertinent information you have on potential attackers. They're ugly as a wild hog, but they work."

"Hey!" Ricky complained, patting Frank fondly. "We might never need 'em, but if we do, we got 'em."

"Like I said, that's some Ricky Shit." Keaton laughed. "Now, let's see about them containers. We got us some time before I'm needed back in the pilot's seat."

Ricky activated his control, and the weapons and mast folded back into the body of the vehicle. He guided it back into its parking slot on its magnetized tracks and shut the bulkhead. Unless one was really looking for the seams, it couldn't be noticed. Jyrall realized it was part of the bulkheads that hadn't been present the first time he'd stepped on board the ship and part of the reason the cargo hold area was smaller. It seemed like a good trade off.

Keaton studied the data pad on the corner of the first container. After a few moments, he pulled a small handheld computer out of his cargo pocket and connected a lead from it to the container's pad. It took a few minutes, and then a faint click was heard.

"They have security on the pad," Keaton informed them. "It'll register every time it's opened. It also has a cargo weight recorded. There must be a scale plate in the bottom of the container. If any of its contents are removed, it'll register that as well. If this thing is full of red diamonds, we can look at them, but I wouldn't suggest we remove any, even if we put them right back. We may be able to get away with it in micro gravity, but definitely not under gravity. I can override the pad to show it was never opened, but I can't get to the plate sensors and override that program unless we have a lot of time to do it, plus we need to put all the contents in something to do it."

"Wait," Larth asked, "you mean it's unlocked already? I don't get to use a pry bar?" He shook his head. "Where's the fun in that?"

"If it's unlocked, don't open it," Jyrall said. "We have to wait until we've landed on Krifay or Miderall."

"Wait? Why?" Larth asked, disappointed, again.

"We open that container, and we may have red diamonds and their dust floating everywhere," Jyrall explained. "What if we miss a couple as we gather them and the weight is off?"

"Aw, hell," Ricky said. "He's right. They'll go everywhere."

"Fine, lock it back up," Larth said, throwing up his paws. He pushed off the container toward the hatch leading into the rest of the ship. "I'm headed to the galley. It's my turn to cook. We got any ketchup on board?"

"Damn right we do," Ricky said, following him, "and mustard, too. What are you going to make? Fish sticks? I like 'em crispy. I know how to make hushpuppies. You ever have hushpuppies?"

"What's a hushpuppy?" Jyrall asked Keaton with a pained look on his face.

"Good eating's what they are," Keaton answered. "Come on, we'll show you. Don't worry, you don't dip 'em in no ketchup."

* * * * *

Chapter Fourteen

"It's going to storm later," Kurrang said the moment the outer hatch opened, and warm, moist air swirled around them. "It's too warm after sunset. They'll likely be quite severe. I'll ensure the handlers chain us down."

"A 10,000-ton Blue Flight needs to be chained down?" Dreel shook his head. "What are you talking about? Storms? Like thunderstorms?"

"Some of the most powerful ever observed."

"How can you possibly know that?"

"I was stationed here a long time ago." Kurrang grinned with one side of his mouth. "I don't remember my time here with fondness."

"Why not?" Dreel asked. "Aside from your assurance that there are storms somewhere in that gorgeous orange and red partly cloudy sky, this seems to be quite a nice planet."

"Of course it looks nice now," Kurrang said with a grunt. "The atmosphere is so unpredictable from solar heating that weather systems on the planet can be horrendous. It may not look like it now, but on the western horizon are the beginnings of storm fronts."

Dreel held back a laugh at the sour look on the TriRusk's elongated face. "You really didn't like it here."

"I believed this planet and its shitty weather was behind me."

"Shitty weather?" Dreel laughed. "You definitely spent some time with Jessica."

"Her colorful language fits some descriptions better than our native tongues ever could."

"Come on." Dreel started down the boarding ramp. "Gnaxx and Maraq are waiting."

"Maraq is the Tortantula?" Kurrang fell into his ambling, all-fours walk next to the large Besquith. "I've only been up close to them once before."

"Disconcerting, isn't it?" Dreel laughed softly. The Flatar and the Tortantula couldn't have been more different species, yet they were bonded for life and, when properly trained, were a formidable weapon. Apart, the Tortantula was far more frightening. The ten-legged spiders came straight from the universe's most evil imaginations. Menacing and massive, they could scare most citizens away based on sight alone. The Flatar were far less intimidating, though in reality, as deadly as their many-legged counterparts. Only a third-of-a-meter tall, Flatar were often overlooked as a threat until it was too late for their enemy. Combined, with the Flatar riding atop the spider in a combat harness and with weapons at their disposal, the lethal teams were exceptional combatants who thrived on chaos and destruction.

For Gnaxx and his counterpart, Maraq, the notion of them working together in a Regional Barracks with the Flatar operating as the barracks commander and the Tortantula as an executive officer wasn't as strange as it sounded. They might be a finely tuned war machine, but they were equally handy administrators and leaders. Of the relatively close regional barracks to start their mission, Toscatta had been at the top of Dreel's list for precisely that reason. If there was one barracks command team who had the attention of their Enforcers, it would be Gnaxx and Maraq.

Dreel didn't really expect trouble from the Enforcers collected at the regional barracks, but he'd learned early on that being an Enforcer was very different than being a Peacemaker, and that sometimes

the two barely managed to co-exist in the same barracks arrangement. Enforcers, at least some of them, tended to believe they existed on a different plane of existence than mere Peacemakers. While
both tended to work alone, or in an occasional pairing, Enforcers
gravitated away from the investigative end of the spectrum toward
full-on operations. Often times, they performed missions far and
above the difficulty level suitable for a regular Peacemaker. The
guild, after studying the way Humans and other species treated such
forces, had shied away from calling them special operations, but it
was a good analog.

Across the tarmac, the collection of twenty Peacemakers of all
species came to their respective positions of attention on Gnaxx's
high-pitched command.

The tiny Flatar turned and bounced toward them. A few seconds
later, the Tortantula pranced forward on its ten legs and took up a
position abreast of Gnaxx. As they closed the distance to each other,
Dreel saw a very tiny, but distinct, smile on Gnaxx's face.

It's been far too long, old friend.

"The other day, I told Maraq that I wouldn't be surprised to see
you out here soon." Gnaxx showed a few more teeth as his smile
widened. "I did make good on our bet, remember."

Dreel grunted but smiled. "You know I can't drink alcohol,
Gnaxx."

"Your allergies are not my concern, Dreel."

The tiny Flatar bounded forward a few jumps, and Dreel knelt on
the ground, extended an upturned clawed paw, and Gnaxx jumped
squarely into the middle. Dreel brought him up to eye-level. The
chipmunk-like creature placed its tiny paws on its hips. "It's good to
see you, Gnaxx. Well met."

"Well met, my friend." Gnaxx nodded, the smile evaporating
from his face. "If you're here, I can extrapolate that it's bad. If

memory serves me right, your friend is a TriRusk. They haven't been seen in a Jeha's age. That's two strikes, Dreel. Why do I feel the third has to do with the Peacemaker recall order?"

Dreel nodded. "It does. But there are other concerns that have to be addressed, and that's best done away from prying eyes and listening devices."

"This whole area is clear and—"

"Inside." Kurrang grunted. "Guild Master's orders."

Gnaxx stared at the large, white-furred creature. "I can understand Honored Rsach's orders perfectly. I don't need to be forcibly reminded, Captain Kurrang."

The TriRusk looked mildly surprised. "I wasn't aware my presence had been announced through StormWatch."

"Not StormWatch," Gnaxx replied. "The surveillance cameras on Araf got a really good look at you visiting Tara Mason. The entire galaxy has to know the TriRusk—well, at least one of you—has been found. There was only one named in the archives we researched. The public ones, no less. You're a known quantity now."

Dreel looked up at his friend. "No matter, Kurrang. They would've known sooner or later."

"It's not my presence I worry about," Kurrang replied. The solemn tone was not lost on Dreel.

"Your colony has the protection of the Peacemaker Guild," Dreel commented. "And ultimately, our mission will secure them."

Gnaxx chittered, "Well, I'm under orders to provide you all the support you need."

"I didn't expect Rsach to communicate that," Dreel replied. "Is your relationship still strained?"

"Does an Oogar excrete wherever it wants?" Gnaxx laughed. "I told him, nicely, that he didn't need to order me to support you and the Enforcers. I expect he knew that, but I told him anyway."

"And he did so nicely," Maraq said, rumbling to life. The deep-voiced translator around the Tortantula's thorax flashed brightly. "Well met, Peacemakers."

"Well met, Peacemaker," Dreel and Kurrang said in unison.

"Let's get inside," Gnaxx said. "Would you at least inspect the formation, Dreel? I've had the whole barracks quaking in fear that the Deputy Prime Enforcer was coming. They're all spit-and-polished to perfection."

Dreel shook his head and laughed in resignation. "Fine. For you, I'll do this."

"Maraq will recall the Enforcers." Gnaxx turned and winked at the Tortantula before looking up at Kurrang. "We'll get you set up in the central briefing room, Captain Kurrang."

"Thank you, Gnaxx," Kurrang replied. "I apologize for my impertinence."

"Well, I'm not going to apologize for being an asshole." Gnaxx grinned. "In times like these, being nice tends to cause unnecessary loss of property, equipment, and lives. As a barracks commander, I'm kinda partial to those things."

After the quick and relatively painless review of the assembled troops, the Peacemakers moved to the central security facility. Dreel was quiet, his mind working, not through the mission's parameters and requirements, but through the fertile fields of memory from the time he'd first met Gnaxx at the academy nearly thirty years before.

The formal education of a Peacemaker was both eccentric and unique. While schooled in weapons and tactics alongside policy and diplomacy, Peacemakers spent time in courses designed to suppress or camouflage their emotions and intentions, either through the timeless practice of dramatic acting, or calming, meditative techniques. Rarely did most Peacemakers show emotion to anyone other than wearers of the platinum badge. Most often, said emotions weren't shown in public, either.

Hence, when Gnaxx leaned forward at his desk, placed his head in his tiny paws, and groaned, it was as authentic a reaction as Dreel had seen in years. For a Flatar, much less an experienced combat leader like Gnaxx, the reaction approached stunning.

"You're kidding, right?" Gnaxx asked, his tiny face hidden behind his paws. "It's that bad?"

"It appears so," Dreel replied. "The guild has spread the High Council to the expanses of the galaxy, and the temporary headquarters has moved at least three times by the standard operating procedures."

Gnaxx sat with his head down. Maraq was the first to speak. "The recall? It's for real? We're going to war?"

Dreel looked at the Tortantula for a long moment. The multiple eyes of the spider-like alien stared implacably back at him, as if searching for something other than the truth. The Tortantula were bred for war. They knew what it meant, and they knew the price that would be paid, if not by themselves, by those headed into combat.

"We've known this day would come, Gnaxx," Maraq spoke slowly. "We've trained ourselves and our students for this day."

Gnaxx didn't look up. "That doesn't mean I have to like it. We've worked for years to get to this point. The guild is in a position beyond reproach, and the damned mercenaries have to make a play. Especially now."

"You knew this was coming, Gnaxx," Maraq chided.

"You just said that, and I did, but godsdammit, I didn't want to admit it, okay?" Gnaxx looked up at Dreel. The Flatar's eyes were dark and bright at the same time. "How soon?"

"Rsach wants your Peacemakers moving as soon as possible," Dreel answered, "but there's a little leeway in the timetable, so to speak."

Gnaxx cocked a furry eyebrow. "Oh, I get it. I'm supposed to wait? Place those under my command at the whim of the—"

"No," Kurrang replied. "Not at the whim of the guild master. We serve the Union, and the *Union* requires that the Peacemakers stand or fall."

"I know that! Don't lecture me." Gnaxx whirled on Kurrang. "You and your kind sat out the fight for a few hundred years."

"And we sit it out no longer," Kurrang rumbled. "Nor do your Peacemakers, Gnaxx. We knew this time would come, as Maraq said. We've been through the plan half a dozen times. Our portion of this effort is well thought out and executable. The outliers, as Dreel pointedly called them, are whether the Enforcers can adapt to operating in small units, and the situation on Parmick. The young ones will stick to their plan. We have no doubt."

Dreel nodded. "It's important they do so, and they recognize that. If they simply started poking their snouts into places they didn't belong, the cover story would fall apart in a matter of days. They'll do what we discussed. It's imperative that we're there to meet them."

"That implies Peacemaker Rekk's intelligence is accurate. The thugs on Parmick could be paying off the Gate Master and the Information Guild," Gnaxx said. His tiny face screwed up in concentration. "They're after profit. That's why they're running shipments every few days. They have two or three crews dedicated to running whatever they're shipping out of Parmick."

"That bothers us," Kurrang said. "All our intelligence assets and a trustworthy Peacemaker on the planet have no idea what they're shipping. All we can assume is that it's related to the mine."

Dreel nodded. "A mine declared exhausted of red diamonds ten years ago. They've got something down there. Could be as simple as gold. There's still quite a market for it."

"That's what the young ones have to find out," Kurrang replied.

Gnaxx nodded. "And we're supposed to recall through all of this? Not do our duty and stop this insurrection once and for all?"

Dreel lowered his chin. "Do you remember in the academy? Counter-diplomacy?"

"Hampf." Gnaxx laughed. "A professor with a sense of humor. Who knew he was so damned right about life in the Galactic Union?"

Dreel laughed, but Kurrang stepped forward with concern on his face. "What do you mean? What did this instructor tell you?"

The laughter stopped, and Dreel's face grew serious. He leaned down, his sharp teeth glinting in the light of the hallway. "Life in the Union means an insurrection has to happen on occasion, and the Peacemakers' role during those times is to let it happen."

"We're not going to let war happen, though, are we?" Gnaxx grinned. "That's why you're here right? The Enforcers?"

"Your Enforcers," Dreel said. "If you've done precisely what I think you've done, they're ready to do something no other Enforcer has ever done."

"And that is?" Maraq asked with a clear hint of a grin in her voice.

Gnaxx glanced over his shoulder and locked eyes with the Tortantula before turning back to Dreel. "You want them to work together, don't you? A small unit instead of individuals."

"And you've trained them to do this, correct?"

"Maybe…" Gnaxx grinned and then burst out a laugh. "Just maybe we have."

* * * * *

Chapter Fifteen

ight Moves transitioned into normal space in the Krifay system, much closer to the single inhabitable planet than most system's emergence points. They were only hours from a trading port, where medium and small ships filled the docks and large freighters orbited above in a wide circular pattern. Many ships were unable to dock, which spoke well of the demand for Krifay's wares. Smaller cargo ships ascended directly to orbit with the main trade item from the processing plants on the planet Krifay's surface and transferred the cargo to the huge freighters.

Keaton looked over at Jyrall, once again in the copilot's seat. Jyrall shook his head, trying to fight through his discomfort. "Are you all right?" he asked.

"I don't know if I ever will be," admitted Jyrall. "I'm doomed to be one of those who suffers from the transitions. It passes quickly, but not quickly enough."

"Well, that should make you feel better," Larth said from behind them. He released one of the straps he was clinging to so he could point.

Past the port, the planet could be seen. It was mostly blue in several different shades. There were a few green land masses visible from this distance. They weren't large enough to be considered continents on most planets. As they got closer, more islands came into view. It was truly a water world.

"It's beautiful," admitted Jyrall. "Just beautiful."

"What?" asked Ricky. "It's mostly water. I don't think its purty at all. I mean, I don't mind a little water. But that right there is a bit much."

"You need to like water a little more," exclaimed Keaton from the pilot's seat, "and wash the dang grease out from between your digits more often."

"Whatever," answered Ricky. They were back in their running argument. "Ain't no sense in washing my paws until I finish what I'm working on. Like I'm gonna wash up and then go get dirty again a few minutes later. It ain't happening. Besides, how am I gonna walk away from something I'm about to get fixed?"

Larth looked over at Jyrall and grinned from ear to ear. "We have the best team ever," he said. "Ever."

Jyrall, feeling better, rolled his eyes, though in reality, he enjoyed the brothers' light bantering. The four of them had gotten to know each other better on the trip through hyperspace, and he felt comfortable with the team as well. "I think it's beautiful," he said again.

"Tell them why," implored Larth. He knew the answer but let his partner tell it.

"Krifay is one of the largest seafood producing planets in the galaxy," Jyrall explained. "Earth seafood, I should say. There are planets that produce their own versions, but this planet was colonized long ago by Humans with the sole intention of farming fish and other seafoods."

"Really?" Ricky asked, looking again at the planet growing in the viewport.

"Really," confirmed Larth. "Apparently, many of the fish species from Earth were able to thrive in this planet's oceans. Along with algae, kelp, and several other seaweeds."

"How did they manage that?" Keaton asked, intrigued.

"The conditions on the planet are very similar to Earth's," Jyrall explained. "Gravity, saline content, currents, temperatures. Everything."

"How can that be?" Ricky asked looking at the planet with a slight squint to his eyes. "What are the odds?"

"It don't matter the odds," Keaton explained. "With as many habitable planets as there are in the galaxy, there's probably several more that match up. Hell, odds are there are many more just because of the sheer numbers."

"They just happened to stumble on this one," Larth explained.

"Decades ago, credits passed hands, claws, feet, paws, whatever," Jyrall said, "and the information was given to a corporation with the financial means to send out a team to verify. More credits were spent, and decades later, this is what you see. A colony thriving, while it provides much-needed food to the galaxy."

"So, what keeps some race from coming and taking it from the colonists?" Ricky asked the obvious question.

"Many races besides Humans in other colonies, whole planets, rely on some of the shipments from Krifay," Jyrall answered. "If it was to ever get attacked and taken over, the colonists would refuse to work. Not many races know how to fish like Humans, especially for Earth fish. Shipments would stop, and several planets, empires even, would spend the credits necessary to hire mercenaries to take it back and allow the colonists to continue to ship the seafood."

"Some things are better left alone," agreed Larth. "Credits talk. Some of their clients would spend vast fortunes to ensure the source of proteins continue to be delivered. The Merchant Guild would get involved. It wouldn't be wise."

"All three of the largest islands have defense systems," added Jyrall. "They also have a navy and ground units. I wouldn't doubt they have some mech units. Not mercenaries, per se, but islanders ready to defend their home, like the colonists at Victoria Bravo. For many of them, it's all they've ever known. There are several generations of Humans from Earth."

"From what we learned at the Academy, there are several other races in the colony from water worlds of their own. Even the Selroth have a presence here. They all live and work together in harmony."

"Have y'all ever been here before?" Ricky asked.

"We have not," confirmed Jyrall, with a toothy smile, "but I've always wanted to visit. The red snapper from this planet may just be the best in the entire universe. That's why I chose this as our stopover, to give Captain Dreel time to get the message and get in place on Miderall."

"So, what's the plan?" Larth asked his big friend.

"The ship's transponder is sending the registration as *Against the Wind*, so they won't know who we are. We'll get permission to land, do a little bargaining, and get a load," said Jyrall. "It's not unusual for smaller cargo ships capable of atmospheric flight to take on a small load. There are several small islands with fisheries that specialize in small businesses. Credits talk here, as you said."

"Got it," Larth said. "We can also buy F11 and let them know we'll be freshening up on our weapons skills and boarder repelling. It wouldn't hurt to buy some weapons or ammo while we're here, as well. They should have stuff for Earth weapons. It'll make it seem legit and allow us to fire weapons without having the local authority come around."

"I'll dump some F11, so it won't look strange that we'd only need a little," suggested Keaton.

"I like the way you think," Jyrall said. "We'll use some of the hard credits we have stashed, not the credits we got from Barlung. We'll add to that when we get the rest, and count it in front of him like a good smuggler would. Trust no one when it comes to credits and all that."

"I'll make the calls now," Keaton said, and he reached for the comms.

* * *

Snapper Isle
Krifay

"You go ahead, mon," the airfield security officer said. "I'll call it in and let dem know you be firing a few rounds off. Just aim dem off de end of de tarmac and toward de water, mon."

"Thank you very much," Larth said. He watched the old tanker truck drive past the man standing near him, toward the few hangers on the small island's airfield. There were two other ships nearer the packing plant being loaded. It would be a while before they received their small load in freezer containers. He turned back to the large man in a uniform of sorts.

The man appeared middle-aged, though it was hard for Larth to tell for, not having encountered many Humans before. He wondered if all the time in the warm environment contributed to the man's unusual uniform. The guard's pants only went to his knees, and his top looked like a wild pattern of red and orange plant blooms of some kind. The man had a belt on, and a holster with a projectile weapon of some type on his hip, along with the badge of authority pinned to his shirt, so it must be a uniform.

Larth watched the man pass Jyrall with a friendly wave and go into a smaller hanger near the others. Larth caught a glimpse of at least one mech in the open bay before the door shut. The man may have seemed friendly, but Larth had no doubt he or those he worked with would come out ready in a fully-armed mech if things went wrong out on the tarmac. He looked closer and noted the cameras half hidden around the property. Friendly, but cautious.

A few minutes later, Jyrall made it to his location. "I bought a freezer container they'll deliver along with the order." Jyrall beamed. "We just keep it in there and strap it into a corner of the hold."

"Nice," Larth said, rubbing his paws together. "Please, tell me you bought crabs."

"Oh, yeah," Jyrall said, "and several other types of seafood. If nothing else, we'll eat great food on this mission, and not have to eat protein bars at all."

They both turned when they heard a land craft approaching. It was a small topless hovercraft with a cargo bed. Ricky was in the passenger seat, with one hand up in the wind, moving it in a fashion that resembled waves. The driver of the craft stopped it and backed toward the open ramp to make unloading easier. Ricky jumped out.

"I got what we needed," he said as he walked around the craft. "This is Mike, he owns the local gun store."

The grey-haired driver got out and came over as well. "Wally here says you're going to fire off a few rounds," the old man said. "I rented a few target holders to him and thought I'd come along and set them up for you."

Keaton came down the ramp after Ricky took his first armload of supplies on board. Together they made two more trips, hauling ammo and large bundles of fresh and frozen seafood up the ramp. By the time they were through, the man had set up the targets. The target holders they'd rented had sensors that sent a signal back to the slate in the man's hands. Paper targets were pinned into place in the middle of the frames.

Larth went first and stood twenty-five feet from one of the targets. In a blur of motion, he drew both pistols from his sides and fired them at his target simultaneously. When both pistol slides locked back empty, he pushed the magazine release on his right, letting it drop as he slid the one in his left hand quickly into its holster, and when his paw came back, he had a magazine in it, which he slammed home into his remaining pistol. He proceeded to empty that magazine. He checked both weapons to ensure they were safe, and turned to Mike to see what the slate had to show about his shooting.

Mike stood staring at the Zuparti. The fact that Larth was a Zuparti wasn't the cause of the stare. The man hadn't even blinked when a Pushtal entered his establishment or when he'd pulled up to one of the largest Besquith he'd ever seen standing beside the ship.

He'd dealt with and fought with many races through the years, both when he was a mercenary, and since he'd retired to run a gun store here on Krifay. He'd never seen a display of speed and marksmanship like that. Ever.

On the screen of the slate, an image of the man-shaped target was displayed. The head of the target was torn to pieces. As far as Mike could tell, every round from all three magazines had hit it in a ridiculously short amount of time. He forced himself to close his mouth.

"Well, okay then," Mike finally said. "I can change that target out if you'd like…"

"Wait," Larth said, "let me try out the other two."

Larth unbuttoned the two buttons on his vest, crossed his arms, and when his arms straightened, his paws held two more of the .380s. He quickly emptied both magazines, checked his weapons for safety, and put them back in their holsters. He took his time rebuttoning his vest, and then looked over at the slate. Mike's mouth was hanging open again. There was a fist-sized hole dead center in the silhouette's chest.

Ricky looked over at his brother and said, "See, I told ya he was a sure 'nuff gunslinger."

"I wouldn't have believed that shit if I hadn't seen it with my own eyes," Keaton assured him.

The brothers went through a couple of power packs each on the other target and were satisfied. Larth gave them a few pointers on their stance and breathing, and by the last pack, they were doing really well. It was time for Jyrall to shoot his CT-75 Paladin.

"All right, Snarlyface," Larth said, knowing Jyrall couldn't complain about being called that. For all Mike knew, that was his actual name. "Let's see that Paladin in action."

Jyrall unsnapped the flap on his holster, freed his weapon, and took aim with a good solid stance. When it fired, the force did cause his arm to raise several inches, but he'd been prepared for it, and was back on target in no time. He fired three more times and put it away.

"Day-um, that'll make your fur rise," commented Ricky. "I believe I could shock somebody with a touch, I got so much static electricity standing by you."

"Um, I believe you shorted out my target holder, Mr. uhh…Face." Mike said, looking down at his slate, verifying there was no reading coming from the target frame, and back up at the Besquith.

"Sorry about that, Mike," Jyrall said. "My associate Gatch will pay for it."

Larth glared at Jyrall as Mike asked, "Which of you is Gatch?" The man looked back and forth at Keaton and Larth.

"The short one," Jyrall confirmed. "His name is Gatch Up."

Larth glared at his friend but said nothing.

"All right," the man said, turning to Larth, "I'm afraid that'll be five credits, Mr. Up. I'll probably have to rewire the whole thing."

Before the man drove off, he looked over at the four of them and said, "I don't know who you really are or if those are your real names, but I know you aren't normal merchants; that much is for sure. I only knew a few men when I earned a living fighting back in the day that could shoot like the little one there. Whoever you are, your secret's safe with me. I never met you."

As they watched Mike depart on the sleek hovercraft, Ricky said, "Well, if he knew what was what, we could have brought Frank and Stein out to play a little."

"I think it's best we didn't," Jyrall said. "He doesn't know who we were, he just knows who we aren't."

"He's right," Larth said with a deep sigh. "I really wanted to shoot the machine guns, even if it was through remote control. Hey, look, here comes the fish." He pointed to the cargo hauler headed their way. "Help me gather up my brass so they can be reloaded sometime."

After the ship was loaded and the freezer wired in to maintain power, they turned to the containers they were transporting. Once again, Keaton hooked his slate to one of them and bypassed its security. Jyrall lifted the lid and drew in a sharp breath. The container was full of red diamonds, as they'd suspected.

None of them touched the contents so as not to disturb the weight measurement plates. The diamonds were beautiful in their own right. All were a deep red color, and there were three sizes of them mixed together. There were also containers of slivers and dust. It was an incredible amount of credits sitting in the container.

"Look at that," Larth exclaimed. "That's more credits than we'll probably ever see in one place ever again."

"Hoo-wee," Ricky exclaimed. "That right there could buy you a biscuit for breakfast."

"Yep," agreed Keaton. "And lunch, too."

"Shit, I reckon," Ricky confirmed.

Jyrall looked back and forth at the brothers, confused. "I should hope it would buy a few meals," he said. "Where are you two trying to eat? In an emperor's palace somewhere?"

"It's a figure of speech, I think," translated Larth. "Well, close it up and reset the security. Let's get out of here. I'm taking Ricky's turn to cook. I have big plans."

After the start-up procedures were performed, they cleared it with the tower and made their way into open space. Keaton loaded the coordinates, and they made the transition into hyperspace, headed to Miderall. Several minutes later, after Jyrall felt better, he noticed the smell of a crab boil. The time in hyperspace wouldn't be so bad this time.

* * * * *

Chapter Sixteen

Pete's Dive Bar
Town, Parmick

Life at Pete's Dive Bar had a predictable routine, which was the only thing positive about being stuck on Parmick and working there. The bar closed every morning at 0300 local. Pete usually left the bar immediately after closing, leaving Cora and her team to finish sweeping, mopping, and washing up the glassware. Most days, they finished by 0400 and clawed their way into the small bedrooms built in the rear of the establishment. Pete's apartment dominated the space, but the women had managed to build five somewhat-comfortable bunks in a space of their own. Pete left them alone, which was the only consolation they had. From the time they went to bed until Pete rumbled to life in the apartment typically ran from 0400 until around 1100 the next morning. The man purposely made so much noise that sleeping any later was impossible. The girls had to be in the bar for work at 1400, and the whole cycle started over. What mattered, on an increasingly important basis to Cora, was their privacy.

May popped back into their room carrying a pot of coffee from the bar. "He's gone again. Headed to the starport, I reckon."

"You didn't follow him this time?" Kellie asked. Her wet blonde hair hung around her face as she held up a chipped coffee mug, which May filled. "Thank you, honey."

"No," May replied. "Lisalle should be watching him, right?"

"I am," Lisalle said with her mouth full of Nileah's homemade bread. They'd been able to scrounge the ingredients from a few traders, and with a bit of luck, and a lot of work, the mechanically minded Lisalle had turned Pete's kitchen stove and ovens to good use. The man refused to serve food—said it hurt his bottom line—but Cora's team had used it to create a touch of home. Part of those modifications had been to splice and hack Pete's Aethernet connections. Lisalle had made short work of his paltry security, and Kellie had connected the city's closed-circuit security cameras to the system shortly thereafter. They could see just about everything, aside from the mine and the inner sanctum of Barlung's offices.

Nileah adjusted the feed and saw Pete limping with his crutch toward the starport. "He's not even halfway there. We got an hour."

"He's supposed to be meeting a distributor today. Some company bringing in liquor from Earth, or so he said," Lisalle said. "There's nothing in his mail about it."

"You don't check our mail, do you?" May replied.

"Only Kellie's." Lisalle chuckled, and Kellie flipped a middle finger at her as she sat down on one of the beds.

Cora made her way in between the sets of stacked bunks. There was a small table between the lower beds. May and Kellie sat on her right, Lisalle and Nileah on her left. The slate appeared on the table, placed in a makeshift stand, and the five of them drank their coffee for a moment without speaking.

The coffee was strong and black. It was almost as good as the coffee they'd had with their company, and Cora had to push the memory of happier times away. There was business to discuss. Cora took a deep breath and let it out slowly.

"Cora?"

She blinked and looked at Nileah. "What is it?"

"You always do that thing—the deep breath and the sly exhale, like you don't want us to know when you have something to talk about."

Cora flushed and her mouth fell open, but Kellie spoke first.

"The Jivool spoke to you, right? You gave him a bottle of water on the house. Pete wasn't too pleased about that." Kellie grinned. "I know you paid for it, but what did the bear say? Don't even think about making a picnic basket joke, either."

They laughed for a moment. Cora waved a hand in front of her face. "I won't. Gods, what a funny day that was." Two years ago, on a mission at Ghart, the company had run into feral Jivool in the midst of a security mission. Given that most of the troops had grown up in the mountains and knew how to deal with bears foraging at night in their midst, most everything was secured in bear bags or large, locking containers. No one knew that the containers hadn't exactly been tested as Jivool-proof, and one of them had managed to tear open a container filled with several large air compressors for maintenance operations. When in flight, the compressors were drained of their contents, but on the ground, the containers served more as a storage locker. For the Jivool, whose claws managed to tear a high-pressure tank open with its six-inch-long claws, it was a very bad night.

May giggled. "I just remember Sergeant Jerund laying on the ground howling with laughter. I didn't learn until later he was quoting Yogi Bear, is that right? A cartoon character?"

"You might still find the old shows on GalNet. It would be on those little kid channels you watch all the time," Kellie chided the younger woman.

"You had to look it up, too." May grinned and they all laughed. As their voices faded, all of them smiled a bit wistfully and turned their eyes to Cora, who'd sat down at the head of the small table. There was business to discuss.

Cora licked her lips and spoke slowly. "I don't know what it means, or why Ledram told me, but the miners are preparing to revolt."

No one said anything for a moment. Nileah spoke first. "Did he *say* revolt, or are they just trying to negotiate? Maybe he meant they were bringing in a Peacemaker or something."

"Peacemakers aren't exactly worried about some backwater mining station taken over by thugs," Lisalle said. She took a sip of her coffee and raised a finger as she did. After she swallowed, she waggled her finger at Cora. "Did he say revolt? Was that the actual word he used?"

"No, he said the conditions and pay were horrible and they wanted to do something about it. He said our 'tools' would be needed." Cora frowned. "That makes me wonder what they know about our gear."

Kellie shook her head. "The containers are sitting in the protected area of the yard. No one's been near them in the last two weeks. Security seals are good, and the camera systems I placed out there are undisturbed."

"He knows we have gear," May said. "What's the big deal?"

Cora looked up at her. "We have CASPers in transport containers. Yes, they have an outer shipping container around them, but anybody with a brain has seen them and followed their registration to us. Five women and five large containers in a high security area? We're working at Pete's and paying a hefty sum so our gear isn't messed with? Most everyone would make the connection we're mercs, honey."

"Which is why Ledram came to you," Nileah said.

Cora shook her head. "I found him getting beaten by Barlung's thugs. They didn't see me. There was nothing I could do for him. I was about to leave the area when Peacemaker Rekk appeared at the end of the street and demanded they stop."

"Rekk? He hasn't been seen in a month," Lisalle said. "Are you sure?"

"I saw him with my own two eyes," Cora replied. "The two thugs started after Rekk and that gave me a chance to get Ledram and his cub out of there. Barlung gunned him down in the street from behind. Killed him in cold blood. He ordered his flunkies to dispose of the body in the smelter and secure his office and effects."

"So the Peacemaker is gone?" May asked.

"Yes," Cora frowned, annoyed.

"No, I meant if he's gone, how long would it be before they send someone to investigate?"

Kellie tapped May on the knee. "We just said they aren't going to care about a little backwater world like Parmick. A new Peacemaker might never come."

"Which brings me back to us being on our own," Cora said. "If the miners revolt, they're going to go after whatever weapons they can find. Our gear would be high on their list. We have weapons, some ammunition, and five pretty decent Mk 7 CASPers out there.

They're going to want them, and it might be better if we were prepared to help them."

"Help them? If they lose—which they probably will, Cora—we'll go down with them." Kellie frowned. "Our best bet is to stay out of this and scrape together more credits."

"I disagree." Lisalle leaned forward. "We can help them defeat Barlung and his collection of thugs easily. They're no match for our CASPers."

"We don't have enough fuel for extended operations," May noted, "and our ammunition levels aren't that high, either."

"That doesn't matter," Nileah said. "The miners outnumber the thugs at least four to one. Presuming the miners get weapons, we have an advantage. Our superior firepower can stop them really—"

"There are mercenary forces out there. Most of them aren't much, but what's to keep Barlung from hiring them to stamp out the miners?" Kellie asked.

"Why can't Ledram and his miners hire them?" Lisalle returned the question.

Cora raised her hands. This was getting nowhere. "Okay, listen to me. I know it's not the best situation, but right now it's in front of us, and we have a warning but no timetable. He could call me to their meeting at any point in time."

"So you've pitched in with him already?" Kellie asked with a frown on her face.

"I haven't pitched in on anything," Cora replied. "I'm trying to figure out what in the hell is going on. I want the rest of you to help me figure this out. We have to do this together."

May nodded. "What do you want us to do?"

Cora looked at them for a moment, making eye contact with each one. May, Nileah, and Lisalle returned her gaze earnestly. Kellie seemed ready to explode, or cry. She was Scots-Irish to a fault and possessed a more than heady temper. Nileah sat quietly, studying her hands. They locked eyes for a moment.

"I want to go home," Kellie said.

Cora sighed and reached out for her friend's hand. Kellie stared at her for a moment, then relented and grasped on to Cora's hand. "I know, Kellie. I do, too. We all do. But right now, we have a chance to get our asses off this planet. I want to make sure we're doing the right thing and—"

Kellie shook her head and laughed. A tear fell from her left eye. "You don't get it, Cora. We'll do what you say. You know what you want to do and, really, we do, too. Devil's advocate was never my strong suit."

Cora shook her head and smiled. "Meaning you already figured the miners need our help, and if they win, we might be better able to buy our way off this rock?"

"Yeah." Kellie wiped the tear off her cheek. "I'll get us fuel and ammunition."

Lisalle spoke next. "I'll have the entire system tapped in a day or so. I need some quiet time to program off Pete's Aethernet connection."

"You got it," Cora said. She let go of Kellie's hand and touched May's bare knee. "You, kiddo; you've got a mission, too. One we need to have done, and only you and Nileah can do."

May squinted at her. "You always tell us to stay close to the bar, Cora."

"That has to change, sweetie." Cora smiled at her. "There are two things we need for this to work. One is a timetable, and that's my job. The other thing that you have to do, because nobody on this rock will really suspect you to be a bloodthirsty mercenary, is gather intelligence. Mainly down at the port and through the traffic control system."

"How do you want me to do that?" May asked.

Cora pointed at May's boots and a backpack. "We'll start with something simple. A few ruck marches around the port fence. Make sure you've got your mask and goggles. Breathing is good, but recording everything you see with Lisalle's toys is even better."

Nileah grinned. "When do I need to start, Sergeant?"

"Right now, ladies." Cora looked at May, Lisalle, Nileah, and Kellie. "All of us have to start now, including me. It'll be time to take the credits to Nay-Thok soon. My part of the recon starts there. Everything is in play now, ladies. Every miner or thug in the bar is a source. Turn on your eyes and ears. No more drinking, either. When this thing is over, I'll buy the drinks, but until then I need you at your full best. You've got mine, ladies. I know I've got a soft spot for miners because of my family, but this might be our best chance to get home."

* * * * *

Chapter Seventeen

D reel and Kurrang moved easily into the heart of the barracks operations center. All Peacemaker barracks followed a similar layout, built in rings or layers that pushed the non-critical office spaces and storage areas toward the outside of the complex. The deeper inside the compound, the more critical the information, weaponry, and supplies that could be found. In the middle of the compound, behind secure doors capable of withstanding a 10-megawatt laser, was the information node. The space was barely eight meters square, and normally only held one communications/intelligence specialist and one officer for the review, preparation, and transmission of StormWatch. As the vault door swung open on perfectly balanced fulcrums, they stepped into the room and found six surly faces staring back at them.

The Enforcers were familiar to Dreel, despite not having seen them face-to-face in more than two years. With more than a thousand in the active force spread across the galaxy, even the Deputy Prime Enforcer couldn't be expected to see them during normal operations. There was nothing normal about their operation now. If anything, the surly faces on the collected Enforcers could very well have been simple apprehension. Most of them only deployed with their intelligence specialists and pilots. Being in close proximity to, or working with, another Enforcer was highly irregular.

"Stand at ease," Dreel said as they walked into the room. None of the Enforcers had moved toward the position of attention, a fact which Dreel noted with a frown. Aside from messy, bureaucratic appearing proceedings, most Enforcers saw the Prime Enforcer or his deputy only in formations and official ceremonies. Their inaction was more a lack of practice than a lack of respect. Neither was passable to Dreel. He snarled, "Is that how you would greet the Prime Enforcer or his deputy? Your inaction tells me you are either apprehensive or disobedient. Neither is appreciated."

None of them moved, which surprised Dreel greatly. He inhaled sharply, prepared to blast them at the full volume of his voice, but Kurrang appeared at his side. The TriRusk stepped forward, grabbed a Jivool Enforcer by the shoulder, and threw him across a control console in one impossibly swift movement.

The remaining five took up defensive postures and glowered at Kurrang with weapons drawn, but they didn't fire. The massive Tri-Rusk sat back on his rear legs and stared at them. "You disrespect your office. All of you. You disrespect your office not because you failed to provide proper protocol to your Deputy Prime, but because each of you have failed to understand we are at war. *War.* Your leaders will undoubtedly ensure each of you understands your place when this is over, but none of you may presume anything from this point forward. Gnaxx says you're prepared to act as one. Your insubordination was total, which leads me to believe one of you has been voted to be in charge of your ad hoc group. Who is it?"

Dreel caught two of them, a young male Caroon and a female Sidar, glancing ever so slightly toward a GenSha in the center. The striped bovine-analog stared at Kurrang for a long moment before looking away in disgust and raising one arm. "I am."

"And your little display of defiance had what purpose?" Kurrang's voice was far more measured than Dreel knew his voice would have been, but the TriRusk had their undivided attention, and that was a good thing. "That you don't want to listen to your superiors? That you believe you have everything you needed to win this war yourselves without orders from anyone? Or was it just foolish incompetence in thinking your numbers and talents were a match for experience and treachery?"

"You can't call us here without reason. We have missions—"

"Did you not hear Captain Kurrang?" Dreel growled. "We are at war."

"The Humans and the Mercenary Guild's conflict—" the female Sidar sputtered until Kurrang raised one massive palm.

"The Mercenary Guild has targeted Guild Master Rsach. They destroyed the consulate on Luna." Kurrang paused and solemnly added, "Enforcer Hr'ent gave his life to assure the guild master's escape."

"StormWatch didn't report the Mercenary Guild's guilt for the attack on Luna," the Jivool said from his seat on the floor. He absently rubbed at the side of his head. "This was a purposeful omission?"

Kurrang nodded. "The official report mentioned terrorists or something equally inane. The guild master didn't want to tip our hand. This instance matches that one. Make no mistake, we are at war, young ones. How you choose to respond to this call, right this very instant, will determine how we fight going forward."

"We know this is not how you were trained," Dreel explained, "but we believe this to be a necessary action. Furthermore, we have reason to believe Kr'et'Socae himself is behind the attack on Victoria Bravo and other recent actions around the galaxy. You've been called together not just to help defend the guild from attack, but to stop what we believe to be a funding operation set up by Kr'et'Socae. You must understand how imperative his capture is—at all costs."

Kurrang's voice rumbled. "Your impertinence and disrespect show a lack of understanding. You reported here because of your duty, which is commendable, but the attitude you portray is not. It ends now."

"Captain Gnaxx told me you could work together. That you'd been trained to do so." Dreel eyed them each carefully. "I'm not certain they're ready for this mission, Kurrang. Perhaps we would do better with Peacemakers, and not ones who've forgotten those who've gone before them."

The GenSha stood straight at an approximation of the position of attention. The others, including the Jivool, who scrambled to his feet, did the same. "Our disappointment with what we knew of the situation fueled our actions to disrespect, Captain Dreel. We didn't understand the greater situation. You have our apologies."

Dreel flared. "I do not want your apology. I want your duty. I want you as the weapons you truly are. I want you prepared in an hour for deployment and combat operations. When I return to this room, anyone not willing to cooperate fully and honor the Enforcer Creed will be sent directly to Ocono as security at the academy until such time as their removal from active service can be affected. Am I clear? You have one hour."

Dreel spun on his heel and stomped out of the room. He felt, rather than heard, Kurrang following close behind. The TriRusk closed the door quietly behind them and caught up to Dreel. The Besquith smiled over his shoulder at the TriRusk, who stared up at him with bright, black eyes.

"You didn't hurt him, did you?"

Kurrang grunted. "Only his pride. Which they needed. Is that an often occurrence in your ranks, Dreel? Disrespect?"

"It's not really disrespect," Dreel continued as they walked. "Nor is their attitude poor with regard to the guild. They honor the guild and the union with their service. Often, though, because they have a unique place and mission, young Enforcers get a superiority complex. That was on full display, even with my leadership position. Barracks commanders report this often, especially when the young ones come in for annual training activities."

"Really?" Kurrang asked. "That surprises me greatly."

"That's why annual training never lasts more than a standard week," Dreel replied. "I trust Gnaxx and his assessment that they can work together, but I also know my friend well. He knew about their attitude and took no effort to correct them. My seeing them was critical, in his eye, to how we deploy them."

Kurrang's maw curled under on one side, the approximation of a grin. "And what does the good captain have in mind for his charges?"

"Option two."

Kurrang brightened. "You're really going to do that?"

"Yes, I believe so." Dreel grinned and revealed his slate. "This came in a short while ago. Our young ones have messaged us through secure channels. They've taken on a cargo mission to Miderall by way of Kifray. Appears to be one of the regular runs from the mining operation, but they haven't ascertained the cargo for fear of tampering. We'll be intercepting them and, for our young Enforcers' benefit, appear to fail spectacularly by letting Jyrall and Larth escape. Perhaps it'll motivate them to work better together, follow combat orders as a group, and help find Kr'et'Socae before he wreaks any more havoc in the Union."

Kurrang was silent for a moment as they walked into the outer ring of offices and spaces. They could smell fresh coffee being brewed, and it made Dreel's mouth water. "Would you care for a cup of coffee?" he asked over his shoulder. The look on the TriRusk's face stopped him cold.

The TriRusk glowered at him. "Just what in the hell was all that? I expected you to be the one to snarl and thrash some resemblance of respect into them. Not me."

"You move pretty fast for an old TriRusk." Dreel grinned and a low, rumbling laugh broke through. He covered his maw with one paw in a vain attempt to stifle the sound. He saw the look of utter confusion on Kurrang's face become one of understanding. "They expected it, too, my friend. By not giving them what they were expecting, it disarmed them, and the real reason came forth. They're Enforcers used to operating in special circumstances with the utmost authority at their discretion. In a time of war, like this, we've changed their missions from individual ones of high importance to a group mission of critical importance. They believed attitude would cause me to violate their trust. Had I done so, they would've been justified in going to the guild master in protest of my orders. As it was, I did nothing. I didn't expect your hackles to rise, so to speak. But the effect was immediate. They looked like they'd seen a ghost."

Kurrang nodded. "I'm surprised at my outburst. I owe them an apology."

"You'll do nothing of the sort." Dreel's smile hardened. "You're a Peacemaker, Kurrang. An exceptional one, and a captain, to boot. You got the drop on them—something they won't let happen again, which is a good thing. They understand the mission, at least the basic parameters of it. That's all we need. I gave them a timetable, and they'll meet it. We can brief them on the way to Miderall."

They started to walk again, and Kurrang shook his head, a sly smile crossing his long maw. "I understand. I shamed them."

"They shamed themselves," Dreel replied. "They'll further shame themselves if they don't meet the timetable."

"So we have an hour to kill. Hence your idea of coffee."

"Once we find those beans being brewed, we'll grab a cup to go. If you think I'm giving them a full hour to get ready, you're mistaken. The Blue Flight is being refueled now. If we hurry, we'll beat the young ones to the station by a few hours."

"And you said Gnaxx was a sonuvabitch." Kurrang laughed as they turned a corner. "He's got nothing on you, Dreel."

Dreel took a deep sniff. The scent of coffee strengthened with every passing step. They were close. He turned to Kurrang and his vicious smile returned. "Guilty as charged, Captain Kurrang. Guilty as charged."

* * *

Night Moves
Miderall System

The ship transitioned into normal space, and once again, Jyrall felt anything but normal. Attempting to ignore it this time, he looked through the viewport at a completely different system than the one they'd just come from. The inhabited planet looked like many others across the galaxy. Blues, greens, and some browns made up its coloring. It was the home planet for a sentient race of colorful avian humanoids.

The Miderall were a vain race, valuing their own sense of beauty above anything else as status symbols. Not only was their plumage wildly colorful, the attire they wore was the same. Jyrall had encountered a few in the past and just couldn't agree with their sense of beauty. He knew Larth felt the same way. Almost the rest of the galaxy did as well, for that matter.

"Can you imagine the colors of the bulkheads in that starport?" Larth asked from his usual spot hanging to a strap behind the pilot's seat. He pointed off to the side at the huge starport in the distance.

"Wait," Keaton said. "Is that thing painted bright yellow or is it me?"

"Who in tarnation would take the time, credit, and effort to paint the outer hull of a space station?" Ricky asked. "Is that top portion…purple?"

"Miderall!" answered both Jyrall and Larth at the same time.

"Well I ain't never…" Ricky said shaking his head.

"Wait until you meet one." Larth laughed. "Though we may not see one. I'm pretty sure they pay others to operate the port. We're supposed to get a berth and contact Captain Geerlargum of the ship *Kithlawur* and transfer the containers."

"Geerlargum?" Ricky asked. "Why does that sound like an Oogar name?"

"Because it is," answered Jyral, feeling better. "It figures. Wherever the red diamonds are going on the next leg of their journey, Barlung probably wouldn't trust anyone else. I wouldn't doubt the next leg takes them to their final location, buyer, or distributor."

"We have to let Captain Dreel know that when we meet him," Larth said. "That meeting will have to be short. Geerlargum has been waiting for us since we detoured."

"I agree," Jyrall said. "I wonder if they'll follow them and interrogate them to determine where the red diamonds are going, or just hit them here in this system."

"Wherever they're going, you can bet it's not good for the situation in the galaxy right now," Larth said. "I mean, why else would they hide the fact that the mines are now producing more than they ever have in the past and not just chips and dust?"

"Good question," Jyrall said. "Keaton, you make the calls and get us a berth. I'll see if I can send Captain Dreel a secure transmission."

"I'm on it," answered the pilot. "It's a good thing we remembered to change the transponder back to *Night Moves*."

* * *

Miderall Trading Port
Miderall

"All right, lock it down," Jyrall said, standing.

The ship was connected to the starport, and the rotation of the outer ring created some gravity in the ship. It wasn't quite normal gravity, so Jyrall took mental notes not to bound when he walked. He suspected the Miderall had designed the port to have a lower gravity than most races preferred so their cloaks and capes could flutter behind them as they moved. Whatever the reason, he was mindful of it.

"Be careful when we exit the ship and move this cargo," Jyrall warned. "The gravity is about three quarters normal."

"You be careful slipping out to meet Captain Dreel," Larth warned. "We'll be ready here. Keaton says the ship we're taking this cargo to is seven berths away, so it won't take an awful long time to move it."

"I will," confirmed Jyrall as he flipped his patch down over his eye and adjusted the strap.

The ramp lowered, and Jyrall walked down into the cargo loading area of their berth. He looked around and turned back to his partner and crew in the ship. "Lime green," he said. "The bulkheads are lime green." He looked up and shook his head. "The overhead is pink. Bright pink." Jyrall walked out of sight as Larth and the brothers laughed.

Jyrall walked into the prearranged location, stalked over to the bar as only a Besquith could do, and ordered a Human drink. "Whiskey," he demanded. He laid a credit on the bar.

He turned and sipped his drink, eyeing the room. He spotted who he was searching for and walked over. "I greet you," he said in his natural language to the sitting Besquith. "What word of home?"

"I greet you," answered the sitting Besquith. "Join me and I'll tell you what I know. It may be that you have been back since I have."

Jyrall sat, looking around the room without being too obvious. He placed his drink on the table and his hand-held slate beside it, right beside a similar slate. The two discussed their home world and clans feuding to determine if they knew others each may know. It was also to ensure they were not of feuding clans and didn't need to fight it out there in the bar. Anyone listening in would have been grateful to learn neither was obligated to kill the other.

If anyone else was deliberately spying on the chance meeting, they would have learned nothing. Home was all the two discussed. Their code was solid and unbreakable, as Jyrall delivered his report while neither of them broke character.

"I must check in on my crew," Jyrall said finally, and he picked up a slate to scan for messages.

"If your crew members are as lazy as mine, you would do well to," agreed the slightly smaller Besquith. He picked up the other slate and appeared to be scanning for messages. Once he read what he needed to know, he set the slate down and tipped back his entire drink. "My crew have loaded the goods, and I must go."

"I, as well," answered Jyrall, standing. He reached down and picked up his slate. "May your clan grow stronger."

"Yours as well," answered the other Besquith. Anyone listening in would have been disappointed to continue learning nothing as the two Besquith turned in opposite directions in the walkway outside the bar.

Jyrall came back to the cargo loading area with two cargo moving platforms in tow. He'd rented them so they could move all four containers at once. He'd discussed it with Larth at length, and they decided it wasn't wise to split the cargo for any amount of time. It would mean splitting the four of them up outside the ship, and it was too risky, given the value of the cargo.

They arrived in the loading area for the *Kithlawur*, a smaller ship than theirs, a short time later. It appeared to be a converted small frigate of some type. Jyrall was unsure if the frigate's weapons systems were still intact. In general, the ship appeared beaten up and barely spaceworthy. Captain Geerlargum and eight of his crew met them after the ship dropped its ramp.

"Took your time, did you?" growled the purple captain. "You should have been here days ago, Varkell."

"Time wasn't stipulated," Jyrall growled right back at him, "only a flawless delivery. We have kept our side of the agreement. I merely ensured no one interfered."

Captain Geerlargum was small for an Oogar. Jyrall towered over the Oogar and peered down at him, challenging him with his good eye. He stared and waited for a rebuttal. None came.

The Oogar turned to his crew. "Check the panels and get it on board." He turned back to Jyrall and pulled out his slate. "I'll send the message back to Barlung once I know it matches up."

One of the crew members called out, "We're good, sir. All four match up."

"There. I sent it," Geerlargum told Jyrall. "With the gate traffic in this system, it should beat you back."

"It better," Jyrall warned. "I expect the second half of my payment when I land." He turned and walked away with Larth and the brothers.

* * * * *

Chapter Eighteen

"**D**id Captain Dreel give any indication of their next move?" Larth asked, curious about how the *Kithlawur* would be intercepted.

"He didn't," Jyrall answered. "I was able to communicate through our prearranged codes, and he picked up my slate and read the report we wrote. He now knows the berth number, the ship name, and the name of our contact, Captain Geerlargum. The instructions for us, which I read verbatim from his slate, were to stick to the mission. We are to continue to ingratiate ourselves until we gain Barlung's full trust and find out why there have been no reports from the local Peacemaker."

"Speaking of which…" Larth paused until Keaton had the ship safely away from the port and was turning toward open space to prepare for transition, "we have yet to even see the Peacemaker. Not in his office or around Town. Nothing on camera feeds, either. I find that really strange."

"I agree," Jyrall said. "When Captain Dreel got to the part in our report about the rumor he was called back to the Academy, he shook his head slightly. I know he was at that part of it because I deliberately put it on the second screen at the top. He pressed the tab to continue, read it, growled softly, and shook his head."

"Well, that clears up that rumor," Larth confirmed. "We need to find out where he is."

"Peacemakers don't just drop off the face of the planet," remarked Keaton. "Something is fishy."

"Yeah, and it ain't supper we're talking about," agreed Ricky. "Speaking of supper, I'm making lobster rolls. Y'all, I like fish as much as the next feller, but when are we having something else, like burgers or chicken?"

"I don't eat meat," Jyrall said. "There was an issue when I was a pup. It's been cured now, but the thought of meat still turns my stomach, hence the fish."

"Aw hell, chicken ain't meat…it's chicken," Ricky countered. "I mean, it ain't red meat, anyway."

"He has a point," Larth said to his partner with a grin.

"Fried chicken is hard to beat," confirmed Keaton.

"Why do I feel like you three are conspiring against me?" Jyrall asked, looking sideways at them.

"It's not easy to get out here," Ricky said. "If we run across any, we'll get a bird or two, and Keaton can fry it up for us. It was one of Pop's favorites."

"If we can purchase some, I will agree to try it," Jryall said. "Try."

"I will too; I've seen it on the GalNet, but I've never actually tried it," Larth said. "I—hey look at that!" He pointed out the view ports.

All three turned their heads to see two small corvettes with weapons bristling coming in from deep space headed toward the trade port behind them. The ships weren't on an intercept path with them, but in the vastness of space, they would pass by closer than was comfortable for most pilots and ship commanders not in actual combat.

"I don't know who they're going after, but at the rate they're moving, it won't be long before they catch them," remarked Keaton.

"I'll adjust our flight to stay away from whatever's happening. I think I'll move our transition time up…to say, right about now. Jump in twenty seconds. Hang on."

Larth and Ricky reached up and held onto straps with both hands, and the four of them prepared for transition. None of them were aware that one of the corvettes now behind them had started to skew turn around when *Night Moves* made the jump into hyperspace. Using its own shunts once again, the destination couldn't be traced.

* * *

Tango Veritas
Vicinity Miderall Emergence Point

"Emergence confirmation," the SleSha Enforcer Zevva called from the pilot's chair. Each of the Tango-class Enforcer corvettes were only slightly larger than the typical Blue Flight, and given the power requirements necessary for hyperspace travel, they required the assistance of a thrust core. "Separation."

From the command chair, Tok, a GenSha, nodded. A tangible vibration thrummed through the ship as it separated from the core and fell away into open vacuum. "*Tango Aequitas*, this is *Veritas*, separation confirmed, moving to intercept."

"Confirmed," Mratt's gruff Jivool voice replied. The normally flippant, easy-going Enforcer had been all business since Captain Kurrang's swift confrontation at the barracks. Mratt never liked being surprised, and having a three-hundred-year-old TriRusk do so must have been embarrassing. "Line abreast and spread to fifteen kilometers. Weapon status?"

Tok rolled his lower jaw around his tongue. The chewing motion looked silly, which he knew, but old habits died hard, despite what the academy instructors had tried to instill. "Ready and hold. No active targeting. Let's not give ourselves away."

"Copy," Mratt replied. On Tok's display, *Aequitas* took up station on the *Veritas'* left wing and slowly increased the distance.

Tok looked over his right flank to the weapons station. "Kravon? Weapons to ready and hold."

"I heard you, Tok. We're ready to fire," Kravon replied. The Caroon's thin lips pressed into a tight white line. "Multiple contacts in the area. I have several making transit for the gate. Any update from Blue Flight?"

Tok glanced at Zevva, who shook her head. "Nothing yet. Captain Dreel has two minutes to hail us before we go actively searching. Prepare weapons bays and stand by for intercept protocols. We'll do this by the book."

"One minute and fifty seconds." Kravon didn't look up from his display. "Can we bring the helm right one zero mark two? It'll increase visibility of the departure corridor by seventy percent."

Zevva was already moving. "One zero mark two," she said. Her multiple limbs worked the controls and forward sensor arrays. "Passive sensor nets engaged."

Tok reached for the control to his own Tri-V. He intended to zoom in on the departure corridor and try to break out the clutter. A klaxon sounded before his forehoof completed the move.

"Incoming message," Kravon said. "Direct laser on button two, standard freqs."

"Encryption?" Tok asked.

"It's one of ours," Kravon answered. He looked up at Tok. "Captain Dreel."

"On speakers," Tok replied. Unconsciously, he shifted in the command chair as the connection enabled. "Blue Flight, *Tango Veritas* on station and ready to proceed."

"Multiple bogeys on departure courses," Dreel's clipped voice replied. "Bearing on first vessel from your position is zero four five mark six. Targeting solution follows."

On the forward Tri-V at Tok's position, a targeting box appeared. "Identified, Blue Flight. Moving to engage."

"All possible speed, *Veritas*. *Aequitas* to rendezvous on my position. Stop that outbound freighter."

Tok straightened in the chair. "Understood. *Veritas* clear."

"Weapons solution loading. Target vessel has picked up speed and appears to be vectoring away from the departure corridor," Kravon said. "Zevva, get us on an intercept."

"Boosting," the SleSha replied. As the ship's engines came to life, there was a palpable pushing sensation that drove Tok's thick frame into his seat. "Maximum thrust."

"Time to intercept?" Tok asked.

"Four hundred seconds. Target is changing course." Kravon paused. Tok strained to see the Caroon leaning forward against the thrust to study his Tri-V station. "Aspect change confirmed. Target is changing course—they're headed this direction and under acceleration."

"Adjust course for weapon deployment," Tok replied. Though nearly six months beyond his last check in a Tango, Tok clearly remembered the protocols and commands for combat operations in the well-armored, fast-maneuvering vessel. Yet nothing about this mission was normal. Instead of two well-trained and experienced pilots manning the other stations, along with a full crew, there were two other Enforcers like himself on board. Operational security was a very important thing, but flying into an intercept without the best crew available seemed rash and dangerous.

Then again, a Peacemaker corvette wasn't much more than a fast attack craft, designed for immediate suppression, but with a host of refined defensive munitions capable of thwarting the larger-rated warships of the various species. Built by the elSha and armored by the Besquith, the corvettes were typically crewed by no more than a support crew of ten for combat missions, and far fewer for Enforcer deployments and retrievals. They'd deployed without any crew at all, and it didn't make sense to Tok, given his five years in the Enforcers.

Maybe Dreel trusts us to perform every aspect of our missions without the need for other support? Why else would we train as pilots? We train for every situation on our own, don't we?

Maybe this is a test of our abilities as a small team?

"Course set. *Night Moves* is picking up speed."

Tok squinted. "*Night Moves?* What kind of a name is that?"

"There are one thousand and twelve possible references," Kravon replied. "The most popular is a Human rock and roll song."

Humans? This far out and under the Mercenary Guild's blockade?

Tok cleared his throat. "Standard neutral pass intercept, Zevva. The minute we're abreast of them, cut thrust and make the turn."

"I know what I'm doing, Tok," Zevva said, bristling.

"*Night Moves* is nose on to us and still accelerating," Kravon replied. "Flank speed achieved."

Zevva glanced at him. "Recommend we cut power."

"Negative. If we show them that, they'll have the advantage."

Zevva shook her head. "Even in vacuum, either we'll have a large turn radius or have to burn a massive amount of fuel to change direction that quickly. We can't just come about, Tok."

"And they know that," he grunted. "Start an intercept turn."

Tok glanced at the display again and watched as the *Aequitas* raced toward its target, an Oogar-flagged frigate named *Kithlawur*. There was no sign of the Blue Flight. Apparently Dreel didn't want to give away their position relative to the target frigate. "Kravon, open a channel to them and have them prepare to receive—"

Forward sensors reported a power spike aboard *Night Moves*, and the ship disappeared half a second later. One moment the rapidly approaching ship was there, and the next it wasn't.

"Hyperspace transition," Kravon said. "I've never seen a shunt power up that fast."

"Breaking off the turn," Zevva called. "Plotting intercept to *Kithlawur*. We'll be behind and above the *Aequitas*."

Tok fumed. "Just get us there."

"The *Kithlawur* is firing at the *Aequitas*," Kravon reported. "It's not tracking Blue Flight at all."

Tok's mind worked through the situation quickly. *Aequitas* was in position to draw the enemy's fire and attention. "Are they firing lasers or missiles?"

Kravon looked up. "Both."

They're not conserving energy for a shunt jump. They're wanting to use the gate.

We have them.

"Missiles to standby," Tok ordered.

"Missiles ready," Kravon called. "Solution targeting *Kithlawur* loaded and ready."

"Two missiles, combat spread. Fire."

"Missiles away," Kravon reported.

Tok jabbed his communications display. "*Aequitas*, we're accelerating in behind you. Two missiles in flight off your starboard side."

Zevva hissed. "Starboard? What's next? Port? Set the mainsails? Secure the forecastle?"

Tok glared at her. "Standard naval terminology keeps things straight in combat! You know this!"

"You've been reading too much again, Tok." Zevva buzzed with laughter.

"Missiles tracking," Kravon reported. "Damage control warnings from the *Aequitas*."

"*Aequitas*, report!"

Another voice came through the speakers. It was the Sidar, Chamyt. "*Veritas*, this is *Aequitas*. We've taken a hit to the CIC. Mratt is down. Weapons are online. Continuing to defend against missile attacks."

"We're twenty seconds from laser range, Tok," Zevva reported.

"Fifteen seconds to missile detonation."

Tok watched the engine section of *Kithlawur* intently. Counting in his head, at four seconds to detonation, the first of their missiles took the brunt of the laser defenses and exploded harmlessly. *Kithlawur's* lasers powered down for a few milliseconds and then recharged to fire again. By the time they engaged the second missile, the distance to the ship's hull was far closer. As the missile exploded under laser fire, the proximity kill features used simple kinetic energy and very dense materials to continue on and rip through the engine section of the Oogar frigate. The ship immediately yawed to the left. A moment later, it's offensive and defensive weapons systems powered down.

"Slow us down and prepare to assume a boarding orientation." Tok was already moving toward the bridge hatch. "Hail Captain Dreel and—"

"*Veritas* and *Aequitas*, Blue Flight. Prepare to board and secure the target," Dreel ordered. "We have assurances you'll be met peacefully."

Tok studied the forward Tri-V screen. The Blue Flight appeared off the nose of the *Kithlawur* and held its position. Kravon unstrapped from his seat and floated toward the hatch. Tok nodded at him and turned to look at the SleSha.

"When you're docked, meet us in the airlock. We'll have your gear positioned."

Zevva didn't look at him. "Docking in two minutes, ten seconds. I'll be ready to board in three."

"Standard load, Tok?"

The GenSha smiled at the smaller Caroon. "Heavy. If there's an Oogar on board, I can't really believe he'd go down without a fight."

* * * * *

Chapter Nineteen

The three Enforcers crowded into the tight space, bristling with weapons. Tok stood in the rear center of the group cradling the multi-barrel chain gun he never left home without. The 6mm cannon could fire up to 6,000 rounds a minute and was capable of using multiple types of ammunition, from flechette rounds, to depleted uranium-tipped, armor-piercing shells. The familiar heft of the weapon felt right and, in Tok's opinion, perfect for his use.

To his left, Zevva hung in space without using any type of holding device. Her long, thin limbs cradled two dart pistols ideal for close-combat action in microgravity. Kravon was similarly armed, though in his left hand, the Caroon carried a combat knife with the blade pointed down from his fist.

"*Veritas*, we are docked and in position. Blue Flight is holding position off the *Kithlawur*'s nose. Their engines are inoperable," Mratt sent over the radio.

"I understand you were injured?" Tok asked in a low voice.

"My arm is broken. I'll remain behind. Permission to undock and provide support by fire?"

Tok nodded appreciatively. "Granted. Let me know when you're on station."

"Affirm, *Veritas*."

Tok tapped his earpiece. "Cha-myt, do you read?"

Across the width of the *Kithlawur* in the opposite docking collar, the Sidar Peacemaker replied, "I have you, Tok. We're standing by."

Tok closed his eyes for a moment, visualizing the ingress of the team.as they'd been taught to do, initially in the academy, and with more aplomb following Enforcer training. There was no indication of what might meet them on the other side of the door. The ceiling-mounted autocannon was online and prepared to fire, and each of them wore the standard BAMF combat armor for their species, though neither Zevva or himself wore a tactical helmet. For the GenSha and their thickly armored skulls, a helmet often proved to be a distraction. For Zevva, her bulbous compound eyes took up the majority of her skull, and operating in the blind was not a SleSha specialty.

"We'll breach first. Zevva on the left, Kravon on the right. If we get hit, Cha-myt and Tavaara will support by fire until we can get to cover. If we get through and you get hit, maintain your position and we'll get back to you. If nothing happens, wait 60 seconds and follow us. Copy?"

"Got it," Cha-myt replied. "No noise from the hatch. Taking cover and preparing to engage the control panel connections now."

Tok watched both Zevva and Kravon attempt to become one with the walls of the airlock. There was nowhere he could go, hence the heavy weapon and the best armor an Enforcer could wear. It could stop almost anything, and for what it couldn't stop there wasn't much to care about. He'd never even feel the impact.

"Verify connection."

Kravon peered at the control panel. "Lock shows open and pressurized. No security locks. Maybe we don't have to breach it."

Maybe.

"Engage the hatch." Tok adjusted his grip on the chain gun and brought the barrel down between the other Enforcers to aim into the space beyond. "Weapons up."

Unconsciously, Tok gripped and regripped the weapon as the circular hatch irised open. There was no resistance. The boarding area appeared to be an auxiliary entry port leading into a space more than ten meters wide. Empty and devoid of cargo pallets, the room gave Tok an immediate impression the ship was either rigged for high-speed transit, or the whole thing was a trap.

"*Veritas*, this is *Aequitas*. I have support by fire off the *Kithlawur*'s starboard side. I have visual with Blue Flight." Mratt's gravelly voice filled Tok's ears.

"Do you have comms with Blue Flight? Can you relay them to me?"

"I can hear you, Enforcer Tok," Dreel replied. "You're clear to advance. The captain assures your safe passage."

"And you believe him, sir?"

Dreel laughed. "We're sitting five hundred meters off his bridge, with sixteen active missile radars pinging his location. He's flanked by a Peacemaker corvette, and has five Enforcers aboard. I believe he understands the gravity of his situation."

Tok grunted, but didn't ask the question that threatened to burst from his lips. They'd already challenged Captain Dreel once and lost spectacularly. Given the time during hyperspace transit, they'd each had time to think about the disobedience they'd shown. For Tok, there was a higher degree of shame than the others. He'd intended to have a frank, sincere discussion of their role, given the recall and the impending war. Enforcers were the best of the Peacemakers, to his understanding, and if anyone should remain on normal duty throughout the galaxy, it should have been them. No one was willing to challenge an Enforcer. Or were they?

The crew of the *Kithlawur* appeared to have submitted for boarding and search by the Peacemaker Guild. They hadn't challenged the notions of probable cause or pressed for any type of search warrant, though that was likely a result of the mere presence of Enforcers. Yet if the crew truly had nothing to hide, or hadn't planned on resistance of any type, shouldn't someone have met them at the airlock?

Tok pushed the questions out of his head and nodded toward the door. Zevva first, followed by Kravon, stepped around the edge of the hatch and took positions flanking the door. Each of them swept the room with their eyes quickly.

"Clear," Kravon said.

Tok pushed forward into the space and glanced around the rectangular room. "Cha-myt, status?"

"Empty room. We have the ship layout downloaded. Forwarding to you now."

Tok frowned. He should have ensured they had the same documentation before stepping foot on the ship. His slate vibrated, and the layout appeared half a second later. To his left was another hatch at the center of the bay. It appeared to connect to a central corridor running to another set of cargo bays.

At least we can link up with Cha-myt and Tavaara.

"Take the hatch to your right, Cha-myt. We'll rendezvous in the passageway before moving to the main cargo bay at the next junction toward the bridge."

"Copy, moving."

Tok nodded at the hatch. Zevva reached up with a long, spindly limb and flicked at an exposed edge on the ceiling. It was enough to propel her forward toward the hatch. Kravon followed and took up a flanking position on the opposite side of the hatch.

"Kravon, can you get anything from the ship? Camera? Sensors?" Tok pivoted and moved again toward the center of their formation with the cannon's barrel pointed at the hatch.

"Negative. Given some time, I can break the encryptions, but I'd rather secure the crew before doing that. Distractions and all."

Tok snorted. One of their instructors at the Enforcer course always said the gathering of intelligence should be left to the professionals. For an operator on the ground, intelligence in place of situational awareness led to death. Cha-myt and Tavaara appeared in the passageway. Cha-Myt took up a position near Kravon, while Tavaara took rear guard with her own large chain gun. For an Oogar, the weapon looked almost like a toy.

"Hatch is clear. Ready to open." Zevva tapped at the control panel. Again, the ship's systems seemed to be laid bare for the Enforcers.

"Do it."

The hatch irised open and immediately Tok tensed. In the wide space beyond the circular hatch, an Oogar stood. There were multiple Zuul and two Sidar around him; none appeared to have weapons, and they stood with their hands and foreclaws in plain sight. Tok noticed all of them had slipped at least one foot through a loop on the cargo bay's floor to remain in place.

"I'm Enforcer Tok. This ship is secured by the Peacemaker Guild. Any resistance from this moment forward will be met with death. Are we clear?"

The Oogar spread his large paws even wider. "Enforcer Tok, I'm Geerlargum, and this is my ship and the entire crew. We request asylum with the Peacemaker Guild, and present the ship to you for search and seizure of its contents."

Tok kept his face still. Searches weren't supposed to be easy. Adding to his confusion, an Enforcer typically didn't deal with requests for asylum. Peacemakers normally handled such mundane tasks, but he'd been trained to do so at the Academy, and it took a few seconds for the procedure to come back. "What's the reason for the request?"

"Protection." Geerlargum's lower jaw worked. "I can provide information regarding our benefactor and the significance of the cargo, if it's what I suspect it to be." The Oogar pointed at the small pallet of containers strapped to the floor between them.

The last part of the Oogar's words struck Tok. "What do you mean? You're not aware of the cargo in those containers?"

"I have my suspicions, but we've operated under the strictest orders not to inspect our cargo," Geerlargum replied. "We have our reasons to obey the one who contracted us to these missions."

"Who is your benefactor?" Tok asked. The entire crew looked away from them as the sound of his voice still echoed in the bay.

"Kr'et'Socae."

Tok felt a bolt of electricity shoot down his spine. *A lead?*

Dreel's voice growled in his ears immediately. "Secure the crew and every last weapon aboard. When they've turned all that over, grant them asylum and have them open the containers. I'm on my way."

* * * * *

Chapter Twenty

Kithlawur

Seized and Flagged by the Peacemaker Guild

Miderall

The portside airlock cycled shut, and Tok waited another two minutes until the *Tango Aequitas*, with the crew of the captured freighter aboard, undocked and shunted for Toscatta. As he waited, the Enforcer cycled and safed the chain gun and prepared to attach it to the bulkhead near the docking port to his ship, *Tango Veritas*. He deftly moved from handhold to handhold to secure his weapon, and then returned through the main circular hatch to the cargo bay. Captain Dreel stood over the cargo pallet with his arms crossed over his black and red Enforcer vest. The look on his face, to Tok, seemed strangely satisfied. It was nothing Tok or any of them had seen before, and on the Deputy Prime Enforcer's maw, the small smile seemed quite out of place.

Dreel's eyes flashed to him. "Crew secured?"

"Captain Kurrang took possession of them. They're returning to Toscatta now," Tok replied. "I took the liberty of sending Tavarra and Kravon with them."

Dreel nodded. "Between yourself and Zevva, and Marrt and I, we can get the *Tangoes* home with no issue."

"That was my thinking, sir." Tok glanced down and gasped. Under a finely netted mat, what appeared to be a veritable sea of red diamonds sparkled up at him. "Gods!"

Dreel chuckled. "I expected to find some, but not this many."

"Why?" Tok asked. Remembering his place, and not wanting to perpetuate the earlier confrontation at Toscatta, he added, "Sir?"

"The mine at Parmick was abandoned several years ago." With his back feet in restraining loops, he bent down to the magnetized pallet and peeled back a small corner of the fish netting. A small hexagonal item appeared in his palm. The elSha stealth device would prohibit anything hearing their conversation. With the device on, Dreel reached out and fingered a small sliver of red diamond. "I'm not much of an authority on currency, but once the mine stopped pulling out fragments like this, it was likely cause for abandonment."

"But a local faction took it over and continues to produce these." Tok took a cue from his commander and pulled himself to a lower position. Zevva had a larger fragment of diamond atop her slate. Pitched forward, her compound eyes were a few centimeters away. It took a moment for Tok to recognize that she had a monocle type device over the lower portion of her right compound eye.

"Based on what we know from the mine's previous owners and their documentation," Zevva said, "they stopped pulling fragments like this out of the mine about six months prior to their abandonment."

Tok peered closer. "It's still too small for currency."

"It is," Zevva said, "but it still has a significant value."

Dreel reached forward and returned the sliver to the mat and pulled up what could only be described as a gem. "This, though, is definitely not something the previous owners would have left behind."

Tok nodded as several pieces tumbled together in his head. "So they abandoned the mine and took a loss, which they likely recouped, with either insurance on the claim or additional mineral rights. They left, and the new owners dug new shafts and found an additional vein."

"Valid possibilities." Dreel met his eye. "I'm reasonably certain the previous owners took their money and ran. From what we've seen, the company was disbanded four years ago. There have been no further operational transactions. As for the mine, when it was purchased, there was a discrepancy in the funding that was publicized and quickly written off as a mistake. A Zuparti corporation appeared to have funded the original sale of the mine, but the Merchant Guild reported that the transaction was billed in error. The real owner of the mine was a private corporation, so the documentation says. The transaction was additionally marked as having occurred under financial duress, which the Merchant Guild protects for fifty years. We have no idea who might actually own the mine."

Tok frowned. "There has to be something, though? Geerlargum said they were working for Kr'et'Socae."

"He told me the same. We're downloading the entire ship's log. This vessel has run fourteen similar loads to this, according to the captain. Most of those loads were much smaller. This was his largest haul yet." Dreel shook his head. "All told, there's around a quarter of a billion credit's worth of diamonds here."

"What?" Tok's mouth fell open. He'd never seen so much currency in one place before, even in the treasurer's offices of several guilds.

"But," Dreel said, "there's another problem."

"What do you mean?"

Zevva looked up at them. "The majority of these are fake."

"They look real," Tok said. "You mean they're synthetic, right? Counterfeits?"

Zevva buzzed, and her antennae bounced in amusement. "Yes. They're really good fakes, mixed in with natural diamond shards. On a back-water colony, they'll pass for currency easily enough. Just add the right type of chit, which is stupidly easy to counterfeit, and you have what appears to be valid, authentic credits to eighty percent of the merchants out there."

"But Kr'et'Socae isn't money laundering? I mean, he's creating the currency using some of the dust or materials?"

"That's part of it," Zevva said. "The fake ones are really obvious to anyone who's ever inspected currency. Take a look."

Tok took the larger stone from Dreel's outstretched hand and placed it on his slate. From the side of the device, he brought out a similar monocular device to the one the SleSha wore and slipped it in front of his right eye. Leaning in, he engaged the slate's fluorescence scanner. Immediately, the slate could tell it was a fake, but he couldn't until he looked closely at the stone. There was a subtle difference in the shape of the diamonds, a telltale indication of a synthetic. "Lab grown. The shape is slightly off, and the fluorescence monitor went off."

"The monitors we have on the slate are state-of-the-art. Those out in the outer colonies? Not so much," Zevva said.

"He's not laundering money. He's attempting to destabilize the currency or the Merchant Guild itself. Neither is a positive course of action." Dreel sighed. "These might be synthetic, but they could fool a sizeable portion of the union. If he could somehow introduce more, we risk economic chaos. Maybe even the collapse of a guild."

"But he likely can't get a better synthetic, right?"

Zevva shrugged. For a SleSha it was an awkward movement. "It depends. He can solve the shaping with better laboratory standards. That's pretty easy. Fooling surface fluorescence is more difficult, but if they looked specifically into synthetic diamonds and how to refine them, they could use a different material and alleviate that issue entirely, perhaps."

Tok nodded as he put the thoughts together.

"Gods!" Dreel gasped. "You said a better material. Like what?"

"There are plenty of good sources of synthetic diamonds. Some of them are very rare and—" Zevva's mouth dropped open, and Dreel nodded vigorously.

"The TriRusk. There are three children with the form of albinism that generates exceptional quality synthetic diamonds. Now that Captain Kurrang's presence is known in the galaxy, everyone will realize the possibility of TriRusk diamonds exists. If Kr'et'Socae discovers *that*, he'll waste no time finding them." Dreel stood and released his feet from the restraining loops. "I'm returning to Blue Flight. The pilots I contracted to return this vessel to Toscatta will arrive in an hour or less. Once you turn the *Kithlawur* over to them, prepare *Tango Veritas* for hyperspace transit to Weqq."

"We're not warning the guild master or the High Council first?" Tok asked.

"Careful, Enforcer Tok." Dreel smiled. "You're starting to sound like a Peacemaker. For what it's worth, I'm executing my duties as assigned. We're proceeding directly to Weqq, where we'll attempt to evacuate the TriRusk."

"What do you mean attempt?" Zevva asked, her curiosity piqued.

"The TriRusk do not wish to leave Weqq, as we protect it. If I tell them they're in danger, and that it's my intent to evacuate them, I expect their leader, Honored Nurr, will decline. She would rather fight to the death to protect their way of life. They've been away from the union for several hundred years, and I'm nearly certain they'd rather die fighting than let anyone or anything have a chance to get the drop on them again."

"Again?" Tok asked. "You mean the Flesset War?"

"I do, Enforcer Tok. I suggest you read up on it during our transit. We have much to learn from history. I can guarantee you Kr'et'Socae already has. Now we must beat him at his game."

* * *

Town Starport
Parmick

"All right, lock it down and let's head into Town to get paid," Larth said. "We probably want to go to the credit exchange again so we can pass by the Peacemaker's office and see if he's back."

The ramp rose on the ship. Keaton used his handheld remote to lock the ship and set the security to ensure it couldn't be operated. In a place like Parmick, security was a wise precaution. Some of the criminal elements and even less reputable mercenaries had been known to steal ships and leave the system, never to be seen again around that sector of the galaxy again.

"We'll need to go by the mining operations office first," said Jyrall, adjusting the strap on his eyepatch. "The rest of the payment is due now. I don't think a crew like we represent would wait very long after touching down."

"Good point," agreed Larth. "Do you think we should have set down closer to the hanger with the guards to kind of use them to help watch the ship?"

There were security guards still roving around the large hanger they'd noticed the first day they arrived. They had no idea what type of ship was in there, or ships, for that matter. Perhaps it was where the finished products from the mine were kept after they were cut by jewelers.

"I think that hanger belongs to Barlung," Keaton said, covering his mouth. "I just saw one of those idiots we trashed walk into it. He was in bandages."

"Yeah, well, him and his buddies can have another stomping if they trip another waitress," Ricky said, glancing their way. "Hell, they can get it again right now on principle."

Larth laughed at the mechanic. "I thought you'd rather turn wrenches than fight."

"I would," Ricky answered, "but sometimes that's what it takes."

"I like the way you think, my friend," Larth agreed.

"Violence is not always the best course of action," cautioned Jyrall.

"When you're undercover as a ruthless gang of smugglers, it is," answered Larth. "To do otherwise is a dead giveaway."

"Why do I feel like you're enjoying this mission far more than you should?" asked Jyrall with a toothy grin.

"Because you're very perceptive, Snarlyface," Larth answered with a skip in his step.

The four of them crossed Town and headed for the mining operations center. The building was near the front of the valley, and they could see the openings to the mine shafts on the wall of the cliffs behind them. The cliffs continued up, becoming the base for a huge mountain with no name. The peak had a very thin dusting of fine white snow at the very top, while the rest of the snow on its slopes appeared as gray as the dust swirling through the lower atmosphere. Instead of gorgeous and majestic, the mountain was bleak. The land beyond was, too. They'd seen from the air that the distant land beyond that mountain wasn't as green and lush as the area near the river and the coast. Any society would be pinned in near the coast and its fresh, somewhat-potable water.

As they approached the building, Larth remarked, "If we have to keep coming over here, we should get a ride. Buy a used hovercraft or wheeled vehicle, something. All this walking is making my back paws ache."

"That's because you have to take twice as many steps as the rest of us." Jyrall smirked.

"Oh, short jokes again," Larth said in mock anger. "At least I don't hit my head coming through a hatch."

"That wasn't funny," Jyrall said rubbing the sore spot. "I saw stars."

"We were in space," Ricky deadpanned from behind his hand, "they're kinda everywhere."

"You, too?" Jyrall asked. "Great."

"Okay, we're almost there," Larth said, serious now. "Everybody look mean."

Without a second glance at the guard standing near the door, Jyrall shoved the front door open and the four of them walked right past the stunned Lumar. Even though he wasn't particularly intelligent, he was smart enough not to hinder the four scowling smugglers. The Lumar shrugged his four shoulders and turned back to stare toward Town. Simple security was obviously his station. Out here, a Lumar couldn't possibly harm the miners or their equipment. The strong, semi-intelligent aliens needed constant instructions. His glance at them told Larth that the Lumar didn't understand why they'd come in the front door anyway. His confusion was all they needed to push inside.

Several Lumar and Goka heads turned at the intrusion. They looked up from the conference table and whatever they were doing. Jyrall noticed two disassembled rifles, their owners cleaning parts. Quickly, three Lumar stood and reached for their sidearms. Before they could draw them, Larth had his out and was covering them.

"I wouldn't do that if I was you," the Zuparti said quietly. The tone of his voice froze the guards' hands.

"Varkell!" boomed Barlung as he came through door at the back of the room. "I've been expecting you, but I didn't expect you to come here to rob the place. I mean, really?" He indicated Larth with weapons in hand.

"A little preventive measure," Jyrall shrugged. "They went for their weapons first. Switch here beat them all to the draw."

"I see that," scowled the Oogar, looking around at his guards in disgust. "Sit down you three—and you two, how many times do I have to tell you to put those back together and get out to the towers!" The last came out as a yell.

"Moving, Boss," one of the Goka said hurriedly. They began to reassemble the weapons, even though all the parts weren't clean yet.

The door opened again, and a Jeha came through holding a small box in several of his upper pincers. Moving in the peculiar fashion of his millipede-like race, he set it on the table, stepped back, took a long look at the four of them, and returned through the door on multiple legs. He never said a word, he just looked at them. It bothered Larth, being observed like he was being sized up as an adversary.

Larth watched the Jeha's eyes the entire time and noted how it took in all the details of the undercover Peacemakers and their crew. Something in the look from the Jeha disturbed him. It wasn't just the fact that the Jeha was curious about the smugglers, it was something else. He couldn't quite put a digit on it, but it was there. There was something going on in the dynamics between Barlung and his technician, and Larth noticed it. Larth caught his partner looking around slowly, taking in the entire room with the sensors in his patch.

The Zuparti continued looking around the room and noted several camera lenses. The three he saw were mostly hidden, but he knew what to look for. There were probably more he wouldn't find with a cursory glance. That was how Barlung and the Jeha had known they were there to bring their payment out.

Larth put his pistols in their holsters and walked over to the box. He opened it, reached in, and counted. Once he was sure it contained twenty-five hundred credits, he closed the box, picked it up, and nodded at Jyrall. There wasn't time to tell whether all the diamonds were real, but he knew most of them were likely counterfeits.

"It's all here, Boss," Larth said.

"Good," Jyrall answered. He looked at Barlung. "Pleasure doing business with you. Let me know when you have another run for us. If nothing comes up soon, we may move on. This place is one big dust ball, and unless it provides a decent source of profit, we'll have to find somewhere that will."

"Don't be too hasty," Barlung said quickly. He appeared excited about the crew's performance and didn't want to miss an opportunity to get them working for him on a more permanent basis. "I'm sure one will come up. I should have a load ready in a few days. I try not to send small loads…of equipment, you understand."

"I get it," Jyrall said. "Like I said before, I don't care what we haul as long as the credits are good."

"As you can see, they are," Barlung said, indicating the box. "Even if you took longer than expected to make the drop. What was that all about, anyway?"

"I always make it a habit to put a stop or two between me and my destination. It throws off anyone who might be following and allows us to take care of any that do. You're not successful long in this business if you don't take precautions."

"Makes sense," agreed Barlung. "It would have been nice to know that before you lifted off."

"You paid me to make a delivery." Jyrall shrugged. "That doesn't mean I have to divulge my methods. We got the goods there and made the transfer with no issues."

"You did," agreed Barlung. "Geerlargum let me know in his message."

Jyrall turned to go, but Barlung called out. He stopped and turned back. Satisfied he was gaining trust, he waited for what the Oogar had to say.

"There may be some other things that come up, jobs for beings with the ability to handle things quietly, if you understand my meaning," Barlung said. He looked over at Larth. "I already know how they are in a brawl, and some of your crew seem quite capable with their weapons."

"We're not mercenaries," Jyrall warned, "if that's what you mean. Too many rules, regulations, you breached a contract, and all that kind of stupidity involved in registering as a mercenary company."

"And that's precisely why I think I may have some jobs for you in the foreseeable future," Barlung said with a grin. "I'll be in touch."

"I'll be waiting," Jyrall said and motioned to the brothers to step out and scan the area. He and Larth followed, leaving Barlung to watch them go.

They noticed more activity around Town than before they left. It was almost evening, and there were more locals about, although none of them seemed in a hurry. It was almost as if they had accepted their lot in life, and they were just moving through it in slow motion.

They received a couple of glares from obvious mercenaries, but no one said a word to them as they passed by. Some dirty miners stopped their conversations as the four of them walked by. Jyrall glanced over but couldn't read the looks on the faces of the various aliens. All of them appeared equally dejected and exhausted.

A few minutes later, they passed the Peacemaker's office. It looked exactly the same. The lights were on, but there was no activity inside. The items on the desk hadn't been moved, and both Jyrall and Larth took note of it.

Up ahead they could see the exchange was still open, like a lot of the places they passed, though it was later in the evening. Larth remarked that a ship must have come in-system, maybe some mercenaries, and the businesses hoped to earn some extra profits.

They walked in and received the same alert stares from the guards. The Jeha at the counter seemed pleased to see them. Larth walked up with the box of credits.

"May I be of assistance?" asked the teller, rubbing several of his upper pincers together.

"Yeah, I need change for a thousand again," Larth said. This time he reached into the box for the chit. The red diamond sparkled in the light as he handed it over.

Once again, the teller pulled out an eyepiece and studied the diamond in the center. He looked up with a strange expression. "Another thousand-credit chit. Would you mind telling me where you acquired this one?"

"Not that it's any of your business, but it came from your boss," Jyrall said over Larth's shoulder. "Payment for a job we did for him. Is there a problem?"

"No problem at all sir," the Jeha quickly said. The chit disappeared, and he provided change hastily. "Is there anything else I can do for you?"

"No, but you can quit looking at our credits like they're fake every time we come in here," Larth said quietly. "I don't appreciate it."

"Yes, sir," answered the now-nervous teller with a glance at his guards.

As they left, the guards found something to look at other than the four of them, and especially the two Pushtal growling softly and baring fangs. They didn't notice one of the growls turn into a snicker as the door shut.

* * * * *

Chapter Twenty-One

Town

Parmick

"You can't keep giggling every time you scare someone," Keaton told his brother as they walked back toward Pete's Dive Bar.

"I can't help it," Ricky admitted, covering his mouth as he spoke, like his brother.

"He's right," Jyrall agreed. "We still have a ways to go to build complete trust with Barlung. We don't want to blow our cover this early in the investigation."

"When you feel you're going to start laughing," suggested Larth, "you can jump at them a little to startle them, and then you have a reason to laugh out loud. It'll help maintain your cover, plus it really will be hilarious."

"You can't just go around scaring others all the time," Jyrall admonished.

"What? Do you hear yourself right now?" Larth asked in disbelief. "You scare the crap out of everyone just by walking into a room!"

"I don't do it on purpose," countered Jyrall. "I can't help it."

"It *does* happen, Snarlyface," Larth continued. "Admit it. Sometimes you find it funny."

"Sometimes the reactions of others are pretty funny." Jyrall grinned and gave up on the subject. There was no stopping a good sense of humor.

"Speaking of funny," Larth said. "See that man up ahead and across the street? The one in the black jacket with the red goggles?"

"I see him," Jyrall answered, looking at the Human without appearing obvious.

"There's something funny about him," Larth said. "He's been watching us. I noticed him before we went to get paid, right before we went into the credit exchange, and now here he is again. He's watching, but trying to be discreet about it and doing a terrible job."

"I don't like it either," admitted Jyrall. "Let's go into Pete's and ask around. Maybe that waitress knows who he is—if he's a local, or if he's someone passing through. For all we know, he works for Barlung and is keeping an eye on us for him."

"Maybe," Larth said slowly, "but I don't know. He's not covered in dust like all the other ones working for Barlung."

"Good point," admitted Jyrall. "You have an eye for the little details. Must be because—"

"Don't even finish that sentence," warned Larth, interrupting him. "I'll kick you in the shin and run."

"I'll snatch you up and your feet will be spinning in the air like that really old animated show you love…the ones with the fast avian and the small Besquith." Jyrall laughed.

"I love those!" Ricky exclaimed. "Dude is always getting blown up by his own traps. He runs off cliffs and has time to stare at the viewer, hanging in midair, before he drops. Hilarious."

"Meep-meep!" Keaton laughed.

A few minutes later, they entered Pete's Dive Bar. There was a larger crowd this evening. Over to one side of the room, at least twenty mercs occupied tables, talking loudly and drinking a lot of beer. The waitresses were busy hustling back and forth from their tables to the bar.

Looking around, Jyrall saw the table they'd sat at before was empty, and the heavy chair was still in place. They walked over and sat down. The buzz on the other side of the room quieted a little, and he noticed a few of them lean together, whispering and glancing their way. A huge man with red hair and a full red beard was at the center of the discussions. Jyrall tapped a claw three times rapidly.

Larth scanned the room without saying a word. Once he found what his partner intended him to see, he reached up and scratched behind an ear. Those sitting across the room were not only talking about them, every one of them was wearing red somewhere on their body. A few had red shirts, one a red cap, the rest wore it more discretely, red goggles pulled down around their neck or pushed up on their heads, or a red patch showing on a shoulder. All of them were armed in one fashion or another.

After a minute, May came over, smiling. "Hey fellas, what can I get for y'all?"

"Four from the tap, please," Jyrall answered, with a grin of his own.

"Honey," May said, "if I didn't already know you were a good un and the kind of fella to defend a gal's honor, that grin would scare me half to death. But y'all can smile at me anytime you want, I'm good with it."

"At least you can walk by them without having to keep your backside away from grabby hands, unlike some others in here," said the dark-haired waitress, wiping off the table next to them. She smiled at the four of them, but it was the tight-lipped smile of one who has too much on their mind and has to remain guarded.

Jyrall, with his Peacemaker training on reading emotions, could see there was more than met the eye with this serious woman. Given the rise in the status of Human mercenaries, Body Language of Humans was a class in itself, and not just a brief lesson. The experience in her eyes and the way she carried herself showed the same way it had the first time he had seen her.

May came back with their drinks, and Larth slid some credits toward her. It was substantially more than the drinks cost. "I like to tip up front," he explained with a wink. "We tend to get good service all night that way."

"Honey, you keep tipping like that, you won't see the bottom of your mug all night," May assured him, making the credits disappear.

Three taps on the table caused Larth to look away from the waitress toward the front door. The same man they'd noticed tailing them earlier walked in and headed toward the big man in the group on the far side of the room. He leaned down and whispered something to him. After a moment, the bearded man appeared to decide and spoke quietly. Three of the men nearest him got up, leaving their drinks unfinished on the table. They walked out, following the informant, while their leader looked at the four of them over his mug.

"That's not good," Larth said, appearing to sip his beer. "There's entirely too much interest in us from that biker-looking guy and his men."

"That what?" Jyrall asked.

"The biker in charge over there," Larth explained. "You need to watch more GalNet shows. You're forever killing me, you know."

"The one with the facial hair?" Jyrall asked. "The sleeveless jacket and the red shirt? Yes. I agree. Something is amiss."

"Missed what?" Ricky asked over his mug, his eyes glancing left and right. "Who missed? What did I miss?"

"Can't take you nowhere," Keaton complained. "He means something ain't right with that whole group of mercs."

"Well, there's a bunch of 'em, but I think we could take 'em if nobody draws a weapon," Ricky said. "If they do, somebody's liable to get hurt."

"If they do, I'm betting it's them." Larth grinned. He eased his chair back a little from the table so he could reach his pistols with no hindrance.

"No bet," Jyrall said. He waved their waitress over when he made eye contact. She walked over from a group of miners just settling in.

"Y'all need something else?" May asked.

"Just an answer to a question, if you know it," Larth said with a disarming smile. "What's the deal with all the red over there? Everybody's wearing it."

"That's Redd," she explained.

Jyrall saw her shoulders rise and fall in a deep sigh as if she were both glad to be talking to them and developing trust in their group. It was a good sign. Jyrall gestured with a clawed finger for her to keep talking, and she did.

"His company is called Redd's Riders," she continued. "They come and go on missions or whatever, but they're based here on Parmick."

"A mercenary company, huh?" Larth said, glancing over at Jyrall.

"If you could call them that," the seasoned woman said from two tables over as she wiped it. She had a look of disdain on her face.

"What do you mean?" Jyrall asked, addressing her for the first time.

"Rumor has it his stepfather owned a registered merc company," she explained, stepping nearer so she couldn't be overheard. "The stepfather didn't survive a mission, and his wife inherited." The woman put up two fingers to simulate quotation marks when she said survive.

"It wasn't long after that his mother died of an overdose," added May. "He inherited the company and has been able to scrape together enough shady contracts to maintain the license. Ain't that right, Cora?"

"Yeah, though I wouldn't trust him or his company to have my six in any situation," Cora stated as she walked off.

"She's right, you know," May said. "I heard he's behind some of the ships disappearing right off the tarmac and stranding some folks here…or at least causing them to spend everything they have to E and E off this rock." She walked away, having noticed a Jivool waving an empty mug.

After a second beer, the four of them stood to leave. Larth noticed one of the mercs elbow Redd. As soon as they were outside, he mentioned it to Jyrall, "Something is up with those mercs, and we need to be ready."

"Agreed," Jyrall said. "Did you catch the words Cora and May used in conversation right before we left?"

"I did," Larth answered glancing back. "Six and E and E."

"Those are both slang used by Humans in the military," Keaton advised as he adjusted the respirator mask to cover his mouth. "We used to hear Pops say them all the time."

"Yeah," Ricky confirmed. "Watch your six means cover the area behind you to protect you, and E and E means evasion and escape. The slang use of them just means watch your ass and get the hell out of somewhere."

"That's what I surmised," Jyrall agreed.

"Those waitresses have been in some form of military," concluded Larth. "I bet all five of them are—or have been—mercs. I mean, I know they each carry a pistol for protection in this town, but they may actually know their business with them."

"No bet," Jyrall said, as usual. "I bet you Cora is their leader."

"Nope, no bet," Larth said. "You're right. She's the leader, and I bet she's a good one, too. It's pretty obvious from the way she carries herself."

They turned to go down the street leading to the airfield gate, headed back to their ship, when Ricky glanced back. "Don't look now, but we're being followed. By about fifteen of them Mercs, if there's one of 'em."

They came through the broken gate and could see another ship, an old frigate parked closer than it needed to be, given that *Night Moves* was parked off to one side and away from the few ships on the tarmac. Even from this distance, they could see an opening in the ship, as if they were loading or getting ready to load something.

"What's that old thing doing parked next to *Night Moves*?" Keaton asked, disgusted.

"It's too close to the front of our ship, that's for sure," Ricky complained. "Look at that raggedy ass ship. Looks like an old Zuul insertion frigate. I didn't know any was still flying. Those things would come into a hot zone and drop troops wherever they were needed. Weapons development made 'em obsolete. They'd get bust-ed up pretty bad before they landed. It got to where they had to land almost too far from the action for the unit in the troop bay to do any good."

As they got closer to their ship, the four of them noticed the old frigate had a silhouette of a Human riding some type of beast on the hull near the front of the ship. It was painted bright red. Out of the opening, three mechs walked down the ramp and stood, motionless.

Behind them, the group of mercenaries kept coming, gaining ground. Jyrall looked back and spoke to Keaton and Ricky, giving them their instructions. Keaton grimaced and gave a reluctant nod, along with his brother. There would be no hesitation in following their orders. Larth agreed with the plan and prepared himself mentally should it have to be enacted. The group behind them may have been headed to their own ship, but it didn't appear so. They'd be ready for them.

As they approached *Night Moves*, Keaton prepared to unlock the ship and drop the ramp. Before he could activate it, Redd called out, "Go ahead and open it and save us the trouble."

The four of them turned to face the Mercs standing thirty yards away. "What are you talking about," demanded Jyrall.

"That ship," Redd said as his men spread to the left and right, hands near their weapons. "You're about to give it to me…and I'll give you your lives. It's real simple, One-Eyed Varkell. The ship, or you die and I'll get it anyway. Your choice."

"What if I choose neither?" Jyrall growled, his hand near his holster. Larth reached up and unbuttoned his vest.

"I don't think you have a choice," Redd said, raising a hand and waving his hand in a small circle. At this, most of his men laughed.

An unmistakable roaring sound washed over them as the three Mk 7 mechs ignited their jumpjets, launched, and flew to land behind the group of men. It was now four against eighteen men…and three mechs. The odds were terrible, even for the two Peacemakers and their Pushtal crew members.

"I see," Jyrall said, his shoulders slumping, losing his swaggering confidence in front of the mercs and his crew. "You want us to lay down with our paws behind our heads or what? How do we do this?"

"That's funny," boomed Redd. "Yeah, you just lay down real nice like, and I'll let you live…maybe." All the Mercs were laughing at this point.

Jyrall, Larth, Keaton, and Ricky laid down on their stomachs. Jyrall wished it hadn't come to this, but there was no other choice, given the circumstances. This would be over soon.

"Hey!" shouted Redd. "Drop the ramp you moron! You're about to piss me off. You do that, and I won't be so fair in our little deal here."

Jyrall leaned up on one elbow and said, "It's a two-step process. One crew member disengages the security protocols, and the other unlocks and lowers the ramp."

"Well, get to it, I don't have all day," the merc commander said, reaching up to scratch his face through his beard.

Jyrall looked back at the brothers. "Do it," he ordered.

Both controls came out. It took a few seconds for Ricky to access his. After about thirty seconds, his input was done. Keaton disengaged the safety measures, waited thirty seconds, and hit the button to lower the ramp. He nodded at Jyrall.

"It should open in another thirty seconds," Jyrall said in a defeated voice. It was the last thing he wanted to do this soon in the mission.

"Well, it's about damned time," said Redd. He stepped toward the ship as the ramp came down. Once it was level with the cargo deck, the big man froze in his tracks, but it was too late.

Frank and Stein were lined up side by side. Both had their main weapons up and rotating antennae raised. Thirty missiles launched from Stein, at the same time Frank's duel fifties opened up in a sustained burst. Jyrall, Larth, and the brothers did their best to get even lower as they lay with their paws over their heads, and their faces down against the tarmac and tucked tight against a shoulder.

Ten missiles struck each CASPer, completely destroying them. It didn't help their cause when several of the fifty caliber rounds came through the men in front of them and struck them as well. They toppled backward from the impacts.

All the men were torn apart by the rounds as Frank swept the weapon left and right until its sensors indicated nothing was standing or moving in the near vicinity. Its mission complete, the weapon lifted skyward in safe mode, the panel with the few missiles in the front slowly closed, and it sat silent, awaiting further guidance.

Stein, after launching its entire rack of missiles, stowed the launcher back into the box on top and sat immobile, out of the fight. A slight whirring could be heard, along with a knocking sound inside its hull.

In the silence following the destruction of the entire merc unit, Jyrall shook his head to stop the ringing in his ears. He looked back and watched Ricky use his control panel to shut down his machines. He slowly stood, and the others followed his lead.

Looking at the remains of the would-be ship thieves, Jyrall shook his head. "Stupid. Such a stupid waste of lives. Still, they brought it on themselves, and we had no choice. Once they got inside the ship and discovered we were Peacemakers, they would have killed us."

"Yeah," Larth said, amazed at the results of Frank and Stein's handiwork. "That was crazy! That shit was so loud! Mechs and bodies were dropping everywhere! That's like something out of the shows on the GalNet. Crazy!"

"At least we know some of that Ricky Shit works," Keaton said. "Damn!"

"Yeah, they work," admitted Ricky, "but there's something wrong with Stein. I need to work on him. His Tommy Guns didn't deploy. Must be a bad hatch or something. I'll work on it."

"What now, Snarlyface?" Larth asked, looking over at his partner.

"We need to clear that frigate," Jyrall answered after thinking for a moment. "I think the entire company was out here, otherwise the ramp would have already been closed on the ship. Looks like Varkell and his crew lived up to their reputation and now own another ship."

"That ship is a piece of shit, just so you know," stated Ricky.

"Let's go do an inventory,' Keaton said. "Who knows what they had on board? Maybe even some more of those mechs."

"Yeah?" Ricky asked, now more than interested in checking it out. "Bet they got somethin' usable in that tub."

* * * * *

Chapter Twenty-Two

Pete's Dive Bar
Town, Parmick

The thunderous noise of weapons fire washed over the conversations in the bar and snuffed them out in a heartbeat. Cora's head snapped up at the unmistakable sound of rocket fire coming from the direction of the starport. In a matter of a few heartbeats, she exchanged glances with the other women. They communicated solely with their eyes. Cora remained behind the bar with Lisalle. Kellie moved quickly between several tables, taking the opportunity to disrupt the curious glances and whispers with the promise of more alcohol. The dirty miners mostly cheered her efforts. A few of the former mercs stared into their beers, either hoping for a break, or fearful they might be next.

Cora caught May's wide blue eyes staring at her. With a tilt of her chin, Cora motioned the young girl behind the bar. Collecting a tub of dishes that wasn't even half full, but enough that she could get away with clearing them from the barback, Cora marched into the kitchen area of the bar and set the tub next to the dishwasher. The aging sanitizing station had been manufactured on Earth sometime in the last century and was held together in multiple places by faulty rubber hoses and the modern equivalent of bailing wire. With a practiced speed she likened to loading the MAC on her CASPer, Cora loaded the mugs, glassware, and dishes into the machine, slammed down the heavy steel door, and initiated the sequence. The entire process would take three minutes. Normally the women used the time for a much-needed break to eat or take care of other business. Instead of taking the time for herself, Cora jogged to the back door of the living quarters, past the snoring figure of Pete collapsed in front of a football match from Earth on a Tri-V, and rushed into the alley outside.

The late afternoon light gave the perpetually gray sky an ominous look, and several columns of thick, black smoke rose into the sunset by the starport. The relatively few citizens and miners on the streets kept their faces down as they hustled along the street. No one looked in the direction of the starport except Cora.

Three minutes isn't enough time. If I had my CASPer, maybe.

Without a second thought, Cora broke into a jog and headed toward the starport, for two reasons. First, her team's CASPers and gear were stored in several storage containers at the port. They were away from where the smoke was rising, but close enough that she was concerned about their welfare. Second, there was a more than idle curiosity rising in her brain with regard to both Ledram's proposition of an uprising against Barlung and his Oogar thugs, and the four seemingly aggressive mercenaries who'd arrived a few weeks before and quickly fell in with Barlung, delivering a shipment of ore from the mine and returning earlier in the day. There was something about them. Cora couldn't quite put her finger on it, and it was May who'd said it best.

"The Besquith and the Zuparti aren't mercenaries at all. Maybe bounty hunters, but they're clearly restrained beyond their normal selves. They try to act natural, but they ain't. And those two Pushtal?

They sure whisper a lot for folks that ain't supposed to talk much. I think One-Eyed Varkell and his crew could be trouble."

As she ran, Cora felt her stomach lurch. She'd watched Redd and his hooligans follow the four unusual smugglers toward the starport not twenty minutes before.

And now this. Dammit.

Try as she might, Cora hadn't wanted to believe the four aliens were anything special, but with their extravagant tips and protective stance over all of them in the rowdy confines of the bar, there was a part of her that believed they might be able to help her team get away from this shitty little world and the so-called life they'd fallen into on Parmick. If they were dead, another victim of Redd's, it wouldn't matter.

Cora turned a corner and accelerated toward the starport. Her goal was a small set of buildings with an upper deck on them that hadn't been used for anything other than the drying of laundry in decades. It wasn't much, but the small structure might be tall enough to let her see the starport. At the bottom of the deck, she juked to the left onto a small inclined wall and prepared to jump, when something snagged her left arm at the elbow and dragged her effortlessly into the shadows at the base of the building.

"Hey!" Cora said as she fell. In a split second of freefall, she recognized that a thick, strong arm had encircled her arm and she was only a meter or so off the ground, with her feet under her. She fell with her knees relaxed, planted her feet on the ground, and whirled defiantly toward her attacker.

Ledram raised his forepaws. "I meant no harm, Cora McCoy."

"Ledram?"

"Yes," the Jivool said. "What are you doing out here?"

"What's happened?" Cora glanced at the rising columns of smoke visible through the deck supports. "We have things stored out there."

"The storage area is safe and secure. Redd and his company followed the four newcomers to their ship. There was an attack. I'm afraid Redd's company is dead."

"What? The entire company is *dead?*" Cora gaped. The four aliens, nice as they were, had to be much more than they'd originally thought. "Gods."

The Jivool nodded. "I didn't see it, but my eyes did."

Cora glanced back to the Jivool's wide brown eyes and caught his meaning squarely. "You're watching everything?"

"As are you," he said. "I've noticed your women taking things in more so than before. I believed you would do so, and you've proved me right. The time draws nearer for action. Can we count on you?"

The earnestness and concern in his voice startled her back to reality. The first question was something her sergeants and lieutenants would have recognized. It came straight from Colonel Talmore himself. "What if your plan fails?"

Ledram's eyes went wider, and he gurgled a laugh. "We have weapons, ammunition, and more forces than Barlung and his thugs can organize on short notice. We can turn the field. Especially with your team's…gear on our side. I hear those suits are quite capable."

How does he know for sure we have CASPers?

Cora kept her face still. There were several possible reasons. The yardmaster could have squealed about the containers and, given their size, shape, and familiarity, it would be easy to discern them as shipping containers for CASPers. Or Ledram could have taken a shot in the dark and hit the mark. Either way, her pause was far more than one to gather a quick response. There was one other possibility for the situation—an opportunity to be seized.

"They have no fuel. No ammunition. They haven't been started or had diagnostics run on them in months. I can't simply get them out of the containers and break them down on the flight line, Ledram."

The Jivool nodded. "I understand, and I'll see what I can do."

"When are you planning to move against Barlung?"

Ledram shrugged. "Soon. We've planned some protests to determine his capabilities to deploy forces against us and, if possible, to determine what he has available in the vicinity of the mine itself. We think that may be the right place to strike first."

Half a dozen scenarios flashed through her head, breaking down the tactical strengths and weaknesses of starting an armed insurrection in the mine itself. None of them were pretty without external support—the kind five fully armed CASPers could provide. Depending on what enemy forces Barlung could manage to coerce or field, Cora believed she and the others could make a difference.

But is that difference enough to get us off planet?

"Don't move without telling us. You won't last ten minutes in the mines without significant support," Cora said. When the Jivool started to respond, she raised a palm to him and heard his maw click shut. "Weapons and massed forces aren't enough, Ledram. You're a miner, not a mercenary—no offense. Simply rushing the guards in the mine might work just fine, but once you're up here in the open, you've got no prayer if he brings in heavy weapons."

"Once we get to the surface and secure the mine, we'll summon the Peacemakers. They'll arbitrate our demands."

Cora frowned. "Peacemaker Rekk's death should have triggered a response. Unless the guild doesn't know, they won't send anyone to help."

"There are others we might persuade," Ledram grunted. "Your friends, perhaps."

"They're not my friends," Cora replied. "I think they're working for Barlung."

And here I am wondering if they're capable of getting us off this rock. Dammit.

"All beings have their price, Cora McCoy." Ledram's maw curled up on one side like a half-smile. "You of all Humans should know that. Get back to your bar before your absence is noted. As I learn more of what occurred, I'll make sure you know."

"There's more to this than what just happened. The ships? The hangar?" Cora pointed. "Barlung's got something out there that nobody can get close to. What happens if it's all weapons and troops? Your insurrection will be the shortest in recorded history."

"Then I suggest we learn more about that. By we, of course, I mean you and your team." Ledram chuckled. "When does the next shipment leave?"

Cora squinted. "How would I know that?"

"You deliver the nightly profits from the bar to Nay-Thok, correct? I'm sure you can find out when the next shipment will be."

Cora nodded. "To get at least some of his thugs or hired guns off the planet, I get it. There's too much we don't know, Ledram."

"This is why we'll launch our protests to see what they do," Ledram said, his voice quiet. "Now go back to the bar. I'll contact you in a day or two at the most. Chances are you'll see what we see, and it'll be enough to plan a move."

With a gentle push on her arm, the Jivool sent her back into the deserted street. Cora ran toward the bar, weaving through the citizens in the street with ease. Ducking into the rear quarters of the bar, she found Pete still snoring in his chair. As she passed their tiny living space, Cora resolved that she'd find a way out of the mess she'd put them in—even if they had to fight their way out.

* * *

Riding High
Newly Acquired Frigate
Town Parmick

"*Riding High?*" Jyrall asked. "That is the ship's name? Are you certain?"

The Besquith was standing behind Keaton as he manipulated the controls and accessed the operating system of the old Zuul insertion frigate. It only took him a few minutes to connect a cable to his handheld computer and force the security programs to allow him complete access.

"I'm sure," Keaton said. "For now, at least. The programming in this pile of scrap metal is child's play. It looks like there's been some reprogramming, but even that is no better than the original stuff."

"Good," Jyrall said. "See what you can find out about the Mercenary License this company holds—or held."

"Sure, it should be no problem." Keaton shrugged. "You want me to create a file with digital documentation showing Redd sold the company and transferred the Mercenary License to you or Larth?"

"You can do that?" Jyrall asked, surprised. He and Larth had received training in basic programing and digital investigation, but nothing like Keaton was proposing.

"Aw, hell, there ain't nothin' to it," confirmed the Pushtal with a toothy grin. "I can date/time stamp it, too. Who do you want to own it all?"

"Intriguing, let me think about it," Jyrall said. "And what in all the known stars is that smell!"

"I think it's the pilot's seat over there," Keaton answered, looking over at the offending station. "Not only did the guy obviously never wash his ass, Ah think he had stomach issues."

Jyrall held a paw over his nose and shuddered. "I think I'll see how the inventory is going back in the troop bay." He left the operations center as fast as he could manage in the unfamiliar ship.

Making his way back to the troop bay, he kept his head low so he didn't hit the top of hatchways. The corridors of the ship were never meant for a Besquith. Up ahead he heard Larth and Ricky talking about the arms room and the bay itself. He couldn't help but grin to himself. *Those two.*

"Yeah, there may be seven CASpers backed into their slots, but that don't mean any of 'em is worth a plug of fresh-chewed tobacco," Ricky explained. "From just lookin' 'em over, I can see there's three of 'em that need major work. Look at that leak! That thing is sitting in a puddle of jump juice. It's a dang far hazard, that's what it is."

"A far hazard?" Jyrall immediately grinned and waved off the question. "Oh, right. A fire hazard."

"Yeah," Ricky said, "the dang thing is sitting in some mighty flammable stuff."

"What about the others?" Larth asked.

"They look all right, I guess," Ricky admitted. "They been shot up some and repaired, but I won't really know unless I run a diagnostic on 'em."

"Can you do that?" Jyrall asked.

"Sure," Ricky answered. "I been helpin' Pops with his since I was knee high to a grasshopper. I still have the program and gear. Keaton wrote some patches to shorten the run-time by half."

"What is a grasshopper? Never mind," Jyrall said, beginning to understand he'd need translations and explanations for a while to come with Ricky and Keaton as part of the team. "How does the arms room look?"

"Not too bad," Larth said. "There are Human weapons, both handguns and rifles, some laser pistols, and a few outdated laser rifles. There's a decent-sized stockpile of ammunition and missiles for the CASpers. I noticed a case of grenades, but I have no idea how old they are. There may be some duds in the box."

"What?" Jyrall asked. On second thought, he decided he might just need a translator for everything everyone else on the team said. "Oh, you mean ones that won't function properly. More GalNet nonsense. Never mind."

"I'm about to go take a look at the ship's weapon systems," Ricky warned. "They probably ain't in good shape, either. There should be some missile racks, a decent main laser, and some defensive stuff—if it ain't been modified. Lord knows where they been getting Zuul missiles."

"What about the power plant and engines?" Jyrall asked. "Have you checked those?"

"That was the first thing I looked at," Ricky admitted. "They need a little work, too, but I'm surprised, to be honest with ya. Some work was done on 'em, looks to be about five years back. Maybe that was when the stepfather was still alive and kickin'."

"Well, that's something, anyway," Larth said.

"Agreed," Jyrall admitted. "I know one thing: the filtration system on this ship is almost nonexistent."

"Yeah, she stinks a bit," the Pushtal mechanic agreed, wrinkling his own nose.

* * *

Mining Operations Building
Parmick

"Slow down, you idiot," Barlung said to the panting Oogar in front of him. "Catch your breath and tell me again. This time I want to understand what you're saying!" The last came out in his customary yell.

Cartrule, one of his lieutenants, was doubled over in front of him, breathing heavily. He had run without stopping the entire distance from the hanger on the airfield to the Mining Operations Building to tell Barlung what he'd witnessed.

"Boss," Cartrule said, finally able to speak again, this time somewhat coherently, "the Redd Riders, they're gone."

"Okay, so they're gone," Barlung said, his anger rising. "You idiot! They come and go all the time. It's a good thing when they're gone. There's too many of them, and they have CASPers, so they think they can act any way they want in my town. Good riddance to them, maybe they'll find somewhere else to base out of.

"I can't believe you come here, interrupting my dinner, huffing and puffing, to tell me something as trivial as that. I should have you work a shift in the mines for your stupidity." He turned to two Goka sitting quietly, cleaning their rifles. "And you two! I swear I'll kill you the next time I catch you goofing off in here pretending to clean your rifles. I've seen you clean them enough to make them look new. Get out there in those towers!"

"Moving, Boss," one of them said, glancing at his fellow guard. They began reassembling their weapons as fast as they could.

"No, Boss," Cartrule tried to explain. He paused. "Can I sit down?"

"You're weak. Sit down," Barlung relented. "You're young, you should be in better shape."

"I think it's the dust," Cartrule said. "It's always hard to breathe. Anyway, what I was saying is that the Redd's Riders are *gone*. They're dead, every one of them."

Hearing this, Barlung paused, the piece of meat he was about to put it in his mouth held in mid-air on the end of a large eating utensil. He slowly set it back on the tray. "Say that again," he ordered.

"The Redd Riders are dead," Cartrule repeated. "I saw it happen with my own eyes. Well, I saw it right after, anyway. I was over at the hangar and heard it. They were all shot up, and three of those big machines were smoking wrecks right behind them. They're gone. There wasn't enough of anybody to save, that's for sure."

"Which of the other two factions did it?" Barlung asked, sitting back. "I mean, I'm glad they did it, it's one less group I need to keep an eye on, but who did it?"

"Neither," Cartrule answered, reaching for a piece of meat on Barlung's tray. He snatched his paw back with the fork sticking out of the back. "Oww!"

After he pulled the fork out, he continued, rubbing his paw. "It was Varkell. Him and his crew. They were standing over the bodies. I saw them walk around them a bit, and one of the Pushtal kicked Redd to check for life, then they turned, walked over to the Redd's Raider's ship, and walked right up they ramp like they owned it."

"If they took them out, I guess they do own it now," surmised Barlung.

"You said they had a reputation, Boss," Cartrule said. "Killing, taking ships, and everything else. It must all be true."

"I believe it is," Nay-Thok said from the doorway to the back office. "I don't have cameras always monitoring that particular part of the airfield. I rotated a few of them after the explosions, and what Cartule told you is true. The Redd Riders are no more."

"I should go over there and thank them," Barlung said, standing.

"A wise idea," Nay-Thok agreed. "Perhaps it's time to have Varkell perform other, similar tasks. We have a few more courier ships. We need not send them away as the runner, perhaps they can be the escort. Geerlargum hasn't checked in to the final destination. I mentioned my reservations about that particular captain, as you recall."

"If something happened to Geerlargum," Barlung said, "it had to happen at the end of his run. His message stated the delivery was made by Varkell, and his last message stated he was minutes from exiting the system, with no issues."

"You go speak to Varkell, and I'll attempt to get to the bottom of the missing shipment," Nay-Thok said, turning away and closing the door behind him.

"Come on, weakling," Barlung said to Cartrule. "We'll walk there. Just for your sake."

* * *

Town Starport
Parmick

"Barlung," Jyrall said with a nod.

Jyrall and Larth stood outside *Night Moves*, waiting for the two Oogar to arrive. Keaton had noticed them headed their way through some of the outside monitors on the ship while sitting in the operations center. He was using their powerful computer system to access what he needed through a relay slate connected to the main computer in the frigate. They'd raised the ramps on both ships and waited.

"Varkell," Barlung acknowledged when he got close enough for polite conversation. He looked around at the devastation of the still smoking CASPers and the bodies lying everywhere, recognizing what was left of Redd and his men.

"To what do I owe the pleasure?" Jyrall asked.

"I heard what happened and wanted to come and thank you personally for ridding me of a thorn in my paw," Barlung said, indicating Redd and the other bodies with a wave. "How'd you know that was a job that needed to be performed?"

"It's the least I could do," Jyrall said. "Switch was able to find out they were becoming a problem for you, so we lured them out and took care of it."

"There's no charge…this time," Larth said, playing up his part.

"I appreciate that," Barlung said to the Zuparti. Larth could see Barlung's trust in him and his team growing with every moment. It made the prospects of Barlung continuing to use them even better.

"At least let me take care of the cleanup," Barlung offered. "You don't need the smell that's sure to come from them outside of your ship—or should I say, ships?"

"Ships would be correct," Jyrall said. "Thanks for that. We'll wait for your cleanup crew to come do their thing, and ensure all the weapons and the three destroyed machines stay right here."

"Trust, but verify." Barlung laughed. "I understand completely. I'll be in touch."

Jyrall and Larth watched Barlung and his lieutenant walk across the tarmac to enter a small door in the guarded hanger.

"You were right," Jyrall said. "That hanger belongs to him."

"I think I'll see about getting a look inside," Larth said, almost to himself. "I bet Ricky has a few drones."

* * * * *

Chapter Twenty-Three

Town

Parmick

At precisely noon, two days following the incident at the starport, Cora made her way through Town toward the mining center of operations. In her left hand she carried a leather-handled satchel that had seen better days as a tank crew toolbox. Strapped to her right hip, openly carried for the first time in as long as she remembered, was her GS-45. A blued-steel variant of the venerable M1911 pistol fitted with an integrated laser sighting system and a high-capacity magazine that held 15 rounds, she'd left it locked in the weapons crate at the starport for fear of losing it or attracting the attention of someone intent on taking the expensive weapon from her.

With the eradication of Redd's unit at the hands of the newcomers, some of the older mercs, and those who'd simply slunk into the background around Town, had decided they wanted to flex their own muscles and get Barlung's attention. Barfights were the first indicator, and on the first night alone, she'd broken up three altercations and been forced to draw Pete's shitty .38 pistol from under the cash drawer.

Before dawn the following morning, the five of them made their way to the weapons lockers and secured additional firearms and ammunition, body armor, and a medical kit. Having the weapons eased

Cora's anxiety some, but the reality was, the tension in Town was palpable enough that on the second evening, the number of regular drinkers and ne'er-do-wells was far below what it would have been the night before payday. Those who did come out certainly seemed to want to fight.

Thankfully, Varkell and his group were quiet for more than twenty-seven hours before they made their way to their usual table and held court for most of the evening. They drank little and talked less. As they gave the surrounding drinkers suspicious looks and bared teeth, all while remaining excessively polite to Cora and the women, a resigned calm came over the bar.

Earlier than normal, the crowd headed into the night. Those who'd wanted a fight left sorely disappointed. Those who wanted peace did as well, because it was merely a postponement of violence, and they all knew it. Town and its inhabitants—miners, mercs, and all those in between—felt the lines being drawn and the implements being sharpened. It was only a matter of time.

They made it back to their little apartment just as the sun was rising over the dusty, dreary town, and Cora sat with them for a moment. With a mug of coffee in her hands, she looked up at the women and told them what they already knew.

"Things are about to get real. It's a fight we didn't want, and it ain't something we can stop, either. I figure we have two choices: either sit here with our heads down and pray nothing happens to us directly, or arm our suits and have them ready to either defend ourselves or the citizens once Barlung's thugs open fire."

They didn't say much for the rest of the morning—just sat with their drinks in the silence and the light from a few candles until the sun rose fully. There wasn't much of a choice. War was coming to the planet, and they had weapons that could ensure their safety and, potentially, save the lives of others. Once Pete had prepared the evening's take, Cora walked out into a clearer than normal morning and actually saw a streak of the light blue sky above the perpetual cloud cover. For a split second, the fast-moving clouds parted enough that a swath of warm sunlight passed over her face, and Cora smiled. As fast as it had appeared, the sunlight flitted away, and she looked down from the overcast sky into the faces of a town primed to explode.

The residents of Town who were off shift were curiously not asleep, nor seeking food or drink. Miners, mainly Zuparti, Cochkala, and Jivool, huddled together in small, nervous groups outside the various shops, blocking the open streets so much that it appeared like a holiday gathering. For as many townspeople as she saw, there seemed to be a proportionally large group of security forces, too. Cora saw several familiar faces among them. Mercenaries without companies and ships had signed on to help Barlung, likely for excessively high short-term payments.

As she approached the mining operations building, the smaller of the Oogar lieutenants, Frooth, shouldered a laser rifle of a type she'd never seen before and made his way toward her. About twenty meters away, she watched his eyes drop from her face to the pistol on her hip. His gait wavered slightly, and it sent a thrill through Cora's spine.

You realize I mean business. Finally.

Frooth nodded theatrically to her. "I'd be happy to take that burden from you, Cora McCoy."

"Not a chance, Frooth. My instructions, and Nay-Thok's, are crystal clear." Cora smiled sweetly at the Oogar, hoping the effect died at her eyes like she wanted it to. "So I'll be passing through to the inner offices now."

The purple bear-like alien frowned down at her. While he was smaller than the others, he still towered over Cora. "I'm interested in something, first."

"What would that be?" Cora answered, even as her stomach churned at the idea of what he might ask.

"Those weapons crates you've paid handsomely to protect in the yard." Frooth's awkward smile returned. "It would be a shame if something happened to them."

Considering the contract on them and the expense we paid? You should be concerned.

Cora clenched her jaw. "Is that a threat to my property that's contracted for protection by the yardmaster, who I believe is one of your employees? I'd hate to have to report that to the Peacemaker."

Frooth laughed, and the sound sent a chill down Cora's spine. "If you were smart, Cora McCoy, you'd consider using whatever you have stored out there to help us maintain the peace here in Town."

Peacemaker Rekk is dead, remember?

The thought stunned her in its clarity and the sudden realization that the rapid sense of panic and violence in the town was in direct correlation to the lack of the Peacemaker's presence. As quickly as she wanted to discount the clarity, Cora recognized it was true. She'd seen the Peacemaker gunned down in cold blood on a city street by the Oogar.

Cora blinked and forced her smile wider. "And what would it be worth to have my gear deployed to assist you?"

"I can pay you, of course. A thousand credits a day."

Cora clenched her teeth to keep her mouth from flopping open in shock. "A thousand credits a day for each of my team? Five thousand credits a day?"

"I can see to that," Frooth replied. "You have my word."

Bullshit. Your word ain't worth that much, Yogi.

Cora shook her head. "I need more than your word, Frooth. A down payment would be nice. I can talk it over with the girls, and we'll give you a decision. If we support you, ten thousand credits up front, and then a thousand credits a day each until this mess is over."

Frooth didn't hesitate. Instead, he reached into a pocket on the bandolier strap he wore over his left upper shoulder. As experienced as she was, watching a seven-foot-tall bear walk on its hind legs all the time was terrifying. "I'll speak to Barlung. Take this as a guarantee."

Cora watched a five thousand-credit chit, the red diamond glinting in the sunlight, fall into the palm of her hand.

"You'll want this back?"

"No." Frooth waved a huge paw in her face. "That's yours to keep, Cora McCoy. If Barlung agrees, and you work for us, I'll ensure you receive more than fair compensation. If not, you can have that as a token of my appreciation."

What the hell?

Cora slipped the chit into the front pocket of her trousers, trying not to feel giddy at the sudden rush of earnings. It was more than they'd earned at the bar in three months collectively. She did the math—ten days of hostilities, or whatever it might become, would be enough to get them off Parmick and help them find a new home. "I'll speak to my team."

"You do that," Frooth growled at her. "I'll need an answer to-night."

Without another word, he stepped out of her way, and Cora walked through the mining office entrance. The two Lumar guards barely noticed her or her weapon.

"Miss McCoy."

The voice came from above her someplace. Cora looked up and saw a speaker recessed into the outer office ceiling. "While my guards seem to have no problem with you wearing a weapon, I do. Please leave it on the outer desk. Neither the guards nor anyone else will disturb it while you are inside."

Cora unholstered the pistol and ejected the magazine with the press of a button. She worked the action to clear it and caught the ejected round as it cartwheeled through the air. Cora casually slipped the round into the top of the magazine and set the pistol and the magazine on the table, all within no more than a few seconds. She looked at the camera and speaker and heard a *click* as the inner office door opened. Without another word or look at the Lumar guards, Cora stepped inside.

"An impressive display, Cora," Nay-Thok said. "I take it your familiarity with weapons goes far beyond that large pistol. I'm curious, though, as to why you feel it necessary to brandish a weapon so openly now."

Cora stared at the Jeha and then gestured at the banks of monitors. "You've seen the town over the last few days. The fights? The violence? That weapon is for my protection, first and foremost, but I like to think of it as a measure of deterrence, given what happened to Redd's Riders and all."

"As in your having a weapon will prevent others from assaulting you?"

"It's worked for years," Cora answered. Nay-Thok wasn't looking at her, and Cora used the moment to look around the cluttered space.

"In my experience, if someone really wants something you have, they'll attempt to take it. Deterrence as a solitary principle fails." Nay-Thok settled against the back of the specially made couch and rippled a dozen of his arms and pincers. "Look at my security forces. They're deterrent for deterrence's sake alone. They have weapons. They have authority. But the likelihood that they would hold their ground in an armed conflict for longer than a few minutes comes down to whether they're loyal to the overarching cause, or if they can be paid enough to assuage their concerns through simple greed. They won't deter violence by doing nothing. Their presence will cause angst. Angst will become wariness. Before that wariness can be accepted, there will be an incident. There always is in these things."

Cora wasn't really listening to the Jeha's monologue. Her eyes found several key pieces of intelligence in a matter of seconds. There were red diamonds, uncut and very small, on a worktable across the room. On a Tri-V display was a complex chemical molecular model. She didn't know what it was, but the words "synthesis match—94 percent of control" stood out. The sight of the small, circular glass dishes used in laboratories—gods help her, she couldn't remember their proper name—suggested an experiment of some type was in progress.

Can red diamonds be synthesized?

Cora filed the question away and looked back at the Jeha just as he turned his eyes to her again. "Wouldn't you agree that the people here will accept this new security, Cora?"

"They're trying to make a few credits." Cora sighed. "Most of them will do anything necessary to maintain their income and security, no matter how bad things get."

"And what about you?"

Cora blinked. "Me? I think it's very clear my girls and I want to get off this planet at the earliest opportunity."

"But where would you go? I mean, Human mercenaries are being rounded up by the Mercenary Guild as we speak. You're not a mercenary, are you?"

Cora felt her stomach contract on itself. "Not anymore, no."

"Good." Nay-Thok rippled in satisfaction. "This pleases me, Cora. I had hoped you would consider more lucrative employment. We have need for employees of your caliber."

Cora nodded. "I already told Frooth I'd consider it."

Nay-Thok chittered a laugh. "Oh, I'm not talking security. I'm talking something much more lucrative and…"

When Nay-Thok didn't continue, Cora followed his gaze to the bank of monitors. She recognized an intersection about two blocks from the Dive Bar filled with citizens of all races as they encircled Barlung himself. Nay-Thok sat forward and tapped at his slate frantically.

"I believe our business has concluded for now, Cora." Nay-Thok didn't look at her. "Get out of this office. I will summon you another time."

Cora spun on her heel and exited the secure inner office. Her weapon and ammunition were on the table, undisturbed. She picked it up, racked the action, and slipped the loaded pistol into her holster. Instead of heading back to the bar, she detoured toward the disturbance, more out of curiosity than a sense of security and understanding.

A few minutes later, she wished she hadn't.

* * *

Town
Parmick

The crowd was six or seven deep, ringing the center of an open city block. Given the many species, there were places Cora could almost see into the center of the square, but not quite. Along the side of the street, there were multiple vantage points where she could climb and see more clearly, but she pressed forward into the throng. Weaving around the smaller alien species, through the veritable cloud of sweat and mine dust, she heard them calling and cajoling at the Oogar.

"Fair wages for all!"

"Safer mines or no more miners!"

"We won't die for your diamond dust anymore."

Some of the epithets hurled were decidedly alien, colorful, and clearly insults, but she didn't know, or care to know, what an Oogar shoved up its ass on a regular basis—among other things.

Cora reached the inner circle and expected to see Ledram in the center challenging the Oogar. Instead, it was a small Zuparti female with a child bundled against its chest in a type of sling. The female chittered and pointed up at the massive bear, her words lost in the cacophony of protesters.

Barlung wore a menacing smile and placed his massive paws on his hips as he stood. He played to the crowd with the ease of a politician. "Have we not paid you good wages for your work? Have we not given you the best equipment available? We've protected your lives and given you profits from a mine they said was defunct. A mine many of you labored in for years under worse conditions than those I've provided you. You want more wages? Find more red diamonds! Find more valuable stones of any type. I'll pay you for them."

"With what?" Cora heard the small Zuparti shrilly call above most of the noise. "With your lies?"

Barlung smiled pitifully down at the female. "What lies?"

The Zuparti raised up her other paw and opened it. Cora saw a large red diamond, worth more money than she could immediately fathom. "This should buy me the world, but it's not worth—"

The Oogar backhanded the Zuparti faster than anything Cora had ever seen. The diamond glinted briefly against the light, and a frenzied collection of aliens piled on each other in a vain attempt to secure it. Barlung stomped toward the unmoving form of the Zuparti.

"Thief!" he roared over her. "No one steals from my mine!"

The Zuparti moaned and rolled over. She looked down into her bundle and screamed. The inhuman noise pierced Cora's ears enough that she raised her hands to cover them.

"My baby! You killed my baby!" A wave of bright crimson blood cascaded from the bundle around the Zuparti's chest and the crowd roared in defiance. The circle around Barlung closed quickly. Frooth and Cartrule appeared through the crowd, each of them carrying huge rotary cannons, which they pointed into the crowd.

"This ends now!" Barlung roared. The crowd did nothing, and the circle drew around the three Oogar. More security forces appeared on the edges of the growing crowd, and Cora realized her mistake. She tried to back away through the crowd, but the wall of aliens around her was impenetrable, and she couldn't see a way out. They pressed forward, yelling and screaming as one. A Cochkala ahead of her fell and howled in agony as dozens of feet and paws trampled its body.

Her heart racing in sudden panic, Cora reached for her weapon, hoping the feel of the pistol grip would calm her nerves. As she did, she looked at the aliens next to her and saw them brandishing weapons of their own.

This isn't happening.

Crack!

The crowd screamed and flinched. Cora realized the sound was from behind them, from down Center Street. It was a single shot from a large caliber—

Crack!

Screams filled the air as Frooth and Cartrule opened fire in the direction of Center Street. Dozens of aliens were hit. Blood of all colors sprayed into the air and across the dusty ground. An opening appeared, and Cora dashed for it. Five seconds later, she was through the crowd.

"Cease fire! Cease fire!" Barlung screamed behind her. "I said cease fire, you morons!"

Head down, arms pumping, Cora ran for the bar. Around her, others were doing the same, trying to find cover. As she turned down the side street closest to the bar's rear entrance, Cora heard the speakers attached to the decrepit light poles throughout Town click to life.

"Martial law has been declared, by the order of Barlung."

Nay-Thok's voice grated from the speakers. "Curfew is in immediate effect for 2100 hours local time. Anyone on the streets without permission beyond that time will be questioned, and risks arrest and detainment. Those individuals responsible for this action will turn themselves in to the mining operations center within the next hour, or security teams will be authorized to go door-to-door to collect them. This behavior will not be tolerated. Martial law is in effect from this moment forward. You have all been warned."

Cora pushed through the rear door of the apartments and found herself staring at the wide barrels of a sawed-off shotgun held by Pete.

The old pirate scowled at her. "What the fuck happened out there, Cora?"

"All hell just broke loose." Cora gasped for breath. Pete lowered the shotgun, and she pitched forward onto her hands and knees. "There was a protest and…" She paused, thinking about the Zuparti's words and the large red diamond in her paw.

Lies! The memory of the female Zuparti's voice, and then her incoherent scream of pain, almost made Cora flinch.

The diamond was fake. Synthetic. Sonuvabitch!

"What, Cora?" demanded Pete.

"Miners protesting conditions and wanting better wages. One of them challenged Barlung, and he swiped at her—a Zuparti with a child. I think the child is injured—maybe dead." Cora saw Kellie and Nileah filtering back into the apartment. For a moment she almost panicked, but remembered that May and Lisalle were at the container and should be safe, for now. "Martial law has been declared. A curfew, too."

Pete lowered the shotgun and sank into a nearby chair, his crutch clattering onto the floor. "It's happened before; won't be the last time, either."

"What do you mean?" Cora stared at him. "This is really bad, Pete."

Pete looked up at her. "No, Cora, it's not that bad. It's the way things are done around here. I wouldn't think about doing anything else but keeping your head down, woman. It might look like all hell is gonna break loose, but it'll be worse for you if you take a side. This'll blow over like the last one, and the one before that."

"Barlung might have killed a child, though."

"That doesn't have the same meaning to most other species it does to you and me." Pete poured a healthy shot of bourbon into a glass and drained it with one swallow. "Stay here, do your job, and you'll make enough to buy your way off this rock while you still can. Stay out of the business of the aliens, girl. It's a losing proposition for us Humans."

The question on Cora's mind froze in place. She met Nileah's hard stare and realized Pete paid them in credits acquired from Nay-Thok. If they were also synthesized, the credits they'd collected didn't amount to just over five thousand. They were likely worthless. She stuffed her hands into her pockets and felt the valuable credits Frooth had carelessly given. It, too, was likely worthless.

Cora kicked herself mentally. She'd been so focused on earning credits that she'd never thought about what might really be happening around her. They were farther away from leaving Parmick than they'd ever been.

Cora walked past Nileah, ducked into the bathroom, and sat on the commode with her head in her hands. She didn't cry, nor did she let anger overtake her faculties.

Instead, she did what Colonel Talmore always told her to do. She shelved her emotions and planned.

Don't make your next move until you can clearly see it and the one beyond it, Cora. You don't dare move until you do.

* * * * *

Chapter Twenty-Four

Town Starport

Parmick

Jyrall, Larth, and the McCoy brothers returned to their ships. They'd attempted to go into town for a casual stroll and a look around, and maybe go by the Peacemaker's office—his whereabouts were still a mystery to them.

"Hell, I don't mind going back to the ship," Ricky said. "I'm hungry anyway. It's almost lunchtime."

"I'm with you," Larth agreed. "There are leftover fish sticks calling my name."

"I'll never understand you two," Jyrall said. "We have a freezer container of some of the finest seafood in the galaxy, and you two want to eat pressed fish sticks from a box." The big Besquith shook his head in shame. "There's something wrong with both of you. It's undeniable."

"I wasn't going to say anything," Keaton agreed, "being's how Larth is my boss like you are. I know Ricky has some programing errors in his head with his obsession over fixing things, but I'm here to tell ya...Larth ain't right. That's a fact."

At hearing the seriousness in his voice, Jyrall burst out laughing. "Yes!" he said between deep breaths. "Yes! You have no idea how right you are, Keaton my friend."

Larth stopped in his tracks and stared at the Pushtal, indignant, as he tried to keep a straight face. Finally he could hold it no longer. The laughter from the two standing beside him was infectious, and he cracked a grin.

"Hey! I resemble that remark," he finally said, starting to laugh. "But I'm good with it."

"It ain't right," Ricky said, "making fun of a feller right to his face and all."

At this, the three laughed even harder, now at Ricky instead of Larth. They started toward their ships again with the occasional giggle from Larth. He looked over and noticed several guards running from the direction of the hanger toward downtown.

"I wonder if Barlung and his guards called for reinforcements?" Larth asked. "That was a pretty sizable crowd gathering."

"It was large enough to make us change our plans," agreed Jyrall. "Maybe we can use it to our advantage."

"If you're thinking what I'm thinking, I say we do it," Larth said, glancing at the hanger, now unguarded.

"Go," Jyrall decided. "We'll get the drone up and monitor. You already know where all the doors are, and there's that window on the far side that's stayed cracked open for the last two days."

"I'm on it," Larth said, "though we couldn't see anything through that window. It opens to the latrine, not the hanger bay."

"The door to the facilities probably opens into the bay," Keaton said.

"Yeah," Ricky agreed. "Ain't nobody in their right mind locks a door to the facilities. When a feller's got to go, they got to go."

Larth took off at a dead run for the frigate. He was moving so fast, Keaton jogged toward *Night Moves*. The Pushtal had to get the ship open so Ricky could deploy the drone he called Buzz while Larth waited under the newly acquired frigate until the small drone could be deployed over the hanger.

Soon Jyrall called out, "Okay, it's over the hanger, and Keaton has activated the scrambler. None of the security cameras will work. Go!"

Larth sprinted for the hangar. It was a fair distance away on the other side of the tarmac. He never once slowed, and was in position faster than the brothers thought he could be.

"Dang," Ricky exclaimed as he observed his screen, "he can flat-out run, can't he?"

"He is quick," agreed Jyrall. "Let's get that thing in overwatch. Keep rotating it slowly so we can see the road from Town, too."

"Hey!" Ricky complained. "Buzz is not a thing. He's a—okay, he is a thing, but you don't have to call him that."

"Fine," Jyrall said, glancing over at Keaton with a wink. "We need to get Buzz watching the road as soon as possible."

"He's ready," Ricky said. "He can stay up for two hours with a full charge. I had to give up some power to operate the camera lenses and relays along with the scrambler. It's the same type of camera your patch uses."

Ricky held the slate and controlled the drone's ascent and direction of flight. Keaton pulled the view from the same signal Ricky was using, so he and Jyrall could watch, as well. Larth stood beside the hanger in the shadows. They saw him pause and glance around to make sure there were no guards remaining.

* * *

Barlung's Hangar

Town Starport

Parmick

Larth stood in the shadows of the hangar, catching his breath. He was confident he hadn't been seen. Watching for guards, he eased down the length of the hangar to the door Barlung had entered two days before. Testing the handle, he found it locked. The guards had been smart enough to do that, at least.

Larth dropped low and peeked around the corner of the hangar. There was no one around. Across the airfield road, he could see a line of storage containers sitting within their own fence. He paused, looking closely at them. Several doors were open, indicating they were empty, as he could see into the one directly in front of him all the way to the back wall. The others he couldn't tell due to the shadows within. After watching for movement and seeing none, he eased around the corner to try the next door.

Larth found this one locked, as well. He decided to enter through the window instead of picking the lock. He dropped low again and looked around one last time to make sure it was clear. Glancing up, he saw the window was still partially open, as it had been for the last two days. He reached up and pushed it open just enough for his small frame to slip through. Larth pulled himself up onto the sill, looked into the room, and crawled inside, making sure to slide the window back to its previous position.

* * *

Storage Container 23
Town Starport
Parmick

"Hey," Lisalle said. "Isn't that your little Zuparti friend over by Barlung's hanger?"

"Where?" May asked, looking up from inside the hatch of her CASPer. "I don't see him."

They were in the back of the storage container in the deep shadows. If anyone drove by, they'd be hard pressed to see what was inside, unless they came inside the fenced off area. It wasn't the ideal situation, but so far no one had discovered what they kept in their secluded and secure container.

"There," Lisalle pointed. "Down low, looking around the corner."

"I see him," May said. "Why, that is the little charmer! His name is Switch, you know. You can tell it's him by that vest he wears. Now what in the world does he think he's doing over there?"

"I don't rightly know," Lisalle admitted, "but he better not get caught over there. Look! He just pushed that window open!"

"Why, that little scamp," May said. "He's gone and climbed right in! We might better let Cora know about this."

"Not until we get all the diagnostics run on these," Lisalle countered. "I gotta know exactly what we're working with as far as the charge and the jump juice status. We already know we ain't got no munitions for 'em to speak of."

"Well, don't let me forget to tell her," May said. "What was that? Sounded like weapons fire!"

"I heard it," Lisalle said, walking out of the shadows to look out the front of the container toward downtown. After a few minutes she said,

"Whatever it was, it didn't last too awful long. Maybe that's where all them guards ran off to in such an all fired hurry."

"You think Varkell and his boys set up a distraction so Switch could get into the hanger?" May asked. "If they did, it makes you wonder a might iffin Varkel and them work for Barlung, or if they might be workin' him, you know?"

"Honey, you may just be on to sumthin' there," Lisalle admitted. "We'll tell Cora and let her decide how she wants to handle that little piece of gossip."

"Let's hurry up and get this done," May said. "One of us needs to keep an eye out and see what he does when he comes back out of that window."

* * *

Barlung's Hangar
Town Starport
Parmick

"Okay, I'm in," Larth said after he put the earpiece Keaton had given him in. "Can you hear me? Crap, I didn't think about that with the scrambler in operation. If you can hear me, I'm in the facilities…and let me tell you now, Snarlyface, this is one mission you better be glad you didn't take on. It stinks in here. I don't know what those guards ate, but it was rotten. My eyes are watering."

"Better you than me," admitted Jyrall into his ear. "I can hear you, five by five. Keaton's scrambling program allows a signal to get through if it has the code entered on the receiver. Just keep a running commentary; I won't try talk to you in case someone is still in the hanger, so you can hear any noises. We have the—we have Buzz over the hanger. There's still no sign of the guards."

"Roger that," Larth said, "I'm stepping out of the facilities; it does open into the main bay. This thing is huge. There are three ships in here. The first looks like an old frigate. What's up with the old frigates everywhere these days? Anyway, I see an old frigate, and what looks to be a large cargo shuttle that's been modified; it has thrusters on it that didn't come with it when it was made, that's for sure."

He continued his running commentary as he walked over to the last ship. It took him a minute or two to get over there. "The third ship is a small shuttle. Wow! It looks brand new. I can still see the name and registration number of its host ship painted on the hull. It's a nice one, except for its size. As small as it is, it looks like the kind on a gunship, where there's not a lot of room in the ship's bay to park a shuttle."

"What's the name of the host ship?" Jyrall asked. "I'll have Keaton look it up and see what we can find out."

"It says *Strong Arm* in Jivool lettering, and the numbers are as follows." He read off the string of numbers.

"Got it," Jyrall whispered to him. "Go ahead and—Larth! There's a hovercraft headed toward the hanger! Get out of there, now!"

"I'm on the far side," Larth exclaimed, "I'm not near a door. I'll try and make my way to the facilities. You give me a running commentary now."

Larth darted under the newer shuttle and crouched in the shadows, easing himself closer to the landing gear. Not hearing anything, he ran to the next ship and slipped underneath. He paused, waiting, listening for instructions.

Jyrall relayed to him, "There are four Goka; they just got out of the hovercraft. It looks like two of them are coming inside, so stay hidden. The other two are moving to the ends of the building, and it looks like they'll post up there. It's a good thing only four of them came back. You have a chance. They're going inside now."

Larth watched from underneath the ship as the door opened and bright light poured in. Two Goka walked in with their rifles at the ready. Before their eyes could adjust to the darkness of the hanger, Larth ran for the next ship and hid behind its landing gear. From there, he was stuck. The guards were between him and the door to the facilities.

"I can't move," Larth whispered. "They're hanging around an old desk over near the facility door. I may have to take them out."

"Hold tight," Jyrall cautioned. "There's about to be a distraction at the small door between the hangar doors facing the tarmac. When they go see what it is, you make a break for it."

"Roger that," Larth said, buttoning his vest back up and thumbing the safety releases for his holsters. Waiting, he ran a digit over the grips of the .380s and realized he was itching to use them.

* * *

Barlung's Hangar
Parmick

Outside the hangar, Squarlik kicked a rock. The Goka was bored. They'd gone into town to help control the crowds, and they hadn't gotten to fire a shot. Now he hadn't even gotten inside duty, though it was clearly his turn. He kicked another rock, disgusted, because nothing ever happened when his posting was outside on the end of the hangar.

Squarlik heard someone or something knocking on the small metal door between the big hangar doors around the corner. He paused a moment, then decided to investigate. Looking around the corner, he saw Bweenkit walking toward the center of the building from the other side. He'd evidently heard the knocks, too. They met at the door, looked at it, then back to each other. Squarlik did a close approximation of a shoulder shrug and tried the knob. It was locked.

Suddenly the door opened, and he was looking at his team leader.

"What?" demanded Figgle. The last member of their team stood behind him with a tired, angry expression on his slimy face.

"What what?" asked Squarlik.

"What do you mean, what what?" Figgle asked, his voice rising. "You knocked on the door."

"We didn't knock on the door," Squarlik said, taken aback. "You did. We both heard three knocks."

"I didn't knock on the door, you imbecile," Figgle said. "Why in the dusty hell that this place is would I knock from the inside? I could just open the door."

"That's true," admitted Squarlik. "If you didn't knock, and we didn't knock, who did?"

"A distraction!" shouted the team leader, looking left and right as he realized the possible ruse. "You two come inside and help us search every inch of this hanger. Check the ships and make sure no one entered them, especially the shuttle!"

He never noticed the facility door close softly behind them or the slightly dented drone observing them from above the two Goka standing outside looking in.

* * *

Storage Area 23

Town Starport

Parmick

What do we do?" Lisalle asked as she watched the two Goka guards enter the hanger.

"I don't know," May said. "If they look, they'll probably find him, unless he's hid real good."

"Do we provide backup and help him?" Lisalle asked.

"I don't know," admitted May. "If we do, we'll have to take out the two guards outside and hope he can handle the ones inside. I don't know if he can; he's so little."

"He's always armed," Lisalle countered. "He wears them pistols like he knows how to use 'em."

"With those .380s, he'd have to hit a Goka in the face," May said. "He'd have to be a real good shot, unless he has some kind of armor-piercing rounds."

"Well, we can't just sit here, especially if he's ends up being on our side," Lisalle countered.

"They may just be on their own side," May suggested, "but then again, enemy of my enemy and all that."

"Well, shit!" Lisalle decided. "Hand me my rifle. I'm gonna need more than my pistol."

Before their eyes, the guard moved around the far side of the hangar, and a hovercraft darted out between the hangar and *Night Moves*, blocking the Zuparti's likely retreat. Moments later, they watched Larth ease out the window, pull it back to its original position, and look around. He ran for the fence at a dead sprint, scaled it, and dropped down on the inside of the storage area.

* * *

Storage Area 23
Town Starport
Parmick

"Change of plans," Jyrall said in his ears. "They've deployed a hovercraft. Get to the storage area and wait for the all clear."

"Copy," Larth replied as he pushed out of the hangar window.

When he hit the ground, Larth looked toward the shadowed openings of the storage containers. Just as he decided which one to hide in, he heard a shrill whistle. He looked to his right and was surprised to see May waving him toward her. With a grin, he ran for the container.

Sliding to a stop on the shadowed metal floor, Larth took a few deep breaths while May and Lisalle stared at him. Behind the women were several CASPers. Both women held rifles like they knew what they were doing.

"Hi," Larth said with his usual grin.

"Well, hey yourself, you little sneak," May said putting a hand on her hip. "Mind telling us why you were sneakin' and peekin' over yonder?"

"Mind telling me why waitresses have war machines hidden in the back of an obviously expensive storage container?" Larth countered, putting his hand on his own hip in exaggeration.

"Oh, no," May said. "I asked you first. Tell you what, I'll tell you mine if you tell me yours."

Quid pro quo, huh? I love this game.

Larth looked up and spoke into the air, "You hear that? What do you think?" he paused a moment and then said, "I agree."

He turned back to the women, but before he could speak, Lisalle asked, "Are you talking to yourself? Please tell me you have an earpiece in or sumthin'."

"I do sometimes talk to myself, but I am wearing an earpiece," Larth answered both questions honestly. "What I'm about to tell you is highly confidential. I'm talking secret squirrel shit here. Before I tell you, answer this—are you and your friends mercenaries?"

"We are," May said slowly after looking at Lisalle. "We're just between companies at the moment."

"Good," Larth said. "You're about to be hired. We're the good guys. We need to meet with all of you. Like right fucking now. How can we make this happen?"

"I knew it!" May said, and hugged Larth against her with her empty arm. Larth didn't stop her. He wasn't that crazy, after all.

"I can talk to Cora," Lisalle volunteered. "If she thinks it's a good idea to meet, we can meet you before the sun rises…at your ship, maybe?"

"Fair enough," Larth said. He turned to go. "By the way, we can include some fuel and ammunition for those as a sign-on bonus." He indicated the machines behind them. "CASPers, right? Those look like Mk 7s, if I'm right. Fairly new, and well maintained. Something tells me you ladies aren't just mercenaries, but damned good ones."

May brightened, and even Lisalle smiled for a change. The young blonde nodded. "It's been a while, but we're ready to get back into the fight."

She looked as if she was about to say something else, but they heard a tinny, amplified voice echoing throughout the starport and the town beyond. As they listened, Larth watched the color drain from the women's faces.

"Martial law?" May asked. "Something really bad must have happened."

Lisalle tapped at her slate. "Cora says to get back to the bar ASAP. Let's close this up and get moving."

May looked at Larth for a long moment. "You're really the good guys? Not joshing me or anything like that?"

Larth's eyes became distant, and she knew he was listening to the voice on the other end. "I've never heard of joshing before, sorry. I'm being as honest as I can be right now. Telling you anything else puts all of us in danger."

"We could go to the Peacemakers?" May asked hopefully.

"Somehow I don't think that's an option," Lisalle said. "We need to go, May."

"Okay," May said. She turned a tight smile to Larth. "How can we get word to you? Martial law is too dangerous to mess with."

"Barlung's idiots with guns will shoot first and ask questions later," Lisalle said. "We have to find another way to meet."

"You heard the Jeha," Larth grinned. "Curfew isn't until 2100 local. That gives us time for a drink. Something tells me not too many folks will be wandering around tonight. If Barlung initiated martial law, there's a very serious threat he's trying to honor. We're going to have to see exactly what he's trying to do before we make our next move."

* * * * *

Chapter Twenty-Five

Cora stood behind the bar at her usual station well before the bar's doors were to open for the afternoon crowd. May and Lisalle sat with Kellie at the bar, having told their story. Nileah and Cora stood silent as May and Lisalle told them about Larth's infiltration of Barlung's hangar and his request for assistance. When Cora told them what had happened in the square, not sparing any details, the three women sat silent as well. For a long time, no one spoke as their individual thoughts threatened to overwhelm them.

Cora reached into her pocket and placed the five thousand-credit chit on the bar. "Frooth gave me this. I believe it's worthless to anyone who knows better. That's the easy part. But Pete's being paid by Barlung's guy Nay-Thok, and there's no telling if any of those credits are real."

"Meaning we don't know if the credits we've managed to keep are any good." Lisalle frowned. "If they ain't, we're more stuck than we thought."

"Dammit," Kellie grunted. "If Varkell and Switch want to pay us, they might have fake diamond credits, too. What the hell do we do then?

271

Cora raised a hand. "We haven't made a decision. The miners have come to us. Well, to me, but you know what I mean. Barlung's thugs are offering to pay us a hefty sum for security—which we know is likely fake. Varkell and Larth claim to be the good guys, but there ain't no tellin' if they really are. I know you like 'em, May. They seem good, but I don't know who to trust outside of our little group."

"What about the Peacemakers?" Nileah asked.

"With Rekk being dead, the best we can hope for is that the Peacemakers realize something's wrong and come looking for him. It's weird; his office looks spotless every time I've been by, the slate on the desk and other things are in the same exact same place as they were the day before. They're cleaned off every other day or so, dusted by someone, I guess, but they don't move." Cora leaned forward on the bar on her elbows. "I know y'all don't want to hear it, but I really think we're on our own."

"I don't see it that way." Lisalle shook her head. "Even if Varkell and Switch pay us in fake credits, they can provide jump juice, ammunition, and gear. You want to help the miners, Cora? We need them. The suits don't have a full load between them."

"We can't trust them."

"We sure as hell can't trust Barlung, either," Kellie said, "and we might be able to trust and help the miners, but they ain't got a pot to piss in. Varkell and his gang took down Redd's Riders. They got all his gear. That's enough ammunition and jump juice to make it a good decision, Cora. We can always find a way out of the contract."

"Only if there was a Peacemaker around." Cora shook her head. Her chin fell to her chest, and she stood there motionless for a moment.

"They're coming by tonight, Cora," May said quietly. "We can talk to them. You can hear it straight from them. But Kellie's right; if we want to help Ledram and the miners, we have to have fuel and ammunition. Without Varkell and Switch, we're not going to have any of that."

Cora nodded and looked at the doors. "We open in five minutes. Let's get the bar ready for business. Keep your eyes and ears open, too. I haven't heard anything from Ledram, and what happened today has to push their timetable forward."

The women stood up from their barstools. Cora saw how tired they were, but in their exhaustion, she also saw dedication and duty. She tapped her holster. "Like always, ladies. Get your weapons on. Lock and load. Let's try and stay ahead of the shitstorm."

* * *

Later that evening, at 2000, Pete yelled last call, and most of the evening's paltry crowd crept out the door. Only two tables of miners remained inside, and one of those tables was a dark-haired Human woman Cora knew was deaf and only communicated by slate. None of the remaining miners ordered another beer. Pete lurched into the rear of the bar and closed the door behind him. He'd been drinking all night and would be asleep in minutes. At 2010, the doors opened, and the massive Besquith Varkell and his crew stomped into the bar. They moved to the central table, where the heavy chair capable of holding the Besquith's weight remained unoccupied, and sat down.

"Four from the tap, if you please," the Zuparti named Switch called out. Cora worked the tap quickly, and May appeared with a tray and took the tall, frothy mugs, readying them for delivery.

"No business until the others leave." Cora lowered her chin. "Not even a suggestion, May."

The young woman's eyes widened slightly, more from the tone in Cora's voice than the actual words. "Yes, Cora."

Cora winked at her. "Be yourself. Just don't overdo it."

May flushed and turned with the tray. As she moved across the bar, one table of miners tossed back their drinks and got to their feet. They trundled their way toward the door, carefully not making eye contact with the one-eyed Besquith or his friends. Kellie cleared their table quickly, and Lisalle made her way to the deaf woman, who waved her off with a smile and paid her tab before heading out.

May approached the table. "Here you go, boys. It's good to see you back again."

The Besquith nodded but said nothing. Larth grinned up at May. "We promise no tight spots this evening."

May giggled, and Cora walked around the end of the bar. She looked at Lisalle. "Check on Pete—lock the door to the apartment."

"You got it." Lisalle made her way to the back quickly, while Cora went to the front door, switched the "OPEN" sign off, and locked the doors.

May handed each of the aliens their beers and turned toward Cora. Nileah placed herself near the door. Lisalle returned from the back of the house and stood beside Kellie, ten paces away in an almost perfect covering position. Cora reminded herself to tell them later. A few months of regular jobs hadn't dulled their combat instincts.

This might just turn out okay, Cora thought.

"Why don't you and the ladies join us, Cora? Drinks are on us," the Besquith growled, and a half-grin appeared on his ragged maw.

"We're not drinking tonight," Cora said, "but thank you kindly for the offer."

Varkell nodded. He set his mug down on the table and sat back in the heavy chair. "I understand you ladies are mercenaries."

"That's right," Cora replied. "Between companies is all. It's quite a story."

"Then I'd like to hear it. The abridged version, though," Varkell said. His long snout curled in a smile. "We don't have a lot of time, and I need to know just how good you really are."

* * *

"I've never heard of Talmore's Ridge Runners." Varkell glanced at the two Pushtal sitting across from Cora. "At the risk of regretting this decision," he chuckled, "have either of you heard of them?"

The two Pushtal looked at each other for a moment. One of them spoke and Cora felt her mouth flop open in surprise. May was the only one who'd overhead them actually speak, and she wasn't quite sure what she'd heard.

"Hell, yeah we have! They was one of the more popular companies 'round our neck of the woods."

Cora coughed and found her voice. "I'm sorry? Can you say that again?"

The Pushtal grinned. "I didn't stutter, ma'am."

"Gods. You sound like you were raised in Georgia," Cora gasped. "Or you're damned good at putting on an accent."

The other Pushtal spoke. While his accent wasn't nearly as pronounced, she could hear the subtle nuances in his voice. "We were. Up north in the hill country. So we do know their company by more than reputation. They were a good crew. I understand Colonel Talmore has passed, though. Y'all have our condolences on that. He was a good man."

Cora flushed. "Thank you."

For a moment, no one spoke. The big Besquith leaned forward on the table and stared at the Zuparti. Cora tried to read the emotions in his face, but couldn't. Fighting her first impulse to sit there and do nothing, she leaned forward.

"You're worried about sharing more," she stated.

"I am. There are too many variables in play here. Seeing what's really going on here is difficult, and knowing who to trust is almost impossible. I was hoping to bring this matter to the attention of the local Peacemaker and—"

"He's dead."

The Besquith rocked backward. "What did you say?"

"Peacemaker Rekk is dead. I watched Barlung and his two lackeys gun him down in the street a couple of weeks ago," Cora replied.

"No one else has said anything about it," Switch said.

"There are only two people who saw it. A Jivool miner named Ledram, and me. Frooth and Cartrule were roughing him up in the street. Rekk appeared, and they stopped beating Ledram and started after the Peacemaker. Barlung was in the alley behind Rekk and gunned him down. He told his crew to incinerate the body and make sure no one messed with his office. Someone's cleaning it every day or two to keep up the ruse."

The Besquith shook his head. "Why would Barlung gun down the Peacemaker if he's trying to be a legitimate businessman?"

"There's nothing legitimate about this business," Cora replied. She reached into her pocket. "Would a thug working for a legitimate businessman throw around a five thousand-credit chit?"

"They might," Switch grinned, "but it wouldn't be good business in the long run."

"Especially when the diamond in the middle is fake," Cora agreed.

Varkell barked. "What?"

Cora took a deep breath. "I deliver the profits from the bar to Nay-Thok, the Jeha who works for Barlung. Day before yesterday, I saw a whole bunch of documentation about diamond synthesis, and more red diamonds than I've ever imagined. There were some real fragments there, but I think Barlung is manufacturing fakes."

The Besquith ran a huge clawed paw over his face. "Is that what the miners challenged Barlung about in the street?"

Cora nodded. "One of them held up a diamond that couldn't possibly have been found in a mine that hasn't produced anything more than slivers in the last several years. They pull all sorts of stuff, metals and gems, out of the mine, but a red diamond the size of a shooter marble? No way."

"Shooter marble?" Varkell looked at the Pushtal.

"Long story. We can explain later, Boss," Keaton said.

The Besquith shook his head, and Cora heard the Zuparti snicker. A moment later, Switch cleared his throat and caught the Besquith's eye. "Is there anything else we should know, ladies?"

"The miners are planning to revolt against Barlung," Cora said. "I don't know when, but they asked for our help. I'm prepared to do just that."

The Besquith stared at the bolted doors for a long moment. "Time is running short, and it appears things here are worse than we thought."

"That's an understatement," Switch said. "We want to hire you ladies. Your payment is the ship we took from Redd's Riders, and all its gear, along with whatever jump juice and ammunition you need for your CASPers. With the miner revolt coming, and Barlung's declaration of martial law, things are going to explode very soon."

Varkell reached into his belt and pulled out a small, hexagonal device. He touched it on the top and a series of lights flashed. When they stopped, he looked up at Cora. She'd never seen a device like it, but it wasn't hard to guess that Varkell didn't want any more of their conversation potentially heard.

"Having allies we can trust," the Besquith growled softly, "is vital. I believe the time for formal introductions has come. Cora, please tell us your team's names so we can become better acquainted."

Cora hesitated. "I'm not sure about working with you, Varkell. No offense meant."

"None taken." The Besquith actually smiled. "I think we'd all like to know more about each other."

May spoke up. "I'm May Bolton. I was a specialist in the Ridge Runners."

"Lisalle Jones." The brunette woman smiled and waved with one hand. "I was a maintenance sergeant."

"Nileah Sevier. Heavy weapons."

"Kellie English. Recon."

They looked to Cora. "I was their squad leader. Staff Sergeant Cora McCoy."

The two Pushtal gasped loudly and flinched. Cora saw all of her team do the same. One of the Pushtal stood slowly. "You did say McCoy, didn't you?"

"I-I did." Cora's hands came up defensively. "Is something wrong?"

"Where are you from Cora?" one of the Pushtal asked. "You picked up my brother's accent as Georgia. Where are you from?"

"North Carolina. Murphy, North Carolina," she said.

The Pushtal whirled on his brother who also stood. "Esther Mae, right?"

A rush of electricity flashed down Cora's back. "Esther Mae McCoy was my grandmother. How in the hell do you—"

"Her younger brother's name was Milton Gene McCoy. He left home at eighteen and headed out as a merc, even spent some time in Intergalactic Haulers. He found us on a mission twenty-four years ago and raised us." The Pushtal were grinning from ear to ear. "I'm Keaton McCoy, and this is my brother Ricky."

"You've got to be shitting me!" Cora exclaimed and shook her head. For a long moment, no one said anything. Cora sat forward with her elbows on the table and her left hand cradling her forehead. "I can't believe this is happening. I have so many questions."

A soft chime sounded from one of the Pushtals' slates, and the Besquith stood abruptly. "We have to leave. There'll be time to further acquaint ourselves, provided the miners don't initiate their insurrection come morning."

"There's just one more thing," the Zuparti said and reached into his vest pocket. "Are we certain this place is totally secure?"

Keaton nodded and tapped his slate. "I'm jamming everything in the area, and that elSha thingie is doubling down on it."

"You're certain about this?" The Besquith grunted. "I'm not sure the timing is right."

"And if things go to hell in a handbasket tomorrow?" Keaton asked. "I mean, it's your call, but we needed help, and we've got it."

"Good help, too," Ricky said. He turned to Cora and winked.

"Partner?" the Zuparti said, looking at the Besquith. "I'm sure. Does that help?"

"You're afraid of nothing." He laughed and reached into the bandolier across his chest. He pulled out a black folding case and opened it. Laying it on the table, the Besquith stood to his full height.

"I am Peacemaker Jyrall. This is my partner, Peacemaker Larth. We're on a clandestine mission at the direction of the guild master himself. Well met."

Nobody moved. Cora saw Lisalle smile. Nileah raised a hand to her open mouth and covered it in a mix of happiness and surprise. Kellie appeared surprised, and a soft grin spread across her face. May squealed and wrapped her arms around the Zuparti's neck.

"He's Peacemaker Larth. Not Switch. Gods, I hope I can remember that," she said through her grin.

Peacemaker Jyrall extended a hand to Cora. "Well met, Cora. Welcome to our team."

"Thank you, Peacemaker."

"Tomorrow," the Besquith raised his voice, "you ladies will take possession of the ship and move your gear from the weapons container to the hull itself. Ricky and Keaton will ensure the ship's security systems are programmed and ready for you. Once we've made sure your CASPers are ready for action, we can discuss our options."

"There's just one outlier," Cora said. "The miners. I'll see what I can do about getting more information from them."

"And we need to learn more specifics about our opposition." Larth pointed at the ladies. "Something tells me you all have lots of information on the mercenaries that roost around here. We'll need to figure out how to skin the Oogar, so to speak."

There was a soft chime, and both Jyrall and Larth looked at their slates for a moment before locking eyes with each other.

"What is it?" Keaton asked.

Larth replied, "That shuttle I saw? From the *Strong Arm?*"

"Yeah."

"It just departed from the starport and is heading to the gate." Larth frowned. "Can you guys figure out where it's going?"

"Well it's too small to use the gate," Ricky said. "Wait. *Strong Arm.* I know that name. That's the gunboat from Victoria Bravo."

"Precisely," Jyrall said. "Can you guys figure out where it's going somehow?"

"No, Boss," Ricky said. "Not without breaking our cover."

"Why not do it the old-fashioned way?" May said. "We can go down to the starport and ask tomorrow."

Jyrall's eyes narrowed. "Why would any of the mercenaries down there tell you anything?"

"You don't know the power of homemade baked goods, Peacemaker," Nileah replied. "I'll get the oven fired up, Cora."

Larth's nose twitched. "What am I missing here? You're going to cook something and take it to the mercs?"

"A little bribery never hurt anyone," Cora replied. "And the second fastest way to a merc's heart is through the stomach. Those Goka are pretty easy to bribe."

"And the first fastest way to a merc's heart?" Jyrall asked. "Credits."

Keaton slapped his brother on the shoulder. "See? We're going to make mercenaries of them yet."

Ricky leaned over to Nileah. "An oven? Like a real oven? Not a zero-G thing?"

"Real. Runs on gas, too." Nileah smiled.

"Would y'all mind if we threw some fish sticks in there?" Ricky beamed.

"Fish?" Cora replied. "We haven't had seafood in months."

"Well, then, once our business is completed, I think a little feast might be in order," Jyrall said. "But until then, we keep our distance, and when we are seen together, it's business. Our identities are secret, and we must all play our roles. Our very lives, and the lives of many innocent people here on Parmick, will depend on this. Can I trust you all to do this?"

Around the group there were nods of assent. Cora saw smiles on the faces of the women, and the Pushtal brothers grinned widely at each other. Jyrall and Larth were quiet, but with satisfied expressions on their faces. She instantly recognized the mood and feeling of the room.

Camaraderie and esprit de corps were subjects thoroughly dissected by Colonel Talmore during his professional development meetings with his leaders of all ranks. Humans, in particular, rally around the idea and thrive on such things. Cora and her soldiers were a team who genuinely cared for each other, like a family. The impossible revelation of a familial connection, not blood but still family, between herself and the Pushtal twins had likely shocked Jyrall and Larth, but it was easy to accept. Ten minutes before they were complete strangers. The realization of a family connection tied them together. In some places Humans didn't necessarily have that type of connection. But in Appalachia, the mere connection of one person to another by blood or close relationship immediately tied a sturdy knot between them.

The kind of knot Cora knew was about to be tested, maybe even slashed at, by the sword of violence.

Cora smiled up at the Besquith. "We'll be ready, Peacemaker Jyrall."

"My name is Jyrall, Cora. And I believe you are correct." He glanced at Larth. "Anything else we need, partner?"

Larth frowned and fiddled with his vest. "Do you ladies happen to have any ketchup in your kitchen of wonders? We're about out."

* * * * *

Chapter Twenty-Six

It was still early morning when Cora and her troops arrived at their storage containers.

Cora, Lisalle, and Kellie ran the start-up procedures for their CASPers. The plan was for them to make two trips from the storage containers to the frigate on the far side of the tarmac, using the CASPers to carry their personal gear. On the second trip, Cora and Lisalle would bring the last two over. May and Nileah had their own mission to accomplish.

The shortest route between their storage area and the frigate took them right past Barlung's hanger and the guards outside it. The route was desperately needed, given that three of the machines were in the red on power. The long trip around was a risk they couldn't take. It was likely one or two wouldn't make the distance more than once.

"Hey," May said to the Goka standing in front of the door facing the road. He was one of six back on duty, one per side of the hanger, and two inside. "Could I talk to your sergeant? We need a favor."

Squarlik stared for a moment at the audacity of the Human female in walking right up to him. Realizing she'd asked him a question, he answered, "This area is restricted. You need to go back across the road, Human. Wait? What favor? And what are you carrying? It smells delicious."

"Well, since you asked," Nileah said as she pulled the cloth from the top of the container. "I made some cookies for your sergeant, if he'll let us bring our gear between these hangers to our ship."

"My sergeant?" Squarlik asked. The Goka visibly sagged, and the women knew why. Sergeants got all the good stuff, especially the inside duty every day.

"Yes, but…" Nileah looked around conspiratorially, "I can give you a few now before you bring me inside to ask his permission. Sergeants don't need to know everything, you know."

Squarlik stood straight, delighted. "I like the way you think. Yes, I'll have a few before I bring you inside."

May reached into the container, pulled out three, and handed the cookies to the Goka. He sniffed them, gave the closest thing a Goka could give to a grin, and stuffed one in his mouth. Dropping crumbs, he chewed rapidly, his mouth making an almost complete circle as it moved. "Mffffttt delisciousssss," he said around his mouthful. After he swallowed the last of the cookie, he placed the others in a small pouch on his harness. "I'll save those for later. Come. We'll speak to Sergeant Figgle. Maybe he'll give me a fair share of the rest."

"I like the way you think," confided Nileah with a wink.

Squarlik walked through the front door into the open bay with the two women right behind him. Closing the door behind them, he led the women over to the desk in the corner. The sergeant looked up from the protein sludge bar he was opening, dropped it, and scrambled to his feet.

Figgle looked from the Goka to the other women incredulously, as if Squarlik had grown an extra head. "What are you doing?" he demanded. "No unauthorized individuals in or around the hanger. How hard is that to understand?"

"But they asked to speak to you personally," Squarlik explained, "and they have a gift for all of us." He attempted to wink at Nileah but the muscles in his race's face couldn't accomplish the feat. Instead he just squinted.

"What gift?" asked Figgle, suddenly interested in the container Nileah was holding.

"We made these as a payment for a verbal contract with you," May said, laying on the charm. "We'd like to move some gear to our ship, and going between this hanger and the next is the shortest route. We thought we'd ask your permission, so the ten or eleven guards you have everywhere outside won't stop us."

"Well," Figgle said as he leaned forward and sniffed deeply. "I don't have quite that many guards, but they are well trained, and exceptionally well led, so they may appear to be everywhere at once, you understand. Are those Human cookies?"

"They are," confirmed Nileah as she took one out and handed it to the Goka. "I made them with the very last of my chocolate; I've been saving it."

The cookie quickly disappeared into the sergeant's face. With crumbs falling, he pronounced them excellent and reached for another. It beat his protein bar by light years.

"Not so fast," Nileah said, pulling the container away. "Will you accept these as payment for allowing us to pass through to our ship? It'll take more than one trip."

"Yes, yes of course," Figgle said, "but I want them all for the payment."

"Well, alrighty then," May said. "Thank you kindly."

Nileah placed the container on the old desk, and Figgle sat down to enjoy more of them. They stood patiently until he'd finished another. He looked up right before he put another cookie in his mouth and noticed they were still standing there.

"You can go now," Figgle said. "Squarlik will let the others know I've given permission." After a moment he said, "Squarlik, you may take them two cookies each."

"Thank you very much," May said. "You do a fine job taking care of your troops. Say, where's that small shuttle? I saw it once before rolling into the hanger. It's real nice. No wonder they have someone like you watching over it."

Figgle sat up straight and looked over to the empty spot on the other side of the hanger. "Yes, yes I do. That ship? It took off last night. Off to find something or other." He stuffed another cookie in his mouth after Squarlik finished counting out cookies.

"Oh," May said, smiling, "well, I hope they find it. Whatever it was."

"I doubt they will," Figgle confided, reaching for another cookie. "I never even heard of what they are looking for."

"That seems so strange to me," Nileah said getting into the act. "A leader of your intelligence knows everything happening in this system, for sure."

"That's true," agreed Figgle, as Squarlik made a face, such as his race could do, behind his leader's back. "But they are leaving this system looking for a… Kurrang. Whatever that is."

"Oh, okay," May said. "Well, thanks again. We'll get to moving our gear now."

Figgle didn't bother to watch them leave. He just continued to stuff his face. After a few more cookies, he pushed the partially open protein sludge bar off his desk into a small waste container and reached for another.

Outside, Nileah turned to Squarlik. "I saw you count ten of those cookies. There's only four of you out here. Nice. You keep thinking the way you do, and you'll lead your own unit one day.'

Squarlik stood straight. "I will. Wait and see. I'll go tell the others to leave you be. What will you be moving?"

"Oh, just some CASPers and stuff. Bye," May said sweetly as they walked away from the Goka guard with his mouth wide open, this time with no cookie in it.

* * *

Riding High
Airfield
Town, Parmick

The last Mk 7 CASPer walked up the ramp to a maintenance rack and backed in. The hatch opened. Ricky was standing in front of it when Cora looked out and prepared to exit. She paused a moment, perplexed by the look on Ricky's face. His brother Keaton stood slightly behind him.

"Hey, Lucille," Ricky said quietly.

"Ricky, my name is Cora, remember?" Cora said.

"I know," Ricky answered, glancing up at Cora. "We're kin, I won't ever forget your name."

"He's talking to your CASPer," Keaton explained. "He names dang near anything he builds or works on."

"Did you work on this one?" Cora asked. "It looked practically brand new when it was delivered for my eighteenth birthday. Is that why it has an extra hour of power in the fuel cell and it holds a little more jump juice?"

"She," said Ricky, reaching out to pat the machine. "She has an extra hour of operational time. Yeah, I did that. A few other little things, too. I was a teenager when Pops and I broke her down and worked on her. Well, I did, mostly. Pops didn't need to climb all over and down inside a CASPer by then. He was gettin' on up there, you know. Lucille was an old girlfriend of his. I always liked that name."

"I've had to work on it—her—a few times," said Lisalle as she glanced at some of the obvious repair sites on the machine.

"Yeah," Ricky said. "That's going to happen if you use 'em right. You just fix 'em again. Looks like you did a good job from here. You want to help me work on the others later? I noticed a hitch in the step of the one Kellie brought in. Probably a servo motor. We can pull a part off one of those Stein wrecked. The bottom half on 'em are fine."

Lisalle beamed. "Sure. Let me get the software updates running on the racks and we'll do it."

Larth put his paws in the pockets of his vest and rocked back on his heels. "Looks like we're all here, Boss. Any words of wisdom before the ladies have to get back to the bar?"

"A few, really," Jyrall said as he sat on a heavy maintenance crate that would support his mass. "Down to business. There are five Mk 7s capable of operations. There are two here that need major work, and there are the three wrecks Ricky says you can still pull parts from. Plus, there are several parts in the maintenance room here on the ship."

"Speaking of ship," Keaton interjected, "the ship is now ready to receive your security codes and other crew recognitions for all the systems to operate. All you have to use is the master code, which will be the first one you enter, and the ship is yours."

"Ours?" Cora whispered as a small tear fell. She wiped it away quickly. "Can we rename it now?" she asked, her voice stronger. Now was not the time for tears.

"You can," Keaton confirmed. "Have y'all already decided?"

"We have," Cora said. "We want to name her *Blue Ridge*."

"Nice," Keaton said with a grin.

"I like it," Ricky agreed. "What are you calling your mercenary company?"

"Our what?" Cora asked, surprised.

"Your company," Larth explained. "Keaton can work a little magic and transfer the license from Redd to you. He can't give it to all of you, I don't think, but he can to you."

Cora turned to the other four women, looking for their input. The smiles on their faces almost made her shed another tear. She was their squad leader, and now she would become their company commander. None of them had any doubt she'd share in the gains of the unit, and they understood someone had to own the company and hold the license. They were too close for jealousy.

Cora turned back to the Peacemakers. "Kin," she said. "We'll be the Blue Ridge Kin. Everyone who is accepted into this company will know from the very beginning, we treat each other like family. No matter where they hail from, no matter their race, they're some kin of ours."

Larth met Jyrall's eyes. "That's family, Snarlyface."

"I actually understood that reference, Larth." Jyrall frowned.

"I'd kill some sumbitch over my kin," Ricky said to no one in particular. "That's a fact."

His statement eased the tension, and everyone laughed at what he'd said and how he'd said it. Jyrall and Larth looked at each other with a satisfied smile. They'd made the right choice with this small unit. It was the profound truth felt by every being on the ship.

Jyrall turned to May and Nileah. "The cameras Ricky slipped into your clothes weren't seen? You're sure?"

Nileah nodded. "They were too busy sniffing the cookies to even give us a second look. Kinda like your unnecessary eyepatch; Ricky told us your secret. Most aliens just accept others as being different and don't pay 'em no mind."

"You have the playback, Ricky?"

"All I gotta do is press play," Ricky said. "The ladies can walk us through what they saw with their eyes, and I can pull all the CASPer cameras, too."

Larth pointed at May. "You said I was a sneak the other day. I think it takes one to know one."

May smiled. "You ain't gonna believe what we learned about Barlung's hangars."

* * *

The reconnaissance data was so thorough that no one minded Cora reviewing it one last time. "Okay, we have the north and south hangars. The north hangar is the one Larth snuck into. We know there are two ships remaining there. The shuttle from *Strong Arm* departed yesterday."

Larth nodded. "It must have met up with a ship and went through the gate. There's no telling where it went."

"We'll come back to that in a minute," Jyrall said. He looked at Cora. "Keep going, please."

"The north hangar has four guards and a really basic security system. Mainly cameras mounted on the exterior of the building. We saw no drones or ground robots there. They obviously just hold the ships there." Cora took a breath. "The south hangar is a little more problematic. They have enough ammunition and weapons to outfit three hundred soldiers of just about any species. With all the hiring Barlung has done lately, that's probably a pretty accurate figure."

May chimed in, her face serious, "There are six CASPers in the hangar, too. They're tucked back away from the entrance, but I saw them. Squarlik let us look in for a promise of more cookies next time we make them. Maintenance racks suggested they were Mk 4s, but they might be Mk 5 capable. I couldn't see what gear they had with them. That whole section of the hangar is a hot mess."

"Which means either they aren't expecting to use them, or they don't have qualified pilots," Nileah said.

"And the armored skiffs?" Keaton asked. "They look real similar to the ones from Victoria Bravo. The ones that tore Force 25 a new ass, if I'm not mistaken."

"I reviewed that video too many times to count," Jyrall said as he wiped the side of his face with one paw. "They don't appear to have the same armor construct as the ones on Victoria, but they are Besquith designed. They're weak when attacked from the rear."

"That's what she said!" Ricky giggled.

The women laughed, and Larth put his face in his paws as Jyrall semi-exploded. "No one said anything!"

"I think that's the point." Larth grinned. "Innuendo."

"In your end—" Ricky blurted, and the group dissolved with laughter.

Jyrall sat with his head in his hands. "Will someone explain that nonsense to me later? Please? I can't take much more of this stupid humor."

Larth pointed at Ricky. "Don't say it again."

"Aw, man."

The group, minus one very large Besquith, laughed.

After a moment, Jyrall bemusedly nodded at Cora and the women. "Thank you for the information. The hangars are definitely a concern. When the miners revolt, we can expect the miners to try and take them."

"Even with the fencing and security?" Kellie asked.

"They'll need weapons. Either they're going to hit the starport to get them, or they'll try to secure them in Town," Jyrall replied.

"Or they're going to try to do this with pickaxes and shovels." Larth frowned. Half a second later, he gasped. "That's at least part of their plan. Contain security forces in the mine while the ladies take out the guards here and secure the hangars. I mean, that's what I'd want them to do. With weapons, and cutting off supplies to Barlung's thugs, they'll have the advantage."

"That would make sense," Jyrall agreed.

"They haven't spoken to me about their plan," Cora replied. Her eyebrows raised. "I'm going to have to push them for that information, huh?"

"To the extent you can without attracting attention, yes," Jyrall said. "And a timetable for their revolt would be nice. The distraction will give us the opportunity to raid Barlung's offices and secure the evidence for counterfeiting currency and whatever else they're doing."

"And the murder of a Peacemaker," Cora added. "I'm prepared to give a statement if you need one."

"We will, but that can wait," Larth said. "You said we'd get back to the ship, Snarlyface. What did you mean?"

Jyrall held up a paw and pointed at the Zuparti. "You're going to break into the Peacemaker's office. We have to get a message out about *Strong Arm's* shuttle having been here. It's a piece of the puzzle to Kr'et'Socae's whereabouts."

"Who?" Cora asked.

Jyrall's lower jaw worked. "A disgraced Enforcer. We believe he's behind what's going on here, and we know he was behind the attack on Victoria Bravo. To what end, nobody knows."

"Let's just say he's accumulating charges and crimes faster than kudzu grows," Keaton smiled at the ladies. All of them grinned in return.

"What's kudzu?" Larth asked.

"It's a plant," Ricky said.

"An invasive plant, also called Japanese arrowroot, that's all over where we come from. It grows over everythin' in its path," Keaton explained.

"Y'all remember how to plant kudzu, right?" May asked.

Lisalle rolled her eyes. "Clear an acre, plant a kudzu seed in the middle of it, and run like hell."

"So it's fast," Jyrall said.

"Keep up, Snarlyface," Larth chittered. "I'll get to work on a recon of the Peacemaker's office. Shouldn't be a problem to get in and out."

Jyrall nodded and pointed at Cora. "Lastly, you ladies need to be careful. Your baked goods notwithstanding, Barlung knows you have a ship and possess CASPers now. He'll try to buy your services, and when you tell him you're with us, he'll either continue to try to buy your loyalty, or he'll suspect we're moving against him."

"What should we do?" Kellie asked. "Play him?"

"No," Jyrall said. "Don't put yourselves in a place where he has anything to hold over your heads. This was a business deal between you and Varkell. If he presses, have him take it up with me. I'll be glad to lay out our arrangement for him. You're my employees, and we're preparing for additional missions supporting Barlung or the highest local bidders. That ought to keep him satisfied. For now, at least."

Cora opened her mouth and glanced at Ricky. "We have a saying about poking the—"

"No more!" Jyrall's stare evaporated into a grin, which turned into a heartfelt guffaw. "I'm glad we banter like friends, but the time is coming very quickly when we'll have to be serious. It may be the only way we walk out of this situation. I'd prefer we all did so together."

The smiles slowly vanished around the room. Jyrall met each of their eyes for a moment and opened his paws to them. "Anything else before you ladies head to the bar?"

May spoke up. "Oh yeah, I almost forgot. There were a few shipment records on the desk that said Weber Six—that's in the Myrcu system, so that's something. But when we asked where the shuttle went, the Goka sergeant said they left to go find something called a Kurrang. Whatever that is."

Larth's mouth fell open, and he and Jyrall stared at each other for moment. "Oh, shit."

"We have to get into the Peacemaker's office immediately," Jyrall said. "This is more than just that *Strong Arm* and its shuttle were here."

"And it all makes sense now," Larth answered. "They're synthesizing red diamonds, but they're not perfect. They're going after a way to do just that."

"I don't understand," Cora said. "What's a Kurrang?"

"Not a what, a who," Jyrall replied. "Kurrang is a TriRusk. Some of their young have a condition that causes them to synthesize diamonds in their waste. Those diamonds were typically used for industrial uses several centuries ago, because they're nearly flawless and can replace actual ones at a fraction of the cost."

"And if Kr'et'Socae wants to counterfeit red diamonds for currency manipulation, only the most experienced gemologists of the guilds would be able to stop him. They'd be traded on common markets, and no one would be the wiser." Larth frowned. "Economic meltdown."

"You think he's doing this himself?" Keaton asked.

"Nah, I'd say that sumbitch is working for the Mercenary Guild." Ricky shook his head. "Never trusted any of them assholes. No offense, ladies."

"None taken, Ricky," Cora replied. "They never thought much of us Humans before the war started. We ain't never thought much of most of them either."

* * * * *

Chapter Twenty-Seven

Mining Operations Center
Parmick

Barlung sat back on his haunches on the floor instead of using a chair. Leaning over the gray metal table, he cradled his massive head in his equally massive paws. His heart pumped blood so hard he felt it inside his ears. Had his eyes been open, there was little doubt his vision would've been clouded purple by the volume of blood swirling in his suddenly aching head.

"They brought you *what?*" he asked.

"Cookies," Figgle replied with a pronounced fidget. "They wanted to use the walkway between the hangars to move their gear, and they paid with cookies."

"And you thought this was an acceptable form of payment?" Barlung raised his head. "You compromised the security of our hangars for Human *cookies?*"

"They never came into the hangars, save for my office," Figgle replied. "The guards watched them move their equipment pallets and mechs the entire time. The whole operation took less than half an hour."

The Goka's words stuck in Barlung's head for a moment. "Did you say mechs? Those women have CASPers?"

"Their equipment containers were sizable enough that it was always a—"

"You confirmed they have them. How many?"

"Five," Figgle said. "They're not in good shape. A couple of them appeared to be as scarred as the Mk 4s in our storage area. The ones Redd would never purchase?"

"I'm aware that Redd didn't want them because of their condition and their age."

"The women's mechs seemed better, at any rate."

Barlung shook his head. The condition of the CASPers didn't matter. The simple fact that they were there meant the women might be in a position to be hired as pilots or, even better, as instructors to teach some of the inexperienced Human mercenaries how to drive the machines. He shook away the thought process. "They moved their equipment to Redd's old frigate?"

"Yes. From what it looked like, Varkell either signed it over to them or gave it to them."

Barlung squinted. "Varkell would do no such thing. He's an astute smuggler who knows what's good for his crew. He obviously hired them."

He left the other thought silent. *Hired them to do what?*

As quickly as he'd thought of the possibility of having the Humans teach other pilots, he realized what Varkell had done. His team was good, but they needed additional muscle. The Human women were down on their luck and without a company or transportation. Varkell had signed them on and provided transportation in exchange for the security and power their CASPers could project in a fight.

That Besquith is sharp. I wonder if he thinks he's sharp enough to challenge me.

He couldn't be thinking that, could he?

Barlung knew from experience that such things were possible. At the earliest opportunity, he'd sit down with Varkell and have a long, one-sided conversation. As long as the mercenary wanted to remain in Barlung's employ, he would have to understand his place. If he wanted to hire the Human women, that was fine, but anything that appeared to be a play for power would have to be dealt with swiftly.

"Well, he might have hired them. It was hard to tell. As the Humans moved their gear, and the two Pushtal scowled and followed them in and out of the ship every time."

Barlung nodded and felt his concern lighten perceptibly. "He's hired them. They need a way off this planet, and he has a bunch of Human equipment he can't possibly use or sell, given the state of the Mercenary Guild right now. He needs help to do so."

"But wouldn't the Humans be worth more if Varkell simply turned them, and all that gear, over to the Mercenary Guild directly?" Figgle asked, his eyes downcast and away from the Oogar.

It was an intriguing thought, enough to make him wonder about what price the Humans could bring to his operation, before he remembered his other commitments. "Varkell's business is his business. If he does something to betray my trust, it'll become my business, but not before then."

"And what of the women and the ship itself?"

"Add it to the security profiles. Ensure there are cameras on it at all times, but don't approach without my orders," Barlung said. "And furthermore, no one is allowed within fifty meters of our hangars again. Accept no visitors and no more gods-damned bribes. Is that clear, Sergeant Figgle?"

The Goka ducked its chin in a bow. "Yes, Barlung."

The inner office door opened, and Nay-Thok wiggled into the room. The Jeha glanced harshly at Figgle before looking at Barlung.

"Sir? I have those numbers you asked me for. Would you care to go over them now?"

Barlung nodded. "Back to the starport, Figgle. Report anything unusual. You have your orders—don't make me repeat them again."

The Goka moved from the room at what amounted to a sprint for the species. Barlung's eyes were almost level with the Jeha's, and the millipedic alien's antennae were rigid with anger.

"Your personnel and their lack of operational security skills are going to end this entire endeavor before we deliver, Barlung."

Barlung snorted. "The mine is secure. I have every hired gun on Parmick working for me in some way, and we continue to pull fragments from the new shafts every hour. My part of this operation is working just fine. Your synthesis plant and its lack of success is the issue."

Nay-Thok chittered and stepped forward. A stunstick Barlung hadn't seen appeared in the Jeha's pincers and hovered in front of his nose. The end of the stick pulsated with purple sparks of electricity. "Remember your place, animal."

Anger coursed through Barlung's blood, but he sat motionless, staring past the stick into the Jeha's black eyes. "Kr'et'Socae will not be pleased."

"On the contrary," the Jeha's antennae danced with laughter, "the additional intelligence gained from the Peacemaker's files have given our benefactor the very real possibility of expanding delivery of our counterfeits into the central core of the Union itself. We're long past the idea of making money off the uneducated backwater colonies of the three arms, Barlung. Kr'et'Socae is going after the guilds. He'll soon have enough cash to buy the loyalty of the Mercenary Guild outright—he won't even have to take it with his forces. But he must feed and arm them for operations, and he will certainly do so. After that, he devalues the red diamond, and the Merchant Guild falls. He can broker for almost anything. I will have given that to him. You'll be rewarded for your work, but let's not forget who has the responsibility for this operation, shall we?"

Barlung grunted. "I am aware of the arrangement you have, Nay-Thok. And mine."

"Good. I want your assurance that the mine and the laboratory spaces on levels four and six are protected by armed soldiers at all times. The miners are going to try something soon. Their pathetic protests and apathetic work are proof positive of that. If you haven't seen that, you're even more of an idiot than I feared."

"I am not an idiot!" Barlung flared. The stunstick inched closer to his face.

"I'd suggest you prove that, Barlung," Nay-Thok replied. "The required shipment will be ready in four days. Begin the transport and loading of the second-class materials to the frigates immediately. Double the guards at the starport, as well."

"The guards will demand more funds."

"Then pay them with the counterfeits. It doesn't matter. We'll be far away when they realize the truth." Nay-Thok moved toward his inner office. "One more thing. I want the mine destroyed when we leave."

Barlung squinted. "We don't have the demolition capability, and *Strong Arm* departed yesterday."

"I'd suggest you figure out a way to destroy all the evidence, then. Your life depends on it."

"And why is that?" Barlung felt what backbone he had flex.

Nay-Thok twisted his head back to stare at him. "It's what Kr'et'Socae wants."

The inner office door shut and locked, leaving Barlung staring at it for several minutes before he stood and moved to carry out Nay-Thok's orders. As he did, the Oogar smiled. A few of his own orders would certainly help his situation.

Chaos only requires a few. Sometimes only one.

* * * * *

Chapter Twenty-Eight

J yrall and Larth headed to the credit exchange. As usual, they were followed closely by Keaton and Ricky, except they were bunched together more than normal. They walked past the Peacemaker's Office and saw it was empty, as usual.

Jyrall, Keaton, and Ricky walked past the narrow opening between the buildings and turned to go into the exchange. Jyrall intended to make change for another one thousand-credit chit to simulate paying his help and perhaps conduct other business.

Staying low in the shadows, Larth eased down the small alley until he reached the only window on that side of the Peacemaker's building. Larth pulled a device out of his pocket and checked to make sure it still showed a green circle on the small screen. According to Keaton, once activated, none of the cameras in the vicinity of the device would record properly.

It didn't scramble the signal, it simply caused the camera to shut down and restart over and over again, simulating a normal malfunction. Glancing up to the corner of the building, he could see the small device. Whoever was on duty would send someone to check the device, and they would find a faulty camera with no evidence of tampering. There was no telling how soon that would be, so he had to move quickly.

Reaching up to the window, he found it locked. Upon closer examination, he felt confident he could slide a small blade in and pop the lock. The building was old and never intended to be secure, unlike the credit exchange next to it. The window rattled slightly as he unlocked it.

Larth slid the window up enough to slip through. Glancing around the small bathroom, he reached up and slid the window back down until it almost locked. He ducked low and pushed the door open, and crawled into the Peacemaker's main office.

He stayed as low as possible until he was behind the desk. Had anyone been watching through the front window, they'd have seen a small hand reach up and pull the slate off the desk. Safely hidden, Larth turned the device on, prepared to enter the overriding master command on the small terminal. All Peacemakers memorized several password overrides, enabling them to use equipment in other's offices or ships in an emergency. This most definitely qualified as such an occasion.

Larth brought up the desired program, entered yet another set of codes, and waited until the StormWatch screen loaded. He quickly typed in the report, classified it for Dreel's eyes only, and hit send. The secure message couldn't be interrupted or broken without proper coding, which only Peacemakers possessed. He'd added the extra measures given by Captain Dreel so not even another Peacemaker would be able to crack it. The precaution was deemed necessary, given that several Peacemakers had been compromised, including the two Larth and Jyrall had stopped during their confirmation mission a year before.

Larth turned the slate off once the message finished sending. The message would find its way with the next ship traveling through the gate and would enter the communications network shortly thereafter. It would be a week before the message could reach its intended recipient. Larth hoped it wouldn't be too late. With a flurry of codes, he erased his use of the slate entirely, and then wiped it clean of any residue from his fur. He made sure to put it back on the desk in exactly the same position. He quickly made his escape through the facilities' door and out the window. Once back in the alleyway, he closed the window, moved to the end, crouched low, and waited.

Several minutes later, he heard Jyrall speaking. "If we don't get the interest that teller promised, I'll come back and have a little wall-to-wall conversation with him."

One of the brothers growled, letting Larth know they were close. He stood up and stepped in with them as they made their way toward the other end of town and Pete's. The group's conversation with Jyrall was about the new account, as if nothing else had transpired.

* * *

Mining Operations Building
Parmick

Nay-Thok held the eyepiece closer to his eye and studied the red diamond intently. Sighing, he put it down and chose another. Glancing up at his monitors, he noticed a black screen in the rotation of cameras. He quickly tapped a command into his terminal and the entire monitor showed the same black screen.

Cross checking the rotation sequence, he determined it was the camera covering the corner of the alley between the Peacemaker's office and the credit exchange. The Jeha tapped a few more commands, and he could see One-Eyed Varkell and his three companions walking down that side of the street. He grew suspicious, especially with the group near the malfunctioning piece of equipment.

He'd noticed them earlier walking past Pete's Dive Bar. Considering the time it should take to make that trip and open the account, the only solution was a faulty camera, but this was one of the newer models, unlike the ones covering the hanger at the airfield. He decided to check something before having Barlung and his guards round them up for questioning.

Reaching for his comm, he called the teller in the exchange. "Did Varkell and his crew come into the exchange?" he demanded.

On the other end of the call, the nervous voice answered immediately and without thinking. "Yes sir, they opened another account with us." He didn't bother to say three of them entered and not the usual four.

"I see," Nay-Thok said, his suspicions eased. "There's a problem with the camera covering the alley. Have one of your security guards climb up, take it down, and bring it directly to me for examination."

"Yes, s—" Nay-Thok ended the call before the teller could finish.

* * *

Pete's Dive Bar
Town, Parmick

Jyrall, Larth, and the brothers walked through the door of the bar and were surprised to see it busy. They made their way to their usual table. As they settled in and waited for one of the waitresses, all four of them overheard a rather large Jivool make a snide comment about reserved seating.

Looking at the offender, Jyrall asked, "You got a problem?"

"If I did, I'd handle it," bluffed the Jivool. Around him several other Jivool laughed.

"Is that so?" Jyrall growled, intent on maintaining his persona as Varkell.

Behind the Jivool, fifteen others at various tables stood, ready to back their commander. At the farthest table, two Miderall stood after looking back and forth from the huge one-eyed Besquith and their commander.

Jyrall did a double take. It wasn't often one saw the avian race outside their home system of Miderall. True to their nature, these two were dressed in bright colors, never designed to go well together. It was all in stark contrast to their pink feathers and their deep orange bills. Around their bobbing necks were gaudy necklaces of purple and gold beads.

Before the situation could escalate, Pete shouted from behind the bar, "That'll do. There will be no more fighting here. Anybody fighting, no matter who they are, will be reported to Barlung himself. Those are his orders and, by God, I'm following them to the letter. So sit down, the both of you."

Still glaring at each other, they sat. The Jivool looked away.

May came over with four mugs from the tap and whispered to Jyrall as she reached over his huge shoulder to place his in front of him.

"Them's some near as bad as Redd was," she whispered. "That's Captain Gimmold and some of his company, the Eye Pokers. They take security jobs mostly. They just came back today and were hired right away by Barlung. About fifty of 'em."

Cora came by and pretended to wipe up spilled beer on the table. "They come and go here in Town. They always strut around like they're a top rate company, but I have my doubts. Mainly they just bully the miners when they're in town. I will say, I've never seen the two in the corner, whatever they are."

"You'd know if you had," Larth whispered over his mug. "I need a pair of dark goggles just to look at them. They're Miderall."

"I think they're purty," May confided. "But they're with a bunch of non-tippers, I'll tell you that."

"When should we let Pete know we're quitting," Cora asked as she walked by, "now that you've hired us?"

Larth grinned. "Depends on what you find out. There's good intel around here."

Lisalle was the next waitress to come along. "Cora's meeting with the miners tonight. Ledram says they're ready to go."

Larth turned to Jyrall, and they stared at each other for a long moment. "You thinking what I'm thinking?"

Jyrall nodded. "I am. There's only time for one beer tonight, for appearances' sake. The miners are going to strike in the morning. I'd guess about two hours after shift change."

"Why do you say that?" Larth's smile faded. "Wouldn't shift change be the right time? More miners?"

"Oh, it would if you or I were planning it." Jyrall took a large sip from his mug and wiped his maw with the back of one hand. "I think their plan isn't much of a plan at all. They'll want to rush the guards, subdue them, and then try to make a play for weapons. They can't be in two places at once—that's why Ledram wants Cora and the ladies to support them."

Larth twitched his head toward the Eye Pokers. "And the miners haven't planned on those forces or the armor May and Nileah saw in the hangar."

"Completely outmatched," Jyrall said.

Cora swept by them. "Meeting is tonight at 1800 GST."

That's 0300 local time.

Before Jyrall could speak, she was gone. He turned and saw May walking up. "Tell her she has to stop them from revolting."

"It ain't no meeting, Varkell. I got their password with the message. They go tonight," Cora said.

"Password?"

"Strength together." Cora frowned. "They're ready to go."

Jyrall sucked in a breath and glanced at Larth. "Miners are familiar with the dark. They'd have a tactical advantage in the mine. That actually makes sense. The early hour might work in their favor, too."

"We still have to do something about that armor." Larth frowned into his mug. "Gonna be a short revolt if we can't stop it."

Jyrall grunted. "Might be a good time for some Ricky Shit after all."

* * * * *

Chapter Twenty-Nine

Town Starport

Parmick

"Okay," Ricky said as he ran the wire from the rack on the motionless CASPer in front of him to the thrown together control box on the tarmac. "That's the last one."

"Are you sure this is going to work?" Kellie asked as she looked at the five machines arrayed in a semi-circle behind the two ships.

"It'll work," Ricky assured her.

"Yeah, well, it better," Keaton said. "This has got to be the Ricky-ist Ricky Shit you ever tried to pull off."

"What?" Ricky asked. "That cuts me deep, man. Real deep."

Ricky finished connecting the wires and stepped back to admire his handiwork. The five working Mk 7s from the hold of *Blue Ridge* were set up with full missile racks on both of their shoulders. Redd and his troops seemed to prefer missile racks for the machines' shoulder mounting brackets as opposed to other weapons. The lack of magnetic accelerator cannons for newer model CASPers typically indicated a poorer company, but the mechs themselves seemed serviceable. Even though there were no pilots for them, they would still be used in defense of the ships, should the need arise.

All their missile racks were tied into the control box Ricky had made. In theory, he'd be able to fire them all in one mass volley.

Keaton had punched a quick program into the control box to enable them to zero in on a substantial heat source. If the skiffs were deployed against them, their engines would provide plenty of heat for the guidance systems to lock on to.

Cora and her troops were in their own CASPers close to *Night Moves*. Before creating the control box, Ricky and Lisalle had spent the evening and most of the night finishing what repairs they could to the ladies' machines. All five of them were fully fueled and armed. Along with Frank and Stein, parked next to the ships, the five piloted mechs and the five immobile mechs, the ships would be well protected no matter what happened during the planned revolt.

"Hopefully you won't need to use them," Cora said. "It's almost 0300 here. The fan's spinning. We'll see what hits it." She disappeared from view as the hatch closed on her CASper.

"I reckon we will," Ricky agreed. He looked over at Frank and Stein, debating if he should move them yet or wait to see if they were needed.

* * *

Mining Operations Building
Parmick

Nay-Thok glanced at the time indicator on the corner of his computer system's main screen. 0258. He should have retired for the night hours ago, but he couldn't sleep. He didn't know why, but for some reason, he still didn't like that the new camera in pieces in front of him had failed when Varkell and his crew were near it.

Combined with the temporary failure of the older ones on the airfield the other day, it was too many coincidences for his liking. Even the cameras in Pete's Dive Bar had been going in and out lately. He decided he'd inspect the offending piece of equipment one last time tonight and speak to Barlung about his suspicions in the morning. Varkell and his crew may be just as they seemed…or they were very good at disguising their true intentions. It wasn't as if Varkell was anything more than a smuggler and criminal—a very good one—but the last thing Nay-Thok needed was for someone to make a play on Barlung and attempt to run the mining colony themselves. A change in leadership, even hired muscle, meant a longer timeline, and that simply would not do.

He picked up the tester in a pincer and the section of the camera's electronics and began testing the connections. Once again, nothing about it made sense. It was as if the small device had been reprogrammed to turn itself off and start up again right before it was fully online, creating a never-ending loop. Deciding it wasn't a connection issue, Nay-Thok decided to hook it up to his computer and take a look at the actual program itself.

Glancing up at his monitors again, he was startled to see several screens go dark, both on separate monitors and one that rotated views of the mines themselves. Levels, six, seven and eight winked out, showing a black screen. He scrambled for the comm to alert Barlung and his guards when every video feed from the mine went dark.

Frustrated, he tried again and again to reach someone, anyone. The entire communications system was being blocked somehow. His small pincers flew over his keyboard, bringing up other views from Town and the mining site. There in plain sight, Nay-Thok watched as several miners took down a security guard with pickaxes. One grabbed the rifle from the dead Lumar and turned, firing upon the newly hired guards Barlung had scraped together. Several Humans and Goka died before mowing down the lone Jivool. Flipping through the cameras that were still working, Nay-Thok saw similar scenes elsewhere. In some, the miners were taken down quickly, in others, several miners now had weapons of their own.

Nay-Thok watched in horror as miners came boiling out of the shafts. Most were using their work tools as weapons, but some held pistols and rifles, clearly stolen from the subterranean guards. The lights leading into the mineshafts flickered out, and all moving machinery ground to a halt. One of the security members had sense enough to cut the power to the mine shafts in an attempt to stem the flow of reinforcements for the miners now on the surface.

* * *

Mining Operation's Building
Executive Quarters Wing
Parmick

Barlung sat up with a start. Shaking the sleep from his massive head, he heard pounding on his door and panic in the screaming voice. He moved to the door and snatched it open. One of the Lumar stood bleeding in front of him. It appeared as if one of his shoulders had been hit with a pick; the upper right hand hung useless.

"The miners!" exclaimed the guard. "It's the miners; they came out of the mines fighting. Some of them came from Town. There's fighting everywhere!" Having delivered the message, the idiot turned and ran in the direction he'd come from to get back into the battle.

With a snarl Barlung returned to his room, moved to the desk, and grabbed his personal comm. Nay-Thok hadn't contacted him yet, which meant the wireless communication system was likely compromised. The camera feeds still worked, though. Barlung had never liked all the cameras and wired stuff, but he realized Nay-Thok had been right to insist on it.

Shaking his head in disgust, he called Frooth. "Frooth! Get your worthless hide up!" Once Frooth's sleepy voice answered, he ordered, "Get Cartrule and everyone we hired to the mines. Use the processing facilities—north and south! They're revolting!"

"Do we kill them all?" Frooth asked, his thinking clearer.

"If they're armed or resist, kill them!" Barlung screamed. "You idiot!" he added.

Grabbing his weapon harness, Barlung paused, thinking. He reached for his comm again and dialed in a frequency. "Captain Gimmold? Come in Captain Gimmold."

"Last calling station, this is the EyePoker Command Net," an alert voice answered. "The captain is indisposed at the moment."

"Well, get him on the line before I reach though this comm and strangle you!"

"Wait one," the voice replied calmly.

A moment later, Captain Gimmold was on the line. "This better be good."

"My credits were good, you better be," Barlung informed him.

"Barlung," Gimmold said, his tone completely changed. "What can I do for you?"

"You can start by telling me what the situation is at the airfield. Are the hangers secure?" Barlung demanded.

"Ours is secure," said Gimmold. "I can't vouch for the other. You have that ragtag group of Gokas guarding it."

"The miners are up in arms over here," Barlung informed him. "I expect it to be under control shortly. I need to know what Varkell and his team are doing. You have eyes in the area. What's the latest?"

"Hold on, I'll get the latest report," Gimmold said.

A few minutes later he was back on the line. "They have CAS-Pers in a defensive ring around the ships facing Town and toward the hangers. It appears as if several others are near the ship. What are your orders?"

"How many?" Barlung asked.

"Ten," answered the Jivool.

"*Ten!*" Barlung screamed. "Impossible!"

"I confirm ten CASPers. Sensors indicate they're powered up but aren't moving." Gimmold reported. He paused for a second. "What are your orders, Barlung?"

The large Oogar flexed his paw around the stock of his rifle and ground his jaw in silent thought. For a moment he tried to place himself in the mind of his potential adversary. But that in and of itself was difficult to process.

The miners were revolting. That much he understood clearly. They were an enemy. What gave him pause were Varkell and his crew. The presence of armed, operational CASPers outside Varkell's ship wasn't a coincidence. Either the Besquith was in on the revolt, or he'd heard the rumblings and decided to defend his ship.

Will Varkell move against me?

Barlung shook his head. It was too early for this kind of action and Varkell had done nothing to suggest otherwise. "The CASPers haven't moved?"

"Correct," Gimmold replied. "What do you want us to do?"

Barlung pushed through the doorway of his quarters, ducking to avoid slamming his head into the jamb, and out into the passageway beyond. The options and possibilities threatened to overwhelm him.

Varkell is defending his ships. He knew about the attack and is defending his ships. That's all it is.

Or he's waiting for an opportunity to pounce on me and rip my throat out.

Rage flashed through his mind, and he slammed a paw into the plastered wall, shattering a large chunk of it. The pain cleared his mind in an instant. Action was needed. The mercenaries were simply paid soldiers, and they needed to be told what to do. Or, more precisely, what to do if the situation deteriorated.

That's what I'll do.

"Gimmold? If those CASPers move a centimeter toward my hangars, deploy your armor and wipe them from the tarmac. If you see Varkell, Switch, or those Pushtal raise a weapon against any of our aligned forces, kill them. If any miners with pickaxes come to the starport, kill them, too. Anything that threatens our forces dies before sunrise. Is that clear enough for you?"

"Clear, Barlung," Gimmold replied. "Armor skiffs are prepared to launch. I have a company of infantry forces standing by. We're going to secure the other hangar and prepare to assault on your order."

"Good," Barlung growled. "Let me know if the situation changes. I have a revolt to end."

* * * * *

Chapter Thirty

J yrall tapped the display on his slate for the fortieth time in the last hour. The display read 0256 local time, and he'd drunk far too many waters and paced the dirty bar floor enough to wear a clear pattern of footprints in the dirt. Sitting in his usual chair in the deserted bar, Jyrall stared at his time display. At 0302, the earpiece in his right ear chimed to life, and a video feed appeared on his slate.

"You awake, Snarlyface?"

Jyrall sighed. "I really don't like that name, Larth."

"I know. That's what makes it awesome." The Zuparti chuckled. "Okay, I promise I won't call you Snarlyface for the next minute or so. Does that work?"

I'm getting too old for this shit.

"Fine." Jyrall rubbed his face with both paws. "What do you have?"

"The miners have started to take the mine. Panic warnings have gone out, and the merc units have started to deploy," Larth reported. "And before you ask, the mercs at the starport haven't done anything. We know they're up and around. Ricky and Keaton can see them milling about, and they're really curious about what we have set up, but they're not moving."

321

Jyrall nodded to himself. "Barlung is playing this cool."

"What did you say?"

"I said, Barlung is playing this cool. Is that not the saying?"

"It is. Where'd you pick it up?"

"I watched some of your movies tonight while I waited. I couldn't force myself to sleep," Jyrall replied. "I figured it was the least I could do to understand what you're always giggling about."

"We don't giggle," Larth replied. His voice cracked into a high-pitched laugh that belied his denial. "I'm impressed at your dedication."

"Thanks," Jyrall deadpanned. "Barlung's waiting for us to move. He'll deploy his security forces at the mine, and they'll start to put down the revolt."

He has to realize that Cora's CASPers and our ships are the outliers. Where we go, he'll commit forces. That tips the scale. Can we do it in our favor?

What won't he expect?

At the Peacemaker Academy, strategy and employment of assets and capabilities was often likened to games likes chess and *niar-bura*. Strategy tended to unfold in sweeping, planned moves, and not always the seemingly random applications of combat power like the way Humans tended to fight. At his side, Cora and her team were Human, and for all intents and purposes, Ricky and Keaton would fight like them, too.

I can use this to our advantage. It's time to force Barlung's hand. He might expect Larth and the brothers and me to go against him. But he's not expecting Cora and her team. Especially when we split them.

"Okay, the miners are fully committed. Security forces are deploying all across the perimeter," Larth said. "If you've got any ideas on when to move, I think now's the time, Jyrall."

I do, too.

Jyrall tapped his slate. "Cora? Can you hear me?"

"I've got you, Jyrall." Cora's voice was as clear as if she sat next to him.

"Do you have a brevity code? I know most mercenaries operate with some type of codes for operations. Would that make this easier for you?"

"Affirmative." Cora paused and the silence grew for ten seconds. Jyrall was about to transmit again when she replied. "There ain't time to figure that out right now. Let's keep it simple and just use our given names."

Jyrall smiled. "That works for me. Ricky? Keaton?"

"Copy, Boss. We got ya," Ricky drawled into the radio. "You, too, Cora."

"We should do a radio check with everyone," Larth quipped.

"No time," Jyrall replied with a shake of his head. For a moment, doubt grew inside him that radio procedures were something they should have planned out in advance.

What else have I forgotten?

"Cora? Make your move toward the starport," Jyrall ordered. "Ricky and Keaton, bring up your control box and have it ready to fire. Once Cora moves out, I expect the Eye Pokers to attack you."

"I'm prepared to go after the operations building," Larth replied. "I'm in position at the mercantile across the street."

"You're in adequate cover?"

"They ain't gonna find me," Larth replied. "I'm ready when you are."

Jyrall checked the hacked feeds on his slate and saw the miners emerging from the elevators and tunnels at the surface, where they ran into a hail of bullets from the security forces. It was time. "Cora, you're cleared to go."

"Copy, Boss. Taking May and Lisalle with me. Kellie and Nileah are behind with the boys," Cora said. As he switched to his tactical feed, he saw their icons move away from the ships and accelerate toward Town. "ETA at the mine is forty-five seconds, prepare for max bound."

"Good hunting, Cora," Jyrall said into the frequency. "Larth? When the ladies pass by and the security forces lock onto them, that's your cue. Get into the operations building and do what you do best."

"I thought you'd never ask, Snarlyface," Larth laughed. "Your minute is up, buddy."

"Boss, I've got movement at the Eye Poker hangar. They're coming," Keaton reported. "We're ready to go."

There was no going back. Jyrall knew what it meant to commit to a mission as a Peacemaker, and while he understood the theories of combat operations, finding himself in command of an armed force was different. Putting his friends into a deadly situation in an attempt to support their mission threatened to turn his stomach. He closed his eyes and performed a simple breathing exercise to calm his body and center his thoughts. Five seconds later, he opened his eyes and saw Cora's icons flashing down the main thoroughfare. He watched his water glass vibrate, the surface of the liquid shimmering as the CASPers thudded past in their bounds toward the mine.

"Larth, go now. Ricky and Keaton, you're weapons free. Anything that threatens our ships—knock it down. Ladies, I believe in each of you, and we're not going to let you fail. Give me what you can, and I'll do the same for you."

"*Stare aut cadere,* Peacemaker," Cora said. "That's what you'd say in this situation, yes?"

Jyrall chuckled into the microphone. "This isn't a typical Peacemaker mission, Cora. How about we go with something more our style, right? Let's get these fuckers and put them down."

* * *

Town Starport
Parmick

Keaton watched Cora lead May and Lisalle away in a bounding sprint. They headed toward the mines in a straight line, engaging their jumpjets to clear the fence surrounding the airfield and save precious minutes by avoiding the gates.

The lights around the airfield couldn't make it as bright as day, but it was enough to see everything on the tarmac. He turned toward Ricky.

"I sure hope you're ready to use that contraption you built," Keaton said, indicating the control box wired to the missile racks. "We just lost a good portion of our defenses. If any of Barlung's goons try and take our ships, we're gonna need 'em."

"I hate to say it," Nileah added into both their earpieces, "but I hope so too. Kellie and I can handle ourselves pretty good in a fight, but there's no telling how many we'll face. We don't have unlimited ammo or power. A standoff would be bad."

"I think it'll work," Ricky stated again. "I bypassed all the safety features, and Keaton's done programmed 'em to go for the heat source. They oughta hit the engines of any skiffs they might use."

"Let's face the hangers, just in case," suggested Kellie.

They piloted their CASPers around the *Blue Ridge*. Ricky watched them go, satisfied when Kellie's Mk 7 moved without the hitch in its step he'd noticed when he first saw it operate. Lisalle had helped him replace the failing servo with a used part from one of the three damaged machines now stored in the frigate.

Looking back at the five mechs standing motionless in a semi-circle, then over to the two tracked perimeter guards he'd fabricated, he decided to move both Frank and Stein around that side of the frigate with them. He punched a few commands into his small control slate, and both machines rolled out following the guidance.

"I've got an idea," Keaton said, and he disappeared into *Night Moves*. A few minutes later he came out and launched Buzz. "We can see them stirring between the hangers from here, but I figure we can sorta keep an eye on everything better this way. I'll move him back and forth from the mines and here. If I keep him high enough and zoom in, it won't be as far to fly to see what's happening."

"Good idea," agreed Ricky. "I think I got him repaired. I had to take the casing apart and pound the dent out of the nose, but he flies straight now."

"Hey!" Keaton exclaimed looking at the camera feed from the drone. "Look at this!"

"Aw, hell!" Ricky exclaimed. "Y'all get ready. Them sumbitches is coming!"

* * *

Equipment Storage Hanger
Town Starport
Parmick

"**B**arlung? This is Gimmold," Captain Gimmold spoke into his comms as he stood in his temporary command center, looking at a view of the airfield and two ships in particular.

"I've got a lot going on," Barlung answered hastily. "Be quick. What's happening at the starport?"

"You asked to be informed if there were any changes with Varkell or any of his crew," Gimmold said. "Three of the CASPers just took off, moving fast toward the mines. They flew over the fence without slowing."

"Good," Barlung said. "He's probably sent them to help put a stop to the revolt. He knows where his next pile of credits is coming from. Let me know if there are any other changes. I'll let you know if I need you to send any of your soldiers to assist."

"I'll be available," Gimmold said. "I'm up for the night now. No sense in going back to bed when daylight comes in a few hours."

"Sir," the sergeant on duty called out, minutes later. "Two of the mechs have moved around and are facing our direction now, along with two small tracked vehicles."

Captain Gimmold sighed, pushed his plate away, and stood up from his desk in the corner. He took a look at the screen the sergeant was monitoring. Hopefully it was just a precautionary measure by the Humans. If things went bad and they decided to attack the hangers, he had the troops and equipment necessary to take them out. But he didn't look forward to a battle against two of the vaunted CASPers,

328 | IKENBERRY & STEVERSON

much less the other five arrayed around the ships. Then again, he did have his latest acquisition, a good deal in his mind, since it still ran.

"What are those?" Gimmold asked pointing to the two tracked vehicles.

"Looks like some type of perimeter detection devices," the sergeant said. "They don't appear to have weapons."

"Good," Gimmold grunted. "At least that's one less thing to have to consider."

The communication system crackled with Barlung screaming, "Gimmold! Varkell's damned Humans have attacked my guards with their CASPers in the center of town! Gimmold!"

Gimmold snatched up the comms and answered, "I'm here. What are my orders?"

"Attack!" Barlung roared. "Take out the rest of those CASPers and kill all of them. If you can, leave the ships intact. If you succeed, the frigate is yours as a bonus. I want Varkell's ship."

"I'll hold you to that," Gimmold said. "We'll take them down."

The Jivool company commander dropped the comm on the duty sergeant's desk and thought for a moment. He would lose soldiers in an attack. His unit specialized in security, not offensive maneuvers, but the opportunity to upgrade to another frigate-sized ship was too tempting to pass on. What he had now wasn't much more than a corvette, which limited the size of his unit. With a larger ship, he could add another platoon or two. If he kept his old one, too, he could add another whole company.

His ship was an older model and needed a lot of expensive work, since the weapon system no longer functioned and the engines needed a complete rebuild. Right now, they worked at seventy percent efficiency. He couldn't get it fixed with the paltry contracts he'd been taking. It was tight just making payroll; repairs were out of the question. It was, however, something he could afford with bigger contracts. At least he had the two new Miderall pilots working for him now. Though what they tended to wear for clothing was an eyesore, they were very good. Perhaps he could split them up and have them train copilots. The Bakulu pilots before them had refused to do so and had finished their contracts and moved on, disgusted with the ship they had to work with.

"Get the leaders here for a meeting," he ordered the sergeant. "Kick them out of bed if you have to. Those damned pilots, too. I want them all here five minutes ago."

* * *

Town Starport
Parmick

Two armored skiffs came around the corner of a hangar—one behind and slightly offset—and headed across the tarmac. They were followed by a dozen infantry soldiers. The Jivool shuffled behind the skiffs for cover. Jivool were tough fighters but would never be considered fast. Because of this, the skiffs moved slowly.

Suddenly the mounted weapons opened fire at the semicircle, and Kellie and Nileah in their CASPers. Anticipating the move, both used their jumpjets to leap out of the way as the pulses hit the tarmac, creating furrows. One of the empty units took a direct hit to a hip and toppled, severing its link to the control box. As it fell, the missile racks emergency-fired at the skiffs, and a fresh round of laser fire rained on Kellie and Nileah. Both CASPers retaliated, and their rounds hit the armor on the front of the skiffs. Behind one, a Jivool dropped, having caught several rounds.

"Hit 'em, Ricky!" Keaton shouted.

Ricky hit the fire control button on his console, and every missile in the racks on the remaining immobile CASPers ignited and headed toward the skiffs. By this time, the infantry troops were firing around the skiffs at the mechs. Nileah took a hit to a shoulder. The protective armor peeled off, but it didn't penetrate. Several of the immobile CASPers took hits as well.

The missiles flew high, coming down to strike the tops and engines of the skiffs. Both were hit, and one of them blew apart when something vital in the fuel area ruptured. Several of the Jivool were flung away and out from behind their cover. Kellie made sure they didn't make it to their feet.

The troops stayed behind the remaining skiff. It couldn't fire, but it still provided cover as it slowly moved toward the ships. They traded shots with Kellie and Nileah, who remained moving targets, firing as they moved in the open. Occasionally the women would take a hit, and they were expending fuel and ammunition at an alarming rate.

Keaton set himself up behind Stein, used the machine's body for a prop, and fired his rifle whenever he saw an opening. Ricky grabbed the control for the two rovers and punched in commands. The hatches on top of Frank opened, and the fifties came up, ready to go. They opened up on the remaining skiff in a sustained burst. Just as it was firing the last of its rounds, four missiles in front launched. They penetrated the skiff's armor and wreaked havoc inside. It ground to a halt on the tarmac.

"What the hell, man?" Ricky exclaimed. "Stein ain't working at all. Are you holding down the hatch?"

"Hell naw, I ain't," Keaton answered firing another round. "I think it took a few of those laser rounds. You'll have to check it later."

"Guys!" Kellie called out. "I've only got twenty MAC rounds left, and I'm almost out of jump juice."

"I've got a few," Nileah said. "There are only two of them left, and I have part of them in sight."

As she stopped her constant movement and took aim, her CAS-Per was knocked sideways, spinning and hitting the ground as a round hit a lower leg, taking it completely off. All the warning lights in her control panel showed red as she shook her head, trying to refocus.

"Shit!" exclaimed Kellie as she fired almost all her remaining rounds at the ancient tank emerging from behind the hanger. Smoke billowed from the exhaust of the machine; its engine had clearly seen better days. Her rounds were hitting the target, but not doing much good. Without thinking, she used the last of her fuel to jump in front of Nileah's downed machine. Kneeling beside her, she had no idea if her friend would survive, she just knew one of the claws was moving, so Nileah still lived.

The sound crackling in their ears, all three heard Nileah weakly ask, "What was that?"

"A tank," Kellie answered. "Looks like an old Zuul one. And I mean *old*."

"Well, it still works," Nileah said. "Believe me. Did you take it out?"

A round from the tank hit Frank, penetrated the front of the machine, and blew through the side opposite Stein, sending shrapnel against the frigate. The tank was slow to load, or the crew was unfamiliar with its workings, but sooner or later it was going to score a direct hit. They needed to do something fast. Ricky scrambled over to Stein.

"Not yet!" shouted Ricky. He slammed his rifle butt again and again against the hatch on top of the machine. He could see where a beam had sliced across, creating a small spot weld, which kept the hatch from opening.

Kellie continued to lay down fire at the tank coming their way. Additional infantry came from the hanger, trudging slowly behind the tank, using the only cover on the open tarmac. She took several hits as she remained immobile, covering Nileah.

"Can you eject?" Kellie called to Nileah.

"Not from this position."

"You're safer there, honey. Stay down." Kellie stood up and brought her MAC to bear on the charging tank. With her left hand, she unholstered the hand cannon on her hip and fired it as well. "Come on, Ricky! A little help!"

With a final blow, the offending piece of slagged metal broke away, and the hatch on Stein opened, allowing the missile rack to deploy. Ricky's digits flew across his slate as he punched in the commands. He and Keaton ducked behind it just before the missiles ignited as one. The heat across their backs was tremendous.

As the missiles left the launcher, the ancient tank fired another round. Kellie in her Mk 7 never felt the hit as it struck her CASPer in the cockpit. The round penetrated, and she was no more. The mech toppled over the legs of the one lying behind it.

Keaton looked at the screen on the slate lying beside him, and through the lens on the drone saw all thirty missiles strike the tank. Even armored as it was, the thirty simultaneous missile strikes penetrated the old machine and several of its own rounds cooked off inside. The turret went spinning off and landed upside down several yards away. The tank burned.

Standing slowly, the brothers looked over toward the ladies. It was apparent what had transpired. "Nileah?" Keaton called.

"I'm here," a weak answer came back, the transmission crackling.

"We're going to try and get you out," Ricky said. Ducking, he ran over to the downed machines. He attempted to use the outer emergency escape latch to open her CASPer, but several beams bounced around him. The infantry troops, sensing no return fire, moved en masse toward them.

"There's fifteen of them headed our way!" Keaton called out from behind Stein. "And I only have four rounds left!"

"My rifle is FUBAR!" Ricky answered back, looking at his shattered stock. He looked over at Stein. "If that damn front panel would ever open, those Tommy Guns would come in handy!" Frustrated, he threw his rifle up against the offending panel on the rover with all his strength. It completely came apart with the blow.

Slowly the front panel dropped, and two Tommy Guns, complete with ammo drums, came up on their stand. Ricky, with his mouth frozen open in wonder, stood shaking his head. He punched in the command and ducked.

The last of the Jivool infantry, having closed the distance, were caught in the open when both weapons emptied their drums of .45 caliber rounds, waving back and forth. The Jivool never stood a chance. Near silence followed, with the occasional sound of metal groaning and popping as the skiffs and tank burned in the distance.

* * * * *

Chapter Thirty-One

Cora pushed hard through the narrow streets of town. As she bounded her Mk 7 CASPer forward, the external cameras caught sight of frightened citizens hiding behind their drawn window shades. Infrared imaging showed many families in the ramshackle dwellings huddling together in protected corners, trying to melt into floors or walls. Jaw clenched, Cora focused on the street ahead, where armed security guards guarded the entrance. A few shot seemingly random rounds into the town itself until Cora swung the IR camera view to the north and saw a nest of several miners on rooftops firing at the guards.

"Hostiles ahead," Cora called over her connection to Lisalle and May. "Let's give them an old school wake up call."

"Copy, Cora," Lisalle replied. "Spreading out."

Cora landed from a bound and broke her mech into a sprint down the central corridor. Behind her, she saw Lisalle and May duck onto parallel streets and do the same. Toggling her weapons controls, Cora opened the compartments on the Mk 7's legs and withdrew the .50 caliber belt-fed cannons. With one in each hand, she checked the distance to the security guards.

Two hundred meters.

"Standby ladies. ETA is ten seconds."

"We're on it, Cora," Lisalle replied.

"Go, Cora, we'll be in position in ten seconds," May said.

Right. Eight, seven, six, five...

Cora pushed against the jump pedals, and her CASPer shot into the sky. As she did, her targeting system went to work, identifying each of the armed security guards in her line of sight. The targets were linked to May and Lisalle's heads-up displays so they could lock on targets the moment they emerged from their corridors.

A few rounds streaked up at her. Cora cycled the MAC on her right shoulder and fired five quick rounds at the five targets. All of them went down. Nearing the apex of her bound, she saw a cascade of fire coming up at her. Most of it was harmless. A few rockets snaked and twirled up at her, but it was nothing she worried about. Braced for landing, Cora saw May and Lisalle emerge from their avenues of approach and fire at the distracted guards. By the time Cora landed her CASPer, the outer ring of security at the mining operations center was no more.

"Nice job, y'all," Cora said. "Phase two."

"There are snipers on top of the building pickin' off miners, Cora," May yelped.

"Hit what you can as we jump over it. The miners haven't fully cleared the surface yet. We gotta get all of them up here."

Cora ran the CASPer forward, closing on the inner ring of security around the operations building. The collected mercenaries and guards appeared much more disciplined with their weapons and ammunition. Rather than the spraying approach their outer ring employed, Cora heard the impacts of small arms rounds on her CASPer.

"Let's go. Up and over." Cora engaged her jumpjets and shot into the air. As she passed over the building, her targeting cursor found three snipers on the north side, and she dispatched them with two shots each. Behind her, May and Lisalle swept the rest of the building's roof and surrounding area. As they landed inside the mine's secure perimeter, miners burst from the two southern-most elevator shafts. A dirty, screaming flood of every race she'd ever seen stormed across the open space toward the operations center and the processing facility to the south.

"What are they doing?" Lisalle asked. "They're not armed."

Cora shook her head. "Ledram has a plan. We have to trust that. There's no one coming out of the central shaft. We have to clear it so the miners can fully take the mine. We can deal with the guards and the mercs once the mine is secured."

May clomped forward in her CASPer, her MAC firing off to their right. Cora whipped around and saw at least twenty heavily-armored infantry assuming hasty fighting positions. As they did, several guided rockets swarmed toward them.   .

"Spread out!" Cora yelled. Handcannons blazing, she darted toward the central shaft and took shelter behind a large pile of slag. May and Lisalle moved in the opposite direction, yet the volume of fire impacting her hiding place didn't abate. In fact, it swelled.

"We're in position," Lisalle said. "Damn, they're throwing out a lot of rounds."

"Doesn't matter, we've gotta—"

Ka-Whamm! Ka-Whamm!

Cora whirled around and saw red-orange clouds swirling up from the southern elevator shafts. The steady stream of miners emerging from below the surface was no more.

Oh, gods.

From the top of the operations building outside the fence, two Goka popped up and fired at May and Lisalle. Cora turned and brought up her MAC. As she fired, the Goka dropped below cover. Cora waited and fired again as they re-appeared. May and Lisalle were exposed and trapped, and she needed to do something.

As she studied the piles of rock and debris, Cora created a plan. "May? Lisalle? Work your way to the slag pile to your right—the big one about ten meters from your position. I'll hit the Goka while you do. From there, we can bound up to take them out and swing toward the security shed from the flank. You with me?"

"Got it," May replied. "Ready to move."

Cora watched the operations building. The two Goka popped up, and she fired ten rounds from the MAC in a couple of heartbeats. "Move!"

* * *

Atop the operations building, the two Goka took cover, not because they were worried about the fire from the Human CASPers below and inside the mine's perimeter, but from necessity.

The senior guard, Spoom, worked the action on his rifle and tried to clear a malfunction for the fourth time. "I get four rounds out and it jams. Entropy!"

"I get less than that," the young recruit, Sitfol, replied. "If Barlung would have let us clean them, this wouldn't be happening."

Spoom grunted again but said nothing. Finally the jammed round came loose, and he slammed the bolt forward to chamber a new round. "Ready."

Sitfol took another five seconds. "Same."

"Up on three. Take out the single CASPer. I'll lay fire on the other two. We'll get them next."

"Got it," Sitfol replied. "Ready now."

"One. Two. Three!"

They popped up during a lull in the incoming fire. Sitfol aimed down on the singular CASPer and squeezed the trigger slowly. He fired twice more, taking his time, and prepared for the fourth shot when the rifle jammed again.

"Entropy!"

Spoom had waited for the two CASPers to emerge again. As soon as they did, he squeezed the trigger, and on the second round, the action attempted to feed multiple rounds at the same time. The result was catastrophic. Once the firing mechanism engaged, both rounds detonated in the chamber, wounding Sitfol with a shower of debris across his upper body and eyes. The explosion spread to the waiting crude ammunition inside the rifle's magazine and detonated the waiting rounds in spectacular fashion, tearing Spoom in half. The explosion consumed the corner of the operations building and threw their makeshift cover and concealment in all directions.

* * *

Larth sensed he was near the back of the operations building, but he couldn't see it. The only thing exposed was his feet at the bottom of the barrel as he ran across the street. He lifted the refuse barrel up off of him and tossed it. He looked back across the road to the alley he came from and down at the barrel. "I can't believe that worked," he said. "I even paused in the middle of the street like in those old Earth movies for no reason. Now that's crazy."

"What worked?" Jyrall said in his earpiece. "Why are you pausing?"

"Nothing. Never mind," Larth answered. "I'm at the back of the operations building. I'll find a way in and get to Nay-Thok. If you don't hear from me for a few, it's because I'm busy. Who knows how many guards are in the building."

Larth looked up at the cameras; both of the ones on this side were aimed out and not down the walls. Confident he hadn't been seen, he glanced at the windows. There were several on the ground level, but they were higher than he could reach. Looking over at the barrel, he grinned. *Doesn't seem like a crazy idea now, does it?* He stood the barrel up below the nearest window.

Peeking through the dirty window, he saw the room was empty. Once again, it was a multi-species waste facility.

Damn, another stinky room. I'm getting tired of this. He pulled out his small blade, flicked it open, and worked it in, popping the lock. Like most in Town, the old building was never meant to be truly secure. He slid the window open, climbed through, and pulled it back down.

The room's floor was much closer to the window, indicating the building sat on a foundation or a basement. *Up or down?* Larth decided on going up. It would be easier to search the building that way. He eased to the door, placed an ear against it, and listened. It took some concentration, and he had to use a Peacekeeper focusing technique to block out the sounds of battle outside the building and listen only for sounds near him and in the room on the other side of the door.

Hearing nothing, he eased the door open, ducked low, and peered into the room. It was a main room with a large stone slab table. In the far corner he saw stairs. He decided to check the other two doors. One opened into a small office, Barlung's by the look of it, with no chair behind the desk.

The other was locked. This time his knife wouldn't suffice. He reached into a pocket on his vest and pulled out his small lockpicking kit. No electronics on the outside of this door, so he got to do it the old-fashioned way. In less than a minute he heard the tumblers fall into place. *Nothin' to it. If being Peacemaker doesn't work out, I have another trade to fall back on. Maybe I can be a truck driver. Whatever that is.* He giggled to himself.

Shhhhhh!

He eased into the room after he was sure there were no noises. It was Nay-Thok's office and workroom. There on the table were several red diamonds of various sizes and a bowl full of red diamond chips and dust. Larth looked briefly at the schematics for synthesizing the fake diamonds, stacked the papers up, folded them, and slid them into the large pocket across the back of his vest.

Multiple monitors on the desk displayed black screens. Only the remote cameras in Town seemed to work. The main screen indicated the computer on the desk was running, along with the monitoring system. He slid a small retrieval drive into a slot on the computer and proceeded to download everything.

There's something awesome about elSha code, you know?

While it worked, he checked the drawers on the desk. The top left drawer was locked. *Not for long.* Inside was a small box. It was locked as well, but he pried it open with his blade. It held a large red diamond. *Now that's real, or it wouldn't be double locked away,* Larth decided. After a second or two of consideration, Larth determined the diamond must be a comparative control against the counterfeits. He tucked the diamond deep into a pocket on his vest and fastened it closed.

He looked over and noticed the retrieval drive indicator light was flashing green. Putting it back in its padded pocket, he went to the door, listened, then peeked to see if it was clear. Surely the entire building wasn't empty. Jyrall hadn't called to say Nay-Thok had been spotted, nor had the brothers at the airfield. Maybe he'd get lucky on one of the other floors. He left the office and moved toward the stairs.

Silently he crept up the stairs. There was a small, dark alcove at the top, with three doors leading away. The doors had a two-and-a-half-inch gap at the bottom, probably to aid in air circulation when it was built so long ago. Larth got down and looked into the rooms. The first room was another facilities room, and it appeared empty.

The second door opened into a long hallway. There were no feet visible, though he could see a few doors leading off from it. The door straight ahead was the one. Larth counted eight sets of feet. Two were rather large and looked to have typical Lumar-styled boots. The others may have been Human mercenaries, he wasn't sure.

They lined the wide hallway as if expecting someone to walk between them at any time. He could tell he was looking at heels at the moment, so he made a snap decision. He stood and turned the latch, barely opening the door. Not enough to crack it, just enough so the catch didn't engage with the door frame.

Larth stepped back to the edge of the stairs, pulled a spare magazine from his holster belt, and slid it across the floor, under the door.

He drew his pistols and took off. A second after it disappeared, he hit the door at a dead sprint. He dropped to his knees, sliding as soon as he cleared the doorway.

All the guards whipped their heads around as the door slammed open, still puzzling over what had skidded past them to hit the far wall. Most were turned away from him, though their heads were facing him, and those were the targets he was looking for.

Larth emptied both magazines as he fired rapidly, double-tapping as he slid. Even the big Lumars dropped where they stood when two of the special high-velocity .380 rounds penetrated their dense brains via the direct route through their faces. Six Human mercs and two Lumar, all in some type of battle armor, lay dead. "Body armor doesn't help when you take one in the face," Larth said as he stood.

He bent to pick up his attention-grabbing magazine, and several rounds hit the wall over his bent back. He dove to the side behind a body and came up, the magazine now inserted in the pistol in his right hand. He caught a glimpse of a Human as the door slammed shut. He emptied the pistol into the door about chest high. He heard someone drop on the other side.

Brushing himself off, he reloaded both pistols. He stepped to the door and pushed it open. There was another Human mercenary with a chest full of holes. Blood seeped through the battle armor in several places. The high velocity rounds had done what Ricky had promised. Not all of them had penetrated, but enough had. Larth looked at the door and noted his handiwork, the pattern of a smiley face there in the wood.

"Have a nice day," he said to the dead merc as he stepped over him.

* * * * *

Chapter Thirty-Two

Diamond Mine

Parmick

The explosion atop the mining operations building lit up the night around Cora's position. There had only been two Goka—that she was aware of—occupying the firing position.

"Covering fire," Cora yelped into the channel.

A second later, May and Lisalle jumped to the top of a slag pile and laid fire from hand cannons and MACs into the security forces building. After ten seconds of constant barrage, the lights went out, and the surrounding forces dove for cover. Slowing their rate of fire, May and Lisalle raked the security forces enough that incoming fire went from constant to sporadic in a few heartbeats.

Time to go.

"Moving. Cover me." Cora turned and jumped over the slag pile she was using for cover. As she shot skyward, she oriented on the mine's central exit shaft. Beyond it, she could see waves of miners emerging from the northern elevator shafts, but there were far too few of them to cause any real damage. The security forces had the advantage in standoff weapons and continued to pick off miners as they rushed from the outlying shafts.

This is going to be the shortest mine revolt in history.

Unless.

If she and the girls could clear the central shaft and allow more of the miners to the surface, the security forces would face greater resistance.

"May? Target the security forces. Lisalle, keep moving forward toward the central entrance. We've got to get down there and open up the mine."

"Copy," Lisalle replied. "May, stay on my right flank, and we'll move together."

"Right with you!"

As they stomped toward the central entrance, Cora came up behind them with both hand cannons blazing. From behind the slag piles, the three CASPers raced across the sixty meters of open ground under heavy fire. A few bolts of laser fire added to the fusillade of rounds that impacted the CASPers and the ground around them.

"Taking heavy fire," Lisalle reported. "Armor is holding."

I love the Mk 7. Thanks, Uncle Milton.

"May, spread out to your right. Let's clear a path for Cora," Lisalle called. On cue, the two CASPers angled to the right as they neared the upper structures of the shaft. As they closed on the mine, Cora understood more of what might lay beneath the surface. The miners used the elevators for entry and exit into the deeper portions and runs. The central entrance wasn't an entrance at all, but the primary extraction point for the diamonds and the slag itself. Everything came up at once, which, she surmised, meant the extraction shaft was larger than the rest.

The bulk of the miners are there. But what's holding them up?

"I'm in position," May called. She was set up behind a large mining car with a thick, bulldozer-like blade on it. Cora watched the young girl bring up her MAC and lay into the security forces, both inside and outside the wire.

Lisalle was next. "I'm on the other side. Set. We have overwatch, Cora. You're clear."

Cora twisted her head. The camera view spun in the direction she glanced, and she found Lisalle in a similarly good position. With adequate cover, they could hold off the security forces until she breached whatever held the miners trapped below.

"Cora. We're set! Go!"

Cora grunted and a thin smile threatened to dawn on her lips. Taking care of her squad was more than a requirement. They were her friends—her family—and she wanted them safe and protected as much as possible. For a combat leader, she knew the instinct was different and strange, but she listened to it whenever possible. Missions came and went, while her people were a constant.

They're as fine as they can be, Cora. Go.

She bounded toward the yawning, semicircular extraction tube. Sidestepping machinery, Cora spied three Goka skittering into firing positions on the upper surface of the tube. With her right hand, she activated the MAC's targeting sequencer. Using the tracking camera on her right eye, the MAC centered on the cluster of roach-like aliens. Cora squeezed her fist as she ran and raked through them. She didn't bother to watch the bodies falling to the asphalt where the CASPer's feet deftly missed them as she sprinted into the mine entrance.

The artificial lights flickered above her, and the long, half-cylindrical space was dark, but there was enough light to see the stranded miners at the bottom, held back by a wide metal gate. On Cora's side of the gate, two hulking figures sprayed the grating with smaller caliber rifles. Their normal low-slung, multi-barreled cannons sat off to one-side, and Cora immediately understood.

They're killing time. Waiting. For what?

Cora stopped and brought up her hand cannons as the two Oogar dropped their rifles and turned to her.

"Is that you, Cora?" Cartrule laughed. "Come to finish our discussion in front of a cheering crowd?"

Cora swallowed. "Stand down, Cartrule. Walk away now, and we'll find a way to work this out so it's profitable for you and us both."

* * *

Town Starport
Parmick

"Easy, easy," Keaton said as he reached under Nileah's arms and pulled her from her CASPer. "We got ya."

She assisted as much as she could by pushing off the back of the inside of the cockpit with her feet. One of her arms hurt too much to use. She suspected it was fractured, indicating the power of the blow her Mk 7 had received when the tank round took off the bottom part of her CASPer's leg—wrenching her leg—and spun her around. Even with the enhancements from the nanites mech pilots received, Nileah was in great pain. She would heal, but at the moment, using it was not an option.

"Easy, hell!" Ricky exclaimed through gritted teeth. "How 'bout quickly?"

Ricky had a long prybar from his collection of tools in his paws and was straining with all he had to hold the hatch open on the cockpit of Nileah's machine. Part of Kellie's destroyed Mk 7 lay across Nileah's, adding weight to the hatch. It was the fastest way to get her out. Her machine's power levels were fluctuating, including the environmental system.

"She's clear," Keaton said and helped Nileah stand.

Ricky let the hatch drop and stood, using the pry bar as a staff to lean on as he caught his breath. "That thing was heavy. Are you okay?"

"Yes," Nileah said. She looked over at her friend's destroyed machine. "Kellie isn't. She didn't make it." A tear slid down her cheek. "She stayed there with me."

"She did," Keaton said softly. "No greater gift…"

"It was a hell of a thing," agreed Ricky. "Damned impressive if you ask me."

"Well," Nileah said, wiping away the tear with a sniff, "she wouldn't have had it any other way." She looked across the tarmac at the devastation. "Do you think that's all of them?"

Keaton picked up his slate. "Buzz is still over the hangers. I don't see any more of the Eye Pokers. I—Hey! Look at that." He pointed to the far side of the hanger with the ships inside.

Nileah stared hard and a thin smile appeared on her lips. "That's the Goka sergeant and his squad. I wonder what they're doing?"

The six Goka seemed to be having an argument, though they had no way of hearing the animated conversation. Antennae waving, the sergeant waved a limb in disgust in the direction of the hanger they'd been guarding, and all six of the squad members climbed into a hovercraft. Instead of going down the road, it turned and started across the tarmac in their direction, moving slowly.

"Aw, hell!" Ricky said. "You still got four rounds? I'll be right back. I need to get a weapon." He ran toward their ship.

Ricky was back holding an older-model shotgun before the hovercraft was in range for it. The Gokas were in range for Keaton's rifle, but he didn't fire on them. Ricky was confused. He handed several magazines to his brother.

"What in the hell you waitin' on?" he asked his brother. "They's coming."

"They're not armed," Nileah said.

"Wait, what?" Ricky asked as he looked closer at the open-topped hovercraft on the screen. Keaton zoomed in close, and the details were clearly visible. "Why ain't they?"

"I don't know," Keaton said, "but we're 'bout to find out. Go ahead and draw down on them, but don't fire." He glanced at his brother's choice of weapon. "Nice, you brought out Pops' Browning Stalker. What you got in it?"

"High brass rifled slugs," Ricky said with a toothy grin. "I figure a ten gauge might just penetrate their shells."

"It might," agreed Keaton. "Your shoulder ain't gonna like it none, though."

Ricky propped the large shotgun on Stein and waited with his brother and Nileah. The Goka in the front passenger side started waving a brown rag of some kind. It was almost as if they were surrendering. The craft stopped a short distance away, and the squad bailed out and stood behind Figgle. The one with the rag kept waving it back and forth.

"I see you, Squarlik," Nileah said. "You can quit waving that thing around."

Squarlik turned toward his sergeant. "See, I told you they'd remember us. We don't all look the same to them."

"Fine," Figgle said. "You were right. You can now be a corporal." The other Gokas congratulated their fellow soldier with pats on the shell. It took a minute for them to settle down.

"Well," Nileah asked, "what's the deal?"

"I'm Sergeant Figgle, of Figgle's Finest," the Goka said. "Well, we are now. We quit our company. I didn't get your name when we met last. Who are you?"

"I am Sergeant Nileah Sevier," she answered, and after a pause, concluded with, "of Blue Ridge Kin."

"Wonderful!" Figgle said. "Another sergeant. We've been mistreated by our previous employers and feel they broke our contract. We were guarding the hanger, and Captain Gimmold and some of his stupid Eye Pokers came in, said Barlung had demanded we disarm, then they ran us out of the hanger."

"So, there's a few of them left in the hanger," Nileah said, filing the information away. "That doesn't explain why you came over here instead of into Town."

Sergeant Figgle stood straight. "We want to come to your side."

"What? Why?" asked Nileah.

"Because you have cookies," answered the Goka.

"Oh, no he didn't!" Ricky said. He laughed along with his brother.

"Okay, I'm sorry," Figgle said with as close to a grin as his race could make. "I saw that on GalNet once. I thought it was funny.

Seriously. We're a new company. As in right now new, and we need a contract. Would you like to hire a squad of experienced soldiers?"

"Experienced at what?" Nileah asked.

"Guarding things mostly, but we are willing to learn," answered Squarlik for his sergeant.

"How can we trust you?" Keaton asked.

"Because we trusted you," countered Figgle. "We came over here after what we saw you do to Redd's Riders and the Eye Pokers."

"You got a point," Keaton said.

"You're hired," Ricky stated. "Is that hovercraft yours? Never mind. I need to borrow it. I'm going to the mines to see if Cora needs some help, her being kin and all. We ain't heard a peep from them in way too long."

"You might want to provide a driver for him," Keaton advised the Goka. "He can't drive worth a flip," he whispered as loud as his normal speaking voice.

"Corporal Squarlik," Figgle ordered, "drive him wherever he wants to go. He holds our contract, even if it is a verbal one."

"You be careful," Keaton said as Ricky and Squarlik got in the old hovercraft.

"Do you have weapons we could borrow?" Figgle asked sheepishly. "We seem to be in between weapons at the moment."

"There's some on *Blue Ridge*," Nileah said. "Come on, I need a pistol with this bum arm, anyway."

"Not until I wrap it and put it in a sling," Keaton said. He turned back to the hovercraft. "Speaking of weapons." He handed his rifle and magazines to Squarlik. "Use this."

* * *

Mining Operations Center

Parmick

The room was some type of lounge. Larth noticed the chairs were designed for Jeha, like the one in Nay-Thok's office downstairs. There was nothing worth inspecting in the room. To the right there was a door. Silently he padded over to it and heard voices. They sounded like Jeha moving away from the door.

Larth snatched the door open and turned, ready to fire. There were three Jeha carrying cases down a hallway leading to an open door in an alcove. He glimpsed Nay-Thok as he turned and started to descend. Before he could fully register what he was seeing, a Jeha walking backward fired some type of machine pistol. Rounds hit everywhere as it rose upward in the Jeha's grip. Fighting it, he pulled it down too hard, and rounds bounced off the floor.

Larth squeezed off two shots as he dove back through the doorway. When he landed and rolled, he felt a burn in his shoulder. *That non-shooting asshole winged me.* He looked and saw it wasn't a serious wound. He crawled over and took a quick look down the hall. The Jeha was dead. Two rounds in the head had done the trick.

Larth stood and stepped into the hall. He needed to catch the other two, and Nay-Thok for sure. He stalked down the hall, kicking the Jeha's weapon away as he went by. "A whole hall full of mercenaries and nothing," he said to himself. "A stupid technician with a weapon he can't even handle, and I take a hit. What the hell is going on around here? I better get it right. I'm about to piss me off is what I'm about to do. You hear me?"

Suspecting one of the other Jeha was waiting in the room below, he walked back to the dead technician, dragged it through the doorway to the alcove, stopped, put his pistols away, and picked up the body. Most of it, anyway. Part of it dragged. With a heave, he sent it tumbling down the stairs. He heard the tell-tale sound of the same type of small machine pistol firing and stepped into the opening as his pistols came up. He put four rounds in the Jeha standing at the foot of the stairs firing into and around the tumbling body. "Idiot." He laughed to himself.

Careful to avoid the gore, he darted down the stairs toward the open front door. Looking ahead, he saw Nay-Thok rounding a corner. All his pincers were down, and the Jeha undulated as fast as he could go, dragging the case by its handle. He tapped his comm. "Jyrall, I'm chasing Nay-Thok into Town. He's faster than he looks, and it's chaos out here. You better be okay! Out!"

Larth took off at a dead sprint away from the building and the whole mining area. He ran through the gate, barely noticing the bodies. He was on a mission. He was going to catch that fake diamond fabricator no matter how fast he was. If the wind would quit blowing dirt in his face, that is. *Maybe it's not the wind. Maybe I'm that fast*, he thought as he kicked it into another gear.

"Meep! Meep!" he shouted as he ran.

Rounding a building on the main street, Larth saw Nay-Thok duck into Pete's Dive Bar.

I got you now, asshole.

He sprinted the block and a half to the door. Without slowing much, he shoved it open and ran in, sure that Nay-Thok was unarmed. Pete, standing in the middle of the room with one hip against a table, fired his shotgun. The slugs hit the door behind Larth, just above his head, leaving two large holes.

Larth cut loose with both pistols before the old pirate could begin to reload, and Pete folded. Nay-Thok was nowhere to be seen. Moving quickly around the bar to the door leading to the rear of the establishment, Larth heard a hovercraft engine spool up. He stepped out the rear door to see Nay-Thok zipping down the back street. Larth holstered the empty weapons, crossed his arms chest-high, and pulled his spares out in one fluid motion.

He fired at the engine area of the old hovercraft until the slides locked back. It slewed as the left side lost the cushion of air it was riding on. It caught the curb, hit a building and crashed. Flames burst from the engine area, and billowing smoke covered the wreckage.

Larth took the time to insert magazines into all four of his pistols, just in case, then he walked up the block, through the smoke to the wreckage. When the wind took the smoke away from it, he looked for the Jeha. Not seeing him, he stepped closer. A strong breeze blew away most of the billowing smoke. The vehicle was empty. The door on the far side was open.

Larth tapped his comms. "Keaton! I think Nay-Thok is headed your way!" Larth started running toward the airfield and Barlung's hangers.

"If he is, we haven't seen him," Keaton answered. "We been kinda busy. Ricky took off like a bat outta hell to go help Cora, and I been taking care of Nileah."

"What happened?"

"They hit us. Kellie's dead, but we held. Picked up a few friends, too," Keaton replied. "Have you heard from Jyrall?"

Larth realized he hadn't. Without breaking stride, Larth toggled his earpiece to a private frequency. "You with me, Snarlyface?"

There was no response. Larth kept running. The big Besquith could take care of himself, and there was only one large target left. It didn't stand a chance.

Gods, I hope I'm right.

* * * * *

Chapter Thirty-Three

Diamond Mine
Parmick

Barlung charged into the mine's perimeter in a rage, scattering guards and miners alike. Gimmold's forces hadn't responded to his repeated calls for support, and the mine's communications systems, along with all the closed-circuit Tri-V and holographic display systems, were down. Radio communications in the VHF band were the only available frequencies, but his newly hired guards and mercenaries didn't all possess the correct equipment. The situation teetered on the edge of collapse.

He looked at the chaos unfolding and saw two fortunate circumstances. The security forces had disabled the southern elevators used by the miners to bring their revolt to the surface, which limited them to the elevators on the north side of the mine. His security forces continued to move toward the elevators by coordinating fire and overwatch. Fewer and fewer miners emerged with their tools to take on the better armed and equipped mercenaries. No more than a few hundred miners appeared to have surfaced, which meant they'd planned to use the central extraction shaft for a mass exit.

In the event of a revolt or similar action, Cartrule and Frooth had a singular mission, and they appeared to have done their job. They'd moved the heavy gates into place and shut down the extraction equipment, keeping the larger passageway closed off. As he approached, he saw two Human CASPers, Mk 7s if he remembered correctly, providing direct fire support for the miners from covered positions.

It's like they're protecting something.

Barlung roared in sudden understanding and charged. The two CASPers immediately turned and began to fire in his direction. Rage filled his eyes with a tint of purple, and he snarled and thrashed as he accelerated toward them. One CASPer behind mining cars was less exposed than the other; he chose the one slightly farther from the extraction shaft and with less protection.

Instinct took the place of whatever reason the big Oogar possessed. As if chasing prey, Barlung's eyes narrowed in precise focus on the CASPer. He ducked behind a slag pile and weaved toward the mech as it continued to fire in his general direction. Yet the rate of fire coming from the Humans slowed down. They were professionals.

But who are they?

Almost as quickly as the thought crossed his mind, Barlung heard a decidedly Human female voice calling out via the CASPer's external speakers. "Miners! Keep moving! Get away from the elevators! Take the fight to the guards!"

He realized who they were in a heartbeat. They were mercenaries, and they were good.

I'm better.

He climbed up a slagpile, not breaking stride, his claws extended for extra grip on the loose rock, and leapt into the night sky. Underneath him, the Human CASPer spun and brought it's weapons up, but she was too late. In close, the CASPer couldn't bring a weapon to bear on the Oogar, and the ursine alien grabbed both of the mech's upper arms and spun it off-balance. As it started to fall, Barlung let go with one clawed paw and brought it back as if cocking it to slash at the armor. The CASPer continued to struggle, and Barlung took the effort as a challenge, and swung.

His claws slashed the outer armor of the mech but did not penetrate. The magnetic accelerator cannon on the Human's right shoulder popped up from its container and swung to sight on him, but never completed its journey. With a roar, Barlung ripped the cannon from its mounts, exposing the underside of the mech's armor, and tossed it into the night. Sparks popped from the severed connections. Next, he found the antenna mounts for the suit's communications systems and tore them away. Turning back to the shredded cannon mount, Barlung reached into the hole and tore the outer shell of the CASPer away.

* * *

May heard Lisalle scream, and she moved from her covered position to try to sight down on her friend's CASPer. "I'm coming, honey. Hang on!"

"May, it's Barlung. He's here," Lisalle called. "I'll hold him as long as I can, but he's breached my armor, and my long-range comms are gone."

May heard her friend grunt and strain. She found a firing position and gasped. The massive Oogar and Lisalle's CASPer almost appeared to be dancing. Close together, essentially arm-in-arm and trying to tear each other apart, they fought for balance and spun wildly. "I can't get a shot, Lisalle."

"I've got him, May. Keep Cora safe."

May bit the inside of her lower lip. She'd always been the youngest and the greenest of the team, and she knew Lisalle meant what she'd said. Orders were orders. But that didn't mean she had to let her friend die, and there were other ways to both keep Cora safe and save her friend's life. Without taking her hands from the CASPer's controls, May switched frequencies.

"Jyrall? This is May. We've got Barlung at the extraction shaft entrance. He's engaged with Lisalle, and Cora's in trouble with Cartrule and Frooth. We need you here. Now."

She got no response.

May sighted down on Barlung and fired as he slashed at Lisalle's cockpit section with a mighty swipe of his paws. Bright purple blood sprayed from a superficial wound on his left chest and shoulder. He glared at her and continued to slash and rend Lisalle's armor.

May pressed closer, carefully firing in bursts even as she left her covered position. Barlung and Lisalle pirouetted again, and she heared Lisalle bark at her.

"Get back in your position, May. Protect Cora. That's an order."

May hesitated and pressed the transmit button again. "Jyrall? Where are you?"

There was a harsh burst of static in her ears, and the Besquith's gravelly voice came in loud and clear. "There's intense electromagnetic interference all around. I had to move from my observation post. Can anyone hear me?"

"This is May. We've got trouble at the extraction shaft entrance. Oogar trouble. Where are you?"

Jyrall didn't answer. Barlung tore away what looked like the entire outer hatch of Lisalle's CASPer. May shot forward, cannons blazing.

"Nooo!" Lisalle screamed as the Oogar prepared to strike.

May brought up her MAC and sighted on the Oogar, but the angle was wrong. Lisalle could easily be hit, and without the armor's protection, she could die.

"Jyrall! Where are you!" May screamed into the radio. Tears streamed down her cheeks as she tried to steady both her hand cannons and the MAC on Barlung's massive chest.

"I'm here," the Peacemaker growled.

A half second later, she saw the big Besquith leap from the top of a nearby slag pile and crash into the Oogar from behind. Lisalle's CASPer spun wildly, finally free of Barlung's grip, and slammed to the asphalt, facedown.

Jyrall and Barlung rolled away from the CASPer and came up facing each other like two prizefighters ready for the final round. Jyrall was covered in gray dust, making his dark fur shine in the dim light of the mine.

"May?" Lisalle's voice was weak, but clear. "May? Are you out there?"

"I'm here, honey. I'll be there in a second, and we'll get you sorted out."

"I'm okay. My systems are down, and I'll have to eject. Have you got an external weapon I can use, or do you still have a rifle in your cockpit?"

May flushed. Carrying a firearm larger than a pistol inside the actual cockpit of a CASPer had been a no-go during their time in the Ridge Runners, and she'd pulled extra duty and forfeited credits on more than one occasion for the transgression.

"All I've got is a 1911," she replied. "That ain't enough."

Lisalle swore a string of almost unintelligible cuss words. For a brief second or two, neither spoke.

"Get moving!" Jyrall roared at her. "Lisalle, stay down and protected until we can pull you out. May, get down there and help Cora. Do it now!

"You heard him, May," Lisalle said. "I'm hurt, but it ain't bad. Back Cora up. You've got this."

May nodded to herself and spun the CASPer on its heels. As she ran for the shaft entrance, she caught sight of an armored skiff taking an impressive amount of fire on the perimeter. She zoomed the camera view in and saw Ricky and a Goka behind the protective armor screening and firing weapons.

Is that Squarlik? You've gotta be shittin' me.

"Go, May," Lisalle groaned into the comms. "Jyrall has Barlung, and Cora's fighting two of those bastards by herself. Get down there and do what we trained you to do."

May grinned. "A little mayhem coming up, honey."

"That's my girl," Lisalle replied. "Go get 'em."

* * *

For the first time in years, Cora felt in perfect sync with her CASPer. Not since the advanced combatives classes at the CASPer course had she fought with a bladed weapon in the mech's hand and been able to effectively wield her MAC. Cartrule and Frooth weren't stupid opponents, though they could have worked together better, in Cora's opinion. Cartrule was fast and ruthless. Frooth was much slower, but much more powerful in his attacks. Cartrule had charged in almost blindly, and successfully avoided her MAC fire. As he closed the distance, he didn't notice her deploy the dual-edged blade from her left hip. When she struck quickly, gouging his left side, the Oogar howled in pain and rolled away.

Frooth believed he had an opening and leapt into the fray, right into Cora's MAC as she pivoted it in his direction and cut loose with a barrage of fire. Where Cartrule's injuries were more nuisance than actual wounding, Frooth took four or five rounds directly in his chest cavity. Yet he came forward with his claws out and his fangs glinting in the light from the tunnel entrance.

"You'll have to do." He paused and looked down at his chest. Eyes on the spreading dark mat of purple blood, he never saw Cora reposition the MAC and fire a single round directly into the side of his head. Grey and black matter sprayed across the tunnel floor as the small Oogar fell lifelessly to the ground.

"You die!" Cartrule screamed from her four o'clock. As she spun, the Oogar was already in the air, his face a twisted mask of rage and pain. He impacted her CASPer's right shoulder, and she lost her balance, but managed to stab upward with the blade.

Cartrule stomped down on the CASPer's left arm with enough force that the inertial dampeners disengaged, and her grip on the weapon failed. The blade clattered to the tunnel floor and slid away from them. She didn't watch it, instead bringing the MAC up to center on the Oogar's face and—

"Grr-ahhh!" Cartrule bellowed as he tore the cannon away in a ferocious yank.

Her mind working quickly, Cora unholstered the hand cannon on her left hip and tried to bring it up as the Oogar's weight shifted. Cartrule sensed the change, though, and he stomped down even harder on the arm.

"*Servo failure left arm. Servo failure left arm.*" The mech's caution and warning system, nicknamed "Bitchin' Betty," like its counterparts from twentieth century aviation, chimed.

Cora tried, but the left arm wouldn't budge. The Oogar's grip on her right shoulder prevented any movement, and he transitioned to kneeling on the arm with almost all of his weight. The alien was too strong for her CASPer to move. Cartrule brandished his claws above her, and she saw him bring his rifle up in his now free left hand.

"Now I finish what I started. Your friends can't save you, Cora."

Cora's gaze danced across the instrument panel looking for any possible advantage. On the comms display, a new direct laser channel opened.

"Cora!"

May.

"I'm on my way. Hold on."

"Shoot him, May." Cora held her breath. "Do it now!"

"Firing!"

Cora waited, but nothing happened. External microphones picked up what sounded like an engine screaming into the tunnel. May's weapon fired a few times, but only appeared to nick the Oogar's abdomen as he kept Cora pinned to the ground. Time slowed down as she stared up into his rage-filled face. He shifted his aim and fired the laser rifle in a wild one-handed burst of what had to be twenty rounds before throwing it aside. Cartrule reached up high with his right arm and brought it straight down, claws punching straight into her cockpit armor. His claws penetrated the armor enough that they tore into her left shoulder and chest. Warning klaxons rang out in unison with her scream.

"Aaarrghhh!" Pain shot through her body, and the suit immediately administered nanites. Cartrule's claws slashed across her flesh, worsening the wound, before he withdrew them and struck down again, this time lower on the hatch.

Her cockpit darkened. The Oogar had managed to disable her instrument panel and the external camera feeds. She was blind and seriously wounded. The Oogar's claws stabbed suddenly into her soft abdomen, and Cora yelped in pain as Cartrule again pulled away. She heard his claws scraping along the cockpit rail, searching for purchase. He would tear it away, and the next strike would get her heart. A single emergency light flickered to life over her right shoulder.

Cora felt tears of rage in her eyes. Pinned down under the Oogar's weight, her CASPer dying beneath her, she eyed the emergency jettison hatch and wondered if she could un-ass the CASPer fast enough to avoid Cartrule. The ejection sequence would certainly knock him off the mech, but there was no way she could move. In an instant, she knew the ebbing pain and coolness in her limbs meant a significant amount of blood loss. There was no amount of adrenaline available in her weakened, damaged system to compensate for the injuries and propel her out of the cockpit.

There has to be another way.

Hands working on the controls, she brought up the auxiliary power. One camera, the feed from her right shoulder, connected in a flickering, distorted image. Above her, Cartrule stood in the same position he had been. His maw was working, and she realized he was talking to her, likely taunting her, but she could hear none of it.

He suddenly looked up, and shock registered in his eyes for a brief moment before most of his head disappeared. Cartrule fell backward, and the weight on her overloaded systems relented. The large barrel of what looked like a shotgun appeared at the edge of the camera feed.

Behind the stock of the shotgun was a Pushtal.

"Ricky!" Cora yelled.

"Hang on, Cora," he replied. "Count to five and eject your cockpit hatch. Go!"

One, two, three, four, five.

Cora stabbed the button, and the explosive bolts along the cockpit rail fired in quick succession. Parmick's oppressive, dusty air quickly filled the cockpit. As the smoke from the ejection sequence thinned on the freshening breeze, Ricky appeared to her right.

"Oh, damn," Ricky said. "You're pretty cut up, Cora."

"Where's May?"

"Her CASPer's face down about twenty meters away. She's okay, but her cockpit hatch won't open. The bastard got off a lucky shot and blew her servos."

"Get her out. Roll the CASPer over and use the emergency extraction system."

Ricky's eyes narrowed. "I gotta get you out of here, Cora. Unless we stop that bleedin', you ain't gonna make it."

"Get May, Ricky. Please."

"I said she's fine, Cora." The Pushtal leaned into the cockpit and gingerly worked the straps holding her inside the mech. "You're a McCoy, honey. We're kin, and there ain't any way in hell I'm gonna let anything happen to ya."

Cora felt his hands working the straps, and the tears that had started with rage and threatened to spill down her face finally came, but for other reasons. For a brief moment she closed her eyes and dreamed of the hills of her childhood. In the lush, green forests she'd left behind there were memories of playing with friends from neighboring farms and chasing her cousins through the chest-high grasses of the pastures adjacent to their homestead. As close as they were, or she wanted them to be, there was something about Ricky and Keaton she recognized at a level much deeper than family. They'd been raised by a man loved and respected in the family, and while she didn't remember her great uncle, she could see what her family talked about so often around the old wooden kitchen table in the two Pushtal brothers.

"We are kin, Ricky."

"You bet your sweet ass we are." He grinned. "I guess I shouldn't really say stuff like that with you, huh?"

She laughed against the pain in her side. "Talking like that just plays to stereotypes, cousin."

"I ain't much for stereotypes, Cora. Nobody fucks with my family." The Pushtal grinned and she returned it.

"That's good enough for me."

A Goka appeared behind Ricky, and before Cora could warn him, the cockroach-like alien chittered, "Cora McCoy, I'm Corporal Squarlik. I understand you're our commanding officer?"

"Ricky?"

"Long story, cousin. Just go with it." He turned to the Goka. "Open the gates, Squarlik. Let the miners out so they can end this shit, will ya?"

"I thought you'd never ask, Ricky," the Goka replied and disappeared from Cora's view.

"Let's get you out of there," Ricky said as he offered her his hands. "Nice and easy now."

Cora winced as she leaned forward enough for Ricky to pivot around her and grab her under her armpits.

"On three," he said, and in her pain, she didn't really hear him count. When the time came, she held her breath and screamed through the pain in her chest and abdomen. As fast as it came, the pain subsided as he laid her on the ground. There was a hiss and a sting from a pressurized needle as he injected her in the thigh. The burning sensation afterward was far worse.

"Combat nanites. You're gonna rest a bit," Ricky said. "Just relax, Cora. We've got you."

As she slipped into unconsciousness, Cora McCoy actually felt herself relax. Since the debacle with the Ridge Runners and being stranded on Parmick, she'd felt continuously in command and responsible for everything around them. She trusted Ricky and Keaton, along with the Peacemakers. They would take care of her for once. With that realization, Cora gave in and let the nanites put her to sleep and begin to stabilize her wounds.

As she faded out, she heard hundreds of voices shriek in the night. The miners were free.

* * * * *

Chapter Thirty-Four

Diamond Mine

Parmick

Jyrall crouched slightly and circled to his left, eyeing Barlung for an indication of the Oogar's next move. In the background, he heard the battle continuing. From what he could tell, the mercenaries still had the upper hand on the miners. It would take massive numbers for the miners to prevail, as they were clearly outgunned. He glanced at the extraction shaft and understood. The miners were trapped, and it was up to Cora to free them, but she was up against Barlung's lieutenants and likely in over her head.

Barlung glanced to his left and grinned. He'd seen something he liked, apparently. Jyrall risked a quick glance. He caught a glimpse of orange and black in the passenger side of a hovercraft with a Goka driving. They were stopped and firing at nearby mercenaries. It had to be one of the McCoy brothers. *They must be trying to get to Cora to help her.*

Suddenly he realized what Barlung was grinning about. About fifty yards away, three Lumar were putting together a large crew-served laser on a tripod. Once it was assembled, the armor on the hovercraft wouldn't stand a chance. After they were through with it, Barlung would order them to cut the Besquith down.

Looking back at Barlung, Jyrall could see the Oogar's attention was back on him. If he looked away again, the big Oogar would attack. With a grin of his own, Jyrall reached down with his right hand, unsnapped the strap on his holster, and drew the CT-75 from it. Barlung's eyes widened; he'd thought the Besquith would fight him one on one with no weapons involved.

Without turning his head, Jyrall shifted his eyes slightly, still looking at Barlung. Holding the hand cannon straight out to his side, he used the small red crosshairs and sight picture now showing on the screen of the patch covering his right eye. He fired a shot directly into the battery pack of the laser before it could be connected. The blast was spectacular, sending the three dead Lumars flying, their bodies mangled. Still grinning and staring at Barlung, Jyrall slid the weapon back into his holster and snapped the strap. *That's some Ricky Shit for you.*

Visibly shaken, Barlung snarled as the hovercraft started moving again. "I don't need a weapon for you," growled Jyrall.

In a rage, Barlung rushed in, intent on slicing the Besquith wide open with a mighty blow. Jyrall shifted to the opposite side of the swinging arm and, using Barlung's blind rage and momentum against him, tripped and shoved at the same time. Barlung, unable to maintain his balance, hit the dirt and rolled like a novice in a self-defense class.

"Pathetic," Jyrall said calmly.

Standing, Barlung brushed the dirt off his face. He deliberately stalked Jyrall, determined to not be made a fool of again. Jyrall stood his ground. Suddenly Barlung lashed out on what he perceived to be Varkell's blind side. The blow was blocked and held by Jyrall's strong arm as he struck Barlung in his exposed ribs with a quick knee the Oogar never saw coming.

Jyrall shoved the Oogar away using the extended arm. Once again Barlung stumbled as he struggled to catch his breath. With a scream he rushed again, arms wide to grab Jyrall and crush him with his enormous strength. It was a move he'd used many times in the past.

Jyrall was ready for it. It was one Captain Dreel had used in training at the Peacemaker Academy, designed to subdue your opponent. Jyrall had learned the counter move by the fourth time he had sparred with his mentor. He dove into Barlung's midsection as the huge arms swiped above his back, missing him. Once again Barlung was on the ground, but this time Jyrall was there above him, ready to strike.

Barlung threw his arms up to cover his face and block the blow. That negated most of the force, but he still received several cuts across his snout from Jyrall's claws in the open hand strike. He had been slapped…and he knew it.

Jyrall got up, quickly stepped back, and waited calmly, breathing a little harder, but not exhausted like Barlung. The Oogar sat up, practically panting, indecision on his face. Jyrall stepped forward, and Barlung flinched, holding his hands up toward Jyrall in defeat.

"Enough!" Barlung yelled. "Enough! What do you want from me? I'll give you anything—everything! You can have it all—the credit, the mines, the whole damn town. Just don't kill me… Please don't kill me. This isn't my town or anything." The last came out in a pathetic whimper.

"I don't want your credits," Jyrall said. He reached into his inside pocket, pulled out the case, and flipped it open. "You're under arrest. Besides, what does a Peacemaker need credits for? You behind prison bars, Barlung; that's what I want. And answers. Lots of answers."

* * *

Town Starport

Parmick

Larth came through the gate of the airfield, running hard. Far up ahead he caught a glimpse of a Jeha entering the hangar he'd broken into. Breathing heavily, he ducked down, trying to run faster. He'd halved the distance when he heard a thunderous roar and saw part of the roof of the hanger tear away.

He dove to the ground and covered his head as pieces of the hangar flew out in several directions. He risked a look. The shuttle with the modified engines blasted into the sky, picking up speed with every second. Larth ducked his head again as debris rained down all around him.

"Shit!" he said, panting. "That's not good."

He reached up and engaged his comms. "Keaton! Can you track that ship? Is it headed to the gate?"

"I'm here," came the reply. "It's too early to tell. I'll set the system to watch it, and we'll know soon enough. Who was on it, and where are you?"

"It was Nay-Thok. I'm near the hangar," Larth said, sitting up. "Can't you see me? Where's the drone?"

"I lost signal from it," Keaton explained. "The shuttle may have clobbered it. You have to be the one to tell Ricky."

"Why me?" Larth said, walking toward what was left of the hanger.

"You're one of the bosses," Keaton explained. "That's above my pay grade. If you're headed to the hangar, watch out. Gimmold and a handful of the Eye Pokers are there, unless they left on the shuttle."

"I'm pretty sure they did," Larth said. "Nay-Thok didn't have time to power it up, run through the launch checklist, and take off by himself. They had it ready to go and were just waiting for him."

REDACTED AFFAIRS | 373

Well, shit.

"I'm going in to check it out," Larth announced.

Standing in the open area where the shuttle had been parked, he heard a noise behind him. He spun around, weapons in both hands. There, emerging from the remaining frigate, were the two Miderall, looking around at the destruction. They wore some of the brightest mismatched clothes Larth had ever seen. One seemed to be wearing a neon lime cape. They walked over to Larth, ignoring his weapons.

One of them spoke. "Fitting, I say it's fitting. An ugly hangar for an ugly ship. I say, an ugly ship." It waved a feathered arm at the destruction.

"And now we're out of a job, you see. A job, don't you know?" the other replied, nodding its beak.

Larth shook his head and grinned. *Miderall. Always repeating whatever they say. Now that's crazy.*

"Whose ship is that?" Larth asked, pointing with a pistol.

"It's the Eye Poker's ship. Eye Pokers, you understand," answered the first Miderall. "We're the pilots. Recently hired pilots, don't you know? Recent."

"Not anymore, it ain't," Larth informed them. He held out his Peacemaker's badge. "What are your names, and are you looking for a job?"

"Well met, Peacemaker," the first said. Both Miderall bowed their heads in greeting. "I am Kalitrontalmonty and this is Narwit-noomilstew. Kalitrontalmonty and Naritnoomilstew, that is."

"What the hell?" Larth said. "That's a mouthful. How about I call you Monty and Stew?

"A nickname, how delightful, a nickname, you see," Stew said. "Yes, we would like a job, we're pilots you understand. Pilots."

"Yeah, yeah, pilots. I get it," Larth said. "Listen, can you move that frigate out of this mess and park it over on the tarmac? Not too close, but close enough to the two ships on the far side?"

"Of course, Peacemaker," Monty answered. They both turned to go back up the ramp.

"A Peacemaker, he is. Peacemaker," Stew said. "Did you see his outfit? Outfit, that is."

"Be quiet, quiet I say," admonished Monty, as they entered the ship. "I'm sure he can hear you. We cannot judge someone on their poor fashion sense. We spoke of this. Spoke, we did."

* * *

Diamond Mine
Parmick

"Turn around," Jyrall instructed.

Barlung did as he was told, and Jyrall put wrist restraints on him. They were designed to hold the strongest of races. Barlung wouldn't be able to break loose; he no longer possessed the will to attempt it. Once he saw the Peacemaker badge, he seemed to deflate.

With a roar, hundreds of miners poured out of the recently blocked shaft. The remaining mercenaries moved toward Barlung. Though he was defeated, it seemed the safest move. They knew they couldn't kill every miner before they ran out of ammunition. The battle was over.

Jyrall screamed loud enough to be heard by the closest of them, "Peacemaker! Drop your weapons and prepare to submit yourselves for investigation and interrogation."

Those nearest slowly complied. It created a ripple effect, and in no time, all the mercenaries were standing with their hands or limbs raised and their weapons on the ground. The miners circling them cheered. It grew louder and louder, and Jyrall began to wonder if they would tear the mercenaries apart before he could question them to determine if they were deserving of mercy. Surely there were a few who'd taken the contract because there were no other options.

Ledram, the Jivool Cora had told them about, climbed to the top of the nearest slag pile and called for silence. "We will do as the Peace-maker asks. Those with arms will sling them or put them away. Justice will be served." The crowd roared again, but weapons were safed, while the cheering went on and on.

Jyrall indicated he wanted to speak, and Ledram silenced the crowd. "See to the wounded—from both sides of this conflict," Jyrall ordered. "Make that happen, Ledram."

Ledram climbed down to organize the effort, shouting orders as he did so.

A battered and shot-up hovercraft pulled up, driven by a Goka. Ricky jumped out and ran to Jyrall. "I gotta get Cora and the girls to the ship for some more nanite treatment. I had to peel all three of them from their CASPers."

"Go!" Jyrall agreed. Ricky turned and ran back to the craft.

As the miners moved away, Jyrall used the comms and saw they now worked. "Larth?"

"I'm here, you ol' Snarlyface, you," Larth answered.

"Did you catch him?" Jyrall asked.

"No, he escaped in that hopped-up shuttle," Larth answered.

"Damn," Jyrall said.

"But, hey, I got the goods," Larth exclaimed.

"Goods?" Jyrall asked.

"Yeah," Larth said. "I downloaded a copy of Nay-Thok's entire computer system, and snagged some schematics and everything."

"Good," Jyrall said. "Well done. Ricky and the Goka are headed your way with Cora and the girls; tell Keaton to get ready with the nanites and med kit. Cora's in bad shape. May and Lisalle are wounded. How are Nileah and Kellie?"

"Nileah is banged up," Larth said. After a short pause, he continued, "Kellie didn't make it, Jyrall. She took a tank round in the cockpit hatch as she was protecting Nileah and the others."

Jyrall sighed and closed his eyes. *The butcher always has a bill, doesn't he?* "Stand…"

"…or fall," Larth finished.

He opened his eyes and watched the hovercraft accelerating toward the starport. "I'll try to locate a physician, maybe one familiar with Humans, and send them to the ship. Meet me at the Peacemaker's office in an hour."

* * * * *

Chapter Thirty-Five

To Jyrall's surprise, the outer door to the office was open. In all the time they'd been there, no one had thought to actually approach the door and try the lock. He felt the skin under his fur flush in embarrassment as he turned the lever and pushed the door open. With a glance over his shoulder, he caught Barlung's eye. The Oogar was powercuffed, the simple device completing a mild electrical charge that involuntarily clenched Barlung's fists and prevented him from withdrawing his hands. Not that it mattered; the defeated Oogar slouched with his head down and stooped through the Peacemaker's door without Jyrall saying a word.

Built to a standard design, the office was simple and almost un-furnished. Inside the front windows, a multi-species conforming couch sat in front of a simple metal desk with a curved edge and several compartments. Like the couch, the desk itself could morph into an ergonomically sound device for any species. On the far side of the desk was a pair of simple wooden benches for offenders. There was a small galley device for water and various hot beverages built into the wall opposite the window, next to a door that led, typically, to the Peacemaker's living quarters. Opposite the door and directly across from the desk was another small room Jyrall hadn't seen from the exterior window, except it wasn't a room. The holding cell was clean and empty, ready for an occupant. Barlung marched up to the cell, his head down, and stepped inside. He turned to Jyrall.

"I'd like to make a statement," Barlung said.

"You'll have all the time in the world, Barlung." Jyrall saw the Oogar's eyes shift to his left, toward the living quarters. With blinding speed, Jyrall drew his Paladin and drew down on his target before even turning his head.

A shocked Human woman flinched backward and dropped a handful of cleaning supplies on the floor, but didn't say anything in her surprise. In a heartbeat, Jyrall recognized her from the bar. He holstered his weapon, engaged the holding cell, and deactivated Barlung's cuffs before turning to her.

Let's see if I can remember Galactic Standard sign language.

He slowly signed, "Who are you and why are you here?"

The woman's hands flashed through the signs, and Jyrall caught enough to piece together she'd been hired by Barlung to keep the office clean for prying eyes.

I see.

She signed again, more slowly. "I can communicate via slate."

Jyrall nodded. She tapped on her slate and motioned for him to speak. He spoke clearly, enunciating every word. "Barlung hired you to clean the office until the Peacemaker returned?"

She tapped the slate. "Yes," a computerized voice replied tonelessly. "Peacemaker Rekk was recalled to the Academy for additional training."

"Barlung told you that?"

She nodded. "Is that not true?"

"Peacemaker Rekk is dead," Jyrall said. He turned to Barlung. "Isn't he?"

The Oogar stood mute. "Answering that could incriminate me."

"You're a barrister now?" Jyrall grinned. "I don't think you're in a position to argue, Barlung."

Barlung sighed and said, "Peacemaker Rekk is dead."

"That was easy, wasn't it?" Jyrall tried not to laugh. Seeing the formerly belligerent Oogar reduced to a scolded toddler was both exhilarating and troubling.

The woman's slate beeped. "What are you doing in this office? How did you know how to use that holding cell?"

Jyrall reached into his utility belt and withdrew the slim black case. He flipped it open and showed her his badge. "My name is Peacemaker Jyrall."

The woman audibly gasped. "Well, now. You certainly weren't what I was expecting."

Jyrall fought to keep his mouth from falling open. The woman spoke in a clear, lilting voice. Her English was strongly accented, and he placed it immediately in the upper British Isles. Not proper Scottish, more of a Highland dialect. "You can talk? And hear, I presume?"

"Both." The woman peeled off her dirty headgear and shook out her shoulder-length dark hair. Her hands removed the equally dirty scarf covering her neck, and she reached into her jacket, withdrawing a familiar case. In an instant, he recognized the tree on the Human's badge as a Scots pine, one of the native trees of Scotland, and what he knew of her fell into place.

"Peacemaker Sinclair, correct?"

"That's right. Nikki Sinclair." She smiled up at him. "Well met, Peacemaker Jyrall."

"Well met, Peacemaker," Jyrall almost stammered. "I'm sorry about your father and the losses of your family. There was dishonor in the deaths of non-combatants."

The woman's face darkened. "I think all Humans are combatants in times like these. But thank you for your sympathy."

Jyrall nodded. "How long have you been here?"

"Six months," Sinclair said. She brushed her hair from her eyes, walked over to the workstation, and booted it up. "When the first reports from Rekk contained redundancies and inconsistencies, the Regional Barracks commander reached back to the guild. In between missions, Guild Master Rsach sent me here to observe and report. Rekk was compromised months ago by his own inaction. He believed the town to be in good hands and never looked deeper into the expansion of the mine and the ruthless means through which miners found their way into its employ."

"You've been undercover this entire time?"

"I have," she said. A smile appeared on her face. "I didn't enjoy the fall, either. You're a recent graduate, am I right?"

Jyrall snorted and returned her smile. "Yes. My partner Larth and I were commissioned two weeks early."

Sinclair nodded. "Now I recognize your names. So your mission last year at the Marloch Trading Station was your commissioning mission?"

"Yes, ma'am."

She laughed. "You don't have to call me that, Jyrall. I am damned impressed, though."

For the first time since the early days of the academy, he felt lost for words. Finally he took a breath and simply said, "Thank you."

Sinclair tapped the workstation, and the Tri-V displays came to life. Several months worth of messages scrolled quickly down the screen, but she paid them no attention. Jyrall watched as she crossed the room to stare into Barlung's cell.

"You surrendered in the hope of amnesty, yes?"

Barlung nodded. "Yes, Peacemaker."

"You're prepared to answer all our questions? To cooperate fully and grant us investigative privilege in exchange for leniency?"

Jyrall marveled at the change in her voice and body language. Nikki Sinclair, like Jessica Francis, commanded respect and attention instantly. Neither had his size or intimidating appearance, but the effect on the Oogar was immediate. If he could have sunk lower in the cell, Jyrall suspected he would have.

"That's correct, Peacemaker Sinclair."

She turned to Jyrall. "I'd like to lead the questioning, if you don't mind?"

Jyrall shook his head. "Not at all. You obviously suspect much more than the transgressions against the people of Parmick."

"Oh, yes." Sinclair nodded and smiled at him again. Her blue eyes glittered in the light from the office. "This whole operation was under Nay-Thok's supervision and performed under the direction of Kr'et'Socae. They've been mining red diamond fragments and successfully introducing synthesized red diamonds into the economy of the worlds on the far reaches of the three arms."

Jyrall felt his mouth pop open. "That's what we transported for you. We've just become aware of this in the last few days. How much did we transfer?"

Barlung nodded. "Four hundred kilograms. Depending on the value we could expect in the different regions, it could have been hundreds of millions of credits into Kr'et'Socae's war chest."

"War chest?" Jyrall asked.

Sinclair crossed her arms. "We don't know for certain that's what the Equirri's up to, but he's organized, manned, and equipped a considerable fighting force. Finding a way to finance it, especially given their defeat at Victoria Bravo, is almost certainly one of his goals. As for the others? That's what we're going to figure out, Jyrall."

The office door behind them slammed closed and startled them both. Jyrall turned around and saw Larth standing in the doorway with his paws on his thin hips. As his eyes darted to the woman, the Zuparti froze, brought his paws up, and pointed. "Whoa now. Just how in the hell can you suddenly talk? Who are you?"

"I could always talk. The ruse was that I couldn't hear."

"And you heard a lot of things, I imagine?"

"Like you're a savant with weapons and nary an ounce of fear in your body," she replied. A smile appeared on her lips. "And you have dreadful taste in GalNet shows."

Jyrall turned to Sinclair and winked with one eye so Larth couldn't see. "Peacemaker Larth, allow me introduce Peacemaker Nikki Sinclair. She's been on-planet for several months, and I've granted her the lead on interrogating Barlung and his associates."

Larth didn't speak for a moment. His eyes remained fixed on Sinclair and his lower jaw worked from side-to-side.

"Larth? Did you hear me?" Jyrall asked.

"I heard you, Snarlyface." Larth frowned. "Nikki Sinclair, huh?"

"That's right, Peacemaker Larth." The woman smiled and extended her right hand in the Human way of greeting.

The Zuparti grinned and shook her hand. "No shit?"

* * *

Peacemaker Contingency Operations Headquarters
Weqq

Tok and the other five Enforcers walked down the boarding ramp of the Blue Flight and into the stifling heat and humidity of the Weqq summer. The moist air was redolent with the scent of loam and thick jungle foliage, and Tok savored it over the pressurized and recycled air of spaceflight. Overhead, thick clouds kept the oppressive sun at bay and made the heat slightly more bearable. It had been too long since he'd relished the heat, and savoring it almost stopped his movement down the ramp.

As the de facto leader of their group, Tok realized Captain Dreel's expectant eyes were watching them exit the shuttle and make their way toward him. He turned over his shoulder. "Form it up, Enforcers. We do this right from now on."

No one said a word, but they formed up behind him in two rows. Tok saw Captain Dreel almost crack a smile, and it made him strangely happy. An Enforcer typically worked alone or with a private aircrew and intelligence support. As such, they tended to shy away from the normal customs and courtesies of their roles. As they stepped from the ramp onto the wide tarmac of the contingency headquarters, Tok thought he heard Zevva buzzing a soft cadence behind him.

Tok approached Dreel and stopped two meters away. He saluted with one hoof to his chest. "Captain Dreel, Enforcer Tok and a party of five reporting for duty."

Dreel smiled and nodded. "Well met, Enforcers. Yet I think you might need to construct a naming convention of some type."

"What do you mean?" Tok asked.

Dreel laughed. "Have your team stand at ease and gather 'round, Tok."

Without a word, the Enforcers formed a semicircle in front of Dreel and stood at their species' equivalent of at-ease. "Enforcers are formed, sir."

"See? That's what I'm talking about, Tok. You're all either some type of team or squad or echelon. Something. From a brevity perspective, we need to work on that. Especially as the situation continues to change, and we prepare for combat operations."

"Here?"

Dreel nodded. "Yes. The TriRusk are at risk, and we have to protect them."

"Can we not evacuate them?" Zevva asked, her voice a low buzz. "Find a place more tactically sound to defend?"

"This has been defended successfully before," Cha-Myt replied. "Isn't this the former MinSha science station Peacemaker Francis defended and then attacked in a Combat Assault Suit, Personal with Tara Mason?"

Dreel nodded. "It is. There are still some remnants of that struggle I'll show you as we prepare. For now, we must meet with Captain Kurrang and TriRusk Leader Nurr. She won't leave this planet, yet she's unsure of our ability to stop an attack on her colony."

"Aren't they hidden?" asked Mratt, the Jivool. "I read the initial briefing, sir. The TriRusk colony is hidden in a cavern system that's almost impossible to locate without highly advanced sensors."

"A true statement," Dreel said, "however, when you're discussing sensors, you're not thinking about the simplest sensors available to most species, with one in particular."

"The Equirri have exceptional visual senses," Tavaara growled. The large Oogar still had one arm in a makeshift splint from their tangle with the *Kithlawur*. The event had caused much consternation among the team when they'd found out they'd been essentially defeated by two very junior Peacemakers. "If Kr'et'Socae comes here and somehow prevails on whatever battlefield we attempt to force him onto, he'll still find them."

"Which means the trap we have to set is critical," Dreel replied. "Now, we'll discuss your mission parameters later, but it's important to address two critical items at this juncture. First, you're not the main effort of the defense. Your role will be the protection of the TriRusk colony itself. There are ground forces continuing to mobilize here, including additional Enforcer units. According to the guild master, elements of the Force 25 rear guard are on their way here, as well as a few other allies. The defense of Weqq is critical for the guild going forward, but the highest priority is to protect the three hundred TriRusk on-planet. They're the only known colony remaining."

"I understand our confidence in an attack must be high for this type of deployment, sir," Tok said slowly, "but from a strategic perspective, do we really think Kr'et'Socae's going to come here just to get the diamonds he thinks he needs?"

Dreel nodded. Tok thought there might have been some satisfaction in the captain's gesture. "Good point, Tok. We really don't know. Planning for military operations means we try to address as many variables as possible. The guild master has initiated a plan that exceeds your need to know. Frankly, I'm not aware of the breadth of his plan, but the High Council is aware and approves. Capturing or killing Kr'et'Socae is the highest priority for our guild. Weqq may not be the most tactically sound ground to do so, but with the TriRusk resistant to move, and our forces still consolidating around the Regional Barracks, this is the ground we choose."

Tok gestured to the headquarters. "Then it's safe to assume the High Council isn't here? What about the guild master and the selector? Or prime?"

"The High Council have evacuated to their designated planets and zones. The guild master's location is classified, but rest assured, he's safe for now. The prime enforcer has a separate mission across the galaxy. Like me, he's charged with rallying forces for combat operations."

"To what end?" Kravon asked. The Caroon's lips pursed into a tight, thin line. "Are we expecting to fight Kr'et'Socae's forces across the whole galaxy?"

"No," Dreel replied with a shake of his head. "We're anticipating a much wider conflict, Kravon. Something that may even challenge the very structure of the Union itself. We've always taken a stance, as a guild, of being able to react and mediate disputes and solve problems after they happen. We no longer have that luxury."

Tok spoke up. "From our studies of doctrine, as you ordered, we need to see the ground we'll defend and coordinate with those planning the defense of the planet itself."

"You're correct, Tok," Dreel replied. "As those forces continue to arrive, we'll do that. As for showing you the terrain, the best way to do that is for you to do it yourselves. You've received the brief on the planet's flora and fauna?"

"Yes, sir," the team chorused.

"Good," Dreel replied. "It's a sixteen-hour movement from here to the TriRusk colony by foot. Get your tactical gear and weapons unpacked, and be prepared to move out within the next hour. Captain Kurrang is expecting you at first light tomorrow morning."

Tok waited to hear someone complain, but it never came. He met Captain Dreel's eyes. "Will we have a guide or any type of navigation guidance?"

"You'll have whatever you have in your kit, Enforcer Tok. What's the point of deploying with gear if you're not intimately familiar with how to operate it?" Dreel grinned. "Besides, after a few weeks of spaceflight, I know all too well that you all want to be outside and physically active before your tempers flare and all that. What better way to kill two Urrtam with one stone?"

"Urrtam?" Tavaara asked. "Are those the feral bird things that eat pretty much anything they come into contact with?"

"Indeed," Dreel said. "But we've taken care of that for you. Weqq is a jungle, though, and there's plenty of other nasty stuff you'll have to worry about."

Tok grinned. "But so will Kr'et'Socae if he shows his face here."

"That's exactly right, Tok." Dreel nodded. "But rest assured, he is coming here. Guild Master Rsach has asked me to see to that myself."

* * * * *

Chapter Thirty-Six

Ngashia

Aventa Region

Rain fell in heavy curtains into the jungle canopy high above and filtered down on Tirr's position in a cold, spattering deluge. In the midst of the concealed position, he took a moment to stand fully on his four legs and stretch his back. Tactical manuals and the instructors of a hundred MinSha infantry schools would have flashed into panic and anger, but common sense and hours of observation led him to believe several things. First, the Dream World Consortium's science team had been asleep in their field expedient hard shelters for more than two hours. They'd posted three Jeha-built security tripods to scan the surrounding terrain for threats, before breaking into some type of liquor, and drinking themselves into a collective stupor.

Tirr knew the systems well, having used them at Weqq before realizing their obsolescence in a driving rainstorm. Second, combined with the dense vegetation surrounding them, the sensors had a maximum effective range of maybe five meters. Two hundred meters away and watching through a much better built and adapted remote drone system attached to the stalks of tall, thin trees high above, Tirr saw everything clearly through the rain and vegetation. There had been nothing of consequence since the last of the team stumbled to bed, howling Zuul love songs. Finally, over the last ten days and after moving more than eight hundred kilometers in several coordinated dropship movements, the DWC science team of Zuul and Veetanho technicians had never bothered to heft a weapon or post a security detail. They believed, wrongly, that what they carried with them mitigated any threats they'd find in Ngashia's jungles.

They'd followed this particular team for three planets. Each of the previous ones were more inhabited than Ngashia, and the team's pitiful security measures there didn't measure up to the strength of a simple cyberlock. What they'd done was tip their methods, and as they'd done nothing to change their strategy, it had been a simple matter to determine their location from the moment they'd arrived.

With *Victory Twelve* parked in a high orbit and squawking a Merchant Guild "do not disturb" code with minimal power sources running, Tirr and his team of female warriors simply scanned the planet for the known frequencies and power sources the team used in their work. Knowing where the team could be found also made things easy. The Dream World Consortium's work in terraforming worlds with water sources was unprecedented, and while Ngashia appeared to be developed enough to support life, and agricultural in its current biosphere, it was one of the few planets in a habitable zone that hadn't been actively colonized. That it was a target of the DWC wasn't surprising, nor was their methodology.

Colonies required fresh water. Most of the oceans found on habitable worlds tended to be mostly saltwater, and while they could be desalinated and made usable, the DWC realized the cost of making potable water from seawater could be spent elsewhere. Fresh water sources were a prerequisite. Once identified, the DWC simply went to the actual source of the river first. From there, they'd study the land and the soil in a few other places downstream to determine changes in the water, looking for something, and then move to the next river. As long as the river in question was more than one thousand kilometers in length, it would be tested. All Tirr had to do was find a source with a tactical advantage and wait. Mountains, particularly those high in altitude and lacking in natural cover, seemed to be what the DWC always tested first, almost like they were working their way down for a reason. It didn't matter; Tirr simply picked his target, moved the team into position without being seen from orbit by the DWC vessels, and waited.

After eight days on the ground, the warriors were restless, but they kept their bearing and focused on the mission. Knowing that the DWC continued to test water on every habitable planet in the galaxy was one thing, discovering the reason was paramount. Time was growing short.

Tirr tapped his slate and sent a silent command to the team. Eight female warriors ringed the DWC position, each no closer than two hundred meters. The simple alarm was meant for them to turn off their communicators and slates as they approached the bivouac site. Rain couldn't fully dampen the electromagnetic spectrum enough to allow radio communications the Jeha sensors wouldn't pick up, triangulate, and engage with direct fire.

As Jessica would say, we'll do this the old-fashioned way.

Vibrating his antennae, Tirr sent the first command. There wouldn't have to be many commands—his warriors wouldn't need them. *Move out. Good hunting.*

He picked up his pack and moved toward the compound. With a twitch of his head, Tirr activated the command link from the multispectral cameras directly into his goggles so he could see the overall picture. Almost immediately, one of the DWC defensive sensors winked off. The second and third followed a moment later.

Tirr, the command console is unsecured, one of his warriors, Sezza, reported with a definite sense of agitation. This was unexpected. The rest of the warriors—rifles and combat knives at the ready—covered the two entrances for each of the hard shelters. Sezza managed to creep into the center of the site to where the test equipment lay stacked for the next day's operation.

Or it's a trap.

Is there any sign of tampering?

Nothing. I've checked it twice. Do I open it?

Tirr ground his lower jaw for five seconds. The greatest risk was in not taking one. If something happened, the other warriors would enter the compound and kill everything with a heartbeat in a matter of seconds. That wasn't the problem. The Dream World Consortium should have been licking their wounds after the debacle at Araf, and they were very clearly up to something nefarious.

Open it.

Panel is active, Sezza reported with her antennae. The pouring rain was the only sound in the entire compound. Tirr moved through the jungle with practiced ease, and passed the first of the three shelters. The warriors there gave him a respectful nod, and had it not been in the middle of an operation, he would have almost swelled with pride. MinSha females didn't tend to take orders from males. He knew their respect to be authentic, though it was granted by his position as the commander of the Royal Guard of Honored Queen Taal, but at the same time, he'd earned it alongside them for the last several weeks. There was no job or task he wouldn't do himself, and they appreciated his efforts and accepted him, almost, as one of their own.

Coming up on your right. Tirr made his way through the center of the silent compound and stood at Sezza's left shoulder. She towered over him, as most female warriors did over their male counterparts, and there was concern in the droop of her antennae.

Look at this. Can you make sense of it?

What is it? Tirr leaned closer.

They were careless. The operating system was running. All I searched was last files opened. This was at the top of the list. Sezza pointed. *They've tested 467 planets in the last year, and more than 11,000 freshwater sources.*

Tirr nodded as he read. His own hand came up to point at the screen as a shiver of worry shot down his thorax.

The top five matches they've identified are listed here. Get an image of this list.

Sezza put down her weapon and leaned in closer with her goggles to capture the data on the screen as Tirr tried to process it.

Earth—Lake Rotorua, southern hemisphere. Snowmass—Lake Pryce, eastern continent. Tilgh-23, all major rivers. Cruxton Prime—Site One, northern hemisphere near Marietta City. Krifay—Section 26A. His compound eyes glanced at the top of the list—the best match of the planets in the DWC database.

Uluru.

Tirr shook his head. *That can't be right.*

What? Sezza replied. *I have the image.*

I'm not sure I believe it. Tapping his slate, Tirr removed a data cable and moved to connect it to a port on the console.

What are you doing?

Uluru. Tirr pointed at the screen. *Force 25 needs to know about this— it matches records in the database they're using to find Snowman. If we can get the coordinates of the planet, even the region of space, we can—*

Sezza raised a claw and blocked the port. *The risk is too great, sir. They'd know we connected to the console. There has to be another way.*

Tirr thought for a moment, wondering what Jessica would do in this situation, and he realized she'd follow Sezza's counsel and advice. The warrior knew the score, too. Just because a door swung open didn't mean it was safe to walk through. There were other ways to get the information they needed, and there were others who needed to know they'd found a clue to Snowman's whereabouts, slim as it was.

You're right, Sezza. Thank you for your wise counsel. We should go.

Sezza twitched her head, and the other warriors retreated into the jungle toward their original positions. Tirr followed, with Sezza at his side.

Orders, sir?

Prepare to withdraw. We'll march to the landing zone tonight. Once the Dream World team moves on, we'll call the dropship down and get off the planet. The Peacemaker Guild needs to know what we've found.

They pushed through the jungle and into the heavier underbrush. Above them, some type of creature screeched into the night. There was no movement or sudden return of light in the compound. The three sensor platforms winked to life and peered uselessly into the deluge. The entire scene remained as if nothing had happened. The MinSha owned the night.

"What have we found? What are they looking to match?" Her voice was low, but concerned.

Tirr shook his head as he set his pack down and rested in the cool rain. He glanced up and found her eyes on him. "I don't know, Sezza. I have a feeling they know something the rest of us don't. I think Snowman does, too."

* * *

Town Starport
Parmick

"What's he doing?" Jyrall asked.

"Shhh, I want to hear," admonished Larth with a grin. "He's interviewing and hiring for his unit. He knows a lot of the ones trying to get on since he's been on Parmick a while; others he's interviewing."

"How do we know he isn't picking soldiers Cora doesn't want?" Jyrall asked, his maw forming a frown. "I don't know about this."

The two Peacemakers were standing on the ramp looking out at Sergeant Figgle as he walked between rows of dirty mercenaries and miners. There were over forty of them assembled on the tarmac.

"He sat with Cora for several hours in sick bay," Larth explained. "When they finished, she said she trusted his judgment, and the rest of the ladies agreed. Besides, Ricky and his new friend are out there with him cutting through the bullshit. They've been at it for hours. Those are all that remain."

"Cutting through the what?" Jyrall asked.

"Never mind. Shhh," Larth said again. "Listen."

"You," Figgle asked as he stopped, looking at a SleSha. "What's your story? I've seen you and him," he indicated the SleSha beside him in the makeshift formation, "around Town."

"We're pilots, Sergeant," answered the SleSha. "I'm Skirith and this is Diamich. We were crew members of Miguel's Monsoons. The bastards left us here on Parmick."

"The Monsoons had their ship stolen right off the airfield, didn't they?" Figgle asked.

"Yes, Sergeant," Squarlik answered. He stood with Ricky behind the formation. He still had the .50 caliber rifle strapped to his back.

"The forever be damned Redd's Riders did it," Skirith said. "I can't prove it, but I know it. A month later, Miguel landed a contract for his company and just left us. He said he didn't have a ship, so he didn't need us, and we were on our own."

"That sumbitch needs an ass whipping," Ricky volunteered. Squarlik attempted to nod with him.

Figgle continued his line of questioning. "Interesting. Tell me, what exactly were you doing around three the morning of the revolt?"

"The weapon fire woke us," Skirith said and hesitated.

"And?" prompted Figgle. "After that?"

"Just tell him," Diamich said. When Skirith said nothing, Diamich went on, "Fine, I will. We were on top of our apartment building, taking shots at the Lumar guards."

"Really?" Figgle asked, rubbing his limbs together. "So you weren't hired by Barlung to suppress the pending revolt?"

"I wouldn't work for him if it was the last job on the planet," stated Skirith, standing straighter and looking directly at Figgle with his multifaceted insect-like eyes. "I'm a pilot, not a slave driver. Those Lumar beat a friend of mine to death last month. I had to take my revenge."

"Excellent," Figgle said. "I was informed several guards took hits from town." Figgle raised his voice. "Who among you were on other buildings doing the same thing?"

Five hands in the final rank went up. All were Jivool. Figgle squinted his eyes and looked over at Jyrall and Larth, standing on the ramp. He would see about these five. He walked around to see them face to face.

"How do I know you're not Eye Pokers?" Figgle asked.

"*What?*" the Jivool practically shouted. "I spit on Eye Pokers and their entire clan. May they all be infested with gikle bugs and the bites fester for weeks. May they—"

"You'll do," Figgle said, turning away.

He walked back to the front of the formation. Glancing back to Squarlik and Ricky, he looked for confirmation. Ricky gave a thumbs-up. Squarlik attempted to do the same. It didn't have quite the same effect. He looked to the left and right at the other five Goka in his squad. None of them had any misgivings.

"All right, listen up," the sergeant said. "I'm prepared to offer all forty-two of you a contract. You're all experienced mercenaries, even if some of you have been mining for a while. I'm not the commander; that would be Colonel Cora McCoy, a Human. A Human female. Does anyone have a problem with that? No? Good. Because in this company, race doesn't matter. Sex doesn't matter. Rank matters, of course, but more than that, loyalty matters. The unit is called Blue Ridge Kin. For some of you, that may lose something in the translation. Let me explain it as it was explained to me."

Sergeant Figgle paused for a moment. "Kin is an English Human word. A southern word for family. If you sign that contract, you *will* become kin. You *will* become family. You *will* be loyal to your family. Now some of you will sign, thinking you know what that means. If you're not sure, you'll find out in time. Others know what it means. It means you'd stand in front of your kin and take the shot meant for them, and they would do the same for you. Think about it." Sergeant Figgle paused again. This time the moment stretched.

Jyrall and Larth watched the faces of those in formation. Some of them had a determined look, the decision already made. Others had a look of dawning realization. More and more of them acquired the determined look. Both Peacemakers, trained in reading facial and body language of multiple species, saw the transformation take place. It was the realization that, if they joined this unit, they would be joining more than a military outfit—they would be gaining brothers, sisters, and cousins. For some, it correlated to clan members and hive mates.

"If you still want to join the Kin," Figgle said, "on my command, fall out and fall in line in front of Keaton on the ramp of *Kellie's Stand*. He'll have you imprint your mark on his slate. I'll witness every imprint. Normally Colonel McCoy or one of the officers would oversee that, but they're indisposed at the moment. I'm the senior NCO in this outfit; you *are* and *will be* my responsibility. You…are my family. Fall out!"

With a shout, all forty-two members of the formation moved quickly to the ship flown from the wrecked hanger and parked near *Blue Ridge*. As they stood in line, those who didn't know others introduced themselves. It was a start.

* * *

"Sergeant Figgle has a way with the soldiers," Jyrall said. "I have to say, I'm impressed."

"He does," Cora agreed. "I'm usually pretty good at figuring folks out when I meet them. My grandmother called it reading their souls through their eyes. She could tell you after ten minutes if someone was 'Good People.'"

"Hell, I like him," Ricky said. "If a Human merc had as much time as a soldier as he does, they'd be a first sergeant or sumthin'."

"I do, too," Lisalle admitted. "Speaking of promotions, I can't believe you made us captains, Cora."

Cora grinned. "To be a mercenary company, there are some rank structure guidelines in place for contracting. The positions have to be filled. Of course you three would be officers. Before we're through growing, I intend to have a full company of CASPers and at least one of regular troops. Figgle will handle them. Don't worry, there are a few experienced mech pilots in the soldiers we just signed on. A few have been through some hard times, but there's a sergeant or two among them. You'll be fine."

"There's one who's actually piloted a Mk 4 before, so there's that, anyway," May admitted.

"Those four Maki have already started tearing down the weapons panel on *Kellie's Stand...*" She paused a moment, thinking of the friend whose name would forever be remembered in the company. With a shake of her head, she continued, "Ricky gave them an idea of what might be wrong, and they went at it."

"Now them boys I really like," Ricky said with a toothy grin. "They even loaded the hovercraft into the bay and said they was going to fix it and arm it with a crew served. It'll be sweet. I wonder what they'll name it?"

They were all sitting around a makeshift conference table aboard *Blue Ridge* for the final brief before leaving Parmick. Jyrall and Larth had received instructions from Captain Dreel through Peacemaker Sinclair. Everyone was sitting, though Cora mostly reclined, as her body was still healing from her wounds. The medical nanites and her enhanced physique were aiding in the process, but she had a way to go yet.

Keaton looked down at his slate. "We're all loaded. We have the weapons, the gear, ammunition, and the six Mk 4s from the hanger loaded up on *Kellie's Stand*. All the Mk 7s are here on *Blue Ridge*. Monty and Stew are piloting this ship, and the SleSha are flying the other frigate. Monty and Stew did bitch about the color scheme in the cockpit area, though. Oh, sorry about that. Probably shouldn't use that word in present company."

"Don't worry about it." Cora laughed. "There is an answer for it. It's one word. Quitcherbitchin'."

"Yep, heard that a few times," admitted Nileah.

"Okay," Keaton continued, "that takes care of the equipment. As far as personnel go, besides the ladies, you now command twenty Humans, seventeen Goka, five Jivool, four Maki, two SleSha, and two very colorful Miderall."

"Unbelievable," Cora said. "From an unemployed merc and waitress to a mercenary company commander."

"You got this, girl," Lisalle said with a smile.

"*We've* got this," Cora corrected.

Larth leaned forward. "So, we go to the secret squirrel repair outpost. The Jeha and the Maki stationed there, along with whoever else is there, will repair and resupply us, and then we go to Weqq?"

"Those are our orders," Jyrall confirmed. "Before we take off, Keaton will give the two frigates a completely new background and transponder codes. They'll have to use the gate. They'll make a stop before continuing on. That system's gate is, shall we say, friendly to the cause, and they can exit with no one knowing their destination or the repair depot's location."

Jyrall continued, "We'll jump straight to the repair depot system ahead of them. Go ahead and have the Mk 7s transferred to *Night Moves*. Most of their repairs will be complete by the time you arrive. From right now, we must be on Weqq in thirty days. Those are our orders."

"We'll be there, and we'll be ready," Cora stated. "The Blue Ridge Kin have a mission. We'll complete the mission."

"I believe you will," Jyrall said.

"That's what Pops used to tell us, even if it was just taking the trash out," Ricky said.

"Yep," agreed his brother. "Complete the mission, boys. Complete the mission."

"Sounds like our unit motto to me," May suggested. Heads nodded throughout the room.

"I have to ask," Cora said, hesitantly. "I know the ships are payment for our contract, but what about the troops? I mean, they have to get paid, right?"

"That reminds me," Larth said. He reached into a pocket and pulled out a large red diamond. It was huge, and worth a fortune. "Here. This will more than pay for parts and repairs to your new ship. I mean your newest ship. If they even charge you. Where we're going first, you're going to get all the Mk 7s repaired, and the six old Mk 4s up and running, too. They'll be all over everything like a swarm. Use the rest for payroll." He tossed it to Cora. "Don't worry, that one's real."

Cora caught the diamond and cradled it in her hands before looking up at Jyrall and Larth. "I don't know what to say."

Jyrall grinned. "Complete the mission?"

"Complete the mission." Cora beamed. "You're damned right, Peacemaker."

"Fuckin' A!" Larth grinned. "I finally remembered it!"

About Kevin Ikenberry

Kevin's head has been in the clouds since he was old enough to read. Ask him and he'll tell you that he still wants to be an astronaut. A retired Army officer, Kevin has a diverse background in space and space science education. A former manager of the world-renowned U.S. Space Camp program in Huntsville, Alabama and a former executive of two Challenger Learning Centers, Kevin works with space every day and lives in Colorado with his family.

Kevin's bestselling debut science fiction novel, **Sleeper Protocol**, was released by Red Adept Publishing in January 2016 and was a Finalist for the 2017 Colorado Book Award. Publisher's Weekly called it "an emotionally powerful debut." The sequel, **Vendetta Protocol**, is due for release in September 2017. His military science fiction novel **Runs In The Family** was released by Strigidae Publishing in January 2016.

Kevin is an Active Member of the Science Fiction Writers of America and he is member of Pikes Peak Writers and the Rocky Mountain Fiction Writers. He is an alumna of the Superstars Writing Seminar.

* * * * *

About Kevin Steverson

Kevin Steverson is a retired veteran of the U.S. Army. He is a published songwriter as well as an author. He lives in the northeast Georgia foothills where he continues to refuse to shave ever again. Trim…maybe. Shave…never! When he is not on the road as a Tour Manager he can be found at home writing in one fashion or another.

* * * * *

The following is an

Excerpt from Book One of the Salvage Title Trilogy:

Salvage Title

_____

Kevin Steverson

Available Now from Theogony Books

eBook, Paperback, and Audio Book

Excerpt from "Salvage Title:"

The first thing Clip did was get power to the door and the access panel. Two of his power cells did the trick once he had them wired to the container. He then pulled out his slate and connected it. It lit up, and his fingers flew across it. It took him a few minutes to establish a link, then he programmed it to search for the combination to the access panel.

"Is it from a human ship?" Harmon asked, curious.

"I don't think so, but it doesn't matter; ones and zeros are still ones and zeros when it comes to computers. It's universal. I mean, there are some things you have to know to get other races' computers to run right, but it's not that hard," Clip said.

Harmon shook his head. *Riiigghht,* he thought. He knew better. Clip's intelligence test results were completely off the charts. Clip opted to go to work at Rinto's right after secondary school because there was nothing for him to learn at the colleges and universities on either Tretra or Joth. He could have received academic scholarships for advanced degrees on a number of nearby systems. He could have even gone all the way to Earth and attended the University of Georgia if he wanted. The problem was getting there. The schools would have provided free tuition if he could just have paid to get there.

Secondary school had been rough on Clip. He was a small guy that made excellent grades without trying. It would have been worse if Harmon hadn't let everyone know that Clip was his brother. They lived in the same foster center, so it was mostly true. The first day of school, Harmon had laid down the law—if you messed with Clip, you messed up.

At the age of fourteen, he beat three seniors senseless for attempting to put Clip in a trash container. One of them was a Yalteen, a member of a race of large humanoids from two systems over. It wasn't a fair fight—they should have brought more people with them. Harmon hated bullies.

407

After the suspension ended, the school's Warball coach came to see him. He started that season as a freshman and worked on using it to earn a scholarship to the academy. By the time he graduated, he was six feet two inches with two hundred and twenty pounds of muscle. He got the scholarship and a shot at going into space. It was the longest time he'd ever spent away from his foster brother, but he couldn't turn it down.

Clip stayed on Joth and went to work for Rinto. He figured it was a job that would get him access to all kinds of technical stuff, servos, motors, and maybe even some alien computers. The first week he was there, he tweaked the equipment and increased the plant's recycled steel production by 12 percent. Rinto was eternally grateful, as it put him solidly into the profit column instead of toeing the line between profit and loss. When Harmon came back to the planet after the academy, Rinto hired him on the spot on Clip's recommendation. After he saw Harmon operate the grappler and got to know him, he was glad he did.

A steady beeping brought Harmon back to the present. Clip's program had succeeded in unlocking the container. "Right on!" Clip exclaimed. He was always using expressions hundreds or more years out of style. "Let's see what we have; I hope this one isn't empty, too." Last month they'd come across a smaller vault, but it had been empty.

Harmon stepped up and wedged his hands into the small opening the door had made when it disengaged the locks. There wasn't enough power in the small cells Clip used to open it any further. He put his weight into it, and the door opened enough for them to get inside. Before they went in, Harmon placed a piece of pipe in the doorway so it couldn't close and lock on them, baking them alive before anyone realized they were missing.

Daylight shone in through the doorway, and they both froze in place; the weapons vault was full.

* * * * *

Get "Salvage Title" now at:
https://www.amazon.com/dp/B07H8Q3HBV.

Find out more about Kevin Steverson and "Salvage Title" at:
http://chriskennedypublishing.com/.

* * * * *

The following is an
Excerpt from Super-Sync:

Super-Sync

Kevin Ikenberry

Now Available from Theogony Books

eBook and Paperback

Excerpt from "Super-Sync:"

The subspace radio chimed an hour later, just as Lew put aside the holonovel with dissatisfaction. There was no such thing as "happily ever after," no matter how many books she read. No one was going to carry her off into the sunset. Lew reached for the radio controls and felt the thuds of Tyler's boots on the deck in the passageway below. He burst onto the bridge and vaulted into his chair.

He looked at Lew. "Identify the transmission."

Lew fingered the controls and read off the diagnostic information, "Standard Ku band transmission from Earth. Origin point known through Houston nexus. Encryption is solid Johnson Analytics with the proper keys."

Tyler grinned. "Boss."

Lew nodded and smiled as well. "Appears so."

Their mysterious benefactor hadn't called them in more than six months, but every time he'd employed them, the take had been impressive. How he was able to garner the contracts he had bordered on magic. Lew thought the man sounded like some kind of Texas oil baron. Despite the technology, his calls were always voice-only, and there was never any interaction between them and whoever he represented.

Whatever he contracted them to acquire was delivered to a private, automated hangar on Luna. The robotic ground crew would unload *Remnant* and send them on their way again. Anonymous cash transfers always appeared in their accounts by the time *Remnant* returned to lunar orbit. The first mission had earned Tyler's company over a million Euros. The following missions were even more lucrative.

Their benefactor went by a call sign, and they talked in codes meant only for their own ears. It should have been a red flag, but the money was too damned good to pass up. A call from him could *not* go unanswered.

Tyler punched a few buttons on his console, and a drawling voice boomed through the speakers, "*Remnant*, this is Boss. Are you receiving?" The transmission ended with a chiming tone that dated back to the early days of spaceflight. The clear delineation of conversation allowed Tyler to answer.

"Boss, this is *Remnant*. Nice to hear from you. How can we be of service?"

A few seconds passed. "Tyler, it's good to hear your voice. I understand you're on a contract flight from our friend in India."

"That's affirm, Boss."

"Roger, you've got a shadow. Are you aware of that?"

Tyler's face darkened. "Roger, Boss. We're aware of the bogey."

By definition, a bogey was an unknown contact with unknown intentions. Should the situation turn bad, the radar blip would become a bandit. Lew checked the telemetry from the unknown ship. There was no change in direction or speed. It was still gaining on them.

"*Remnant*, the trailing vehicle is not your concern. I have a change in mission for you."

Tyler shook his head. "Negative, Boss. I have a contract."

"*Remnant*, I bought out that contract. The shadow on your tail is the *Rio Bravo*, under contract by me to get Telstar Six Twelve. You're going high super-sync."

* * * * *

Get "Super-Sync" now at:
https://www.amazon.com/dp/B07PGS545X.

Find out more about Kevin Ikenberry and "Super-Sync" at:
https://chriskennedypublishing.com.

* * * * *

Printed in Great Britain
by Amazon

14113544R00241